Other Books by Karen Baney

Prescott Pioneers Series
A Dream Unfolding
A Heart Renewed
A Life Restored
A Hope Revealed

Contemporary
Nickels

Prescott Pioneers Book 1:

A Dream Unfolding

By Karen Baney

Prescott Pioneers Book 1: A Dream Unfolding
By Karen Baney

Publisher:
Author Services International, LLC
3317 S Higley Road
Suite 114-288
Gilbert, AZ 85297

www.karenbaney.com

Printed in the United States of America

ISBN-978-1456512316

*To Mom – the most beautiful
butterfly ever. Looking
forward to our next duet.*

Yes, my soul, find rest in God;
my hope comes from him.
Truly he is my rock and my salvation;
he is my fortress, I will not be shaken.
Psalm 62:5-6

Chapter 1

Cincinnati, Ohio

July 15, 1863

"Gunshot wound!"

Hannah sighed at the tense sound of her husband's voice filtering down the hall from the parlor to the kitchen. Though she clearly heard the urgency in Drew's tone, she took a moment to remove the half-baked biscuits from the heavy iron stove, lest they burn before she returned. This would be the third batch of baked goods she would toss this week so she could assist Drew in the surgery with one medical emergency or another.

Biting back a second frustrated sigh, she removed her cooking apron to don a fresh one. Tying the apron strings around her back, she entered the chaos of Drew's surgery room. The heavy shuffling of feet echoed in the small room as four men grunted under the weight of the injured man. The acrid smell of blood hit Hannah full force. She recalled the days when the odor and sight of blood caused her stomach to roil. Nearly two years working by Drew's side cured her of some of that sensitivity. Heart pounding rapidly, she prepared the ether cone, anticipating the forthcoming request.

"Get him on the table." Drew calmly instructed the men carrying the wounded bank manager, Mr. Davis. As he turned to face her, his tone remained steady, "Hannah, I need the ether now."

Hannah's breath caught in her throat as she looked into Mr. Davis's panicked eyes—her earlier frustration vanished. Whispering words of comfort, she placed the cone over his nose and mouth, silently counting out the seconds. Around the third second, his thrashing stopped and his body relaxed into an unconscious state. She let out a shaky breath, relieved by the sight.

Drew's lanky form bent over Mr. Davis's left leg as he intently studied the blood soaked trousers. Hannah offered Drew scissors and he cut the pant leg to better see the wound. The bullet was lodged in

Mr. Davis's thigh. He placed a tourniquet above the gaping hole to stop the flow of blood. Hannah mopped up what she could with rags silently praying for their patient and for her husband's skill. As he requested the small forceps, she handed them over. Watching, she could not help but admire his steady hand and careful movements as he removed the bullet with the forceps. Gently he removed the bullet.

As she administered another dose of ether, Drew threaded a needle with his long slender fingers, seemingly unaffected by the gravity of his task. He doused the wound to clean it before starting slow deliberate strokes with the needle to stitch the hole shut. His concentration was so intense that he barely noticed her dabbing the sweat from his forehead. Once he finished with the stitches, he wrapped the leg in bandages before checking for other signs of injury.

"I don't see any other wounds," Drew said meeting her gaze as he washed the blood from his hands. His expression remained unreadable. "Please sit with him for a minute while I speak with the men who brought him in."

As Hannah pulled up a chair next to Mr. Davis's still form, she caught most of the conversation playing out in the parlor, though slightly muffled from the distance.

"Bank robbery," one of the men replied in response to Drew's query.

Gasps echoed in the small parlor that served as a waiting area for patients, followed by the hiss of rapid whispering. Hannah, knowing who was scheduled for appointments, imagined their shocked faces at the unexpected announcement.

"Will you let Mr. Davis's wife know he is here and resting comfortably?" Drew requested.

The men replied affirmatively before the sound of their feet faded behind the closed front door.

"Bank robbery," Hannah muttered, surprised someone attempted such in the middle of the day in their peaceful town. She chided herself for thinking of Cincinnati as a town. With the large number of German immigrants arriving daily to work in the meat packing factories, her childhood home was quickly becoming a large city.

She checked Mr. Davis's pulse again which returned to normal. The faint smell of ether hung in the air, intermingled with blood, causing her to take shallow breaths. Drew returned to the room with a deep frown on his face, obviously concerned by the news. As he listened to Mr. Davis's breathing, she started cleaning and sanitizing the room and instruments, trying to hold her emotions at bay just a little longer.

As soon as she finished mopping up the trail of blood from the parlor to the surgery room, she jumped at the sound of the front door bursting open again.

"Phillip!" called out Mrs. Davis as she ran into the room. "Oh, Phillip!"

The frail woman gasped at the sight of her pale husband sleeping. Hannah breathed a sigh of relief that she completed the cleaning before Mrs. Davis arrived, fearful for the woman's constitution. Glancing down at her blood splattered apron, she hoped to go unnoticed, certain the sight would send Mrs. Davis into a fit of apoplexy.

Drew spoke in calm soft tones as he clapped his hand over the older woman's. "He will be just fine. He is resting now, but should be awake later this evening. I would like to keep him here for a few days to make sure he is doing well, and then I'll send him home to your capable care."

"Thank you, Dr. Anderson," Mrs. Davis replied, blotting her tears with a handkerchief before taking a seat next to her husband.

Quietly exiting the room, Hannah paused inside the doorway of the kitchen. The intensity of the preceding hours drained her energy as the emotions rushed forward. Leaning her head back against the wall, she let the tears roll down her face. *Please let the image of Mr. Davis's fear-stricken face fade from my mind quickly.* The look had been so intense that she felt his fear as if it were her own—not in the moment she looked at him, but now as she returned to the calmness of her kitchen.

Wiping the tears from her face with the back of her hand, she removed the stained apron and threw it into a bucket to soak. Picking up a clean apron, she returned to the now half crunchy half soggy biscuits next to the oven trying to push the morning from her mind. She threw the biscuits into the waste and started on a fresh batch.

Carefully, she measured out the flour and buttermilk. The familiar actions of baking soothed her edgy nerves. Using the technique her aunt taught her, Hannah rolled out the biscuit dough and cut round forms, repeating the steps until all the dough formed raw biscuits. Numbly she continued through the motions until lovely golden brown biscuits emerged from the oven.

As Drew saw his last scheduled patient for the day, Hannah started her afternoon routine of tidying the clinic. Starting in the parlor at the front of the house, she straightened chairs and dusted the furniture. From the parlor, she turned left into Drew's office since both surgery rooms on the right were occupied, one by Mr. Davis and the other by Drew and his patient. Hannah dusted her husband's desk and stowed the patient charts in the largest drawer at the bottom of the oak desk. Taking a seat, Hannah flipped through the stack of bills. There never seemed to be enough time to see to everything. She needed to spend some time updating the ledgers soon.

She listened as Drew escorted the last patient to the parlor. She entered the now vacant surgery room, wiping down all the surfaces. Once the room was cleaned, she checked on Mr. Davis again. He was still resting peacefully, his wife clutching his hand as she sat in the chair, her chin resting against her chest either in prayer or in sleep.

Walking down the hall to the kitchen at the back of the house, Hannah began supper preparations. She felt most at peace in her kitchen—her domain. Perhaps it was from the few years she spent by her loving aunt's side learning how to bake and cook, those domestic skills her mother had not instilled before her passing.

Shaking off the mounting melancholy, she shifted her thoughts back to Mr. Davis's care. Following the meal, she would send Drew upstairs to their bedroom to get some rest. She would take the first shift watching Mr. Davis and then, sometime in the middle of the night she would wake Drew to take over.

At times like these, she wished Drew would hire a nurse. Hannah barely kept up with the laundry, cleaning, and meal preparations without overnight patients. Whenever a patient required round the clock care, she fell woefully behind in other chores. What would she do when she had children to care for?

"Barnes," Drew greeted, with some hesitation, as one of the city's policemen entered the clinic alone. Being one of two doctors in town, Drew often patched up robbers or drunken brawlers before Barnes hauled them off to jail. Occasionally he even visited the jail when Barnes deemed it too dangerous to bring the criminal to the clinic.

"What brings you here?" Drew asked, still unable to shake his concern that Barnes accompanied no one.

"May I have a word with you and Mrs. Anderson?"

Drew showed him to his office where their conversation could remain private. Once the bulky man took a seat, Drew quickly fetched Hannah. The lack of sleep from the night before did not help his increasing nervousness about the policeman's unusual behavior.

As Hannah took a seat, Barnes said, "We have your brother, Thomas, in custody down at the jailhouse. He was identified as one of the men in yesterday's attempt to rob the bank."

Drew felt his throat constrict and his heart started beating rapidly. He had hoped Thomas wasn't involved.

Sinking into the remaining chair, he asked, "What happened?"

"From what we pieced together," Barnes' deep voice added to his air of authority, "it looks like Thomas, along with Sam Rogers and Ed Rogers, stormed the bank yesterday afternoon as one of the patrons was leaving. They pulled their guns on Mr. Davis and forced him to open the safe in the back room. Mr. Davis kept a loaded revolver in the safe, so once he opened it, he turned the gun on Sam and shot him in the foot. Then Ed fired on Mr. Davis."

Still stunned, Drew nodded. He didn't want to believe his brother was party to this crazy affair, crossing the line from rebellion to crime.

"After Mr. Davis was shot," Barnes continued, "all three men took off, leaving the money behind. A few pedestrians noted the direction. We followed the trail and it led us to the Rogers' house. We arrested all three men. Like I said, they are in jail and will remain there until a judge decides what is to be done."

Drew looked over at Hannah. Her eyes widened with concern. Thomas had rebelled for years, though never so boldly. Disappointment washed over Drew, quickly follow by guilt. If only he had been able to get through to Thomas. Maybe this would not have happened.

Ever since their father died, Drew's brother could not contain his restless spirit. Thomas started hanging out with the Rogers brothers and things went downhill from there. The Rogers brothers bullied classmates during their school days and as they aged, they got worse: petty theft from the mercantile, vandalizing businesses, and picking fights with anyone who would pay them mind. When Thomas started staying out late and carousing with Sam and Ed Rogers, Drew did not hesitate to warn Thomas of the dangers of his actions. Closing his eyes, Drew clearly remembered the day he confronted his brother.

Drew woke to a thudding sound on the stairs. Sitting upright, he remained completely still, trying to determine if what he heard was real or imagined as his heart pounded against his chest. *Thud.* There is it was again.

Slipping from the bed, Drew carefully crept to the closed bedroom door. Slowly he cracked it open, just as a muffled curse reached his ears. *Thomas!*

Stepping from the room, Drew pulled the bedroom door closed behind him, so as not to wake Hannah. At the top of the stairs he made out Thomas's limp form lying prostrate across several of the stairs. The stale cigar smoke and sickening sweet smell of whiskey clung to his brother's clothing. As Drew approached, Thomas looked up and cursed again.

At first, Drew thought Thomas was merely drunk again—a frequent occurrence. But when he tried to help him up, Thomas recoiled and moaned in pain. Drew led him down the stairs and into the surgery room for a quick examination. Lighting the oil lamp, Drew saw the extent of his brother's injuries. Besides the swollen black eye, his face and knuckles were covered with numerous cuts and scrapes. His ribs were also bruised. This must have been his worst fight to date.

"You must stop this Thomas," he warned his brother, keeping his voice low. "The drinking, the gambling—it is only going to lead to trouble."

"What do you care?" Thomas roared.

He grew weary of the familiar accusation. Thomas always thought Drew didn't care—Drew always tried to show his concern. He was letting him live here. Wasn't that proof enough that he cared? As his anger rose, so did his voice. "Look at yourself. Night after night you come home drunk or—"

"You have no right to lecture me! I'm old enough to take care of myself and do as I please. Mind your own business!"

"It is my business, as long as you are living in this house!" Drew volleyed back. Taking his brother in had been a mistake. He thought providing a home and some structure would help Thomas give up his wild ways. Instead, no matter what Drew did, Thomas threw it in his face.

"Don't act like you are doing me a favor, Drew," the hatred poured from his brother's lips. "I know what you are doing. You just don't want to feel guilty for leaving me here while you went to medical school. But you should! Living with Uncle Peter was awful!"

"Uncle Peter did his best to help you grow up with some discipline."

"Don't defend that selfish old man!"

The argument escalated until Hannah appeared in the doorway. When she looked from Drew to Thomas and back again, Drew shut his mouth mid-sentence. Thomas frowned, cursed, then turned and stormed out into the night.

He hadn't seen his brother since.

Hannah's dainty cough brought Drew's attention back to the discussion with Barnes.

"Dr. Anderson," Barnes continued as he stood and walked to the front door, "I suggest you consider getting legal representation for your brother."

Closing the door behind Barnes, Drew snorted. He refused to bail Thomas out of trouble again. Aware of the waiting patients,

Drew ushered Hannah back to his office and closed the door, wondering just how much they overheard.

"What are you going to do?" Hannah asked her anxiety evident.

"What can I do?" Drew replied, acknowledging his own helplessness in this situation. "He is a grown man and he is not my responsibility any longer."

"Will you get an attorney as Mr. Barnes suggested?" she asked, her voice full of compassion.

"No!"

Seeing the shock on Hannah's face, he quickly explained, "At some point Thomas must choose his own way—he already has. He made that clear more than a year ago. There is nothing I can do or say that will change anything."

Drew ran his fingers through his hair in frustration. His heart broke again as he thought of how disappointed his father would be. Perhaps his father passing on was a good thing. At least he would not witness his youngest son's destructive behavior.

Sunday morning, Hannah put the finishing touches on the roast and slid it into the oven. Bounding up the stairs she quickly untied the apron from her waist. Standing before the mirror she brushed out her long strawberry blonde hair then twisted it into a chignon at the base of her neck inside the decorative black netted hair piece. She smiled, pleased with her appearance.

"You look lovely," Drew commented as his pale blue eyes surveyed the light blue calico dress before resting on her eyes. Color flushed her face with the intensity of his appraisal.

"Come here," he added, pulling her close. "Your eyes look bluer than the sky in that dress." He brushed lips lightly across hers in a brief kiss.

Releasing her, he asked, "Looking forward to Emily's visit?"

"I can hardly wait," Hannah answered giddily.

As Hannah preceded Drew down the stairs, she could not contain her excitement over the planned Sunday dinner guests—Levi and Emily Werner. It had been two months since Hannah had seen

Emily. Earlier this week, Levi stopped by the clinic to let Hannah know Emily would be back to church this week, having recovered from her morning sickness. Hannah missed her best friend dearly, so she invited them for Sunday dinner.

Emily and Hannah grew up on adjoining farms several miles outside of Cincinnati. Hannah could not remember a time when she and Emily weren't friends, despite being such opposites in looks and personality. With her dark curls and flashing nutmeg brown eyes, Emily charmed everyone, from the most reserved students to the toughest bullies in their school. As she grew older and began filling out her dress, boys noticed her long before noticing Hannah—not that any had noticed Hannah in school. Walking to and from school together, Hannah often found herself in the role of quiet listener to Emily's constant chattering about what Amanda Taylor wore that day, or how the pigs on the farm gave birth to a large litter, or who danced with who at the last barn dance. Perhaps if Emily had set her mind on memorizing her lessons at school and not on such things, she would have made higher marks and Hannah would have spent less time trying to help her catch up.

Besides helping Emily with her school work, Hannah found in her a friend with whom she could confide her deepest sorrows, especially following her mother's death. Even when her father sent her away to live with her aunt, she wrote letters to Emily almost weekly. When Hannah moved back to the farm with her father, years later, she easily picked up her friendship with Emily. Sadly, she was the only constant person in her life.

As Drew pulled the carriage to a stop down the street from the large whitewashed church building, Hannah scanned the crowd for her tall friend. Spotting her, she raised her arm for a quick wave after Drew helped her to the ground. Emily turned without acknowledging Hannah and entered through the large dark wood doors. *Perhaps she just didn't see me.*

Placing her hand in the crook of Drew's arm, Hannah smiled, confident nothing could ruin her good mood in anticipation of a wonderful afternoon.

Once inside the church, Hannah watched as Emily and Levi took their seats in their normal pew. Drew led Hannah to the same pew. As soon as Drew and Hannah sat, she leaned forward to greet

Emily, who immediately, without word, stood and followed her husband out of the pew.

"Emily, wait—"

"We'll talk later," Emily hissed as she glanced back over her shoulder with a frown.

As Levi and Emily took a seat on the other side of the sanctuary, she couldn't help but feel hurt by her friend's angry response. Had she unknowingly done something to offend Emily?

When Drew stiffened next to her, she glanced in his direction. The couple on the other side of him stood and moved elsewhere. Soon, the pew in front of them emptied, as long time friends scattered to the edges of the room like marbles spilled on the floor.

Looking up at Drew she saw the stoic expression etched on his face.

"What's going on?" she whispered, still trying to understand how they may have offended so many people.

Drew shook his head curtly.

When the music started, she shifted her gaze to the words in the hymnal, not needing to read them, but needing to hide her growing sadness over the rejection of her friends. Her voice sounded forced as she tried to sing praises to her God. Inside, she felt anything but gratitude.

Hannah shifted in her seat as the service dragged on. Her attention waned.

As the last strains of the final hymn echoed in the wooden room, the pastor stood and gave a blessing. The sound of booted feet heightened as the crowd exited the church. Not waiting for Drew, she hurried to catch up with Emily outside.

"Emily, we've been sitting together for years. Why did you move this morning?" Hannah asked as her friend tried to dodge her for a second time. "Aren't you coming to dinner?"

"No, we are not," Emily replied emphasizing each word, not looking Hannah in the eye.

"Are you not feeling well?"

"I am feeling fine," Emily said, glaring at Drew as he came to stand next to his wife.

Hannah held her breath, hoping Emily might elaborate on her strange behavior.

"If you'll excuse us," Emily snapped as Levi started leading her around Hannah again.

Confused and hurt by Emily's behavior, she reached out, placing her hand on Emily's arm. "Please tell me, what I've done to offend you?"

Emily's dark eyes flashed with anger as she turned to face Hannah. Brushing Hannah's hand from her arm, she said, "It was our money, Hannah. We sacrificed and saved for years for that money. Levi took on that second shift at the meat factory so we would have enough for a home of our own to get out of that horrible squalor."

"I don't understand—"

"No, you don't understand. And neither did Thomas. He just thought he could walk right into that bank and take what we worked so hard for." Emily wagged her finger in Hannah's face, causing her to take a step backwards. "And him, a worthless, gambling scoundrel! Never worked an honest day's labor in his life. But, he thought he could just take what wasn't his."

"I understand your anger with Thomas, but—"

Levi, who stood with arms folded across his barrel chest, finally spoke, directing his comments to Drew. "A doctor is nothing without his reputation and yours is tainted by your brother's wild ways. Tell me, Drew, did he try to hide out at your clinic when his plan failed?" Anger shrouded his words.

Drew dropped his arms to his side, stepping closer to Levi. "How could you think such a thing?"

Hannah bit her lower lip, hoping Drew and Levi would not come to blows. She was certain Drew would not win against the much larger man.

"Everyone knows you've been bailing him out of trouble for years. Well, this time the people of this city are not going to stand for it," Levi responded through clenched teeth.

By now, several other couples gathered around listening to the heated conversation. Friends, who greeted her with a hug and warm smile last week, looked on with hatred carved on their faces. Tears threatened at the corners of Hannah's eyes as the pain of betrayal heightened.

"There is nothing to get upset about," Drew pleaded, looking around the crowd. "I have not seen Thomas in over a year."

"That's not what Mrs. Pierce said!" one woman from the crowd shouted. "She said she saw a man who looked like your brother going into the clinic late that night."

Hannah frowned, balling her fist at her side. *How can they believe that busybody over my husband?*

"If anyone did enter the clinic that night," Drew's voice boomed, "it was without an invitation."

"So you don't deny what Mrs. Pierce said?" Levi pulled Drew's attention his way.

Running his hand through his short sandy hair, Drew said, "I'm saying that it is possible someone could have entered uninvited without our knowledge."

Emily raised her voice above the growing murmurs, "It doesn't matter to me if Thomas entered your house with your blessing or not. I for one," she said, resting her hand on her protruding belly, "will not be birthing my child at your clinic or with your assistance."

Hannah's tears streamed down her heated face as Emily's words pierced her heart. How could Emily say such a thing? She talked for months about how wonderful it would be to have her best friend by her side as she labored to bring her first child into this world. Now, the friend who stood by her in a school yard full of bullies was acting the part of instigator. Did their friendship mean so little?

"And I won't be stopping at your clinic for Franklin's medications!" another older married woman shouted.

"When my niece has her child, I'm telling her to go to Doc Henderson!" A typically quiet man shouted.

As others added in vehement voices their promise to no longer visit Drew's clinic, Hannah watched his face harden. Closing his eyes, he bowed his head.

Don't give up, Drew! Her heart shouted.

When he lifted his head again, he held out his elbow for Hannah wordlessly. With a firm nod to her, she read the silent message: it was time to go. In the midst of angry murmurs circling about them, Hannah followed her husband to their carriage. As he took the seat next to her, his eyes faced forward. His jaw set in a hard line. His shoulders slumped in defeat.

Chapter 2

Drew slapped the reins hard against the chestnut mare's back, directing the carriage from the church yard. He heard rumblings that many of his patients were upset at him over Thomas's crime. But, he had not expected this—the whole church rising up in anger against him.

Worse than their anger was the disappointment he saw in Hannah's face. She expected him to put up a fight. Unfortunately, fighting with his patients—with his friends—would not change their minds about his presumed guilt.

Pulling the carriage to a stop in front of the clinic, Drew hopped down and rounded to the other side. Holding his hand out for Hannah, his eyes locked on her red-rimmed ones. Her gaze quickly darted away. As soon as her feet settled safely on the ground, she released his hand, rushing up the walkway.

Taking a seat in the carriage, Drew navigated the busy street until he arrived at the livery to store the carriage and board the horse. He welcomed the walk home, hoping Hannah might recover before he arrived.

His stomach churned as he replayed the scene from the churchyard in his mind. Levi's words repeated over and over. *A doctor is nothing without his reputation. Yours is tainted by your brother.*

Such harsh, unforgiving words with little hope of reconciliation. Could Drew possibly salvage his reputation, or was it too late?

Perhaps they were a bit justified in their anger. Up until last year Drew had sheltered Thomas and covered for his troublesome behavior. He should have stood up to Thomas sooner, voicing his concerns. Or he should have asked Thomas to find his own place to live.

But, Thomas was his brother. He couldn't turn him away no more than he could turn away injured patient. Thomas was his only family left. He felt responsible, bound by brotherhood. Even if Thomas's actions destroyed Drew's reputation, he could not stop caring and reaching out—even if Thomas continued to reject him.

As he approached the clinic, his steps slowed. A brief memory from the morning after the robbery flitted through his mind. When he entered the kitchen in the early morning, after relieving Hannah from watching Mr. Davis, he recalled thinking something seemed out of place. Though he never figured out what...

Was it possible Thomas really had entered their home after his crime? Surely he would have heard something, as he sat vigil with Mr. Davis.

The savory aroma of the roast greeted Drew as he opened the door. Pausing, he shook off his frustration over the seemingly impossible situation. Cautiously, he walked down the hall towards the kitchen, looking for Hannah. She stood with her back to him, staring out the window over the sink.

As he cleared his throat to announce his presence, Hannah's sniffles turned to sobs. Closing the distance, he turned her towards him then wrapped his arms around her waist. She buried her head against his chest. Several moments passed with Drew stroking her hair, not knowing what to say.

Hannah leaned back and looked up at him. "How could they blame us? We had nothing to do with Thomas?"

He swallowed several times, searching for an answer.

A frown crossed her face. "Why didn't you defend us?"

Drew released his hold on his wife as his shoulders slumped in defeat. "What should I have said?" he replied, more harshly than he should have. "Nothing would have persuaded them to think differently."

Hannah propped one hand on her hip, forcing her elbow to jut sharply away from her body. It was the posture he most despised in his wife as it often preceded an angry outburst.

"Are you going to just let them walk away from the clinic? Are you going to close the doors, Drew?"

Her lack of faith in him hurt. "Give it time. Things will turn around. They will forget their anger."

She turned and pulled the roast from the oven. Slamming it down on the top of the stove, her voice low and tenuous, "What if they don't?"

Pursing his lips tightly, he hoped they would forget soon. He couldn't consider what would happen if they didn't.

In the weeks since the bank robbery, no patients came, save for Mr. Davis. He recovered quickly from the gunshot wound. Odd, how the victim of his brother's crime entrusted his care to Drew, yet the rest of the city lost trust in him. If the city's opinion failed to change, his days of practicing medicine in Ohio were over. He could not support his wife on one patient a month—much less the children he and Hannah hoped would come soon.

With no patients to see, Drew dodged oncoming carriages to cross the street to the mercantile. After greeting Francis, the owner, he paid for a copy of the daily newspaper before returning to the clinic. Flipping through the pages, he scanned the headlines for the latest developments on the Union's progress which reminded him of his decision over a year ago. Instead of enlisting to serve in the Union, he remained home—to the townsfolk's dismay. Newly married when the War Between the States started, he hesitated to leave his wife. He knew the city still needed a doctor whether or not the country warred. So, he stayed. Then six months ago, Doc Henderson moved to town. Some members of the community started pressuring Drew to reconsider, now that two doctors practiced in the area. Still, he remained steadfast in his decision.

Again, he found himself on the receiving end of the city's ire. They were not forgetting. They were not forgiving. They did not want to hear the truth that Drew had nothing to do with Thomas's actions. Instead, their opinion seemed more immovable as time went on.

Drew tried to change their minds. He met with several influential men from church. None of them were swayed by his discussion or by his track record of providing excellent care. He needed to make a decision soon about whether he should give up medicine or if he and Hannah should move. Staying seemed less of an option.

Running his hands through his hair, Drew realized he let his mind wander and had absorbed none of the news he was reading. Placing the paper aside, he rubbed his hand along the edge of his large oak desk. The prick to his finger interrupted the movement as a small sliver embedded his skin. Turning his hand over, he scrutinized the sliver, too deep for him to remove without assistance.

Following the aroma of freshly brewed coffee, Drew entered the kitchen. He stood silently in the door admiring his wife while she mixed dough of some sort. Her long strawberry blonde hair was secured in a fashionable chignon at the base of her slender neck. The work dress hung perfectly on her petite frame with the bow of her apron accenting her tiny waist. Unable to resist the urge, he snuck up behind Hannah. He then grabbed her by the waist and pulled her into an embrace, breathing deeply of her scent. Something about just holding her calmed him.

Hannah welcomed her husband's nearness, though unexpected at this time of day. As she turned to face him, he held out his hand palm side up. She looked from his lithe fingers to his face, raising an eyebrow in question.

He shrugged his shoulders sheepishly. "I seem to be in need of your expert nursing."

As he pointed to his finger, Hannah saw the small sliver. She ran upstairs to retrieve a needle from her sewing basket before returning to her poor injured husband. He stood where she left him, still holding out his hand.

Hannah took his right hand in her left, aware of how small and dainty her hands looked against his. His smooth hands bore no sign of roughness—only the gentle unmarred hands of a doctor, strong and steady. Taking the needle with her right hand, she gently worked the sliver from beneath his skin. Once free, she placed her lips on his long finger kissing the spot softly.

Drew curved his hand under her chin. The sweet action caused her to slowly straighten and look into his eyes. The love reflected there warmed her heart.

With his hand still resting lightly under her chin, he drew her lips closer to his own. Hannah melted into his arms as he kissed her soundly. She shared the love she felt for her husband by responding. When Drew slowed the kiss, Hannah leaned back in his embrace. She trailed her dainty fingers along his jaw line as she stepped away smiling.

Moving to the stove, she poured him a cup of black coffee. Handing the mug to Drew, Hannah giggled and shooed him back to the clinic, a satisfied sigh escaping her lips.

Ah, he loved this woman. Drew thought as he took the offered coffee. *Now how to provide for her with no patients and a dwindling income?*

Sitting down at his desk again, he picked up the newspaper and turned to the middle. An article about the growing gold town of La Paz in the new Arizona Territory caught his eye. The article stated that shortly after Arizona officially became a territory in February last year, gold was discovered along the Colorado River in the southwestern part of the territory. They estimated several thousand miners now lived in the area. The rapidly growing town needed doctors, lawyers, boardinghouses, laundry services, and more.

Doctors. Drew's eyes lingered on the word. Maybe, if they left soon, he and Hannah would still have enough money to relocate to the West. If he could find a buyer for the office, then they would be in a better position to move to the territory. Removing a sheet of paper from the stack on his desk, Drew started listing things they would need and estimated how much it would cost. Excitement built as he thought of a new adventure, starting life over where no one knew them. Or their family ties to a bank robber. This had to be the answer to his prayers. He would speak to Hannah soon about moving to La Paz.

Hannah finished kneading the bread dough then put the loaf of bread in the oven to bake. Unlike in the past, this loaf would bake without interruption, she thought ironically. As she cleaned the kitchen, she could not stop worrying. She noticed the lack of patients coming to the clinic in recent days. A week passed since he saw his last patient, a middle aged man who died from the infected abscess on his side. No others graced the steps of the clinic since.

Emily refused to talk to her, plunging the knife of rejection deeper. Last week, Hannah showed up with the small quilt she sewed for Emily's expected child with the fabric scraps they picked out together. When Emily opened the door, she crossed her arms angrily, not saying a word. Hannah tried to hand her the gift. Emily slammed the door shut—not taking the package from Hannah's shaking hands. She set the gift on the porch, before hurrying down the sidewalk, her vision blurred.

If Emily, her closest friend, failed to forgive them, how could she expect more from acquaintances?

She checked the bread, which browned nicely, so she pulled the loaf from the oven, filling the room with the sweet aroma. Setting it aside to cool, her thoughts returned to their dilemma. What could she do to convince the community that neither she nor Drew supported Thomas's actions? How could she help bring patients back to Drew's clinic? *Lord, show us what to do.*

The immediate answer she hoped for drowned in unbearable silence. Had even God turned his back on them?

Hannah poured herself a cup of coffee as tears pooled in the corner of her eyes. As they spilled over, she brushed the moisture away. Opening the back door to the porch, she sat in her favorite rocking chair coaxing it into motion with the slight push of her foot. Sounds of the busy street out front floated back to her hidden retreat. The August breeze blew a few tendrils of her hair loose kissing her skin softly with a hint of the cooling temperatures to come.

Slowly rocking back and forth she considered what she and Drew might do. The sick and injured needed good doctors, especially since so many doctors left for the war. Any town with a reasonable population could support a doctor. Perhaps she and Drew could find such a town nearby in southern Indiana.

While not the same as Ohio, Indiana might be a suitable

substitute. Hannah always dreamed of raising her children in the same town where she grew up. Yet, her barrenness greeted her daily, taunting her with the hopelessness of never seeing her dream fulfilled. And, now the current situation made staying in her homeland nearly impossible. Yes, perhaps Indiana would suffice.

Slowly she stretched, letting her fears and disappointment melt away as each muscle pulled taut before releasing refreshing relief. Getting up from the rocking chair, she headed back into the kitchen to put the finishing touches on dinner.

The hearty fragrance of beef stew and freshly baked bread usually brought Drew into the kitchen before supper, but not today. She set the table then went to his office to fetch him.

As she crossed the threshold from their living quarters to Drew's office, she saw him bent over his desk studying something on the page before him. So as not to startle him, she gently laid her hand on his shoulder. Almost unconsciously, he reached up and softly caressed her hand, his eyes never leaving the paper. After a few moments in silence, he dropped his hand and pushed back the chair to rise.

"Supper is ready," she whispered.

"Shall we, Mrs. Anderson?" Drew winked, then offered his arm in the manner he did when they were courting. His eyes twinkled with mischief.

"Let's, Mr. Anderson," she replied with a smile as they headed to the kitchen table.

After Drew finished saying grace, he began, "I've been thinking about what we can do, since so many of our patients are now going to Doc Henderson. I read in the paper a few days ago that there is a need for doctors elsewhere, and I thought— "

"Maybe we should move," she interrupted, pleased that he came to the same conclusion as she had moments ago. "I'm sure there is some small town in southern Indiana that would be perfect for us. I mean, I don't want to leave, but things are not turning around. People are not willing to forgive us for Thomas's involvement in the bank robbery."

Drew paused, spoon half way to his mouth. A puzzled look wrinkled his brow. "I truly did not think you would be willing to leave. I, too, was thinking we could relocate…but a little farther west…to the Arizona Territory."

Clank! Hannah's spoon hit the side of the bowl before dropping down into her lap leaving a dark trail of stew on her green calico dress. She paused for a moment to recover both her spoon and her senses. *Arizona Territory! That's so far away. What is he thinking?*

Trying to keep the panic from her voice, she asked, "Why the Arizona Territory? Why not someplace closer?"

"I agree that we could go someplace closer, but I don't believe that is where God is calling us."

Of course he would bring God into this, she thought wryly. Not that she would discount God's prompting—she just hated to leave Ohio.

Drew continued, "There is a gold mine town called La Paz along the Colorado River in the western edge of the territory. The town is growing rapidly and is in need of doctors. If we leave soon, we should have enough money to get there. If we can sell the house before we go, we would be in better shape."

Drew reached across the table to squeeze her hand. Hope and excitement graced his features. His voice pleading, "Don't you see? We could start over. A new life. No one will know us or our past. Or Thomas's past."

"But don't you want to be close enough to support Thomas as he goes to trial?" she squeaked, trying to find some way to stay closer to her beloved Ohio—where both her parents were buried, where she met Jesus, where she hoped to raise her children.

Drew frowned at her suggestion, withdrawing his hand. His voice took on a hard edge as he replied, "He made it clear that he no longer wants my support or, as he would see it, interference. He is a grown man and he needs to manage his own life. I refuse to let his actions destroy our future." His voice softened, "Moving west gives us the anonymity we, and our future children, need to be free from what he has done. I think it is for the best that we move to La Paz."

Hannah paused, several emotions filling her heart at once. She grieved for Drew's lost relationship with his brother. She feared the unknown dangers they would face on such a long journey. She would miss her home and her friends, even if many were no longer acting like her friends. Could she live in a gold town? What kind of rough men would be there? Would there be any reputable women there?

Frankly, she cared not, for she desperately wanted to remain here. "We cannot possibly move so far away."

With slow, deliberate movements, Drew deposited his spoon on the table. "Yes, we can."

"Have I no say?"

Drew's lips pressed into a thin line, matching the deep lines in his furrowed brow.

"I want to raise our children here. Our friends are here," her desperation grew. "Those that are angry with us could still change their minds."

"Hannah, stop!"

The forcefulness of his command halted any further words from forming. Folding her hands in her lap, appetite gone, she bowed her head, waiting for him to speak.

"We will be leaving in a few weeks." The cold words chilled her heart.

"So, you've decided then," she whispered.

"Yes," came the curt reply.

Standing, Hannah grabbed her bowl of barely touched food and tossed it in the waste pail. Drew remained seated, finishing his meal, while she began cleaning.

How could he be so unreasonable? Why not someplace closer? Hannah continued to stew over the decision as Drew left her kitchen. She did not agree with his decision. She did not understand it. There were so many other options. Yes, he said he thought God was leading them there. But, if He was, wouldn't she feel some sense of rightness in the decision?

Nothing about this seemed right to her. Instead of being settled in their new home in a few weeks, they would travel for months. How long would such a journey even take? How dangerous would it be?

The next morning Drew woke before the first sunrays peeked through the window in the upstairs bedroom. A bird whistled cheerfully from its perch on the tall maple tree next to the clinic. *Thank you, Lord, for this beautiful day. Calm my fears about this move. Help Hannah to have the courage and strength for this. I know she is sad to leave, but be with her. Help her to know your hand is in this.*

He slid his long legs over the side of the bed and stood, glancing back as Hannah began to stir. Her hair billowed as a soft cloud around her face. His breath caught and his heart swelled within his chest at the beautiful sight. He could hardly believe she was his wife. He loved her so dearly. She deserved the security she craved, and Drew vowed to see she would receive it—even if they must travel across the country to find it.

He washed up and dressed for the day before rushing down the stairs into his office. Certain there would be no patients again, he planned to use most of the day preparing for the move. Sitting at his desk, he made a mental checklist of things to accomplish for the day which included a trip to both the mercantile and the barber shop. Oh, and he also needed to stop by Doc Henderson's.

By the time he finished planning his day, the aroma of frying bacon wafted into his office beckoning him to eat. His stomach growled as he entered the kitchen. Hannah handed him a plate of fried eggs, toast, and bacon. Pouring himself a cup of coffee, he sat down at the table.

"I'm going to head over to Doc Henderson's this morning to invite him for supper tonight."

"Is this a social visit?" she asked, pushing the food around on her plate. Her sullen expression and lack of appetite concerned him. Was she still upset about the move?

Pushing his own question aside, he answered hers, "Since our clinic is larger than his current office, I thought I would give him the opportunity to make an offer."

"Alright, I'll be sure to make some pie for dessert then," Hannah replied softly still not making eye contact.

On any other day, Drew might try to draw his wife from her dour mood. But, his own worries vied for attention. Should Doc Henderson show no interest in the clinic, Drew thought it doubtful the house would sell before their departure. Someone outside of the medical profession would have to convert the surgery rooms and he suspected few potential buyers would welcome the extra work. Perhaps Mr. Davis would agree to act on his behalf if the house failed to sell.

Once finished with the meal, Drew kissed Hannah on the cheek then he retrieved his hat from the stand in the parlor. The street was relatively quiet this early in the morning so he quickly covered the short distance to the mercantile his father once owned. He smiled in greeting to Francis, the man who purchased the mercantile from Drew. He waited for the older man to finish with a customer before approaching the counter.

"Drew," Francis said, "What can I help you with this morning?"

"I came to see if you might have any information on traveling west."

"Hoping for a fortune in gold?" Francis teased.

Drew shook his head. "Specifically, what might one need to know to relocate to the Arizona Territory?"

Francis rubbed his hand across his chin, as he often did when considering a customer's request. After several minutes, he pointed Drew to a stack of books with specifics on westward travel. Flipping through the pages of several, Drew chose one to purchase.

"If you are serious about heading west you might want a copy of the schedule of departures from Fort Leavenworth. That is where most of the big westward bound wagon trains are leaving from these days."

Drew took the pamphlet and slid it in the front cover of the book. Thanking Francis for his assistance, Drew departed for his next errand.

With book in hand, Drew walked a few doors down to Mr. Tilley's barber shop. Sitting in the chair, he asked Mr. Tilley numerous questions about his brother's westward journey. Mr. Tilley explained that his brother's family boarded the steamboat here in Cincinnati and took it to Fort Leavenworth. Once there, they purchased supplies for the journey, including a wagon and team. When the haircut concluded, Mr. Tilley jotted down the contact information for the wagon train master his brother used.

As Drew started towards Doc Henderson's clinic on the other side of town, he considered the timing of the move. According to the schedule, the next wagon train departure would be in mid-

September. If they left in two weeks, they should have enough time to get to Fort Leavenworth and purchase supplies for the trip. He would bring his medical supplies with him. Hopefully he could convince Hannah to only bring the absolute necessities—certain that space would be limited in the wagon.

Slowing his pace as he neared Doc Henderson's, Drew bounded up the stairs and into the crowded waiting room. Inwardly he cringed when greeted with the unwelcoming glares of the patients. Doc Henderson's nurse looked up and smiled as Drew moved further into the room.

"Dr. Anderson, what can I do for you this morning?" she asked.

"I've come to speak with Doc Henderson for a moment, but I see his is quite busy, perhaps I should—"

"Drew, my boy!" exclaimed the elderly doctor as he led the previous patient to the door. "What brings you here this fine day?"

One mother with a colicky infant, presumably tired of waiting, scowled at Drew as he answered, "I was hoping to speak with you for a brief moment."

"Come on back."

Feeling the piercing looks against his back, Drew followed the doctor into his private office. "I would be honored, Doc, if you would join us for supper this evening. I have a few things to discuss with you."

"Certainly. You know I love Mrs. Anderson's apple pie. Any chance she might be planning to bake one today?"

"Well, I guess you'll just have to stop by around six to find out," Drew countered. He enjoyed the friendly banter with his colleague.

Doc Henderson eagerly agreed and wished him a good day as Drew ran the gauntlet of testy folks in the packed parlor.

With the whispers and frowns from Doc Henderson's patients, he no longer doubted his decision to leave. The townsfolk refused to trust him again, though the trust broke through no fault of his own. Anger boiled to the surface. How could Thomas be so selfish! Did he have any idea what his actions were costing his brother?

That evening, Doc Henderson arrived promptly at six. Drew greeted him warmly and showed him into the parlor. While Hannah finished preparing supper, they filled the time with talk of the medical profession.

When Hannah stepped into the parlor, Doc greeted her, "Mrs. Anderson, so good to see you."

"Doc, I have a surprise for you," she said, leading the way to the quaint table in the kitchen.

"Tell me, did you make some of your famous apple pie for dessert?"

"Of course. I know it's your favorite," she replied taking her usual spot to Drew's right.

Doc Henderson smiled, obviously pleased by the news. Drew motioned for him to take the seat on his left. Taking his place at the head of the table, he bowed his head and offered thanks for the meal, silently asking God to motivate Doc Henderson to buy the clinic.

Following the simple, albeit selfish, prayer, Drew started, "Well, Doc, as you know in recent weeks the townsfolk have made their displeasure with my brother's actions more than noticeable. I have not had a single patient for some time now."

And the last one died—that frail politician that suffered from an infected abscess. What if his last patient turned out to be his very last patient—if he could never practice medicine again? He tried to ignore the nagging thought, refocusing his attention on his guest.

Waving a drumstick of chicken in the air to accent his words, Doc Henderson said, "A shame it is too. I keep telling folks, there is no wait over here." Remembering the chicken in his hand, he took a large bite. His eyes lit with awe as he slowly chewed, overtly enjoying the savory flavor.

"I know and we appreciate your encouragement." He smiled, more from Doc's joy over the meal than from his words. He, too, enjoyed Hannah's fried chicken. "However, Hannah and I have decided to move west to the Arizona Territory. There is a great need for trained doctors in the booming gold towns and we believe a fresh start would be best."

Doc swallowed a mouthful of food. "Are you certain? That is a terribly dangerous territory. No place for a gentlewoman, such as your lovely Hannah."

"Yes, our decision is final. Preparations are underway and we leave in early September." Drew wished he felt as confident as he sounded. "Now, for the reason I asked you here this evening. I wanted to offer you the opportunity to purchase the clinic."

"Well, I am pleased you spoke with me first. I would be interested in purchasing the clinic—" Doc paused for affect. "—but not for myself. My nephew Mark plans to join me when he finishes medical school. He should have been here already, but he decided to stay on for a few additional classes. He plans to arrive in December. This clinic would make an excellent gift for a young doctor craving independence from his old uncle, don't you think?"

Drew nodded his agreement, as he finished the last bite of mashed potatoes and gravy from his plate. Hannah stood and began clearing the plates from the table, still saying nothing. When she brought slices of the apple pie for each of them, Drew saw a frown flit across her features before she pasted on a rather forced smile.

"Mrs. Anderson, thank you for the excellent meal," Doc Henderson beamed. Then turning to Drew, he added, "It is a wonder that you are able to keep so trim. I would not be so fortunate if I were married to such a marvelous cook."

Hannah's smile turned genuine at the compliment as Drew laughed at Doc's teasing. "It is a miracle."

After Doc finished off two slices of Hannah's sweet apple pie, Drew showed him around both the clinic and living quarters. Then the two men returned to the parlor to finalize the arrangements of the sale. As Drew escorted Doc Henderson to the front door, he could scarcely believe things were falling into place.

Chapter 3

North Texas

August 28, 1863

The day started like any other on the ranch, early and full of work. After feeding and watering the horses, Will began rubbing down Jackson, his tawny brown stallion and best friend. There was something calming about the routine action.

Routine. That was just what William Colter longed for this day of all days. But today would be anything but routine, because today he would bury his father. Will's breath caught as the thought passed through his mind. Moisture gathered in the corners of his eyes. He blinked several times rapidly, willing the tears to stay at bay. "Ranchers don't cry son," he recalled his father saying when his mother passed a few years ago. "At least not in front of the cowboys. You must be in control and run the ranch with strength."

Sage advice from the man he admired so.

Clearing his throat, Will hastily saddled Jackson. His six foot frame easily mounted the majestic animal. This morning he dressed in typical rancher garb—sturdy jeans, his trusty leather cowboy boots, and a blue button down cotton shirt stretching across his broad chest. His light tan hat covered his dark hair. Most days, he wore a handkerchief over his nose to keep from choking on the dust kicked up from the cattle, but he forgot it this morning, his attention scattered.

As he neared the far pasture, he spotted the ever faithful Benjamin Shepherd. Ben was a kindly cowboy, sitting astride his black mare, Sheila. Why Ben named his horse Sheila was still a topic of debate among the hands. Some think that Ben was once sweet on a Mississippi gal named Sheila. Others suspected the mare was named after his dear ol' ma.

Regardless of the reason behind the horse's name, it seemed contradictory to the rough appearance of the man. Almost twenty-five years ago Edward Colter, Will's father, hired Ben as the foreman of the Star C Ranch. The two men formed a trusted friendship over the years. When the Colter brothers, Reuben and then Will, were old enough to ride and rope, Ben taught them the skills. When Will was younger, he used to think Ben a giant at almost six feet tall. His broad shoulders nearly spanned the door frame of the bunkhouse. His legs were as thick as a tree—at least to a child they appeared so.

"Didn't expect to see you out here this morning, boss," rumbled Ben's deep voice, pulling Will's attention back to the present. "Shouldn't you be gittin' ready to head in to town to bury your pa?"

Will always felt like he should respond to Ben with a "yes sir" or "no sir" like he did with his father. Countless times the elder Colter reminded him that was not necessary as the rancher's son, and definitely not at his twenty-nine years of age. Still, Will respected Ben greatly, and found the old habit hard to break. Uncertain how to reply, Will merely grunted.

"The boys and me got things under control out here, so you can tend to the family," Ben reassured, as he turned his horse back towards the long-horned steers grazing contentedly in the warm sun.

Being dismissed, Will turned Jackson back toward the ranch. What had he been thinking to ride out there? He should have known Ben would frown upon his presence rounding up the cattle today. Giving Jackson a kick with his boots, he urged the animal into a trot. Maybe he came out here because he needed the time to think. He did his best thinking in the wide open spaces sitting in his style saddle. And his mind was going far faster than Jackson was covering ground this morning.

Watching his father die was not something Will cared to remember. But the memory pressed forward, obscuring the flat pasture in front of him. Two days ago, Edward Colter was the perfect picture of health for a man in his late fifties. Trim and well-muscled. Used to long hours in the saddle and the difficult labor of working the ranch. Though since mother passed, father spent more time at the ranch house and less time in the pastures.

Tears stung Will's eyes as the unwanted images from his father's last morning alive danced across his vision. Father insisted on accompanying Will out to see the herd. As the summer started to fade, the time drew near to send the cattle to market. His father told him he wanted to see with his own eyes the fine work his youngest son had done growing the herd.

At first, everything appeared normal with the herd as they grazed on the sweet Texas grass. Then the fearful sound started—a low rumbling giving way to a crescendo of thundering hooves. The cattle frantically stampeded towards them. Will kicked Jackson forcefully, moving him northward out of the way. His father chose the opposite, more fateful direction, not clearing the onslaught of crazed animals in time. When Will turned, expecting to see his father right behind him, his stomach sank to the ground. He only caught a brief glimpse of his father before the herd swallowed him and his horse.

Swiping at the tears now freely falling down his dust coated face, Will prayed that God would let the horrific memory fade. No one should watch his father die in such a painful manner.

By the time the herd cleared and Will made it to his father's side, Edward squeezed a few words of praise for his son past his battered lips.

"You have made me prouder than any man has a right to be," his weak voice etched the sentiment into Will's soul before taking his last breath.

It was awful—slinging his father's bloodied and beaten body over Jackson's back, taking him to his home for the last time. Will snorted at the injustice of such an experienced rancher dying in an unexpected stampede. None of it made any sense. Edward Colter should have lived his life to old age, bouncing his grandchildren on his knee. But none of that would come to pass.

Will wished he could dwell on what should have been. Instead, his own future had become a jumbled mess in the wake of this loss. What would he do now that his father was gone? Would Reuben let him stay at the ranch? *Doubtful.* Did he want to stay, being reminded of his father's last hours each time he rode out for the day?

What he wanted might not make a difference. Depending on the terms of his father's will, the best possible situation Will could find himself in would be half owner of the Star C Ranch, though that was unlikely. Reuben, five years his senior, as the first-born son, would likely inherit the ranch. Given the option of staying under Reuben's arrogant leadership, or striking out on his own, Will preferred the latter.

Other than appearance, the two Colter brothers shared little in common. Where Will learned everything he could about ranching, Reuben wanted little to do with the labor of working the ranch. He would rather sit in the ranch house plotting and scheming how he could get richer quicker—by any means necessary. Will lived with a deep faith like his parents. Reuben scoffed at religion, unless he could find a way to manipulate it for his own benefit. Will developed a keen business mind as well as the ability to work the stock. He was an expert with his rifle and his rope. While Reuben learned these skills as a young man, he wanted nothing to do with the dirt and dust of the outdoors.

As Will neared the house, he slowed Jackson's pace to a lope. He looked up to see Julia retreating indoors. At sixteen years of age, the youngest of the Colter clan was just over thirteen years younger than Will. While there had been other children between Will and Julia, they died as toddlers or were stillborn. His mother had not expected to have any more children, but was thrilled at Julia's birth.

Growing a bit too quickly into a woman, Julia favored their father more than the brothers did. She shared his bright blue eyes and sandy brown hair. The curls were a trait from their mother. Like their father, she was shorter than Will and Reuben, coming only to Will's chest. Her petite waist and curvy features were starting to be noticed by the young cowboys, sparking Will's protective instincts. She shared Edward Colter's zest for life—everything was an adventure. She idolized Will and he spoiled her, teaching her to shoot, ride, and rope as good as any of the hands. In recent years, their father insisted she spend less time following Will around and more time in domestic pursuits. She resisted at first, but eventually settled into her new role.

He dismounted and tied Jackson to the hitching post. Absently kicking the dust from his boots, Will walked through the front doorway, making his way to his room to change into his Sunday best. By the time he joined the family, Julia was already situated in the wagon. She held Reuben's toddlers in her lap. Reuben helped his wife, Mary, up to the front seat of the wagon. Scowling at Will, he climbed up next to his wife without a word. Reuben slapped the reins and the wagon lurched into motion, groaning in protest.

Will mounted Jackson and followed along wordlessly. He learned a long time ago that the fewer words passing between him and Reuben, the more peaceful the day would be. Glancing over at Julia as he rode alongside, they locked gazes. Her eyes were swollen and red-rimmed from crying. She attempted a smile, but it was strained. He could only wonder what changes would be in store for both of them, now that the family patriarch was gone.

Wagons and horses lined the streets near the small white church on the edge of town. Many ranchers and townsfolk already crowded into the graveyard next to the church. Edward Colter was well respected, so Will expected the large number of mourners. Will found a spot to tie his mount, then hurried to help his sister from the parked wagon. The family took their place at the front of the grave site where the pastor waited. Will stood next to Julia across from Reuben, Mary, and the two squirming children.

The service was short, but respectful. The pastor read from Psalms 23, while Will recited it quietly to himself. The Lord really was his comfort and he knew his father was dwelling in the house of the Lord even this minute—no matter how he longed to have his father still at his side. Julia reached over for his hand, but he put his arm around her instead as she tried to wipe the tears from her face. One of the ladies from church sang "Amazing Grace." When she finished, Will took Julia by the hand and led her back to the wagon through the crowd.

Back at the ranch house, the women from the community prepared a meal for the family. Although Will longed for peace and quiet, he appreciated the gesture. Many of the area ranchers and townsfolk came for the meal as well. Each person offered their condolences and shared stories of his father. It was good to hear how much his father meant to these people.

Reuben seemed relatively unaffected by the events of the day. As Will watched from a corner, his older brother worked the room to his own advantage. Of course, Reuben would never do anything to lessen the perfect perception others held of him. He slyly used the mourners' sympathies to garner support for his latest scheme—whatever it may be.

Will, disgusted by his brother's display, moved to the background where he could observe without engaging. Looking around the room, he watched Julia in deep conversation with her best friend, Caroline. He hoped the time Julia spent with Caroline would lift her spirits. She had been inconsolable since he brought their father's lifeless form home.

Another wave of sadness washed over him. Seeing that no one would miss him, Will ducked out the front door. He needed some time alone. Taking Jackson by the reins, he led him into the stable, removed the gear and began brushing him down.

Will would miss his father—he already did. His wise counsel kept Will from many a foolish decision over the years. He hoped to run his own ranch as well as his father. He led by example, full of integrity. His men respected him. His children—at least Will and Julia—loved and adored him. The townsfolk and neighboring ranchers thought highly of him. Will prayed he would be much like his father.

As he breathed in the scent of hay intermingled with horseflesh, his thoughts turned to his sister again. This was going to be toughest on Julia. She needed a father's love, especially since their mother was gone. Who will protect her? Who will find her an honorable husband in a few years? Would Will be able to take her with him, wherever he went, to protect her?

Not having any of the answers to his many questions, Will dejectedly returned to the ranch house and to the waiting throng of mourners. One thing was certain, the coming days would bring change.

Monday morning dawned early. Three days passed since they buried their father, and today was the day they would hear Edward James Colter's will. Although none of the children knew the specifics of their father's last wishes, Will was certain each of them would be well cared for. As he donned his usual jeans and work shirt, he glanced out the window. Reuben already waited out front with the wagon and his horse. *He must be eager to leave.*

Julia sat sullenly next to Reuben, looking down at her folded hands in her lap. Will quickly mounted the saddled horse tied to the post and led the way to town at a gentle pace. The short distance to town passed quickly. Reuben pulled the wagon to a stop in front of the attorney's office. After helping Julia down, he led the way into the building, leaving Will trailing behind.

Reuben took the seat directly across from Mr. Gainsly, Attorney At Law. Julia sat to his right. Will leaned against the wall furthest from Reuben, crossing his arms over his chest. He rested his right leg over his left, settling the toe of his right boot on the floor.

"Shall we begin," stated Mr. Gainsly. In his gravelly monotonous voice he read the will. "To my first born son, Reuben James Colter, I give full ownership of the Star C Ranch land and house. The herd and stock are to be equally distributed between Reuben and my second son, William Edward Colter—"

"What!" Reuben shouted, pounding his fist down on Mr. Gainsly's desk, causing Julia to jump at the abrupt motion. "Why should Will get half of everything?"

Will stood upright, uncrossing his arms. Facing Reuben, he said in a low voice through gritted teeth, "I have as much right to half of the ranch as you do. If anyone should be complaining about the terms, I should—since I am to get none of the land or the house."

Reuben stood, puffing out his chest. The act made him look ridiculous in his fancy brown suit and bowler hat. Anger creased his face and his tone became harsh, "I am the first born son—"

Will moved closer. "A fact of which you remind me of constantly. Still, that has nothing to do with father's last wishes."

Reuben took a step closer towards Will, the two separated only by Julia still seated in the chair. Mr. Gainsly looked horrified by the confrontation between the two brothers and Julia began sobbing.

She reached up and touched Will on the arm. In a soft voice she said, "Please, stop."

Will looked from Mr. Gainsly's discomfort, to Reuben's fierce anger, to Julia's pleading. Returning his fisted hand to his side, he took a step back, closer to the wall. Nodding towards Mr. Gainsly, Will said in a flat tone, "Please, continue."

Mr. Gainsly looked from Will to Julia to Reuben. "Very well, then. Mr. Colter," he said referring to Reuben, "please take a seat. I understand that our loved one's last wishes can be a bit of a shock— sometimes they make choices we may not agree with. I assure you, your father was very clear, wishing to be as fair as possible for all three of you."

As Reuben returned to his seat, Mr. Gainsly continued reading, "Other than a sum set aside for Julia Catherine Colter, my daughter, the remaining financial holdings are to be equally divided between Reuben and William," he paused, looking to Reuben. Reuben growled, but remained seated. "If Julia has not yet reached her majority, Reuben will be her guardian and the trustee of her stipend."

Reuben's face went from anger to delight in a few short seconds, prompting Will's distrust. Why did that news please Reuben? He barely seemed to notice her, though they lived under the same roof. Was it controlling her money? Or was there something more?

Finally, Gainsly's irritating voice halted. The room remained silent for a few short seconds before Reuben made his wishes known.

"Please see to the details of dividing the money," Reuben commanded with his usual air of superiority. "If there is nothing further, let us be on our way."

Standing, Reuben, in an uncharacteristic display, waited for Julia to control herself. Looking at Will over her seated form, Reuben gave him a bone-chilling glare. If Will had any doubt about his brother's feelings towards him, that look clearly communicated his loathing. When Julia finally rose, Reuben led her to the wagon without waiting for Will. As Will walked out of the attorney's office, Reuben already set the wagon in motion towards home.

On the ride back to the Star C with the dust of the wagon in the distance, Will considered his options. With half of the financial holdings and half the herd, he could make a nice start somewhere else. He knew there was no chance Reuben would let him stay. The animosity between the two brothers was too great. Will was the conscious Reuben never wanted. Perhaps there was a nearby rancher looking to sell out. That would allow him to stay in Texas and keep watch over Julia.

His thoughts went back to Julia's new guardian. Why had father left her to Reuben's care? Will shook his head, knowing the answer. Father never saw the darkest side of Reuben, so he would naturally leave Julia to his eldest son's care, especially since he left the land

and house to him. While he left Will with financial holdings and a herd, he did not leave him a home, limiting his ability to provide for Julia. Though he understood it, he disapproved.

Instead of stopping at the ranch house, Will continued out to the pasture to work. The more he thought about his situation his aggravation rose. In one short day, Will went from being the rancher's second son, to owning half of everything—except the land and house. A part of him understood why father did not leave him a home, yet a part of him resented it. Perhaps if he and Reuben acted more like brothers and less like enemies, father would have left them both the Star C. But, his wise father knew a partnership between his two sons would never succeed. This knowledge failed to take away the sting. He spent his life putting his heart and soul into this ranch and now he would have to leave.

He rallied from his thoughts, hearing the sound of an approaching rider. Ben must have spotted him, because he rode toward Will while he was still a hundred yards out from where the herd was grazing.

"Whoa there!" Ben said as he reined Sheila up next to Will. "How was the meeting in town?"

Will spent the next hour explaining the highlights of his father's estate and his own reaction to the news. When he finished, he confided in Ben. "Leaving is the only option, but where?"

"Startin' over is going to take some doing," Ben commiserated. "Remember in the spring when yer pa was talking about the Arizona Territory and those reports he heard of good grazin' land throughout the place? Maybe we could drive the cattle out there and set up a ranch."

Did Ben want to go with him? "We?" Will asked. "You don't have to come with me, Ben. You know Reuben won't be happy."

Ben's sour expression told Will what he thought of that. His features softened as he continued, "You'll be needing someone to watch yer back and I figured since I've been doing it for this many years, what's a few more."

"Well, I would be glad to have you along." Truthfully, Will could not imagine making a move without his old friend. "Your idea of going to the Arizona Territory has merit, if you think your old bones can hold out for that long," Will teased.

"Humph." Ben grumbled, heartily patting Will on the back. "I can still out ride you young 'un. Speaking of riding, think it's about time to get to work."

Will fell in behind Ben as he led the way out to where a few strays ambled further from the herd. Positioning his horse outside the strays, he gently guided them back to their place in the herd. The heaviness of the week's events wore on his mind and he lost track of time as he diligently watched the longhorns.

As the sun lowered in the sky, Will suddenly realized he came dangerously close to being late for supper. He pointed Jackson toward the stables covering the distance quickly. After caring for the stallion, he washed up outside, then made his way to the table. The ire written on Mary's face told him she considered him late. Mumbling a quick apology to his sister-in-law, he took his seat.

As Reuben assumed their father's seat at the head of the table, Will felt anew the loss. Things were definitely changing at the Star C, no longer under the watchful stewardship of his father.

Julia and Will bowed their heads, expecting Reuben to say grace. Hearing the clank of dishes being passed, Will looked up at Reuben, confused. Julia's head also snapped up, a questioning look on her face.

"What are you gawking at?" Reuben snapped. "You know I don't hold for any of that religious nonsense. If you feel it is necessary to offer up empty platitudes to your so called God, then, by all means, pray away." He waved his hands in the air in a disdainful manner. "It won't stop us from starting supper."

Sitting in his father's seat was expected. Dismissing God was not. Will's blood began to boil. Reuben really had some gall.

Julia closed her eyes and must have offered up a silent prayer, since she did not reach for any food immediately. Will was too angry to pray right this minute. Hopefully, God would understand. He grabbed the potatoes and dished some onto his plate with more force than was necessary. Taking a deep breath, he tried to cool his temper. He knew Reuben was purposely being spiteful, trying to get a reaction from him.

"When will you be leaving, Will?" Reuben said snidely.

The words hit Will as hard as if Reuben slapped him across the face. And so the jockeying begins, he thought wryly.

Mary's jaw dropped. Obviously, Reuben said nothing to her about the possibility of Will's departure. Julia dropped her fork and shot a look Will's direction of both surprise and pleading. For once, even the two children were silent. All motion stopped and every eye focused intently on him.

Will clenched his jaw and stated evenly, "What makes you think I'm leaving?" He hated when Reuben tried to manipulate him.

"Of course you are leaving, William," Reuben sneered. "I'm simply giving you the opportunity to inform this family of when you will be ready to leave." He paused, changing to a more benevolent tone. "If you'd like, I can choose the timing, although I don't think you would be pleased with my choice."

The metal of Will's fork dug into his skin as his hold tightened in proportion to his rising temper. *We only just went to the reading of the will this morning and he's already trying to force me out.* He should have been prepared for this, but he hadn't expected Reuben to play this card so soon. "I haven't made any definite plans yet."

"You have two weeks," Reuben replied, as he gingerly popped a bite of meat into his mouth. The smug, confident look on his face served only to further Will's irritation.

"What!" Will shouted as his face grew heated. He dropped his fork and stood so rapidly that he knocked his chair over, his temper getting the best of him.

"Sit down Will and stop acting like you are surprised. Surely you are aware that I do not hold any sentimental feelings for you." His dark glare punctuated the statement. "I want you off my property in two weeks."

The dismissive tone was more than Will could take. He lunged toward Reuben. "What gives you the right to dictate orders to me?"

Reuben pushed back his chair and stood nose to nose with Will. "I am sole owner of Star C Ranch and *I* do not wish to have you here any longer." Will felt the heat of his brother's breath on his face. Reuben continued with a more chivalrous tone, "It is out of concern for Julia that I am allowing you to stay that long. Make no mistake, William, you are no longer welcome on *my* property." With the last words he inched closer to Will, never breaking eye contact.

It took all of Will's strength not to sling his fist at his brother. Perhaps it was Julia's gasp at Reuben's statement that reminded Will it would do no good to put up a fight. Or maybe it was the steely, sinister look in his brother's eyes that held him back. Regardless, his appetite vanished and his temper flared. Will stepped back, turned on his heal, and stormed out the front door.

Chapter 4

Well after dusk, Will returned to the house. He stalked straight to his room, relieved Reuben seemed to be otherwise occupied. The ride did little to help Will solve his problem. Two weeks was not much time to plan a move if he knew where he was going, much less if he had no idea where to go. Pacing the length of the room in the small space between the bed and the dresser, his boots clomped loudly against the wooden floor. His mind continued to mull over his circumstance, but he came up with no solutions. Perhaps a trip to town tomorrow would be wise. At least he could see if there was news of anyone looking to sell out.

A soft knock on the door brought his feet to a halt.

"Will?" Julia whispered.

"Come in," he answered as he opened the door.

"I found these while going through father's bedroom," Julia said, handing Will a stack of letters. "The first several look like information about the Arizona Territory. I think they are personal letters, but perhaps you could review them? I also found several of mother's letters. If you don't mind, I would like to keep those."

Will heard the unuttered request to keep this bit of information from Reuben. Reuben would only try to use these letters to his advantage, finding some way to manipulate him or Julia. It was best to keep both sets of letters from him, unless some information directly pertained to the Star C.

He took the bundle and slid it under his pillow, nodding in agreement to her request before returning his attention to his sister.

Julia bowed her head, her long curls hiding her face from his view. She stared at the worn wood floor making no move to leave, or to speak. Knowing his sister's moods well, he asked, "Would you like to take a walk?"

Nodding, she turned and led the way outside and away from eavesdropping ears.

The dark night sky shimmered with sparkling stars as Will and Julia walked towards the corral. The cowboys' laughter from the nearby bunkhouse floated across the air. The horses in the stable next to the corral snorted, settling down for the night. As Will leaned forward against the corral, he breathed deeply, smelling the fresh night air spiced with a light fragrance of hay. He placed one foot on the lowest rung before propping his arms against the top rung. Julia stood next to him, leaning her arms on the top rung in a similar fashion. They stood this way for several minutes before either spoke.

"I don't want you to leave," Julia lamented. "I will miss you terribly."

A few more seconds of silence passed before she asked, "Where will you go? Do you have to leave so soon? Can't you talk to Reuben and ask for more time?"

Will sighed in frustration, knowing her last question was completely unrealistic. If he pressed Reuben, he was likely to get even less time rather than more.

Taking a minute to gather his thoughts, Will recalled the conversation with Ben this morning, and then remembered the stack of letters Julia handed him. While he had no opportunity to read those letters, Will was struck by the coincidence. Both were about the Arizona Territory. *Lord, is this from you? Is this the answer I have been searching for?* For the first time since his father passed, Will felt a hint of peace. Perhaps the Arizona Territory would become his new home.

"Well, I will probably head out west," he said, finally answering Julia. "Rumor is that there are good ranch lands in the new Arizona Territory. It's something father was looking into last spring."

Several silent seconds ticked by before Julia sniffled.

Turning to face his sister, Will said, "Julia, you know I can't stay here at the Star C. I'm not sure I would even be able to stay in the area. I'll have to find someplace where I can support myself. Ranching is what I know, so I will go where I can do that."

"But I don't want to stay here with Reuben. He is so cold and calculating."

Will stifled another sigh. She feared Reuben as much as he feared leaving her with him. Feeling helpless to change the situation, Will tried to offer her encouragement. "You know he has always treated you with respect, Julia. It is me that spurs his hatred. With me gone, he will be more bearable." He prayed.

"I hope so." She paused, her voice getting softer, "It's just that, who will I talk to?"

Will half smiled, knowing Julia never wanted for a listening ear. But, he appreciated the sentiment all the same. He loved that his little sister adored him. "There's Caroline. And Mary can be pleasant at times."

Again the silence stretched. Will looked up to the flickering stars in the black night sky. Would the stars in Arizona look the same? Would he really be able to make a home there?

Julia's whispered words cut through his thoughts. "I didn't think I would lose everyone I care about at the same time." Her voice broke and the tears came.

Moving to her side, he put his arms around her, resting his chin on the top of her head. Will empathized. It would be difficult leaving his dear little sister behind. It was a loss they would both feel deeply. Losing their father would leave emptiness, but this would intensify the loneliness. He waited silently for many minutes until Julia's sobbing subsided.

As the laughter from the bunkhouse died down and the lights dimmed, Will became aware of the hour. "It is getting late," he said, leading Julia back to the house.

After seeing Julia safely to her room, he returned to his own. Lighting the oil lamp on the stand next to his bed, he retrieved the bundle of letters from under his pillow. Lounging on his bed, he pulled the first letter from the stack. It appeared to be from one of the advance military scouts to the region. Will was surprised his father actually received the letter, especially since Texas was no longer part of the Union. There were five or so letters exchanged between his father and the writer who remained anonymous in his returned correspondence.

Eager to confirm his thoughts about the territory, Will read the letters. He learned about several areas of land in the southwestern region that had been Mexican ranch lands prior to the Gadsden Purchase. Several new ranches were already sprouting up. Tucson was a growing city and some of the outlying areas were suitable for farming and ranching. This area had a large Mexican population.

Most of the whites were former southerners, so he might be welcomed there, though he did not consider himself a southerner.

The author stated the Hassayampa River in the north central territory would also support ranching. The last letter on the topic indicated a small group of miners discovered gold in the area, which was gaining the attention of the appointed governor of the new territory. This was one of the regions being considered by the governor as a potential location for the capital. A small fort was scheduled to be established by the end of the year. The writer described this region as, "…an area ripe for settlement. The large open grasslands are mostly suitable for cattle ranching. The grass is of a hearty nature, able to endure in a relatively dry climate. Any cattle of a durable nature should thrive here. The rolling hills filled with grass lead way to river valleys and mountains topped with dense forests of pine, cedar, and other strong woods. The discovery of gold will likely cause an increase of prospectors to the area in search of their long deserved fortunes."

Will's interest piqued. This Hassayampa River area sounded very promising. In one of the letters, the author outlined a rough route from Santa Fe to the river. He should be able to drive the cattle from here to Santa Fe, then on to the new territory.

Yawning, Will remembered the late hour. After folding up the letters and storing them in a safe place, he turned down the light. Even though his mind was full of ideas and planning, exhaustion won and he fell asleep almost instantly.

After discussing the letters with Ben and spending time praying over the decision, Will gained confidence that the move to Arizona was the right one. He had much to get done in the next few days, as Reuben's imposed deadline rapidly approached.

This morning was the day he and Reuben agreed to divide the herd, per the instructions dictated in their father's will. Since they were not due to head to market for a few weeks yet, the herd was at its largest.

As he neared the herd, the lowing of the cattle became welcome background noise. Dust swirled around the longhorns and the cowboys as the animals moved slowly forward. Something seemed different this morning, though Will could not pinpoint what caused him to think that.

"Herd looks a mite unusual," Ben stated as Will reined in next to him.

Then Will clearly saw the difference. All of the weaker thinner cattle stood on the right and the strongest, fattest longhorns stood on the left. Never in all of his years ranching had he seen such an unnatural formation.

Hearing hoof beats approaching, Will glanced over his shoulder. Reuben, flanked by several of the seedier cowboys in his employ, rode towards the herd. Reuben looked stiff and uncomfortable astride his mare. It had been years since Will had seen his brother on horseback and in the pasture. He was obviously out of practice.

Once he and his men arrived, Reuben tried to assert his wishes on how to best divide the herd. "I think we should ride up the middle of the herd. I'll take what is on the left and you take what is on the right."

What was Reuben up to? Did he really think Will was ignorant? Stifling a snort of disgust, Will stated, "Let's have Ben cut the herd as usual. Then we can count off equal numbers for each of us."

"I disagree," Reuben retorted. "My proposal is quite valid."

Will moved his mount alongside Reuben's. Leaning in towards his brother, he said in low tones, "I'm not oblivious to your scheme, Reuben. Unless you want to hop off your mare and settle this man to man, I suggest you stop this nonsense."

"Are you threatening me?"

Narrowing his eyes, Will kept his focus on his shifty brother while directing his words to Ben. "Let's get started."

Before Reuben could object, Ben issued instructions to the cowboys, following Will's guidance.

The process took a significant portion of the day. At first Reuben blustered complaints with each good steer directed to Will's herd, but after seeing the impossibility of the situation, he acquiesced. Several of the cowboys commented on how evenly matched the two herds were. Will was very pleased with both the quality and quantity of longhorns. In addition to half the herd, totaling three thousand head, Will took half of the breeding stock and horses.

Relieved that one major task was completed, Will turned his attention to the next hurdle—cowboys to drive the herd west.

Once word spread of his departure, several of the younger cowboys expressed an interest moving west. Including Ben, he had four men to drive the cattle. That number would barely cover point at the front of the herd and flank riders in the middle of the herd for one shift. He needed at least six more men just to cover two shifts for all the positions. In addition, he would need to get a chuck wagon, a cook, more horses, and a wrangler to care for the horses. All of this posed a difficult challenge in the short timeframe left, especially considering many ranchers would be going to market soon. He would also need a good number of supplies.

Although nearing supper time, Will rode into town. He arrived shortly before the general store closed, so he hurriedly posted hiring notices. He also made arrangements for some of the needed supplies. Darting out the door, he headed to the livery to purchase the chuck wagon. He would return to pick it up tomorrow.

Before leaving town, he heard a ruckus down the street and went to check it out. Several cowboys and ranchers that frequented the saloon stood outside discussing some topic heatedly in the street. Staying on the edge of the crowd, Will caught enough of the conversation to learn that the Union blockaded the main cattle trail to New Orleans. They were cut off from supplying the Confederate Army with much needed beef. The crowd grew agitated, throwing down curses on their former northern countrymen. Seeing tempers spiraling out of control Will made his way back to the ranch.

While he did not relish the impact this bad news would have on his fellow ranchers, it could benefit Will. He would be leaving at an opportune time, headed toward other markets. This may make hiring less difficult, now that many area cowboys would fear for their jobs.

"Boss," Ben greeted as Will stepped on to the ranch house porch the next morning. "We have some trouble."

With the deadline just over a week away, trouble was not something Will had time to deal with. He raised his hand to the back of his neck, trying to rub some of the growing tension away. Resisting the urge to grit his teeth, he asked, "What now?"

"Seems some of the cattle are missing," Ben replied.

He groaned, dropping his hand back to his side. "How many?"

"At least a hundred head."

Will sighed. How could he keep from losing cattle to Reuben—for he was sure that is where the missing cattle would be found—and keep up with all he had to do to prepare for the move?

"See if you can discreetly get them back," Will stated. "Then find some way to mark them so we don't have this issue for the next week and a half. Try to keep Reuben out of it, if possible."

Ben asked, "You thinking we should rebrand 'em?"

"No. We don't have time for that." Will failed to keep the frustration from his voice. "Talk it over with Pace and see if you can't come up with something temporary."

Ben nodded. Mounting Sheila, he pointed her towards the herd at a trot.

Will stood still for a moment, wishing again for more time. How could he pull everything together in such a short time? The impossibility of the task nipped at his confidence.

Pulling himself from hopelessness, he headed to the stable and geared up Jackson. He had to stay focused on the long list of things needing accomplished and not give in to worry and fear. Leading his horse from the stable, he met up with Pedro, one of his men, for the ride to town. Each hoof beat brought him one step closer to crossing a few of those items from his list.

Once at the livery, Will helped Pedro harness the oxen he purchased to the supply wagon. Then they rigged the chuck wagon behind it. Bringing up the rear was Pedro's horse tethered to the chuck wagon. Pedro drove the double wagon to the store, then helped Will load the supplies he bought the day before.

Heaving crate after crate into the wagons was a tiresome job with only the two of them. Unfortunately, Will could spare no more than one man from watching his herd—and he could not really spare the one. He desperately needed more than the five hands—otherwise this move would not happen. He still had roughly ten days, which seemed to be ticking by swiftly.

Having managed the cattle drives for the past eight years, Will knew how to plan for the drive. However, this was more than a routine drive to market. This was a permanent move to a relatively unpopulated territory, bringing with it a myriad of unknowns. He knew supplies would be hard to come by once they arrived, so he had to account for that.

He never traveled on the western trails, so water availability might be a problem. While he could carry enough for the men in the wagons, he would never have enough room for water for the stock. The letters to his father mentioned several watering areas between Santa Fe and his final destination. But, he had no information about what the conditions would be like between here and Santa Fe. What if there was no water? The season had been unusually dry. Could the Canadian River be dry in some areas further west? How far did the Canadian flow? This whole situation was madness.

Grunting under the weight of the last crate, Will dropped it into the supply wagon. He just needed to keep moving forward. *Please, God, help me get this all done.*

As Pedro pointed the loaded wagons back towards the ranch, Will mounted Jackson and directed him towards the Larson's ranch. Horses were the next obstacle and hopefully George Larson would be able to supply what he needed. Larson Ranch maintained a well-deserved reputation for breeding the highest quality horses in north Texas—perhaps even the entire state.

Reining in Jackson by the stables, Will was greeted by his sister's friend Caroline, the oldest of the Larson girls.

"Will, what brings you our way?" the young blonde asked, setting a full basket of eggs on the ground near her feet.

"I came to speak with George about purchasing some horses," Will replied. "Is he around?"

Caroline nodded towards the stables, "He's is in the back." She paused, before asking, "How is Julia?"

"As well as can be expected. You should come for dinner after church on Sunday. I know she would welcome your company," Will suggested.

Caroline smiled with excitement. "Please tell her I plan to do just that. Wait here while I fetch Papa."

Seconds later, George Larson emerged from the stables trailed by his daughter. Caroline stooped down to pick up the basket of eggs. Waving at Will, she turned towards the house.

George Larson held out his hand in greeting. "Caroline said you are looking for more horses. I say that surprised me, given the number the Star C purchased just a few months ago. How many are you looking for?"

Will shook the offered hand then explained his situation and the planned move to the Arizona Territory. He finished by saying, "Since Reuben inherited the ranch, he has been throwing around his authority. I have just over ten days left before he wants me off the land."

George's expression grew grim. Having been close friends with Edward Colter for many years, he was no doubt troubled by Will's news.

Will continued, "I need an additional twenty horses for the drive." At least that is how many he would need if he could hire all of the necessary men. The pressure of the clock pushed heavier on his mind, ramping up his anxiety.

"I'm sorry, Will, but I don't have that many. Best I can do is five. The others we have in training right now have been paid for by other ranchers."

Will's shoulders slumped at the news. Five was a quarter of what he needed. "Is there any chance we could work out something with the other ranchers? If they don't need the horses right away, would they be willing to wait?"

George thought for a moment. "Well, I might be able to get you one or two more if Wilson agrees to wait. But, I can't promise anything. You know how much our horses are in demand, especially this time of year."

"Could you let me know by Sunday?"

"Sure. I'll talk with Wilson tomorrow. Then we'll let you know in church."

Will thanked George for his compromise before taking his leave. Five to seven horses was not what he hoped for. He would have to settle for lesser quality animals from the livery for the remaining number, if he could even secure that many. And those horses would not be accustomed to the cattle, which could pose a risk for his men—not that he had enough men yet.

Pulling Jackson to a stop outside the corral, Will frowned. Bates, the man he hired yesterday was just now saddling his horse. He should have been out with the herd hours ago.

"Bates!" Je called the cowboy to him. "Why aren't you out with the herd?"

The young man looked down, not meeting Will's gaze. "I was. But... Um... Mr. Reuben called me up to the house."

"For what?" Will growled, suspecting he would not like the cowboy's answer.

"Mr. Reuben offered me more money if I hired on with him for the drive to market," Bates replied before nudging his horse towards Reuben's herd, not giving Will a chance to argue.

Clenching his fist tightly, Will envisioned punching his brother in the face. Reuben's treachery knew no limits. Stealing his cattle. Hiring men out from under him with the promise of more money. Kicking him out with only two weeks' notice. What next? Would he set fire to Will's new wagon and supplies? Would he make him sleep in the barn for the next ten days? Why did he insist on making this more difficult than it already was?

Tying Jackson to the hitching post, Will stormed into the ranch house and directly into Reuben's office. He had to put a stop to this. Now.

Reuben jumped as Will flung the door open so hard it slammed against the wall.

Not attempting to hide his irritation, Will demanded, "We need to talk."

"Certainly, brother. Have a seat."

Will stood, arms crossed, behind the chair. "What are you trying to prove, Reuben?"

Eyes wide with feigned innocence, Reuben replied, "I have no idea what you are talking about, William. Perhaps you would care to explain?"

"I am talking about the cattle. I am talking about hiring men that I have already contracted. I am talking about your divisive tactics to sabotage me!" Will glared at his brother, resisting the urge to connect his fist with his brother's jaw.

"William, what a wild imagination you have," Reuben said as

he propped his elbows on his large walnut desk, tenting his fingers. "You and I have already divided the herd. If you are having a difficult time managing your half, that is not my concern. As far as hiring your men away, I have some vacancies left from the men *you* have hired away from *me*. It is not my problem if you refuse to offer a fair wage."

Will's nostrils flared as he took in a deep breath. Of course Reuben twisted this all around on him. He expected nothing less. Seeing no peaceful resolution to their conflict, Will turned on his heel.

Pausing in the doorway, he muttered, "If you stopped interfering, I would be out of your way sooner."

His brother's laughter echoed down the hall behind him. "Ten days, William, that's all you have left!"

Chapter 5

Texas / New Mexico Border

September 14, 1863

The dust kicked up by the slowly moving cattle stuck to Will's already coated face. Three days into the drive and he longed for the cleanliness of home already. But, he had no home. Not yet. Two months of travel, based on his best guess, stood between him and someplace that would not feel like home, but must become home.

Miraculously, by the end of Reuben's two week deadline, Will was prepared enough to leave the Star C behind. He hired eight men, a wrangler, and a cook. Less than the ideal number, but enough.

Will snorted as his dark eyes darted across the horizon over the backs of longhorns munching on grass, oblivious to the long journey barely underway. Less than ideal could describe just about every aspect of preparing for this drive. Not the preferred number or quality of horses. Not the perfect amount of supplies. Not well informed about the route. Not well prepared for the unexpected. Not the most experienced men.

Eight men, a wrangler, and a cook. And him. The small number of men for this size of herd meant everyone would be working extra hard. Other than his longtime friend, Ben Shepherd, the crew was composed of some very young men, some very rough men, and some very inexperienced men.

The warm sun beat down on Will causing sweat to form beads on his brow. Dabbing his forehead with his handkerchief, he tried not to dwell on the overwhelming challenges before him. Whether he wanted it or not, he was now a full-fledged rancher—responsible for the lives of his hands and his stock. He had done this many times before, but always under the security of his father's guidance. It was a burden shared among the three Colter men. Now, this was his to bear alone.

Not alone. The small quiet voice reminded him. He was never alone. He knew that promise well. God just seemed a bit distant right now.

Sweeping his gaze over the herd and cowboys, Will's eyes rested on the youngest hand, Jed Campbell. So very young. Just barely sixteen, hardly old enough for such a long drive across miles of wilderness. Jed hadn't even matured to the point of growing facial hair, Will thought as his lip turned up in a half smile.

Yet, when Jed showed up at the Star C asking for work four days before the departure, Will found it difficult to turn the young man away. He had been swayed by Jed's story. Two years prior, he had been orphaned when his family was killed by raiding Indians. At the much-too-young age of fourteen, Jed began working on a ranch in south Texas, learning the skills necessary to ride tall in his saddle as a cowboy. When he heard of a rancher planning to head west, he made his way to north Texas to join Will's group.

Jed stood half a foot shorter than Will. His arms seemed so much thinner and weaker than the cowboys Will worked with for many years. At first, Will thought the skinny kid might not be strong enough to rope a cow to the ground. After putting Jed through several tests, he realized he was stronger than he first appeared. He had potential and would make a good flank rider in the middle of the herd, paired with Elijah Malone, one of the more experienced men from the Star C.

"Shouldn't you be sleeping?" Ben's voice invaded Will's thoughts. "You're not on for a few hours yet."

Will grunted. He always needed a few days to get used to the odd hours of the cattle drive. Moving the cattle by night provided better conditions for grazing by day. The entire crew moved alongside the cattle from eight at night until six in the morning, traveling in the cooler dark of night. The first shift was on from six to one, while the second shift slept. Then, at one in the afternoon, the second shift took over until the first crew joined them at eight. The schedule, while best for the cattle, meant that the men had to sleep in full sunlight.

"How's he doing?" Will asked, nodding toward Jed.

"Good. A little nervous, but he's settlin' in."

Will followed Ben's gaze towards Miguel Ramirez, the only cowboy to respond to the advertisement at the store. Though he spoke limited English, he seemed to be rather experienced. He handled the drag position at the back of the herd well, effortlessly rounding up strays.

A wordless nod and half smile from Ben confirmed he was pleased with the Mexican's work.

The other member of the first shift, Pedro Morales, manned the out-riding position, keeping an eye out for trouble by riding far ahead of the herd. Coming from the Star C, Pedro was one of his most dependable and experienced men. Pedro first hired on with Will three years ago. Though of Mexican descent, he spoke English well. He came from another ranch in eastern Texas that went under. He made his way west from ranch to ranch looking to hire on. When Will met him, he eagerly offered Pedro a job, pleased with his experience. Will was grateful Pedro remained loyal, choosing to head west with him instead of staying at the Star C.

"Go get some shut eye," Ben said, resuming his position at point, which normally required two men. Will couldn't spare a second man in the position, being as short-handed as he was. "And encourage those young pups on second shift to do the same."

Will nodded, feeling some of the weariness seeping into his bones. Two of his new men, Daniel Owens and Samuel Whitten, sat at a makeshift table playing a round of poker. The two seemed more interested in cards than sleep, until it came to the late night hours. He caught Owens dozing in his saddle last night—a dangerous mistake. If he slipped from his horse, he could be crushed under the steady movements of the herd—dead long before anyone realized he was missing.

An image of his father's bruised, limp body flashed before his eyes. As much as he wanted to explain the image in detail to Owens to stress the importance of remaining alert at night, he hadn't. He didn't trust himself to keep the hitch from his voice, as the memory was still too raw.

"We've got four hours before we're on," Will said, pulling his horse to a stop in front of Owens and Whitten. "I want you two alert this afternoon and on through the night."

Red crept up Owen's neck to his face as he threw his cards down. Whitten grumbled something under his breath, setting Will on edge. Neither man earned his complete trust yet.

"Care to repeat that?" Will challenged the nineteen year old pup, trying to solidify his authority.

Pursing his lips tightly, Whitten gathered the cards and walked toward his saddle and bed roll with no further protests.

Will's concern about Owens and Whitten grew the longer they were on the trail. He knew so little about the two men. When they showed up just days before Will had to leave, he hired them out of desperation. They came together, saying they had worked on a ranch elsewhere. Their story was vague and Will had neither the time nor sufficient information to verify where they came from or their references. Both reeked of alcohol and smoke, causing Will to suspect they came straight from the saloon. Nothing about the pair made him comfortable. Something seemed out of place. He only hoped it had not been a mistake to hire them.

The fourth member of the second shift, Jethro Pace, already stretched out on his bedroll with no prompting from Will. Soft snores confirmed he slept. At least Will didn't have to worry about Pace, as he proved himself capable and trustworthy years ago at the Star C.

Sliding down from his mount, Will handed the reins to Matthew Covington, the new wrangler, as he removed his saddle. Covington was definitely younger than most of the cowboys in the crew. While he looked like he was fourteen, he was really seventeen—Will had asked just to be sure. The wrangling job would whip him into shape and bulk up his frame in short order. Working with the horses was a much tougher job than most young men realized, until they spent day after day on the trail. The cowboys rotated through two or three horses in one day. It would be Convington's job to feed, groom, water, and see to the horses' medical needs.

Dropping his saddle to the ground, Will shook out his bed roll. Easing to the ground, he settled his hat over his eyes. Noisy clanging of pots and pans from the chuck wagon chaffed his nerves and kept sleep way.

The cook, Daniel Raulings, was a character. He insisted on being called "Snake" because if you got on his wrong side, that's what he served you for dinner. Despite his cantankerous nature, he came highly recommended from a neighboring ranch. Snake was close to Will's age, maybe a year or two younger. His lanky form was no hindrance to driving the chuck wagon. So far, the men had been very pleased with his cooking abilities, even if the process of cooking seemed rather loud.

He couldn't pin all the blame on Snake for his lack of sleep. Too many thoughts of home—of his former home—consumed his mind.

Leaving the ranch two days ago was more difficult than Will expected. The brief picnic with Julia in his last days on the ranch warmed his heart. It gave him a chance to say good bye and encourage her that God would work things out in her life. It had been so easy to dispense the advice which seemed much harder to believe when it came to his life.

Those last few days, he also spent a fair amount of time reminiscing. He had so many fond memories of his father. He remembered the joy that shown in the senior Colter's eyes when Will successfully roped his first steer. The fun joking between them when Will started to inch taller and taller, eventually surpassing his father's height. He recalled the many Christmases around the hearth listening as his father read the story of Christ's birth.

The memories of his mother were equally poignant. Ah, the first time he fell off a horse his mother had set and bandaged his broken arm, seeing no need to take him to the doctor since it was a clean break. Then there was the way she conspired to make every birthday a surprise, even in adulthood. For his twenty-fifth birthday, four years ago, she and his father had purchased Jackson from a renowned horse breeder. It was his mother who arranged to stable the animal at a nearby ranch for the few days prior to Will's birthday.

And there was little Julia. Such a sweet and unexpected joy for her parents. Will easily recalled most of Julia's childhood, since he was thirteen when she was born. At first he was mad that the baby was a girl. A boy would have been much more fun. But as she grew older and followed him everywhere, he just treated her like a boy. He smiled as he thought about the time he taught her how to rope. They practiced with her rocking horse, a gift from their father. She was determined to do well, so she practiced every chance she got, spending more time roping the rocking horse than riding it. Mother was upset one Sunday when she discovered little Julia had brought her rope to church. When asked why she would do such a thing, she just smiled and said that a rancher should never be without two things, his gun and his rope. She obviously listened to the repetitive admonitions of her father.

Forcing his eyes closed beneath the shade of his hat, Will tried to push the thoughts of home aside. He needed sleep, or he might be the one dozing in his saddle tonight.

Four short, restless hours later, as Will and his shift finished packing up their bedrolls and selecting their mounts, he heard some commotion near the herd. Looking up, Will saw a rider fast approaching. Miguel waved furiously a hundred yards out, covering the distance to camp in a hurry. Just as he pulled up near Will, a *whooshing* sound flew past Will's head. Turning to see what made the sound, he saw an arrow stuck in the chuck wagon's side board.

"Indians! Indians!" Miguel yelled in his thick accent.

In a second, the danger registered, prompting Will to reach for his Sharps big fifty rifle. Letting go of the reins for the horse he was almost ready to mount, Will counted the men as most of the other first shift cowboys rode in. Each man quickly dismounted, pulling their rifles from their sheaths. Arrows fell in showers all around them.

"Take cover!" Ben shouted as he dove behind a rock.

Whoosh, thud. Another arrow made contact with the chuck wagon, reminding Will he was still out in the open. Adrenaline kicked in as he ducked behind the closest boulder.

"Snake, you have a rifle over there?" Will asked as he saw him crouch behind the chuck wagon.

Rifle fire coming from the wagon answered.

Propping his rifle on the top of the boulder, Will raised his head just enough to sight in one of the enemy. Squeezing the trigger released the bullet from its chamber, sending the butt of the gun kicking back against his shoulder. The bullet pierced the naked chest cavity of one of the natives, throwing him from his painted horse.

Peering around the edge of the boulder, Will trained his gun on one of the savages that kept Covington and Pace pinned down some yards away with little cover. Just as the Indian released an arrow, the bullet pierced his arm, causing him to drop his weapon. The arrow made swift contact, penetrating Pace's arm. As Pace cursed loudly in pain, he shifted his revolver to his other hand, sending the shot of death through the offender's skull.

Covington shook violently as he tried to reload his rifle. With no protection, he and Pace remained the primary focus of the attackers. Another arrow flew past the young wrangler's head, causing him to drop the cartridge from his unsteady hands. The arrow landed in the center of Pace's thigh, bringing on a new string of insults, followed by the rapid firing of his pistol. By the time Pace needed to reload, Covington finally managed to secure a usable cartridge in his rifle.

Owens shimmied his way over to Will, sharing the protection of the large boulder. As both Owens and Will fired off another round, Pedro and Whitten took cover behind another large rock near Ben. There was no sign of Jed or Malone, yet.

As Will tried to pick a target, arrow volleys filled the sky with the deadly projectiles, making accurate aim impossible. Horses galloped in rhythm to the breakneck pounding of his heart. High pitched shrieks from the enemy added to the strained atmosphere. He fired randomly at the nearest sound, hoping his shot connected.

To his right, Snake flattened himself on his belly under the chuck wagon to get better aim and provide more cover fire for Covington and Pace. Covington moved behind Pace at his command, still unable to control his turbulent shaking. Pace continued firing at buckskin-clad savages.

Pedro, being fast at reloading the mussel-loading rifles, handed reloaded rifles to Whitten. Whitten then fired while Pedro reloaded the next rifle. They continued rotating rifles to get shots in quicker. Will was never more thankful for his breech loading rifle, for he fired off three times between each of Whitten's shots even though he could no longer take careful aim.

Still, there was no sign of Jed or Malone.

As the number of arrows flying around him began to decrease, Will peeked around the rock protecting him and Owens. The smell of spent gun powder hung heavy in the air. His heart pounded loudly in his ears as he tried to take a steadying breath. Surveying the area, he noted several dead Indians scattered in awkward positions on the ground. Just as he inched out from the cover, he saw him—an Indian boy, not more than sixteen—with an arrow pointed directly at Will's heart. He was going to die.

Before Will could consider his options, the bow and arrow limply slipped from boy's fingers as he fell forward. A muffled sound—did he say help?—reached Will's ears as the boy hit the ground hard. Several arrows protruded from the boy's back. The scene confused Will. Had they hit one of their own intentionally?

Still uncertain, Will swiped his left hand across his chest, confirming the expected arrow never made contact.

Two more shots rang out before the remaining renegades fled, taking a large number of cattle with them.

Letting go of his held breath, Will called out to rally the men and assess the damage, his heart still pumping hard from his close encounter. Ben, Pedro, and Whitten appeared fine. Although Whitten looked a mite pale. Covington sat next to Pace rocking back and forth—numb, and clearly in shock. The ornery Pace sat with his teeth gritted, picking the arrows out of his bloody leg. Snake was at his side in an instant with knife and medical supplies ready to relieve him of the unwanted adornments.

Will snapped his head towards the sound of rapid hoof beats pounding closer. Jed rode toward them leading a horse with Malone slumped over covered in dozens of arrows. A good bit of blood soaked the side of Malone's mare. Ben hurried over to assist. Shaking his head slightly, his grim expression told Will that Malone was gone. Jed nearly tumbled off his horse. His face pale, streaked with tears. Will was sure this brought back some painful memories for the boy who lost his entire family to an Indian attack.

Stirring from the dreadful scene before him, Will leaped into action. "Pedro, Miguel, Whitten, and Owens—go control that herd! Take the breech loading rifles and extra bullets with you. At any sign of trouble shoot twice and we'll send more men out. After you're sure it's safe, send Whitten back with the head count. Ben, check the wounded Indians. You know what to do."

The men scattered into action. Snake appeared to have things under control with Pace, judging by the string of profanity spewing from his mouth as each arrow was extracted. Will ushered Jed over near the group and began to look for injuries. There was a lot of blood on him, but Will could not find any wounds. It must have come from Malone. Jed waved him off, so Will took some time to help Covington.

"Stand up, son. Let's get you some water," he said as he led Covington over to the wagon a few feet away. After Covington took a few sips, he heaved, dumping the contents of his stomach at the toes of Will's boots. Will sat him down next to the wagon to drink more water, slower this time. Gradually his shaking subsided. When he appeared settled, Will left him to help Ben.

"Looks like we've got six dead Indians, and this wounded one," said Ben, pointing to the boy that nearly killed Will.

Still perplexed over why they shot one of their own, Will knelt to take a closer look. The boy had sandy colored hair, much lighter than any Indian he had ever seen. He noticed several bruises on the boy's arms and his bare back showed several scars. Was it possible he was not an Indian, but a captive? Something just did not make sense.

As Ben took care of the dead, Will borrowed some whiskey and bandages from Snake. Taking his own knife, he began the slow process of removing the arrows from the boy's back. He cleaned the wounds with some whiskey before bandaging him up. Not sure where else to put the boy, he left him there for now, kicking any weapons from his reach.

Standing slowly, Will made his way to the horses. Looked like two of his best horses were badly wounded, so he led them a short distance from the camp. Then, as much as it pained him to do so, he put them down. He already had fewer horses than what was ideal for this length of a drive. Losing two would mean fewer fresh mounts for the rotation.

As he stepped back into camp, Whitten rode in to report.

"We've been able to account for all but three hundred head. I'm going back out to help the boys in case we run into any more trouble," Whitten stated as he turned his horse around.

Mounting his stallion, Will asked Ben to take care of things at camp, including the young Indian. He followed Whitten out to the herd, needing reassurance that things were under control. With Malone gone and Pace injured, that left him with only four men for the first shift and two, plus him, for the second. Even if he assigned only one at flank, that left him one outrider and one drag rider, leaving the point position at the front of the herd unmanned. He would have to shuffle men around so he could pull double duty to cover the gaps.

Once the cattle were secure and out of danger, he went back to camp to check on things. After dismounting and tying his horse with the others, Will pulled Ben aside.

"We're down one man, two horses, and three hundred head," he confided. "Is there any chance Pace will be able to ride?" The question sounded absurd to his own ears as it left his lips.

"He ain't looking so good. Lost a lot of blood. Snake says he passed out before he had all the arrows out. Time will tell, but don't expect him to be much good for a while."

The losses of the day started gnawing at Will. He refused to listen to the voice trying to tell him he failed and he let down his men. They needed a strong leader, like his father, right now. Will knew he had that same strength within him. He could do this. He had to.

"We will need to rig up a litter for Pace and for the Indian boy," he said.

"Some of the boys are not gonna take to having an injun travel with us," Ben advised.

Will struggled to keep the tension from his voice. "What would you have me do? Leave the boy for dead? Did you see his injuries? That bruising and the scars are not a sign of him being a valued member of their party. *They* fired on him."

Ben put up his hands in surrender. "I don't think we should leave him. Just saying that some of the boys that have had bad run-ins with Indians may cause problems."

"Get a litter rigged up for both the boy and Pace." Will barked out his order, the stress of the situation getting the better of him. "Then we need to start packing up to hit the trail tonight."

"Okay, boss," Ben's curt answer caused Will to regret his tone.

Stalking away, Will found Covington and instructed him to help Snake pull camp so they could be on their way by night fall. He had the drivers come in when everything was packed and ready to go. They held a brief burial for Malone, before Will addressed the cowboys.

"We've lost three hundred cattle, two horses, one man, with another severely injured. We were shorthanded before this, but we will all have to do extra until we can get to Santa Fe for help. We are moving on with the drive tonight."

Will paused, no nonsense look planted on his face. "The Indian is not to be harmed. Is that understood?"

A chorus of "yes sirs" echoed in reply before they resumed their duties. The compliant words from Jed did not match the look of hatred on his face.

Chapter 6

Kansas Prairie

September 16, 1863

As the wagon master called "catch up," Drew hurried to round up his team of six oxen. Despite having left from breakfast earlier than any of the other men, he struggled to hitch the oxen to the wagon while a chorus of "all set" sounded around him. He would be last again.

You better pull your weight. No one's gonna help you out there on the open plains. The admonition from Eli Jacobs, the assistant wagon master, echoed through his mind, causing his fingers to fumble with the harness. Since he and Hannah arrived at Fort Leavenworth, Eli made his concerns clear. The man did not think Drew capable.

His first morning in Fort Leavenworth, Drew wasted no time locating the wagon train headquarters. With only a few days to purchase all the necessary supplies, a team, and a wagon, he made the most of every second. Standing in front of the large barn-like doors, he contemplated entering through them, until he noticed a smaller door off to the right. Pushing the squeaky wood door open, he stepped into the seemingly out of place room with a small desk pushed against one wall. The opposite wall housed another doorway, opening to a large barn area filled with sacks of grain, livestock, and gear.

Drew waited patiently for a few minutes for the owner of the desk to return. When the tall broad-shouldered man entered from the barn, Drew introduced himself, immediately unsettled by the man's less than welcome reception.

"Normally, we don't take inexperienced fellas like you," Eli stated, as he carefully scrutinized him. Willing his heart to beat in a normal rhythm, Drew feared being turned away before the journey began. "But, seein' how you're a doctor, the boss decided it would be okay. I'll help you get organized and make sure you get everything you need, but once we get on the trail, you'll be on your own."

Drew nodded, unable to speak around the lump in his throat.

"There's just two of you, right?" Eli asked.

Drew cleared his throat. "Yes, my wife and me."

"Do either of you know how to use a rifle?" Eli narrowed his eyes with the question.

Embarrassed that Hannah knew how to shoot, but he did not, Drew purposefully kept his answer to a simple, "Yes."

"Good, cause you and the missus will have to be able to defend yourselves."

"Now, about the supplies," Eli started. "First, you need to get a wagon and a six-team of oxen. Then, a tent, rifle, pistol, four hundred pounds of bread stuffs, two hundred pounds of meat, two hundred pounds of flour..."

After that conversation, Drew felt Eli's patience wear thin as he taught him how to harness and drive the team of oxen. His ignorance continued to strip away his dignity and confidence well into this third day of their journey.

You'll be on your own. We don't take inexperienced fellas. The words taunted him as he fastened the last part of the gear.

Drew quickly climbed onto the hard springboard seat of the wagon, calling "all set" as he picked up the reins.

The man in the wagon in front of him shouted back, "About time!"

Heat rose to his cheeks as he released the brake. The wagon master shouted "stretch out." Slapping the reins against the team's back, he breathed a sigh of relief. At least this was part of the morning ritual he could handle with some measure of confidence. The tight circle of wagons slowly elongated into a line as the cool breeze tickled his neck. When the wagon master hollered "fall in," Drew directed the oxen to take their assigned place in the line of wagons.

The past few days on the trail tested him almost to his limit. As the son of a storekeeper, and then as a doctor, the most strenuous physical activity he performed was lifting and unloading crates of supplies. Never before had he worked with livestock. Never before had he hoisted a barrel full of water several feet above ground and into a wagon, much less three barrels. Every task he learned to perform strained his already weary muscles.

Then there were his hands—most definitely the hands of a doctor and not someone used to driving a team all day. Last night, when Hannah handed him his supper plate full of charred food, he nearly screamed out from the pain as the plate hit his raw, bleeding palms. Hannah saw him flinch and, after giving him a piece of her mind—the long string of words giving him hope that she still must care—she rubbed a soothing salve on the wounds. Then she wrapped them in rags. This morning, Drew dug through their things until he found a pair of gloves to wear over the bandages. He paid dearly for his foolishness in waiting this long to wear the gloves.

As the wagon crept along the rutted, dusty road, Drew glanced over at Hannah's rigid posture. She was still angry. He was certain of it. She never had been angry with him for this long before. Of course, he had never tried to uproot her from her home either. Ever since he announced they would be moving to La Paz, Hannah barely spoke to him. When she did, it was with eyes full of disappointment, disdain, or dejection. No smiles graced her lovely face—not in nearly a month. Not in the weeks they spent packing. Nor in the few days traveling by steamboat from Cincinnati to Fort Leavenworth. Nor in the days spent in Fort Leavenworth. And certainly not since the wagon train moved out.

How long would she remain distant, carrying a grudge against him? What could he do to coax a smile again? As much as he wanted to mend what was broken, at the end of each arduous day he had no energy left to smooth things over with his wife.

She wasn't the only person mad at him. Drew saw the looks of other settlers traveling with them. Whispers stopped as he neared. Piercing eyes followed his every movement. His shortcomings were painfully obvious. He was completely ill-equipped for what was required of him. Perhaps he would never fully adapt to this type of grueling labor.

Even Hannah seemed to be struggling to adapt to outdoor living, as evidenced by the dreadful, unappetizing meals. He assumed the meals she prepared would be hearty and fulfilling, much like he had come to expect back home. There she had been an amazing cook—never was anything less than sumptuous. However, on the trail that was not the case. Each night she served a foul combination of half raw half charred food. If only his empty stomach and exhausted body would be as forgiving as he. He needed satisfying nourishment if he was going to make it through this.

Restful sleep eluded him, too. The hard ground gave no comfort. The thin shelter of the tent did little to muffle the strange noises of the prairie. Rambunctious, and often inebriated teamsters employed by the freighters, added to the noise late into the night. Wolves or coyotes howled, sounding closer as the hours ticked by. The peaceful dark of night he expected turned out to be nothing more than fanciful images in his mind.

The flat, unending Kansas prairie failed to offer solace. Miles and miles of tall buffalo grass hissed in the wind. Trees confined themselves near river beds, offering little break to the chilling wind. Other than the few towns and sporadic houses they passed on the first day, there had been little sign of civilization or variation in the landscape.

Worse yet, he missed practicing medicine. He loved talking to patients, answering their questions and alleviating their symptoms. He loved birthing babies, watching as new life entered the world. He even liked patching up more severe wounds, like Mr. Davis's bullet wound, and doing whatever he could to help the healing process along. While unknown illnesses terrified most doctors, Drew thrived when confronted with such a challenge, drawing on his experience or researching new remedies and theories that might aid in curing the patient.

All those years of training, studying late into the night, prepared him to be a confident physician…that sat atop a wagon without a patient in sight.

Discouraged, Drew glanced at Hannah again. He wished, not for the first time, that he would be able to make her proud.

Hannah sensed Drew's eyes on her. As she turned toward him, his head snapped forward, seemingly interested in the miniscule progress of the oxen.

The silence ate at her. How had this wordless, tense chasm formed between her heart and his? They were husband and wife. They were supposed to love each other and want to be with each other. So why did she feel like jumping down from the wagon and running far from his presence?

Moisture tickled the corners of her eyes. Maybe he didn't love her anymore.

Her aunt would tell her that was impossible. Love doesn't die. But, Hannah knew otherwise. After all, Papa stopped loving her—the day Mama died—so could Drew.

Growing up, she knew that both her parents loved and adored her. She felt it in the morning hugs and evening bed-time stories. It was there when Papa lifted her off the ground and twirled her around as he came in from the fields at the end of the day.

Both Papa and Mama wanted more children and often spoke of their hope for another child. Finally, Mama announced one day that she was with child. Hannah would have a younger brother or sister soon. Papa cried—for joy he told her—because they had waited twelve long years for their family to increase.

Only that joy faded, too quickly, when Mama began having pains only a few months into the pregnancy. When the doctor confined her to bed rest, Hannah overheard him telling Mama she had been irresponsible in trying to have a child at her advanced age of forty.

For months, Mama remained in bed, following the doctor's orders without complaint. Each month the doctor visited, he said the pregnancy was progressing, but there was too much cause for concern. She needed to stay abed.

A month before the baby should have arrived Mama went into labor while Hannah was at school. When she arrived home, the doctor's carriage sat out front. Her mother's screams filled the air. For hours Papa paced the small space between the stove and the table in the small farm house, ignoring Hannah. With each scream, his pacing turned more frantic.

For over a day, Hannah listened, helpless and terrified. Finally, the screaming stopped.

"There should be a baby's cry," Papa said, reaching for the bedroom door latch.

The door flew open as the doctor stepped into the room. "I'm sorry," were the only words he uttered before Papa pushed him aside.

"No!" Papa yelled in a guttural moan as he fell into a heap next to Mama's side.

Confused and frightened, she stepped into the doorway. Her mother's pale body rested stiffly on their bed. Looking around the room, Hannah could not find the baby. The only thing she saw was her lifeless mother and enormous amounts of blood stained the sheets. The doctor, realizing she slipped into the room, quickly pulled her back into the kitchen as Papa's sobs grew louder.

"I'm sorry, little one, but your mama has passed away," the doctor whispered, closing the door to allow her father to grieve in private.

The next hours and days had faded from Hannah's memory. She didn't remember the funeral.

What she did remember was her father working long hours in the field. He left before sunrise and returned late into the night. If she hadn't lain awake each night to be certain he returned, she would have thought he abandoned her entirely.

Weeks rolled into a month. His behavior remained the same. Until one day, when she came home from school, he sat at the table sipping on a mug of coffee, staring off at nothing in particular. As she entered the small room, he looked up.

"Pack your things," he said coldly before standing and walking out the door.

Not knowing what else to do, she followed the emotionless order. Several minutes later, with her bag in his hand, he led her to the waiting wagon. He lifted her into the seat without a word. Then he drove her to his sister's house.

"Take her," he said to Auntie. When her aunt started to protest, he cut her off. "I can't bear to look at her…she reminds me too much of…" his voice cracked.

For three years, Hannah lived with her aunt and uncle, without a single word or visit from her father. Then one day, shortly after her fifteenth birthday, he came as mysteriously as he left. With minimal conversation, he picked her up and took her back home.

The next few years ticked by slowly. Her father barely spoke to her outside of what was necessary to keep up with daily chores and the running of the farm. He hardly looked at her. He never hugged her. He didn't love her any more.

Daily, Hannah threw herself into her school work and her chores. Many afternoons she cried on Emily's shoulder, not understanding why her father didn't love her. She longed to go back to live with her aunt. At least there she felt like someone cared.

Then, after Hannah turned eighteen, her father died suddenly. Bad heart the doctor said. She was an orphan with a farm—crops still in the field.

Her uncle came and advised her to sell the farm, suggesting Hannah move to town and take a job at the local mercantile. She did precisely that.

The first two years after her father's death, Hannah spent her days working at Francis's store and her Sundays begging God to heal her broken heart. She wanted to understand why her father stopped loving her, why he had abandoned her. But, she couldn't. Friends told her that he must have been to overwrought with grief. Perhaps his heart broke beyond repair.

None of that mattered to Hannah. She once had his love and attention. Then, it was gone.

Did the silence from Drew mean that he no longer loved her?

Hannah sighed, looking across the grass-covered prairie. Maybe she held some blame for the distance. She had been less than receptive to the idea of moving to La Paz. After the dinner with Doc Henderson, she tried to convince Drew that moving so far away was ludicrous. The heated argument ended in her vowing to keep her opinions to herself. He would not budge.

The thing that bothered her the most about Drew's immovable stance was that he continued to tell her the move was God's will. If that was true, then why didn't she have any peace about it? She tried. She prayed and prayed and prayed. She asked God to help her set aside her feelings and seek Him in this situation. Yet, she still had no peace.

Then again, she had not fully set aside her feelings. She hated leaving Ohio. She despised Thomas for robbing the bank that started so many difficult circumstances into motion. She fought against Drew's decision—at first with words, then later with her silent resistance.

Another sigh rose to the edge of her breath. She quickly swallowed it away. Regardless of her feelings, she and Drew were moving to La Paz in the Arizona Territory. She would have to start over, again, in a new place with new people.

The slowing of the wagon pulled her from her frustrations. As Drew set the brake, Hannah quickly hopped down, without waiting for his assistance. Since he struggled so much with the team, she figured it would only slow down the process and deepen her embarrassment if she waited for the gentlemanly gesture.

She watched him from the corner of her eye. Even several days into the journey he seemed to have to concentrate very hard to remember how to properly unyoke the oxen and set them afield to graze for the afternoon break. It pained her to watch. Having grown up on a farm, she learned long ago how to hitch a team and how to care for livestock. She knew she could be done in half the time. And the first day on the trail, she made the mistake of trying to help him. He snapped at her, telling her that none of the other men needed help from their wives, so why should he?

Hannah pulled the small bundle of food from the wagon. Each morning, following a hot breakfast, she prepared food for the midday meal. Typically, she set aside some bread, dried beef, cheese, and other cold foodstuff. Only breakfast and supper were hot meals.

A good ten minutes after all the other men finished setting the oxen out to graze, Drew joined her on the blanket she laid out next to the wagon. She poured them both a cup of water, handing one to him. When he reached up to take the cup from her, his fingers lingered against hers long enough to give her pause. A tentative smile graced his lips as tingles traveled up her arm. Releasing her hold on the cup, she quickly sank to the blanket, turning her attention to dividing the meal.

She handed Drew his meal and waited while he blessed the food. As soon as the prayer concluded, Hannah nibbled on the bread and dried beef, still fearing the silence between her and her husband.

"Have you met any of the other women?" he asked.

"No," she replied sharply. What did it matter if she spoke to the other women on the wagon train? She doubted any of them were headed to La Paz. And she did not really want to make friends that she would just leave again. And she wouldn't be in this position if he had decided Indiana was far enough. It was so unfair.

Drew finished chewing his mouthful of food. As he turned to look at her, his eyes clouded.

"Hannah," he said, reaching over to gently lay his hand on her arm. "I didn't mean anything by the question. I'm just trying to…I hate this distance between us." His blue eyes bore through her defenses. "I miss talking to you."

Tears burned her eyes. Maybe he still loved her.

"Anderson!" Eli Jacobs shouted, stopping her from responding to Drew. "A word with you."

Drew set aside the rest of his uneaten meal and jumped to his feet. Then he walked a few yards away to where the wagon master stood. As the two men conversed in hushed tones, Hannah began packing up their things, her earlier despair returned.

"Are those your oxen, Anderson?"

Drew nodded, unable to keep his nerves calm.

"Haven't you noticed this one," Eli asked. "He is favoring his hoof. If you don't take care of that soon, you're gonna have a lame animal."

Heat flooded Drew's face, growing hotter as Eli showed him how to care for the injured hoof. How was he supposed to know what to look for? He never worked with livestock.

He tried to pay close attention to Eli's instructions, but the image of Hannah near tears distracted him. What was happening between them? What had he said to cause her to cry? Looking over at his wife, he caught her dabbing those tears from her face with her lace handkerchief. Guilt jabbed his heart. He was alienating his wife. He was failing miserably at leading them to their new home.

"Doc," Eli's irritated voice arrested his attention. "Did you get all that?"

Drew nodded, wanting to appease the man.

"Good, then go to it."

Blinking, he realized his bluff had been called. Trying to

remember the very first thing Eli showed him, he placed his hand on the ox's back, sliding it towards the animal's hind quarters.

When he bent down to lift the ox's injured hoof, Eli chastised him. "Pay attention this time."

Drew forced his attention on Eli's every movement, carefully repeating the steps in his mind. Each time Eli mentioned what he should look for, he stored the information away for future reference. This time, when Eli asked him to examine the animal's foot, he responded by performing most of the steps correctly.

By the time the hour and a half midday stop elapsed, Drew's confidence faded even more. Eagerly, he climbed aboard the wagon, glad to be free from the embarrassment for a few minutes. He felt so inadequate, unable to manage the team. What would he do if one of the oxen went lame? Where would he get another ox? How much would it cost? What would happen if he could not find a replacement? Would Eli make them stay behind?

Chapter 7

Hannah's hope continued to fade throughout the afternoon. Her thoughts kept returning to the distance between them, plunging further towards despair as the day grew longer and Drew seemed preoccupied. Twice she tried to start a conversation with him, only to see his attention wane quickly.

By the time he pulled the wagon to a stop for the evening, she turned her energy to gathering firewood, glad for the distraction from her thoughts. Her eyes darted back and forth across the tall prairie grass, looking for signs of wood peeking through. The only thing that caught her attention was the round dark brown lumps resembling cow dung, only larger and less odiferous.

Walking farther from the camp, her gaze continued searching, still finding no firewood. Perhaps she would have to forgo the hot meal and pull from their stock of dried beef instead. As she turned back toward camp she noticed a cluster of women gathered around a plump older woman.

"Listen up, ladies!" the older woman shouted. "From here on out, it's doubtful we'll find firewood."

Hannah started to walk away from the crowd with shoulders drooping. Drew told her they would have fuel enough to cook hot meals daily. She had not planned to spend the bulk of the trip without fire. And what about staying warm at night? The temperature already dropped several degrees in the few minutes since they stopped traveling for the day.

The older woman's next words stopped Hannah mid-step. "We will have to use buffalo chips to fuel our fires."

"Buffalo chips?" Hannah asked, relieved to discover they would have fire after all.

"Yes, dried buffalo dung or 'chips' makes an excellent fire," the older woman replied with a kind smile.

Then she proceeded to show the crowd of women how to kick

over the chips with the toe of her boot. Next, she picked up and carried the chips in the fold of her apron. Some women outright refused to pick up the newly discovered form of fuel. Others hesitated, but eventually came around. Hannah, figuring Drew preferred a hot meal, decided to follow the older woman's example. When her apron looked as full as the older woman's, she returned to camp.

As she started to build the fire, the older woman who told them about buffalo chips walked by. Hannah caught her attention and introduced herself. "Thank you for telling us about the buffalo chips."

"Glad to help, dear," the older woman said with a warm smile before introducing herself as Betty Lancaster.

"How did you know about them?" Hannah asked.

"Oh, my sweet Henry and I traveled through some of the plains on our way to Missouri as a young couple," Betty said. Her black and silver streaked hair and the wistful expression implied the journey she spoke of transpired many years ago. "Twas difficult learning how to live outdoors. The first few days I missed my stove something fierce."

Warmth flushed Hannah's cheeks as she looked down at the pile of buffalo chips at her feet. Her voice softened as she spoke. "I haven't quite figured out how to cook the food evenly yet."

"I would be happy to help you, dear," Betty smiled sympathetically. "It's quite different from cooking over a stove. Give me one minute and I'll be back to help."

As Betty scurried to the wagon next to Hannah's, one of the Shawnee Indians, hired by the wagon master, brought by several chunks of fresh venison.

"Now, dear," Betty said, as she reached for a skillet, "just watch me."

Taking the venison, Betty liberally seasoned it on both sides. Then she placed it over the fire. Hannah watched carefully, noting each step Betty took and the placement of the skillet to the fire.

"Those first few days on the way to Missouri, I thought my poor Henry might starve, my cooking turned so terrible," Betty laughed as she started preparing the beans.

"Henry?" Hannah asked.

"My husband. 'Bout fifteen years ago he passed on."

"I'm sorry."

Betty patted Hannah's hand. "Don't be, dear. He's with his Lord in heaven smiling down on us now."

"Tell me you are not travelling across the wilderness alone."

"No, no. My son, Paul, is with me. He's been a great help since Henry died. Took over the farm when he was nothing but a lad of seventeen. Been taking care of his 'ol ma ever since."

"Is his wife with you?"

"Oh, no, dear. Paul is not married. Don't rightly know why. Guess he just never found the right woman," Betty said cocking her head to one side. "There, now," she said pointing to the food. "Just turn the food often and everything will come out just right."

As Betty stepped away from the fire, she added, "After supper, why don't you and your husband visit with us? Might make this long trip more bearable."

Hannah nodded her agreement as she gave the beans another good stir.

A few minutes later, a weary Drew deposited the last of the full water barrels into the back of the wagon. Having gained confidence in her outdoor cooking skills, Hannah quickly dished him up a heaping plate of food, pleased that nothing seemed burned or undercooked. When she handed it to him, he smiled.

"Looks delicious," Drew said. He wolfed down the meal before holding his plate out for seconds.

As she dished up more beans, she said, "I thought we could visit with our neighbors in the wagon next to us after supper."

Swallowing his food, he answered with an edge to his voice, "Not tonight."

"They are really nice—"

"I said not tonight," he interrupted, brow furrowed deeply.

Hannah pursed her lips tightly as she grabbed the empty plate from Drew, confused by his adamant refusal. Shaving off a few curls of soap into the water warming over the fire, she tossed the rest of the dishes in. She had not realized how much she was looking forward to getting to know Betty and Paul, until now. Frustrated, she scrubbed the pot with fervor.

Glancing over her shoulder, she watched for a few seconds as her husband struggled to put up the tent before returning her attention to the pot. Serves him right, she thought. This whole journey was his idea. He's the one that decided they should move across the country to a wild territory full of unknown dangers. Maybe it was fair that things were not easy for him.

Anger boiling over, she lifted the pan she used for washing dishes. She carried it outside of the circle of wagons. Flinging the pan in the air with all her might she watched in the dim light as the water splashed out in an arc before it matted down a small area of the grass.

Tears burned the corners of her eyes. She was tired. Tired of being angry with Drew. Tired of his contrary behavior. Tired of this blasted wagon. She missed her home. She missed her kitchen. She missed her friends.

And she missed Drew—the happy, confident man she married.

Blotting her eyes dry with the corner of her apron, Hannah stowed the dishpan in the back of the wagon. As she neared their campfire, she saw no sign of Drew, though soft snores sounded from the tent. Despite the early hour, she pulled back the corner of the canvas tent and entered, taking her place next to her already sleeping husband.

The next morning Drew stretched his back once more, before leaning over to harness the oxen. Glancing nervously at the darkening clouds to the west, he hurried to take his place on the hard springboard wagon seat. Even though he retired earlier last night, he still felt exhausted and sore.

About an hour into the day, he felt the first drop of moisture. Hannah wordlessly left the seat, climbing into the shelter of the canvas cover seconds before the skies opened, spilling heavy sheets of cold rain over the prairie. The water soaked through his clothes quickly.

As the oxen slowed, Drew slapped down the reins trying to coax the animals forward. Within minutes, the former dusty rutted road became slick and gooey, coating the wheels with mud. More of the mud stuck to the wheels with each rotation.

Suddenly, the wagon in front of him came to a stop. The driver climbed down, then proceeded to scrape the gooey mess from each wheel spoke. Perhaps if he did the same thing, his team would struggle less.

Setting the brake, Drew jumped down from the wagon, his feet slipping on the mud. Quickly he reached out for the side of the wagon, just before his hind end landed in the mess. Rain pelted the top of his hat with audible *splats*, before shooting off the brim down his back. Walking around to the back of the wagon, he kicked out the oozing muck from between the spokes of the wagon wheel. He repeated the action for each wheel, until they were all empty. Carefully, he pulled himself back onto the wagon seat, released the brake, and started the team into motion again.

Another mile or so passed in misery. As the wagon grew heavy with a new coat of mud, he pulled it to a stop. Easing himself down off the seat, he removed the mire from the wheels once again. Back in the seat, Drew smacked the reins to move the oxen. The wagon rocked forward a few inches before settling back. He checked to make sure he released the brake. It was free. Another slap of the reins yielded the same results. The wagon was stuck.

"Hannah," Drew hollered over the deafening sound of the downpour, barely keeping the irritation from his voice. "Take the oxen."

When his dry wife appeared on the seat in a rain slicker, he climbed back down.

"When I yell, start the oxen moving."

Hannah nodded before he turned and walked around the wagon. He yelled and she set the oxen in motion. There! The back wheel hung on a deep rut, which only deepened with each attempt to move forward. Standing behind the wagon, Drew pushed with all of his might to help free the wheel. His boots slid on the viscous mud. The wagon did not move. Trying again, he braced his back against the wagon, pushing with his legs. Again nothing happened. It was futile. He was not strong enough to move it.

"Need some help?" a deep voice asked as a large broad-shouldered man approached with a sturdy looking plank of wood.

Drew nodded, keenly aware that he would not be able to get the wagon moving without this man's help. As he hollered for Hannah to move forward again, the man stuck the lever in the ground behind the immobile wheel. Grunting from the exertion, he put his large shoulder against the long piece of wood. Drew pushed against the back of the wagon at the same time. Between the two of them, it was enough force to break free.

"Thank you!" he shouted over his shoulder before rushing up to the front of the wagon. Hannah pulled it to a stop just long enough for him to jump back on board. Taking the reins back from her, he motioned her to go inside out of the downpour.

The rain continued throughout the morning. When they stopped for the midday meal, Drew stripped off his soaked clothing, changing into something dry. He donned a rain slicker before taking his place back on the seat. Even with the change of clothes, he shivered in the damp cold.

Just an hour before they set up camp, the rain ceased. A huge sigh of relief escaped his chilled lips. Hopefully they could build a fire tonight so he could warm up.

At camp that evening, Drew eagerly devoured another delicious meal. Apparently, Hannah worked out her troubles with cooking outdoors, he thought, patting his stomach in a satisfied gesture. Good thing, too. After the strain of the day, he felt his body liven as the nourishment took hold.

After Hannah finished the dishes, he suggested they meet the people in the wagon behind them. He wanted to thank the broad-shouldered man for his help this morning.

Smiling, Drew called out a greeting before introducing himself.

"Pleased to meet you, Mr. Anderson. I'm Paul Lancaster. And this is my ma, Betty."

Betty already engulfed Hannah in a hug, surprising Drew.

"Dear, is this your husband?" Betty asked.

"Yes," Hannah answered before turning toward him. "You have Betty to thank for helping me figure out how to cook over an open fire."

"Well, I am indebted to you."

Paul set two more crates on the ground, motioning for him and Hannah to be seated.

"Where are the two of you headed?" Drew asked.

Paul answered, "We are moving to the Granite Creek area of the Arizona Territory."

"Paul hopes to set up a placer mine and I plan on running a boardinghouse," Betty said.

"Won't there be too much to do by yourself?" Hannah asked.

"Oh, Paul will help most days. The mining is more of a hobby than a means of supporting us." Turning to Drew, Betty asked, "What about you?"

"We are moving to the gold mine town of La Paz."

"Drew is a doctor," Hannah added, sheepishly.

Betty's face brightened. "Dear, you should think about heading to the Walker settlement with us. Rumor is that the new governor of the territory might locate the capital there. I'm sure they could use a doctor."

"Ma is right," Paul said. "What we've read about the Granite Creek area, it is much more civilized than some of the other gold towns."

"And, Paul heard from the wagon master that once we arrive at Fort Larned, we will wait for the new governor and his party before continuing west. Why, you will already know half the town!" Betty exclaimed.

"Wouldn't that be great?" Hannah joined in with their enthusiasm.

Everyone turned their attention towards him. Running his hands through his hair, Drew hated to douse their excitement. "Well, La Paz has a pretty large population—one that can easily support a doctor."

From the corner of his eye, he saw Hannah's shoulders sag.

"Yes, but it is also a booming gold town," Paul countered, "with many unsavory characters. Not the best of places to raise a family."

Drew frowned. "Didn't you say that Walker and his party were miners? And you would also be mining?"

"All of the Granite Creek miners sign an agreement with basic rules to live by, sort of laws, if you will. That's why Ma and I chose the area."

"If the governor is going there," Hannah's soft voice broke through the silence, "maybe we should consider it."

Drew whipped his head towards his wife, clenching his jaw.

The warning look he gave her went unheeded.

"If the capital is there, the population would be growing—"

"We are going to La Paz." His voice sounded louder than he intended. The look of shock on Hannah's face stabbed his heart. He hadn't meant to be harsh.

"Well, we will enjoy your friendship," Betty said, patting Hannah's hand, "for as long as the good Lord sees fit."

Though the conversation darted on to other subjects, Drew's irritation with Hannah remained. He knew she did not want to make this move. But, questioning him in front of strangers was disrespectful. And not at all like her.

Waiting for an opening in the conversation, Drew yawned. Seeing his chance, he stood, thanking Paul and Betty for their hospitality before seeing Hannah back to their tent.

"Why won't you even consider Granite Creek?" she asked him as soon as they were in the semi-privacy of their tent.

In a hushed, angry whisper, he responded, "We have our plans. Why do you continue to press this?"

Lowering to the ground, she crawled under the covers. "Because, maybe I don't think God is calling us to La Paz like you do."

The words stung. She did not trust him to make the right decision for their family.

Drew thought of a million sharp answers as he kicked off his boots and stretched out on the ground. Instead of speaking a single one, he rolled onto his side away from her, letting his silence speak for him.

Self-pity bubbled up. When had things gone so wrong? When had Hannah started to criticize his every decision? He stifled a snort of disgust. When Thomas robbed the bank—that is when things turned upside down.

Thomas. A pang of guilt stabbed Drew as he thought of his brother. The last time he saw him was a few days before he and Hannah left Cincinnati. Making the excuse of running an errand, he left the clinic without telling Hannah his true destination. Hiring a hackney, he arrived at the jail that housed his brother, the criminal. The stench inside the jail overwhelmed his senses and almost gave credence to the voice telling him to forget his brother.

But, he could not. Guilt hounded him for days. All he could hear was his father's voice asking him over and over to take care of Thomas. Even though Thomas was a grown man, the promise still haunted Drew.

Following several sleepless nights, he decided to visit Thomas, though completely unprepared for the image that awaited him. When the jailer stopped in front of a cell, Drew barely recognized his brother. His sandy brown hair looked unkempt, caked with dirt. His threadbare clothing sported a similar look. Blue eyes sunk into his head, leaving dark circles. Haggard and weary.

The conversation was much like Drew expected. When he tried to engage, Thomas shot back angry retorts, even accusing Drew of gloating—over what, he did not know. Frustrated by the accusation, Drew told him that he and Hannah were moving to La Paz.

Unquenchable desire to lash out spurred him on. He confronted Thomas, making his own harsh accusations against his own flesh and blood. He told Thomas that he cost him the clinic and his livelihood. In his anger he said things he greatly regretted.

Once he finished venting, Drew turned to leave, shooting a pathetic "goodbye" over his shoulder. It was the kind that leaves one wondering how things might go should they ever cross paths again.

Then, unexpectedly, when Drew reached the end of the long hallway, Thomas gave a chilling laugh followed by his own emotionless goodbye. The reaction cut Drew deeply. What he intended to be a clearing-of-the-air, turned out to be a disaster.

As Hannah reclined next to him wordlessly, he stirred from his burdensome. He could do nothing to repair that relationship now.

The mild shaking of Hannah's body alerted him that his wife was crying. He should do something. He should say something to comfort her. Yet his own fractured emotions kept him from trying.

Piled on to the guilt and self-recrimination, loneliness wedged in. He missed Hannah's smiling face. He missed the way she used to brighten when he entered the room. It was like he was the most important man. Her reaction bolstered him, added to his confidence.

Now in the absence of her smile, her soft touch, the light in her eyes, he felt insignificant and undone.

Just reach out. His inner voice chastised vehemently. *She still needs you.*

Hovering his hand in midair over her shoulder, Drew hesitated. Her shaking stopped. Had she sensed his hand mere inches away? Wavering and indecisive, he listened. Soft, steady breathing of sleep reached his ears. Slowly he moved his hand back to his side as the loneliness threatened to suffocate him.

Chapter 8

New Mexico Territory

September 19, 1863

The dust stirring from the cattle stung Will's tired eyes. In the two days since the Indian attack, he slept not more than an hour or two. Even his exhaustion could not diminish the bright pink and orange streaks splaying across the horizon, chasing the last remnants of night from the sky. God must have known he needed the little bit of peace that always rose up from his soul when witnessing such a glorious sunrise.

Other than this brief moment, peace seemed a distant friend— the kind that never wrote. The burdensome responsibility he bore ushered the refreshing peace to the corner of his heart. His men needed him to stay strong. He had to do whatever it took to get them and the cattle to the Arizona Territory safely.

Only things weren't exactly going as planned. With one man buried on the side of the trail two days ride behind them, and another looking like he might soon join his friend, Will fought against the strong sense of failure pushing through his fatigue. If given the choice, he would rather have both men healthy and in the saddle. No one *wanted* to be attacked by Indians.

Nevertheless, they had been. And now it was his job to pick up the pieces and get everyone to the next milestone—Santa Fe—as quickly and safely as possible.

How could he do that when every tired muscle begged him to slip from his horse and sleep the day away?

Stifling a groan of frustration, Will turned his horse from the flank of the herd to camp. Maybe his mind would function better once his stomach was full.

Pulling the chestnut mare to a stop next to the other horses, he dismounted in a wobbly manner, his feet almost buckling under him. Resting his hand on the horn of his saddle, he steadied himself before unbuckling the straps. Lifting the saddle from the horse that had given him too much trouble last night, he carried it away from the horses as Covington took over the horse's care.

That horse, who he fondly dubbed Hilda, was one of the mares he bought from the livery back home. She had not been cattle trained and seemed to be adjusting to the cattle very slowly. Last night she nickered and whinnied far too much, setting the longhorns on edge— and Will. He was too tired to deal with a skittish horse. But, he rode Jackson most of the day before, maybe a bit too long before giving him a rest. When he asked for a mount, Covington suggested Hilda since she was the freshest.

Tossing his saddle on the ground, Will fought against the temptation to lie down without breakfast. Instead, he forced his feet towards the makeshift table where Snake dished out breakfast.

As he neared the table, a flash of silver caught his eye. Owens worked quickly to stash the flask, but not before it registered in Will's foggy brain.

Slamming his palm down on the table, Will said, through gritted teeth, "Owens! What do you think you are doing?"

Feigning innocence, Owens shrugged.

In no mood to deal with insolent behavior, Will leaned forward into the man's face. The smell of alcohol invaded his senses. "I will not have my men drinking on the trail!"

"Calm down, Boss. I'm not on until this afternoon. How else do you expect me to fall asleep in broad daylight?" Owens said, his eyes narrowing to tiny slits.

Adrenaline shot through Will's body, bringing him fully awake. He struggled not to hit the man as he tested Will's resolve. Reaching his hand to Owens' inside vest pocket, Will took the flask, opened it, and dumped the contents into the dirt. Then he handed the empty flask back to Owens.

"I expect my men to have a clear head while we're on the trail."

Owens' face turned beet red. When he started to stand, Whitten clapped his hand down on his shoulder. The forthcoming response died on Owens tongue when Whitten shook his head in warning. At least the fool listened to his friend, Will thought, walking from the scene.

Splashing cold water over his face, Will blotted the soothing liquid away with the sleeve of his shirt. For a brief moment he closed his eyes, calming his temper before he did something stupid, like firing Owens. Replacing his hat on top of his head, he took the bowl of grits Snake offered. Leaning against the chuck wagon, some distance from his men, he ate slowly. Exhaustion tugged at him. *Lord, I just need to make it to Santa Fe. Give me the strength to get us there.*

Finishing the last bite of grits, he dished up more. Grabbing a clean spoon, he walked to the litter where the young Indian boy lay sleeping. Taking a seat next to the sleeping boy, Will could not shake the feeling that there was something unusual about him. His angular jaw line and tanned skin gave him the appearance of being part Indian. Yet, his fairer hair suggested otherwise. The scars on his back told the story of painful abuse. His thin arms and legs gave him the appearance of a young boy of twelve or so. But, the dusting of facial hair on his chin inferred he might be older.

Regardless, sitting here staring at him would not answer Will's questions or help him figure out what to do with him. Reaching over the boy, he gave him a gentle shove.

As the boy's eyes fluttered open, he shrank away from Will, fear widening his blue eyes. He has blue eyes, Will thought.

Softly, reassuringly, Will asked, "What's your name, son?"

No answer.

"Do you speak English?"

A slight, almost imperceptible nod was his answer. His recoiled posture still spoke of fear and distrust.

Holding the bowl of food towards the boy, Will introduced himself. "Name's Will Colter. Would you like some food?"

Slowly the boy reached out to grasp the bowl with shaky hands. Once he had a firm grip, he quickly pulled the bowl close to his chest, shoveling the food in as if he had not eaten for weeks.

"Take it easy," Will warned. "There's plenty more if you are still hungry. Don't want to make yourself sick."

The boy slowed his eating, keeping one wary eye on Will.

"Looks like your wounds are healing nicely," Will commented, not sure why he continued with the one sided conversation. Maybe if he kept talking, the boy might see he had nothing to fear.

As the boy swallowed his last bite, Will held out his hand for the empty bowl. The boy gave it back, letting go quickly as if it were on fire. Standing, Will refilled the bowl with more grits and grabbed a hard biscuit. When he returned, he gave both to the boy. The second round of food disappeared as quickly as the first.

"If you're feeling up to riding, I'd like you in the saddle today. It would help us cover more ground."

The boy nodded.

Will waited another minute, hoping the boy might show some sign of speaking. Hearing nothing and needing to move on with his day, he turned to leave.

"Hawk," the timid voice spoke.

Will looked over his shoulder. "Pardon?"

The boy responded with more confidence this time. "My name is Hawk."

"Well, it is nice to meet you, Hawk. See Covington for a horse and saddle," Will said, pointing to the wrangler. Maybe in time, Hawk would learn he could trust him.

After returning the empty bowl to Snake, Will led Jackson from the herd of horses. As he lifted his saddle from the ground, a shadow fell across his back.

"Boss, why don't you sit this shift out?" Ben suggested from atop his horse. "I'll make sure the boys stay in line."

Will started to argue, but the look in Ben's eyes said there would be no winning this argument. The man could be downright stubborn when he put his mind to it. Pulling his saddle off the horse, Will searched for a spot to stretch out. He threw his saddle down on a fairly flat area. Then he shook out his bedroll. Settling down on the ground, he used his saddle as a hard pillow. No sooner did he close his eyes than he heard a scuffle over by the horses. He propped himself up on one arm to take a better look, his weariness begging him to do otherwise.

"What do you think you're doing?" Jed's voice accused. "You ain't stealing our horse."

"Boss told him to get a horse from me," Covington said.

"Right, I'll bet he did. Don't know why he didn't just shoot you on the spot, you savage." Jed shoved Hawk.

Will groaned. The last thing he wanted to deal with right now was a fight between his men. He waited another minute, hoping the situation would resolve itself.

Hawk stood his ground rigidly. Not speaking. Not backing down. Not breaking eye contact with Jed—such a different reaction from his earlier fear of Will. Jed's face turned red and he clenched his hands into a fist. Will was about to stand to separate the two, when Jed stormed off.

Seeing the confrontation was over, Will rested his head on the saddle and closed his eyes. The stress of the past few days faded as he fell into a peaceful slumber.

The sound of clanging pots some time later pulled Will from sleep. He must have slept the entire day, given the sun's position in the sky. Stretching, he shot a look Ben's way to let him know what he thought of being left to sleep so long. He really shouldn't be upset, he obviously needed the rest. It's just that he felt responsible for being short-handed. He stood, shook the dust from his blanket, and rolled it up, tossing it aside.

Ambling up to the makeshift table, Will took a seat with his men. "Hawk, why don't you join us?" he said to the boy hanging back from the rest of the group.

All conversation stopped as every head snapped in Will's direction. Jed shot him a look of death. Owens' jaw went slack. Only Ben managed to keep a stoic expression.

Hawk hesitated, and then took a seat near Will and away from the others.

"How's the herd today, boys?" Will asked, not needing to hear an answer. The men understood the unspoken command in his look, judging by the lack of eye contact. Choosing to play along, they muttered varying comments about this cow or that steer.

The strained atmosphere lingered through the meal. Ben bantered back and forth with Will trying to lighten the mood. When Jed finished his meal, he jumped up from the table with the pretense of helping Pace, shooting a defiant look over his shoulder.

Will couldn't blame Jed for being upset, knowing he lost his family to Indians. He'd seen this kind of hatred and bitterness before. He just hoped Jed wouldn't do anything foolish.

Following the meal, the men packed up camp and rolled out. Will motioned for Hawk to join him in the flank position within the herd. Now that Hawk was healthier, Will needed to figure out what was to be done with him. Should he teach him the cattle trade? Or perhaps the young boy had a family to return to. Either way, he wanted to learn more about the young man named Hawk.

"You ever worked with cattle, son?"

"No sir."

"Well, I am sure you can pick it up quickly," Will said, scratching at the three days of growth on his chin. He never much liked growing a beard and would find a way to remedy the itchy mess soon.

After a few minutes of cattle lowing and horse hooves thudding, Will picked up the conversation again. "Where are you from?"

Silence.

Will tired of pulling words from Hawk. Looking him straight in the eyes, he said, "Before I hire a man, I like to know a little about him, you know. See if I can trust him to take care of my cattle."

"H-hire me?"

"Yes. That is unless you have some other pressing job offer."

"No sir." Hawk stammered, "I mean yes, sir, I would like to work for you."

"So where are you from?" Will prodded.

"My pa was a sheep farmer in Texas." Hawk finally opened up. "He married my ma, a Kichai squaw, before the rest of her people were sent to the reservation. We lived on the ranch in east Texas along the Red River. Several years ago, I was captured by the Apaches, the Indians that attacked you. I did not want to go with them the day they attacked, but they said they would hunt down and kill my ma. I went with them because I had to."

The sadness in the young man's voice left Will wondering if there was someone still waiting for him in Texas. "Do you want to go back to Texas?"

"There is nothing left for me there. The second year I was with the Apaches, I learned that my ma had been sent to the reservation to live with her people and that my pa had died. I have nothing."

"Well, you got the job, if you want it," Will said, taking compassion on the young man.

"But, I don't know anything about herding cattle," Hawk said, his shoulders slumping.

"We'll teach you. We usually have a few young, somewhat

inexperienced men on the drive. You just watch me and Ben and you'll be fine. How old are you anyway?"

"Sixteen."

Another really young man. Jed, Hawk, Owens, Covington, and Whitten were all under twenty. But, with Malone gone, Will really needed help, albeit inexperienced. They were still a few days out from Santa Fe and he would not be able to hire more men until then.

Will spoke with Hawk a few more times throughout the night, explaining what to look for when driving the herd and when at camp. The boy seemed eager to learn.

When dawn tinged the sky deep red, Will knew they were in for some weather. Shortly after setting up camp for the day, the heavens broke loose in a downpour. Days like this were the most miserable on the trail. About the only thing a cowboy could do, was don a slicker to try and keep dry. No one would be getting any sleep today.

Snake and Whitten moved Pace from the litter to the chuck wagon to keep him dry. Hawk seemed to be recovering rapidly but Pace was not as fortunate. He was delirious throughout most of the night. Some of his wounds festered, despite any ministrations. Snake told Will this morning that he was concerned the young man may not make it to Santa Fe. *Lord, please keep Pace alive until we can get him better care.* He hated the thought of losing another man.

The general mood of the cowboys was agitated, as was often the case in a day full of rain. Tempers were short. Both dinner and supper were cold unappetizing fare, since the downpour prevented Snake from building a fire. Everyone was cold. Everyone was tired. Everyone was wet. As they pulled up camp, tensions rose to a boiling point. Will wasn't sure how it came to be, but when he looked toward Jed, he saw the young man with his pistol trained on Hawk.

"You devilish savage! I know you killed my family. You are good for nothing and I'd sooner kill ya than see your face another day!" Jed vehemently exclaimed, pulling back on the hammer to cock the gun.

Without thinking, Will ran full force, connecting his shoulder with Jed's side. As the two fell to the ground, the thick mud coated Will's jeans. In the fall, the gun flew from Jed's hand and landed out of reach. An angry Jed swung his fist, landing squarely on Will's jaw, the strength of the blow catching Will off guard. Falling to his side onto the tacky muddy ground, Will quickly recovered. Throwing his weight back toward Jed, he pinned the younger man's back to the ground. Jed started to swing with his left hand, then stopped mid-air—only the mud flung from his hand to Will's shirt. His eyes darkened but he dropped his arms to his side, losing his muster. Will stood, then yanked Jed to his feet. Hauling the young cowboy by his shirt collar, Will dragged him a short distance from camp to have a man to man discussion with his hot-headed hand.

Will used his height to intimidate the young man. "What do you think you were doing back there?"

"I was taking care of that murderous savage," Jed answered moving closer to Will, standing toe to toe.

"What makes you think he is a murderer? You don't know anything about him!"

"He killed my family."

"I doubt that," Will scoffed, trying to show the man how foolish he was being. "He is your age. Was there a young man your age with sandy colored hair that day your family died?"

Jed shook his head and crossed his arms. He responded, "No. But them Indians are all the same. They hate white folk and go around trying to wipe us out. I was gonna git him before he could git me."

Stepping closer to Jed, Will frowned. "That kind of hatred has no place on the cattle drive. That's the kind of anger that distracts you and is gonna get *you* killed."

Jed involuntarily took a step backwards, his anger still evident. "How can you take his side? How can you let him stay with us?"

"Because, I believe God sees every man as valuable, whether half-Indian, Mexican, or some white man who had his family killed by Indians," he replied in a calm even tone. As he scraped the mud from his pants, he continued, "Every man stands on his own merits and what he does with his life, not on his heritage. When you stand before God one day, you will have to answer for yourself, just as I will for myself, and Hawk will for himself.

"Make no mistake, every man will be judged and it won't be by you or by me, but it will be by the Almighty God. Those men that killed your family will be judged for what they did. No amount of your anger is going to add to that judgment. The only thing your hatred will do is get you hurt or killed, or full of guilt for killing an innocent man. Is that what you want on your hands? The blood of an innocent man? For what? To satisfy some revenge that will never bring your family back?" Will was so frustrated with the young man and hoped he was getting through.

Jed stood, arms still crossed, in a defiant posture for a few minutes while Will's words washed over him. Then, slowly, the man became a boy again, his pain and loss evident. Will could see he was just beginning to let some of it go. It wasn't everything he hoped for, but it was a good start. Jed uncrossed his arms and let them fall to his side.

"I want them back," he whispered.

Will placed his hand on Jed's shoulder, much like his father did when he was Jed's age. "I know, but what is done is done. We can't change the past. We can only change how we decide to move forward."

The silence stretched for several minutes and Will dropped his hand to his side. Sensing the boy needed to say more, he waited patiently.

"It was so horrible—what they did to my family. They rode into the ranch," Jed explained, his eyes in a far off place as he stuffed his hands in his pockets. "First they took my sister and did unspeakable things to her before they snapped her neck. She was just ten years old. What kind of monster does that? Then they went into the house. I could hear my mother's screams, but I was frozen in place, out of sight in the barn. Then the screaming stopped and they set fire to the house. When my pa came riding in, they threw a tomahawk at him, hitting him square between the eyes and knocking him off his horse. Then they took his scalp. I thought for sure they would come for me next or they would burn the barn and I would die in the fire. But then, they just left. The house burned to the ground before I thought it was safe enough to come out. My whole family was dead. And I saw it all."

Jed's anger faded, replaced by a few drops of moisture rolling down his face. His shoulders slumped forward as if weary of carrying the awful weight. When he looked up at Will, his eyes silently pleaded for something. Maybe forgiveness?

His words soft, Will said, "Jed, it is not your fault."

The young man stared off into the distance, not believing it.

"It is not your fault. There was nothing you could have done that would have saved any of them and not gotten you killed, too."

"Wish I could believe that." His voice was devoid of bitterness. Instead, it was filled with hope.

"Give it time." Putting his hand on the young man's shoulder Will gave a gentle squeeze. "God doesn't blame you and if you ask him, he will forgive you for this guilt you are carrying around. You don't have to carry it any longer."

Jed snorted. "God let them take my family away. I want nothing to do with him!"

His shout echoed in Will's ears as he ran from camp.

Chapter 9

The rain continued throughout the entire day and well into the night. The sweet smell of rain mixed with the pungent odor of wet cattle and horseflesh. The longhorns kicked up mud as they plodded forward on their journey westward. Will shivered from the cold, soaked to the bone despite his slicker. The other cowboys appeared as miserable as he.

Finally, a few hours before dawn, the rain stopped. Off in the distance lights dotted the foothills of the mountain. Santa Fe was in sight, at last. As they set up camp for the day, Will thanked God for reaching this milestone of the journey. Not only did Santa Fe represent the opportunity to rest and resupply, it allowed Will a chance to hire more men.

Life on the drive challenged the hardiest of men. The drive stimulated changes in attitudes and opinions—if it failed to claim your life first, Will thought.

He remembered his third cattle drive. The first two progressed uneventfully, but the third introduced Will to the dangers of the drive in an unforgettable manner. He was barely twenty years old. He and the cowboys of the Star C herded the longhorns to the New Orleans market. On that drive—the worst the Star C Ranch experienced—they ran into a warring band of Indians just days into the drive. They lost three men in the fight, and two more due to infection before the week was out.

For days they drove through a downpour of rain, much worse than what he and his men just experienced. When it came time to ford the swollen river with the cattle, all the cowboys were exhausted. No one had more than a few hours of sleep each day. Riding point, Will entered the river first. Weary, he summoned every ounce of strength to hang onto his horse. Then a swell of water rushed down the river, catching him unsuspecting. He fell into the churning water, unable to stop his rapid progress downstream.

Knocked into steer after steer, he struggled to fight the current. As his energy evaporated, Ben lassoed him, pulling him to safety. The river that almost claimed his life, claimed two horses and several head of cattle instead.

By the time they reached the market, only four men and three thousand head of cattle remained, numbers significantly reduced from when they started the drive. Will remembered sleeping for days before attempting the trip home.

He came face to face with his own mortality through that experience. Prior to that drive, he acted arrogant and cocky. And he filled his weekends with the pursuit of self-gratification, not something he relished today.

Instead of taking his life, that cattle drive changed his life. After the near death drowning, Will's father took him aside. His father embraced him and prayed over him, thanking God for sparing his life. From then on, he figured he should start living a moral life. Shortly afterward, he began his personal relationship with Jesus, and he had his father to thank. When he returned home, his father delegated the responsibility of managing the drive to Will. A few years later, his father admitted watching him become a man on that drive.

Rubbing his jaw in thought, he stopped when his hand moved over the sore lump still healing from his encounter with Jed. As Will thought about his men on this drive, they faced similar struggles. He understood growing up on the trail. Since their conversation, Jed acted differently. He still held on to some of the anger and resentment, but he wasn't lashing out against Hawk anymore.

Covington's insecurity still plagued him. He needed a lot of encouragement in his ability in handling the horses well. The more experienced men like Whitten, Miguel, Pedro, and Owens seemed to take things in stride. And there was Ben—a godsend. Having someone with his experience on the drive really settled the younger men.

Hawk seemed to be opening up a bit. He and Covington talked during down times. Jed still seemed uneasy around Hawk, as did Owens and Whitten. Perhaps in time they would all come to see him as a peer.

With no rain clouds in sight, Snake rigged a clothes line of sorts from the chuck wagon, so the men could hang their wet clothes out to dry. Each man owned a few changes of clothes, mostly because of the permanent move at the end of this drive. Will located dry clothes and changed. It felt good not be sopping wet over every inch of his body.

Looking around at all the things drying in the sun, Snake teased, "How much stuff did you ladies bring with you?"

A couple of the cowboys answered back with some pithy comments. At last, spirits lifted, bringing joviality back to the crew.

Concerns over Pace's injuries weighed heavily on Will. When he checked on Pace before sunset, he was unconscious and had been for the better part of the day according to Snake. He lost all color, his skin taking on a translucent appearance. Some of his wounds improved but the one on his left arm steadily grew worse and infected. Pace weakened daily, unable to keep down any food. Snake said he was feverish and needed better care soon.

Will motioned Ben to join him as he checked on Pace again this morning.

"We gotta do something, Boss," Ben said. "He ain't gonna make to Santa Fe."

"I know," Will replied grimly. Then, having an idea of how to give the wounded man a fighting chance, he asked, "Do you think we could spare someone to ride him on into Santa Fe on the litter today?"

"It'll be slow going, but would get him there by nightfall. Otherwise, we're looking at tomorrow morning at best."

Owens volunteered for the assignment. Will, Ben, Snake, and Owens each grabbed a corner of the blanket under Pace's limp body. Grunting from his bulky weight, the men lifted him from the wagon and settled him onto the litter. Will handed Owens a stack of money for the doctor and lodging before sending them on their way. He hoped the decision proved wise.

Will and Whitten dismounted their horses and tied them to the hitching post in front of the adobe structure with the placard reading "doctor's office." The air felt a few degrees warmer than the chill outside as they entered the building. Will blinked, waiting for his eyes to adjust to the dimmer light. Owens stood and greeted Will.

"Doc has been in with Pace all night," he reported.

A beautiful Mexican woman appeared from one of the rooms down the hallway, followed by a tall man. The man stopped in front of Owens.

"Mr. Owens," he greeted. "Mr. Pace is still unconscious, but appears to be doing well."

Owens introduced Will and Whitten to the doctor.

The doctor said, "I had to take his left arm. Though I hated to do so, it likely saved his life."

Will spoke up, "Thank you, Doc, for taking care of Pace. When will he be ready to ride out?"

The doctor shook his head. "I'm afraid he will not be well enough to ride for a month or more, assuming there are no further complications."

Will expected as much. Having decided the next course of action on the ride in, he held out two stacks of money. "One of these should cover Pace's expenses while he is in your care. The other is his wages. I hope I can trust you to see he gets this."

"This is more than enough for his care. I thank you for your generosity. And yes, I will see he receives this," he said, waving the other stack of money in his hand, "when he is well enough to leave. It should be plenty to cover him until he can pick up some work."

"Thank you again, Doc," Will said touching his finger tips to the edge of his broad brimmed hat. As sorry as he was to hear Pace lost his arm, he was thankful to see he was in good hands.

Stepping back into the bright sunlight, Will motioned Owens and Whitten to follow him back to the center of town. On the way to the doctor's office, they passed several businesses, including the store, butcher, restaurant, livery, and more.

Will pulled his mount to a stop in front of the store. Stepping inside the building, the friendly shopkeeper greeted them. He retrieved the long list of supplies from his front shirt pocket. Unfolding it, he then handed the list to the shopkeeper. He mentioned he would stop back the following morning for the filled order.

Since he purchased a five month supply of various food stuffs suggested by Snake, Will required two additional wagons and a team of oxen before returning in the morning. The livery owner happily sold him the team and wagons, agreeing to board them for one additional night.

Next, Will planned to hire a few more cowboys. He hoped to find experienced men, but would settle for anyone who could ride a horse. The shopkeeper suggested the restaurant down the street, popular with the local cow hands. Heavily spiced air assaulted his nostrils as he entered the establishment. His stomach growled. Motioning for Whitten and Owens to sit, Will waited for a young senorita to take his order. A man, who looked like he might be a rancher, entered the building.

Will stood and walked toward the rancher. "Will Colter," he said extending his hand. The man shook his offered hand with a firm grip.

"Alexander Morrow. What brings you to Santa Fe?"

"We are passing through on our way to the Arizona Territory," Will replied.

"Heard there's some good pasture land out that way."

"Heard the same. Would you know where I might find a few men willing to hire on for the rest of the journey?"

"Well, good cowboys are hard to come by. Most of the men I've hired recently came from wagon trains headed west—men who decided Santa Fe was far enough. There's one such train camped near the west side of town. They'll probably stay for a few days since they just arrived."

Will asked, "You know anyone who might be looking to buy a few head of longhorns?"

"Depends on how many you want to sell. If it's just a few head, the butcher down the street would probably take them. If you were thinking of a hundred or more, then try Fort Union—though it's more than a day's ride north of town. Sometimes they take the steers and let them graze until they are ready to slaughter 'em. You should get two hundred a head, may be more."

At Will's wide eyes, the man chuckled. "Prices are real good this far west and they get better the farther you go. At least if you're on the selling side of the transaction."

He thanked Mr. Morrow for the information. When they finished their meal, Will sent Whitten and Owens out to the wagon train to ask around, while he walked down the street to the butcher. Looking to part with roughly a dozen cattle, he secured the sale with the butcher. He made arrangements to deliver the longhorns the following morning.

Mounting his horse, Will headed west out of town to meet up with Owens and Whitten. As he approached, Whitten spotted him.

"We didn't find anyone who wants to sign on to go to the Arizona Territory, but we did find a man interested in selling his Herefords," Whitten said.

Owens added, "He's got about twenty head or so. Good breeding stock."

While Will could use men more than additional cattle at this point, this news intrigued him. Back in Texas he and his father spoke several times about adding Herefords at the ranch. The beef this breed supplied demanded higher prices. Longhorns were gaining an unfavorable reputation along the trails for spreading disease. Whether well-founded or not, the fear of disease would change the cattle industry. Bringing a small herd of Herefords with him, would allow Will to eventually move away from longhorns all together.

"Did he say how much he wants to sell them for?" Will asked.

"That's the crazy part. He's just looking for forty dollars a head. That's less than they are going for back east," Whitten answered.

Puzzled, Will asked, "Did you see them? Are they diseased or otherwise unhealthy?"

"Yeah, we saw them and they're in excellent condition," Owens commented.

"The man said he wanted to settle here and work for someone else. Lost his wife on the way out and doesn't want to go further. Figures he can provide for his children better here than in California," Whitten said.

Offering the man eight hundred dollars for the twenty head seemed like thievery, but the man quickly agreed to the price and thanked him for taking the small herd off his hands. Will and his men rounded up the new cattle and drove them back to the rest of the herd.

Even though he had more cattle than this morning, he still did not have any more help. Hoping to catch a few hours of sleep, Will laid out his pallet. Before he started to lie down, Miguel rode up with two unfamiliar men.

"Boss," called out Miguel. Pointing to the two men next to him, he said, "vaqueros," the word the Mexicans used for cowboys.

Piecing together conversation half in English and half in Spanish, Will figured that the two men were looking for work and had been *vaqueros* for several years. Will outlined the terms of work and they shook on it. Raul Espinoza and Diego Ruiz officially joined the crew.

The next afternoon, Will instructed Jed and Hawk to saddle up for town. On the ride in Jed remained silent, riding behind Will as he and Hawk passed the time chatting.

Once in town, Will instructed Jed to go pick up the wagons and team from the livery while he led Hawk to the general store.

"Figure it might be best if you had a few changes of clothes," he said as they entered the rough adobe structure.

Hawk's blue eyes rounded in surprise. "But, I don't have no money."

Will smiled. "Consider it part of your wages."

The young man quickly picked out a blue cotton button down shirt that resembled a smaller version of the one Will wore. He also grabbed two pairs of jeans and a slightly faded red shirt. After they were sure the clothing fit, the store clerk helped him pick out a pair of leather boots and a hat.

"Why don't you change into one of your new get-ups," Will suggested.

When Hawk returned from the back room, he looked like a full-fledged cowboy—and much closer to his actual age. Anyone passing him on the street would be hard pressed to think some Indian blood flowed through his veins. The broad grin on Hawk's face was worth the trip. Will figured it earned him a few more steps up on the ladder of trust.

Jed joined them a few minutes later with the wagons pulled around to the back of the store. When he caught sight of Hawk, his jaw slacked open.

"Sure don't look like an injun," Jed muttered under his breath before he grabbed a crate from the stack and shoved it into the wagon.

Over the next few hours, the men loaded the two wagons. Once the task was complete, Hawk drove the double wagon and team back to camp while the other two men followed on horseback. Will planned to leave Hawk in charge of the supply wagons for the remainder of the journey, as he was still learning the skills necessary for driving the herd.

Since Santa Fe was the last major sign of civilization along the way, Will announced that the men could have the night off if they wanted it. Pedro, Miguel, Raul, and Diego volunteered to stay behind to watch the herd. The rest of the cowboys eagerly rode into town. Deciding to keep an eye on the young men, Will joined them at the saloon. Although he hated the smoke and the noise, a beer sounded rather appealing.

As he tied Jackson to one of the hitching posts in front of the saloon, his heart beat faster. The wooden doors flapped back on double hinges as men entered the building. Just the sight reminded him of the man he was nearly a decade ago. He frequently sought refuge in similar establishments back home, drinking the night away—sometimes spending it in the arms of a soiled dove.

Pushing the doors open, he quickly took in the familiar scene. Some half-clothed woman banged out a raucous tune on the tinny piano. Clusters of men gathered around tables trying their luck at poker. Miserable, lonely men seated at the bar, swayed to the music or stared into the dark amber liquid. Women with brightly painted lips and too much bosom showing, hung over the railing above, calling to men with their enticing siren's song.

Will swallowed, unnerved that even after so much time his pulse would quicken just being in such a place. He would just hide out at the bar. That's it. No cards. No women. His stomach lurched from nervousness.

Taking a seat at the bar, he ordered his refreshment. The very drunk man seated next to him struck up a conversation. "Wherrrr youuuu headed?" The slurred words were barely understandable.

"Arizona Territory, the north central area."

"Got a bit... journey ahead... youuu there. Probably...'nother month or soooo."

Could it really be that close? Just another month?

Will smiled before taking another swig of his drink. As his glass made contact with the bar counter, a scantily clad saloon girl came up behind him, her cheap perfume causing his eyes to water.

Draping her arms around Will's neck, she asked, "Can I help you with anything, handsome?"

As she spoke in lilting tones, she ran her hands across Will's chest eliciting a reaction from him. Suddenly the air seemed thicker, harder to breath. It would be too easy to give in to the desire coursing through his veins.

He cleared his throat begging his body not to respond. Grabbing her hands, he removed them from his chest. Annoyed with his own physical reaction, he firmly commanded the soiled dove to move along. At his frown and obvious disinterest, the woman scurried away to find another more amiable patron.

Maybe it was not such a good idea to come here. Downing the last of his beer, he went outside to clear his head. Leaning on the railing of the porch in front of the saloon, Will took several deep breaths.

Years ago when he made the commitment to God, he gave up pursuing what the young woman offered. If she caught him after another beer or two, would his self-control still reign? *Stupid, stupid, stupid.* He chastised himself for coming this close to yielding to temptation. What kind of example was this for the young cowboys in his employ?

"Boss," Jed asked, "is it time to go?"

Will turned to see Jed, Hawk, and Covington all coming out of the saloon. They must have seen him exit. Doubly glad he had not done anything he would regret, he said, "I was thinking of heading on back. We'll be pulling out tomorrow afternoon and this will be our last opportunity to rest up. You may stay if you want." He didn't want to dictate to the men how they could spend their free time.

Hawk spoke first, "We'd like to go back to camp, too."

Jed and Covington nodded their agreement before untying their horses from the hitching post. Most young cowboys welcomed a night, a very long night, at the saloon. Well, Will was proud of their decision. It certainly showed a maturity beyond their young years. Mounting his horse, he led the way back to camp.

Sometime, very late into the night, Whitten, Snake, and Owens returned. Will heard the racket they made stumbling over themselves. They were most definitely drunk. Come morning they may regret their decision.

Will rolled over on his side, praying the rest of the journey west would be uneventful and swift.

Chapter 10

Fort Larned, Kansas

October 8, 1863

"Morning," Drew greeted Hannah, his voice infused with excitement.

She managed to force a somewhat pleasant response from her lips, though she did not feel it. For weeks, they maintained a cool cordial distance—speaking only enough to coordinate daily life. As she turned her back to him, she let the tears fall as painful memories of her father's distant coolness pervaded her thoughts. How had her marriage turned into a mirror image of that strained and hurtful relationship?

Drew came up behind her. "After breakfast, we'll head over to the Indian camp across the river."

Nodding in response, she continued with her breakfast preparations, not pleased with the idea of entering the camp of some five hundred Indians with nothing more than her husband and an interpreter.

Yesterday morning, Hannah had been sewing with the other women from the wagon train when the large group of Indians arrived. Their needles ceased their dizzy fluttering, as did their tongues, when the chief and his small party entered the fort. The impromptu sewing circle watched in silence from their vantage point near the barracks, ignoring the young soldiers dropping off more clothing that needed repaired. Instead, they strained to hear what the strange natives said to the Officer of Indian Affairs.

Before the officer escorted the Indians into his office, Hannah heard enough of the conversation to understand that the tribe was suffering from malnutrition and disease. They traveled many miles to Fort Larned, seeking aid.

Then, after supper last evening, the fort's commander stopped by to speak with Drew. Though they spoke in soft tones, she could tell from Drew's compassionate look that the commander knew he was a doctor and was making a request that he assist the tribe. After the commander left, Drew asked if she would join him in the morning.

Now that the breakfast meal was complete, Hannah had no more excuses to delay. She hurried, securing her long hair into a chignon as her husband waited patiently with his medical bag. The pins slipped in her shaky fingers, making the task take longer than normal. She had never seen such a large number of Indians in one area before. Now she and Drew were about to willingly walk into their midst.

Crossing the primitive wooden bridge, she begged her wobbly legs to be still. The closer they got to the camp, the more rapidly her heart pounded within her chest. Walking close to Drew, she took a deep breath to calm her nerves.

A small old woman with leathered skin approached Hannah, speaking with unfamiliar sounds and words that meant nothing to her. The old woman reached for Hannah's arm, but she shied away. Seeing her reaction, the old woman turned away.

Pressing closer to Drew, she tried not to stare at the bizarre people and structures. If not for their obvious malnutrition and illness, Hannah might have been frightened by the some of the stern looking braves. She heard stories of whites being murdered and horrible atrocities committed by such natives. Were these men safe?

Not only was their appearance foreign, with their dark eyes and jet black hair, but their dwellings were also unusual. Several long poles leaned together at the top while forming a wide base at the bottom. A large animal skin lay over the wooden frame with a flap on the side tied back, acting as a door.

As Drew led the way inside one such dwelling, Hannah held back a gasp. The first patient was a young man, lying on a primitive bed, covered in layers of buffalo pelts. His dark skin looked pale even in the shade of the tent. Sweat beaded on his forehead as his body shook. Drew handed his bag to Hannah.

Speaking to the interpreter, Drew asked, "May I remove the covers?"

The interpreter spoke with the young man, who nodded in reply.

As soon as Drew lifted the covers, the smell of rotting flesh hit

Hannah full force. She coughed trying to quell the rising nausea. Placing her handkerchief to her nose, she took shallow breaths. Drew coughed as well, hinting at his own struggle for control. Hannah dared to look at the wound again. The young man's abdomen was covered with thick puss and flies. The wound must be weeks old. How had he survived this long? Gagging at the sight, she excused herself.

She barely made it outside the tent before losing the contents of her stomach. Having seen many foul things in her time assisting Drew, she thought she would have a stronger constitution. But the stench overwhelmed her. Drew joined her, bag in hand, in a matter of minutes. At her questioning gaze, he shook his head slightly, confirming her assessment that the young man would not live many more days.

Drew offered her his arm and she welcomed his steady strength as the interpreter led them to the next tent. A young woman lay, screaming in the throes of labor. When he asked how long she labored, the young woman's mother replied that she had been this way for more than a day. Drew sought permission to examine the young woman, speaking in soft tones.

"The baby is breech," Drew explained. "I will have to turn it."

The interpreter spoke rapidly in guttural sounds to the older woman. She responded with a frown followed by angry words. Hannah did not need to understand their language to know the older woman was not pleased with Drew's suggestion. She started wagging her finger at Drew. Then, she pointed at Hannah and nodded her head.

"She says woman do this. Not man," the interpreter said.

Hannah's eyes went wide and she looked at Drew. She started to protest the idea forming in her husband's mind, but the concern in his expression stopped the words slipping from her lips.

"Hannah, you have to do this, since they won't let me. I will talk you through it."

"I can't turn the baby!" She shrieked in panic. Surely her husband must have lost his mind.

"If you don't do this, this woman and her child will likely die."

As her breath went shallow, her head began to swim. *Please don't make me do this.*

Drew grabbed her forearms and shook her. "Calm down."

She had to get her panic under control before she swooned. Taking a deep breath, she squared her shoulders.

"You can do this," he said, locking gazes with her. "I will be right here."

She begged God for strength and courage. "What do I do?"

As she knelt before the woman, Drew was so close behind her; she could feel his warm breath on her neck. Whispering in her ear, he coached her through the process. She barely registered what she was doing, so terrified of being responsible for someone's death.

He continued speaking softly to her. "That's right, Hannah. You are doing good. Almost there. Good."

Turning his gaze towards the young woman, he said, "Now push!"

A few hearty pushes later, and the baby arrived. Hannah knew what to do from here, having assisted with many births before. Once the baby boy was cleaned, she settled him into his mother's arms. The young woman smiled and thanked Hannah.

As Drew helped Hannah from the tent, she caught the sparkle in his eye.

"I am so proud of you," he said softly, then squeezed her hand. The small gesture of approval tasted like sweet honey to her wounded spirit. He still cared, despite the chasm between them.

Walking toward the next patient, Hannah hoped she would not be called on again. Her hands were still shaking and her stomach refused to settle completely each time the reality of what she'd just done entered her mind.

Thankfully, the rest of the afternoon she only assisted Drew, like she had in the clinic back home. He examined so many patients that she lost count. Several suffered from dysentery and malnutrition. He gave instructions to the men on how to help prevent dysentery. Some of the other patients he examined had weeks old injuries, similar to the first young man, though not as severe. He treated some, while others he left medicine to dull the pain and ease their suffering.

As she walked next to her husband on the way back to their wagon, Hannah glanced over at him. The spark of joy returned to his eyes, warming her heart. It was good to see him practicing medicine again.

After spending a few days with Drew caring for the Indians, she returned to the daily gathering of the women, relieved to be away from the disease and sickness. To assuage the boredom, the women under Betty's leadership took in mending for the single men in the wagon train, including the military escort and the military from the fort. One of the women led a Bible study, reading and teaching from various passages while the other women kept busy with their mending. A few of the men from the train occasionally sat nearby to listen while fixing harnesses. Even some of the military hung around the group pretending not to listen.

Nearing the end of their third week at Fort Larned, Hannah felt restless, no matter how she occupied her time. The first few days at the fort were a blessing, giving her time to wash their laundry and see to some mending. But they still had so much ground to cover, and she long ago ran out of tasks needing her attention. She just wanted to be on their way. The November date Drew originally projected their arrival would be impossible now.

A noise drew her attention toward the east. One of the army scouts rode back to the fort at a frantic pace. That only meant one of two things—trouble or more settlers. Hannah hoped for the latter.

"It's the governor of the Arizona Territory. His expedition should arrive later today," the scout reported to his commanding officer.

A shout of joy erupted from the bystanders. The military personnel leaped into motion. The settlers all began talking at once. Some speculated their departure in a matter of days. Others wondered what the governor's group would be like. A contagious excitement permeated the fort, causing Hannah to forget the monotony of the past weeks.

A few hours later, the governor's party, of twenty wagons, arrived with great fanfare. The commander of the fort lined up his men in formation. They offered a salute to the governor and his men. The governor spoke briefly, thanking the commander for his hospitality and the crowd for their enthusiasm.

After an afternoon of celebrating the new arrivals, Hannah's curiosity piqued when they camped near the Anderson and Lancaster wagons. Following the evening meal, several members of the governor's party joined the campfire Drew built. Betty and Paul scooted closer to Hannah, making room for their new guests.

"Jonathan Richmond," a young man said holding his hand out to Drew. He had dark wavy hair and dark eyes. He appeared confident, despite his short stature.

Taking the offered hand, her husband responded, "Drew Anderson. This is my wife, Hannah."

Paul introduced himself and his mother before Mr. Richmond asked, "Where are you folks headed?"

"Granite Creek area in the Arizona Territory," Paul said. "My mother and I are looking to open a boardinghouse there. We're trying to convince the good doctor to join us."

"Doctor?" Mr. Richmond asked. "I am certain the area could use a good doctor. The governor has received reports that there are a number of sizable mining camps in the area. Fort Whipple is to be located nearby as well."

Hannah held her breath in anticipation of Drew's reaction. He adamantly refused to consider the idea each time Paul mentioned it over the past few weeks.

Drew said, "Well, we started the journey west with the thought of settling in La Paz, but the idea of Granite Creek has merit. How big is the population there?"

Sucking in a quick breath of shock, she tried to mask it as a cough. Was Drew actually considering changing their plans?

"Right now there are not more than a few hundred miners in the area and a small outpost scouting for the fort's location. However, a large number of folks traveling with us are looking to settle in the area," Mr. Richmond said.

"What else do you know of the territory?"

"The Granite Creek area and the southern part of the state are well suited for cattle and sheep ranching. There are already reports of ranchers moving from Colorado and Texas to the southern end of the state. The two biggest towns are La Paz and Tucson, though the latter has a significant Mexican population still. Much of the territory is sparsely populated with Indians. The governor calls this the last great wilderness. We are hoping to encourage many settlers into the area."

Mr. Richmond shared other news of the governor's plan, likely an attempt to further convince her husband of the beneficial nature of settling in the Granite Creek area.

As Hannah and Drew retired, she could tell by his distracted behavior that he mulled over everything their new friend discussed. Even though she wanted to ask if he was now thinking about changing their destination, she did not out of fear of adding to the lingering tension between them.

The next morning, despite Hannah's eagerness to depart from Fort Larned, she managed to paste on a smile and help Betty with mending and sewing things for the governor's party. Much to the traveler's dismay, the wagon train master announced earlier that they would remain at Fort Larned for several days yet, allowing the new arrivals a chance to rest and tend to any necessary cleaning and repairs.

One evening, the governor, having heard from Mr. Richmond of Drew's profession, invited them to dine with him and his advisors. Hannah heard that the government officials had their own chuck wagon and the cook was accustomed to preparing extra food for whomever the governor wished to join them. She was nervous. She had never met any men in power before and was not sure what to expect.

Drew offered his arm. "You look lovely this evening," he whispered in her ear.

After all this time of being at odds with each other, his unexpected compliment brought heat to her cheeks and remorse to her soul. With those few simple words, he disarmed a large part of the defenses she erected around her heart. She knew she shared some blame for the distance between them. She held on to her anger for much too long.

"Just think, Hannah," Drew said with excitement as he led her towards the governor's camp, "we're traveling with the governor's party. We are witnessing history!"

Still caught up in her own thoughts, she made no comment. Perhaps she would talk to Drew tonight—ask for his forgiveness— see if they might be able to return to the friendly banter and quiet love they shared back in Ohio.

"Pay close attention to what is said tonight." Drew's eyes glittered as his enthusiasm grew. "These are the things we'll tell our children. When they ask us what the governor looked like, we won't want to disappoint them."

Hannah smiled at the glimpse of the happy man she married. She loved his excitement for adventure. That look in his eyes now reminded her of the day he first kissed her. His look had been so intent—a mixture of love and something else—excitement over the prospect of a glorious future. That look melted her heart now as it had then.

As they arrived, Governor Goodwin greeted them. "Dr. and Mrs. Anderson. A pleasure to meet you."

"Likewise," answered Drew shaking the kindly man's hand.

Governor Goodwin's light colored eyes complemented his fair blonde hair and thick blonde handle bar moustache. When he smiled, his whole face lit up. He exuded confidence and seemed quite at ease with the large group of diners. Hannah found something rather familiar about him but failed to place it.

During the meal, Hannah and Drew met the Secretary of Territory, Richard McCormick, with his shocking bright red hair. They also met the judges who would serve in the three districts of the territory. They learned that Mr. Richmond was to be one of the court clerks.

"We heard that your party was due to arrive over a month ago," stated a man Hannah recognized from their wagon train. "What happened?"

"We were delayed in Cincinnati," Secretary McCormick explained. "Goodwin here is not the first governor of the territory. Governor Gurley was the gentleman the President appointed. However, he took ill and passed away in Cincinnati, Ohio. We were delayed several more weeks to make proper arrangements and to await instructions from the President."

It suddenly dawned on Hannah where she had seen these men before—Mr. Gurley was Drew's last patient before they left Ohio. He died from an infected abscess. Drew must have realized the same, for he said, "I believe you gentlemen brought Mr. Gurley to see me for assistance."

Recognition dawning, Governor Goodwin said, "Yes, yes. You were the doctor across the street from the mercantile in Cincinnati. I recall now someone mentioning you were headed west. Thank you for all you did to ease Mr. Gurley's pain in his last days."

"You're welcome. I'm just sorry I wasn't able to do more," Drew said.

Waiving his hand to close the topic, Secretary McCormick said, "So, you made excellent time getting to Fort Larned. How long ago did you depart from Cincinnati?"

"We left nearly six weeks ago. Taking the steamboat to Missouri, we were able to cover much ground quickly."

"Dr. Anderson, where is your final destination?" Goodwin inquired.

"We plan settle in La Paz."

"La Paz, hmmm," Secretary McCormick muttered. "Have you considered settling in Granite Creek?"

Hannah smiled at the Secretary's innocent question, knowing Drew must be weary of hearing it.

"Others have mentioned the better qualities of the area," Drew said.

"Well, I'm certain there are doctors already in La Paz," Secretary McCormick countered. "Granite Creek, while not much now, will grow rapidly if Goodwin here has his way."

"Richard, you know I have yet to select a location for the capital."

"Yes, but you know that is the most sensible location."

The governor appeared annoyed with Secretary McCormick's persistence. Fortunately, one of the judges in the party steered the conversation to less controversial topics before an argument ensued.

The men continued to talk of plans for the new territory, but Hannah's attention waned. Too late, she missed stifling a yawn.

Secretary McCormick must have noticed. "Dr. Anderson, perhaps we should not take any more of your time and allow your lovely wife to retire." She didn't miss the glint in his eyes indicating the concern was sincere.

Thanking the governor for the meal, Drew helped Hannah up and they walked back to their wagon.

"Doctor! Doctor!" a sergeant yelled as he rode toward them.

"Here!" Drew called back.

"Come quick. Lieutenant Harrison has been shot."

Drew jumped up into the wagon to gather some of his medical supplies. With a nod to her, she followed. They ran toward the military section of the camp as fast as they could. She hiked up her skirts to keep from tripping. Both were panting heavily by the time they reached the injured man. Taking a few deep breaths to steady herself, Hannah stood ready to help as Drew flew into action. The wound appeared to be just below the man's rib cage on his right side. She dug in Drew's bag for something to soak up the blood so he could better evaluate the injury. Once they slowed the flow of blood, he removed the man's coat and shirt. The bullet wound did not appear very deep.

Hannah looked at the young lieutenant's face. Amazingly he was still conscious. His eyes were clouded with pain and his jaw was clenched shut. His face was pale, but other than those indications, he made no noise or movement. She had seen grown men with less severe wounds screaming in agony, writhing from pain. She respected his ability to control his pain.

"Give him some ether so we can get this bullet out."

The lieutenant started to protest but a quick look from Drew silenced him. As soon as he was out, Drew quickly found the bullet. Then he disinfected the wound and wrapped it up.

Hannah cleaned Drew's instruments as he spoke to the lieutenant's commanding officer. "I think the bullet missed any vital organs. It wasn't deep, so he should recover. Keep him warm and call me if he wakes before I come back to check on him."

Once back at their tent, they retired for the night. Twice Hannah stirred when Drew went back to check on his patient during the night. Each time she waited for his return and each time he reported that the lieutenant slept soundly.

At dawn, the sergeant stood outside the tent, concern edging his voice. "Dr. Anderson, the lieutenant is awake, but he ain't looking so good."

Hannah prepared to join Drew, but he motioned for her to stay behind. She said a silent prayer for God to be with Drew.

Since she was awake, she decided to go ahead and start the day. The wagon train was scheduled to pull out in a few hours, so she packed up the tent. She would have Drew load it in the wagon when he returned. Knowing this would be the last opportunity to easily bake bread for some time, she set about the task. Just as the bread finished, he returned. The worried look on his face said volumes.

"He's got an infection. I did my best to cleanse the wound, but it is festering nonetheless. He's going to require close attention." Drew ran his hands through his hair, a sign that he was struggling with something. "I hate to ask this of you, Hannah…you must drive the wagon."

She just stared at him, wide eyed, not certain she heard him correctly.

"I'll help you pack up, but then I need to ride in the military wagon with the lieutenant. If he takes a turn for the worse, they may not have time to ride back and get me. I'm sorry…"

Hannah held up her hand to stop him. "I can do this. I was just caught off guard. Back on my father's farm I had to handle the team on occasion. Please, don't worry about me. I'll ask Paul for help. You just take care of your patient."

Drew lightly placed his hand on her cheek. "Thank you. I will join you for supper tonight." Pulling her close, he sealed the promise with a kiss that heated her from fingers to toes. Amazing how he could still elicit that reaction from her after two years of marriage.

"I'll be praying for you," she said as he finished loading the last of their things in the wagon. He smiled and left.

Even with Paul's help hitching the oxen, she was still slower than most. When she climbed up to the wagon seat and called "all set," she realized her voice was one of the last. Nothing to be done about that. At the wagon master's call to "fall in," Hannah took her place in the long line of wagons. It was a routine that quickly came back, despite having stayed at the fort for a month.

The gentle sway of the wagon calmed her nerves. She wished she had thought to wrap her hands, for she could already feel the blisters starting to form.

She smiled as she thought of Drew's kiss. Love for her husband swelled in her heart. She was sorry for being angry with him for so long. She was sorry for not trusting him to know what was best for their future. From this point forward, she vowed she would change.

Chapter 11

For four days, Hannah saw very little of Drew. He came for supper each night, checking on her, before returning to his patient. In the few short minutes they shared together, she learned that Lieutenant Harrison continued to struggle to fight the infection. Drew shared his concern over the continual traveling—the constant jostling worsened Harrison's condition—but he understood the need to press on. She continued to pray for the young man.

Since she drove the wagon all day, Betty took over meal preparations. The motherly figure made enough to feed her and Drew. Between Paul and a few other men, Hannah had all the help she needed caring for the oxen, getting water, and all the other daily chores Drew typically handled. She felt a little guilty when she found out the men worked extra hard to get water along this stretch of the river. It was not flowing freely, so the men had to dig into the Arkansas River's bed for the life giving liquid. Yet, none complained.

Climbing into the wagon, Hannah wrapped an extra blanket around her body. The temperature turned colder, the air crisp, and the skies alluded to snow. Over the past few days, the landscape changed from flat endless prairies to a gentle slope towards the Rocky Mountains. They were in Colorado now and would be nearing Fort Lyon in a few more days.

Again, the complete silence of driving the wagon alone seemed endless. Hannah tried not to let it bother her, but her mind would not be still. And the topic brought a bit of pain. Why was she childless? Day after day the question rattled in her head, accusing. The past few days, it hounded her incessantly. Why hadn't she and Drew had a baby? They had been married for over two years now. They had plenty of opportunity to conceive, but had not. Was there something wrong with her womb? Was she one of those misfortunate women who were not capable of having a child? Was it Drew? How long would it be? Why would a babe not come? *Lord, you know how much I want to give Drew a child. I don't understand. Please help me. I want a child so badly. My arms feel empty day after day. I was so certain we would have a child by now. When, Lord, when?* On and on her thoughts interlaced with her prayers. She wanted to be a mother more than anything.

Her thoughts must have etched deep lines in her face, for when the wagon train camped for dinner Betty pulled her aside for a few minutes.

"What's wrong, dear?"

Sighing, Hannah said, "I have been dwelling on my childlessness for days now."

"Oh, is that all dear? Don't worry. At least that's what the good book says. You are not to worry about tomorrow, that's God's job." Betty smiled and patted her hand as if that would make Hannah's mind stop.

"But, Drew and I have been married for over two years. All of my friends back home had a wee one in the arms by now. Why not me?"

"Dear, babies come in God's time, not ours. Many women go years before their first babe is born. It doesn't mean there's anything wrong or that God doesn't have it in mind to give you a child. He's just taking *his* time with it."

Wrapping her hands to keep the blisters from getting worse, Hannah thought about what Betty said. Maybe her fears were unfounded. Maybe it was just a matter of waiting for God's timing. Knowing that didn't make the waiting any easier.

That evening, once she had the wagon positioned in the customary circle, Hannah jumped down, startled at the unexpected sound of Drew's voice.

"Hello, beautiful," he said, pulling her into a tight embrace.

"Drew, I've missed you." Not caring that they could have an audience, she kissed her husband.

Groaning, he pulled away. "I've missed you too."

"How's the Lieutenant ... Harrison was it?" she asked as Drew began unhitching the oxen.

"He is doing much better. He turned the corner this morning."

"Will you be coming back soon?" Hannah asked, hopeful that

the lieutenant would not continue to need round the clock care. The dark circles under Drew's eyes made him look older. He needed to rest. And she wanted him back with her.

"No. He still needs a great deal of attention."

Once he had the yoke removed from the oxen, Drew led them out to graze. As he returned to camp, Hannah thought he might collapse from exhaustion. Instead, he sat next to her, thanking Betty for the meal.

As Hannah took a seat next to her husband, Paul said, "The wagon master said since we lost so much time at Fort Larned, once we arrive at Fort Lyon, we will only stay a few days. We'll press on and won't stop for an extended time until we reach New Mexico."

Drew sighed, his weariness evident. Hannah knew he was concerned for his patient. This was definitely not the news he had been hoping for.

The stay at Fort Lyon was only a week, much to Drew's chagrin. He hoped they would stay for a few more days, as the lieutenant's return to health proved slow—and because Drew longed to be reunited with his wife.

He felt terrible for leaving Hannah to fend for herself for the past fifteen days. Guilt stared him in the face as he thought of her driving the wagon alone day after day—a job he should be doing. The assistant wagon master's warning that he needed to manage things on his own plagued him. While the lieutenant was making positive progress, he was not healthy enough to be left alone. Drew thought he might be able to ask one of the women to care for the young man, but they seemed to be busy caring for their own families, or they were employed by the army or freight teamsters to cook and clean and would not leave their job.

Though the tension between him and Hannah eased during this time, Drew still longed to talk to her—to make sure she was doing well and reassure her that he loved her. The weeks prior to this separation had been difficult. He tried reaching out to her, but she put up a wall. The first sign of a crack in that strong defense came when he asked her to turn the Indian woman's baby. She listened to each of his instructions and followed them precisely, despite her obvious fear. If they hadn't been across the river from their own camp, Drew would have taken her in his arms and showered her with kisses. Instead, he gave as much encouragement as he could.

Hannah seemed to be softening the night the lieutenant was shot. She even smiled at him before the dinner with the governor—and again several times during dinner.

Her bold kiss the day before they arrived at Fort Lyon made his heart somersault within his chest. The barriers around her heart seemed to be falling. She was letting him near again and it felt good.

Yawning, Drew longed for just a few hours of uninterrupted sleep. He couldn't remember the last night he slept for more than an hour or two at a time. Prior to the lieutenant's injury, most nights were fitful, filled with concern of what was to come. Second guessing his decision haunted him. Did he make the right choice for Hannah? For himself? Should he do as so many others suggested and follow the governor's party to Granite Creek?

Lieutenant Harrison stirred, capturing his attention.

"How are you feeling?"

Harrison cleared his throat and hoarsely responded, "Like I've been shot." A smiled played at the corner of his eyes.

"Ah, well, that's understandable."

"Can I ask you a question?"

Drew nodded.

"The other day when I was dying," he said, holding his hand up to stop Drew from arguing the point. "Don't say I wasn't, for I know I was. When you laid your hands over the wound and prayed, why did you do that?"

Drew hesitated. He knew that prayer worked. He prayed constantly when working with patients. Whenever he felt he had done all that was humanly possible, he would often get a sense that he should place his hands over the wound and pray for healing. Sometimes God chose to heal, and sometimes he didn't. Drew knew he was not responsible for the outcome, he was just supposed to obey. How to explain that to the young man? "I was asking God to do for you what I could not."

A frown crossed Lieutenant Harrison's face. "Why would God

care to heal me?"

Drew didn't know how to respond, so he waited, anticipating that Harrison had more to say.

"I don't deserve to live. I have led men into battle in this terrible war to kill their fellow Americans. It doesn't matter if the government says the southern states are the enemy. We are all brothers. I have instructed men on the most effective way to surround and kill as many of the so called enemy as possible." He paused as if wrestling with a great weight. "I have even fired into a group of men, of which my own cousin was standing, to have it end in what my commander called a victory. That is not what I call it. Why would God want to save a man like that?"

Drew's heart went out to him. This War Between the States pitted brother against brother, or in his case cousin against cousin. What do you say to someone who has experienced such tragedy? *Lord, please give me the words.*

"Because he loves you." Drew was surprised by his own response, but went with the Lord's leading. "It is not because we deserve it. None of us do. It is simply because he loves you. If you ask him for forgiveness, the Bible says that he will give it to you. He will not hold it against you. He will freely make things right with you. All you have to do is ask."

The lieutenant's frown remained in place. Drew wanted to say more, but remained silent. He knew each person had to come to God in their own time and in their own way.

Finally, after several minutes, the frown lessened. Instead of acknowledging what Drew said about God, the Harrison simply asked for some water. A few sips satisfied him. The sway of the wagon had a lulling effect. His patient's eyes grew droopy and he fell asleep again. Drew decided he would make a point of praying for the young man's troubled heart in addition to his healing.

Four days later, in the evening, the wagon train pulled into Gray's Ranch at Picketware, Colorado. The Grays were known for their hospitality and the ranch had become a sort of way station along the Santa Fe Trail, according to the lieutenant. They entertained travelers so often they built out a dining area and had a full time cook for the sole purpose of feeding guests.

Drew's legs felt heavy with exhaustion as he walked toward the dining hall. If it hadn't been for the governor specifically requesting he and Hannah join him for dinner, Drew would have opted to skip the meal altogether. The lack of sleep was past taking its toll. He knew he needed to rest soon, or his body would force the issue. Seeing Hannah waiting for him brought a smile to his lips, although it didn't quite reach his tired eyes.

"Hannah."

She reached up and pecked him on the cheek. "You look positively exhausted. Are you sure you want to dine with the governor?"

He shrugged and offered her his arm.

"At least say you will come back to our camp tonight? If the lieutenant is not well enough to be left alone then let's see if someone else can care for him." Concern etched Hannah's face.

Perhaps he should do as she suggested. "Who do you propose we get to watch him?"

"Betty said she would for the next few days. You really need to rest. I know how you get when you have patients that need care, but in this case I think you are pushing yourself too far. It shows."

Leave it to his wife to set him straight. "Alright."

"Good, I'll talk to Betty."

Once inside the large room, he held the chair out for Hannah. Taking the seat next to her, his stomach growled. When was the last time he ate? Probably supper last night. He couldn't remember. The conversation went on around him, but he found his attention fading. He felt Hannah nudge his arm and realized someone must have asked him a question.

"Pardon?" he asked, waiting to see who responded.

"How is your patient?" Mr. Richmond asked.

"Doing better. He still has a ways to go, but he should recover fully."

The governor's men told stories about the Granite Creek area in the Arizona Territory, but Drew was having a hard time paying attention. Sleep was nudging harder. He simply nodded, as the hostess removed their dinner plates. She replaced his with a piece of cake with a candle.

"What's this?" he asked, slightly perking up.

"Happy Birthday, Drew," Hannah said, smiling sweetly at him.

What day was it? The third of November. Yes, he was so tired he hadn't remembered his own birthday. But, from the look on Hannah's face, she had. "Thank you, Hannah."

The odd assortment of government officials wished him well, as he blew out the candle. The cake was fluffy and moist. How had Hannah managed to arrange this special treat? She was full of surprises. The hostess brought pieces for everyone, so Drew didn't feel guilty devouring his piece. When the dessert was finished, the governor's group made no move to leave. Drew, on the other hand, was fighting to stay awake. He and Hannah bid the men farewell before heading back to camp.

Hannah already had the tent up and the bedding laid out. The weariness washed over him. He headed straight for bed, but was surprised when she followed. It was still early. As they lay down, she snuggled up close. He felt comforted by her presence. Placing his arms around his wife, he fell fast asleep.

As Hannah stirred a pot of beans over the warm fire, she glanced up at the mountains towering on both sides of the flat land where they made camp. A few small abandoned cabins stood near one of the slopes, rumored to have been built by a wagon train stranded in the pass last winter. She hoped their wagon train would not suffer the same fate.

Following supper, Mr. Richmond joined their campfire, excited by the discovery of the cabins. Speaking to Paul and Drew, Mr. Richmond said, "We found nothing noteworthy in the first few cabins we entered. Nothing more than a few utensils or the remains of a cooking fire."

Hannah and Betty both paused in their conversation, sensing Mr. Richmond was about to regale them with some interesting tale.

"Then, in the last cabin," Mr. Richmond continued, "we came across obvious signs of the former inhabitant—mainly in the form of the native woman's severed head."

Hannah's stomach lurched at the visualization. Certainly, Mr. Richmond realized she and Betty were sitting nearby.

"Her body," Mr. Richmond said, "was lying a few feet away. She had been scalped and left not more than a day ago."

As Hannah gasped, Mr. Richmond turned to look her in the eyes.

"Um…Mrs. Anderson, I am most sorry," he fumbled for an apology as Hannah stood. "I did not realize you were listening. Please forgive me."

Hannah merely nodded, before running just past their wagon. Her stomach roiled as her mind became consumed with fear. Not more than a day ago that poor woman had been brutally murdered in one of the cabins a few yards away. Was her murderer still lurking in the shelter of the forest? Would he attack the unsuspecting wagon train? Would they wake up in the morning to a massacre?

"Dear, are you alright?" Betty asked.

Hannah nodded, taking a few deep breaths of crystalline air to calm her stomach. "Do you suppose," she asked Betty, "that they are still out there?"

"Who, dear?"

"Whoever did that… horrific…" Hannah stopped abruptly, trying to push the image from her mind.

Betty placed an arm around Hannah's shoulder. "I wouldn't worry, dear. We have a camp full of brawny men and mounted cavalry. We couldn't be safer."

Hannah wished she felt safe.

Drew woke the next morning to the aroma of breakfast cooking. He jumped up and dressed hurriedly. How could he have slept so late? He needed to go check on Lieutenant Harrison, whom he neglected for several days now.

"Morning," Hannah said as he opened the tent flap. "Breakfast is almost ready."

The dark circles under her eyes testified to her restless night. Drew was furious at Mr. Richmond for recounting the terrifying story in Hannah's presence. And his prayer that she might not suffer nightmares seemed to have gone unanswered.

Seeing that most of the other tents were packed, Drew set to the task. He was ashamed to always be the last ready. Once finished, he sat down for the meal. Hannah handed him a heaping plate which he ate quickly.

"Betty said Lieutenant Harrison is doing well. She's going to ride with him today and insisted that you stay here."

Handing the empty plate back to Hannah, Drew gave her a quick kiss on the cheek and thanked her for the fine meal. He started to turn to retrieve the oxen, when she placed a hand on his arm.

"If you need more rest, I can drive the wagon today."

Though the offer was sincere, he could not stop the guilt that bubbled up. He should be taking care of her. He should be driving that wagon. And he would, despite the exhaustion from the weeks of little sleep. Shaking his head, he went to find the oxen. By the time he returned, Hannah had everything cleaned and stowed. He went through the motions of hooking up the team. Once the wagon was ready, he helped her up then took the seat next to her.

The road was much rockier since the train turned south from Fort Lyon. They slowly climbed the steep mountain. The oxen worked hard to pull the wagon up the difficult grade.

Suddenly the trail narrowed to just a few inches wider than the wagon. On the side next to him rose a sheer rock wall. The other side of the trail dangerously dropped off to the valley far below. When the road curved sharply, Drew's pulse quickened as he tried to keep the wagon on the narrow road, getting the front pair of oxen to start turning at the awkward angle.

Hannah shrieked as the wagon lurched.

"Hold on tight!" Drew shouted, concentrating on driving the wagon.

"Drew—the wheel!"

The wagon tilted precariously as only three wheels remained on the road. Drew's breath caught in his throat as Hannah gripped his arm with frightful force. Slapping the reins down hard, he got the oxen moving quicker. He had to get that wheel back on the road before the contents of the wagon shifted the weight—pulling them down over the side.

Another jolt of the wagon bounced Hannah too close to the edge of the seat. Glancing at his wife, he saw her holding on for her life as one leg dangled over. Panic rose.

Pulling hard to the left, the oxen navigated the last part of the insane curve. The wagon lurched again. The final wheel returned to solid ground. The harsh movement threw Hannah into his side.

As the trail straightened and widened, Drew stopped the wagon and jumped down. Moving to the other side, he helped his crying wife down. His breath returned to a normal rhythm as he buried his head in the small space between her neck and shoulder, clutching her tight.

"I thought I might lose you," he whispered, kissing her forehead, her nose, her lips.

When her tears subsided, and his own beating heart calmed, he helped her back into the wagon, getting far from this Devil's Gate as he could.

By the time the wagon camped for the evening, Drew's nerves stretched to their limits. He wanted to lie down and sleep for days, but the team needed care and he still hadn't checked on Lieutenant Harrison.

Once the team was unhitched and corralled, he went to check on his patient. Lieutenant Harrison was out of the wagon and sitting up nearby. When he saw Drew he stood.

"Dr. Anderson," he greeted with a warm smile.

"Please, call me Drew. How are you feeling?"

"Very good, sir. Mrs. Lancaster is a wonderful nurse, even if she can be rather insistent. Wouldn't let me just continue to lie about." The lieutenant chuckled.

Drew asked him to sit. Checking the bandages, he was surprised at how much the wound healed in the past few days. There was no sign of any infection. *Praise God.* He bandaged the injury again glad he could return to his own camp.

"Let me know if you have any troubles. Otherwise, just take it easy for a few days. I'd like to see you stay with the wagon and not return to horseback yet."

The lieutenant nodded. As Drew stood to leave, Harrison looked him in the eye and said, "Thank you, for everything."

Drew suspected he meant more than just doctoring. Shaking the man's offered hand, he smiled.

For the second night in a row, Hannah shot upright, wide awake long before dawn. Her heart raced and she labored to pull air deeply into her lungs. The image of a floating head speaking in staccato words faded as her eyes focused on the canvas tent protecting her from the elements.

Hannah had been running through a narrow valley, flanked by high mountains. The Indian woman's floating head chased her, screaming at her in guttural nonsensical sounds. As Hannah ran, she stumbled over a body—what looked like Drew's body, only his head was missing. She tried to cry out for her husband, but her voice would not move past her throat. Then, she ran past the body. As she looked back, she failed to see the valley dropping over the edge of a cliff until it was too late. She fell. Just when she should have hit the bottom of the cliff, she woke up.

The dream had been so real, so taunting, so frightening. She was convinced she was going to die on this forsaken journey.

Chapter 12

Arizona Territory

October 24, 1863

"That's not how you do it!" Jed shouted at Hawk, pulling back on the reins as he moved his black mare within inches of Hawk's mount.

Will shook his head, stopping Jackson so he could watch. The two men or boys—he wasn't really sure which they were—were at it again.

"I was close!" Hawk shouted back, reeling in the poor attempt at a lasso loop, sitting atop his white gelding.

"No you weren't. You'd never get that calf back with the herd goin' at 'im like that."

"Well, I ain't been doin' this more than a few weeks," Hawk replied, setting the wound up rope over the horn of his saddle. "I'll bet you were just as bad when you first started."

"What'd you say?" Jed leaned forward in his saddle.

"I said you were probably worse when you started!"

Leaping from his saddle, Jed knocked Hawk from his. Both tumbled to the ground. Hawk landed on his back. As he gasped for air, Jed pounded his fist into Hawk's jaw. Quickly, Hawk recovered, flipping over so Jed was pinned to the ground.

Will remained still as the two wrestled each other, half tempted to break up the fight. As long as neither tried to kill the other, he figured it would be best to let them work out their differences.

"Reminds me of two other young men," Ben commented, pulling Shelia to a stop next to Will.

Snorting, Will asked the question to humor his old friend, "Yeah, who?"

"You and Reuben."

"Let's hope this works out better for both of them."

The sound of a gun unsheathing drew Will's attention back to the fight.

"What are you doing?" Jed shrieked as Hawk pointed the gun at Jed's head.

Will and Ben dismounted, running towards the two. He never suspected that Hawk would do something like this. If he had, he would have put a stop to this sooner.

Shoving Jed's head down to the ground with his open palm flat on his forehead, Hawk pulled the trigger seconds before either Will or Ben could stop him. The bullet whizzed past Jed's nose, severing a rattler's head from its body. The rattler's head, having already been poised to strike, landed on Jed's shoulder causing the color to drain from his face.

Both men sat motionless for several minutes, Jed's chest heaving from either the exertion or the shock.

"Shoot! Hawk just saved yer life," Snake hollered from his vantage point near the chuck wagon. "Ain't never seen nothing like that. He done cut that hisser in half! Hee, hee." Slapping a hand hard on his leg, Snake's loud laughter was quickly swallowed up by the largeness of the flat plain.

Holstering his revolver, Hawk stood. He held out a hand to help Jed up. Jed brushed the dead snake head from his shoulder and took Hawk's offered hand, still dumbfounded by the ordeal.

"Where'd you learn to shoot like that? I'd have blown off half yer face," Jed said in awe.

"My pa taught me," Hawk answered, brushing the dust from his clothes.

Without a word of gratitude, Jed mounted his horse and took off towards the flank position in the herd—his inner conflict written all over his face.

"That was close," Ben murmured only loud enough for Will to hear. "Thank the Lord that boy didn't have his heart set on doin' Jed harm."

Nodding, Will let go of his held breath.

"Mount up, boys!" Ben shouted, rallying the men to their horses for the start of the night drive.

Sighing, Will turned Jackson towards point, ready to be moving further along the trail. Ben was right. It was a good thing Hawk did not want to harm Jed. If only he could be sure Jed felt the same way.

In the weeks since their last scuffle back outside of Santa Fe, on the surface Jed seemed to tolerate Hawk. He had not drawn his gun on the half-Indian again—in fear of Will's wrath. Perhaps he was warming up to Hawk.

Arriving at the front of the herd, Will turned to face the herd and men, waiting for the rest of the men to take their places. Seeing everyone was ready, he nodded for Pedro to ride ahead, scouting for any sign of trouble.

The drive from Fort Wingate, New Mexico, to the Arizona Territory had been quite scenic, Will mused as he settled into his saddle. The valley floor was covered in light yellow-green grass and dark green scrub brush. To the north, red, orange, and rust banded mountains rose from the valley floor for thousands of feet into the air. Eroded by wind and rain, deep grooves and crevices hid their untold secrets in the shadows, untouched by the sun. The further they traveled, new mountains rose from the south, banded in white, grey, and rust, with the green of scrub brush dotting the top and sides.

The landscape they presently drove through was flat, with still more of the tall grass and scrub brush. They had not encountered much water or firewood in the past few days on the open plain. They would need water soon.

The thundering of the longhorn's hooves provided a steady beat to accompany the sweet melody flowing from his lips. Will liked riding point best. There was less dust kicked up and it made singing much easier. The song, one of his mother's favorite hymns, floated in the cool night air. His baritone voice sounded somewhat foreign to his ears, as the words came from his soul.

"Nearer, my God, to Thee. Nearer to Thee. Though like the wanderer, the sun gone down, darkness be over me, my rest a stone. Yet in my dreams I'd be nearer, my God to Thee."

As the sun fell lower in the sky, leaving a dark blue haze settling over the plain, Will felt like the wanderer. Cast far from his Texas home, he roamed the desert wilderness in search of his new home. This pervasive sense of not belonging would fade, he hoped, once he discovered his new home in the Arizona Territory in just a few more weeks.

He wondered many times over the past months why God uprooted him from the Star C and sent him across the wilderness. If nothing else, he would finally have a ranch of his own. Yet, he felt something bigger, something more awaited him.

Ending the song with one last chorus, Will made it his heart-felt prayer. *Let me be nearer to Thee.*

The following morning, as the sun woke from its sleep, Pedro rode back towards Will. Though he was not in a hurry, he appeared a bit earlier than Will was expecting. Nudging Jackson forward, he met Pedro half way.

"Found water, Boss," Pedro announced. "Just another mile or so up. Flowing water, too."

Will nodded, relieved to know water was nearby.

"Good spot to camp," Pedro added.

A smile stretched across Will's lips. "Go tell the others."

Within twenty minutes, the cattle were happily settled next to the Little Colorado River drinking their fill. As the chuck wagon pulled to a stop, the men dismounted their horses. Those who were on first shift transferred saddles to fresh mounts, while the rest set up camp.

Will walked towards the river. Taking off his worn leather gloves, he touched the water with the tips of his fingers. Chilly water gave him a second's pause for the idea forming in his head. The sun already warmed the coolness from the air. Perhaps a quick bath would be worth it.

Headed back towards his saddle and bedroll, he searched for his other change of clothes. Wadding them into a ball, he made his way to the chuck wagon.

"Think we'll camp here tonight. Looks like a good place for a short break," he said to Snake.

Snake nodded in reply.

Within a few short steps, Will stood at the water's edge again. Tossing his hat aside, he quickly stripped down. The playful rogue in him ran head long into the water, not letting the chill change his mind. As the cold of the water registered, he sucked in a quick breath. Dunking his head under, he scrubbed his hair, working out the months of dust and grime.

As he came up for air, a splash of water assaulted him in the face. Wiping the water from his eyes, he saw a grinning Hawk darting away. Laughter surrounded him. As he looked around he saw Jed, Hawk, and Covington making a ruckus in the river. Seems they had the same idea.

The iciness of the water seeped into his bones, warning Will it was time to leave. Wading back to the edge he caught the tail end of a conversation between the three young men.

"Where'd you get those scars?" Covington asked. Their earlier joviality died with the abrupt question.

"From the Apaches," Hawk's quiet voice replied.

"There's too many scars on your back to have all come from them," Jed said, with an edge to his voice.

As Will began to dress again, thankful for the warming sun, Hawk's face hardened. "They were very cruel to me. Didn't like half-breed Kichai any more than the white men."

Jed muttered something Will could not hear.

"They tortured me!" Hawk shouted back. "They hated me. They whipped me for entertainment." Standing square-shouldered blocking Jed from Will's view, he added, "Don't you get it? I'm not one of them. I hate them as much as you do."

As Hawk turned towards the river bank, Will took note of the shame covering Jed's face. Both Jed and Covington stood there in silence for several minutes before either headed back to the bank. As soon as Hawk was dressed, he hurried away from the other two young men, walking along the river.

"Way to go, Jed," Covington smarted off as he pulled on his last boot.

"I didn't know," came the sheepish answer.

"So what're you gonna do about it?"

Slapping his hat down on his head, Jed replied, nonchalantly, "Dunno."

"You're something else," Covington said, throwing his hands up in the air. "Did it ever occur to you that the two of you have more in common than anyone else in camp? If it were me, I'd try apologizin' then make him my friend."

Will silently agreed with Covington's sage words, still going unnoticed by the two men. As much as Jed and Hawk fought, they were the most alike. If only Jed would lose that chip on his shoulder, the two might become friends.

Stuffing his hands in his pockets, Jed kicked the dirt with the toe of his boot. When Covington walked away, Jed stood there for several more minutes, deep in thought. Then he turned in the direction Hawk took, leisurely strolling along the river. Maybe Jed would take Covington's advice after all.

Picking up his filthy clothes, Will headed back to camp. He tossed them in a pile for Snake to wash.

Grabbing one of the empty water barrels, he rolled it down towards the river. Once full, he rolled it back up the gentle slope and heaved it into the back of the wagon before finding the next empty one.

On his way back to the wagon, a cloud of dust to the east caught his attention. Leaving the barrel, Will grabbed his rifle and checked the ammunition in his revolver.

"Boys, ready your weapons!" he shouted. "Covington, ride out to Ben. Tell him we've got company. Hawk!"

When Hawk came running, Will continued, "Saddle up a horse. See if you can't figure out who our visitors are."

Hawk nodded. Sliding his rifle into the sheath on his saddle, he rode off in the direction of the dust cloud.

"Watcha thinking, Boss?" Whitten asked.

"They're moving fast, whoever they are."

"Indians?"

"Don't think so. Seems they would be a bit more covert," Will replied. He had no doubt the visitors saw the bright white canopies of his supply wagons. Not to mention the large herd of cattle. They would be hard to miss in this flat open land.

He surveyed the camp and nearby river for a good place to take cover, just in case the riders were hostile. Not many options. The bank was too shallow of a slope to provide any cover. While a few short trees littered part of the bank further upstream, they were too small for a major offensive. The only other option would be hiding behind the wagons.

"Whitten, you and Owens go hide in those trees. Snake, Jed, stay close to the wagons. If something starts, take cover there," Will commanded.

As he propped up his leg on the crude bench by their small table, he waited for Hawk to return. Covington and Ben rode in.

"Don't know if they're friendly or not," Will informed Ben.

Just after Ben dismounted, Hawk returned. "Military."

"Blue coats?" Ben asked.

"Yup. Riding at a fair pace. Not too hard, though," Hawk answered, sliding down from his mount.

"Well," Ben replied, "Let's hope they're friendly to a bunch of Texans."

Will hoped so, too, for there would be no way to conceal their origins once he spoke with his distinct drawl.

For nearly a half hour, Will waited for the military group, realizing then the distance had been deceptive. At last, the group sent one rider ahead.

"Howdy," Will greeted the rider, keeping his guns close, but maintaining a peaceful posture.

The young man, still atop his horse, returned his greeting. "The captain wants to know if we might be able to join your camp for the evening."

"Be fine," Will said.

The scout thanked Will, before riding to report back to his captain.

A few minutes later, camp buzzed with activity. The captain and his ten or so men joined the camp. Snake started preparing supper. Jed, Hawk, and Covington hung around the younger military men, excitedly plying them with dozens of questions. Ben and Will sat at the table, offering the captain a brief respite.

The short captain took the offered seat, setting his forage cap aside, running fingers through his dark wavy hair. "Didn't expect to run into you," Captain Jarrett said, "for a few days yet. The commander at Wingate said you'd been through awhile back. Less there's another Texas rancher driving west of here."

Will hesitated, not sure how to take the comment. "Moving cattle can be slow at times."

"What brings you out here?" Ben asked.

"We're scouting for possible locations for a fort. Looking for something around where the Walker Party settled near Granite

139

Creek."

"A fort, eh?" Ben said, rubbing the salt and pepper beard gracing his chin.

"The governor should be arriving in a few months, along with a number of settlers. General Carleton adamantly insisted we be ready to protect the territory's newest citizens."

"Protect them?" Will asked.

"From the Apaches and Navajo. They have been causing all manner of trouble to the south. Raiding farms. Murdering all the inhabitants, including women and children. Generally making things pretty difficult for new settlers."

Taking a swig of coffee, the young captain continued. "General Carleton wants to make sure the start of the governor's tour of the territory is as uneventful as possible. So, we have come ahead of time to get familiar with the land and the natives—to be prepared for the worst."

"Good to know there'll be some military nearby," Ben stated.

"Where abouts are you headed?" Jarrett asked.

"Granite Creek area," Will replied. "Looking to find some good cattle land. Settle down and start a ranch."

Jarrett looked intrigued. Thoughtfully, he rubbed his chin. "You know, food and other supplies have been nearly impossible to get into this territory, especially enough to supply the California Volunteers posted throughout. With the recent drought in Sonora, some of our contracted food supplies are not showing up as promised."

Will raised an eyebrow, wondering why Captain Jarrett shared this information.

"A rancher, like yourself, would do well if he decided to supply beef to the military and could guarantee a regular supply."

Keeping his face devoid of the excitement welling within, Will nodded. "How soon do you think the fort will be established?"

"Probably not until near the end of the year. We have the next month or so to scout the area before we select a site. I'll need to make a trip back to Wingate before the final selection is made."

That would give Will ample time to make it to Granite Creek, select some land and get established before the new fort would need a steady supply of beef.

"Might you be interested in such a proposition, Mr. Colter? Can I pass your name on to my commander?"

"Sure," Will said, recognizing the wonderful opportunity before him. "Like I said, I'll be settling near Granite Creek. When you folks get the fort established, send word there and I'll come out and meet with you to discuss terms and the like."

The rest of the evening, Jarrett talked of Colonel Kit Carson's escapades against the Navajo. Jarrett seemed to think things would escalate in the coming month. Since they were almost out of Navajo territory, he assured Will they should see little trouble from them.

As the captain and his men prepared to retire for the night, Will sat on the ground near a small campfire. Accustomed to riding all night, he was not the least bit tired. If they could just make it the rest of the way to Granite Creek without trouble, he would be pleased. Then he would pick out a nice patch of land and settle down.

Settle down. The words stirred something deep within Will. Soon, he would have his own ranch—the dream he had since childhood—the one he put on hold after his mother passed, so he could help his father. Finally, that dream was in sight.

Chapter 13

Santa Fé, New Mexico Territory

November 14, 1863

The five days of travel between Fort Union and Santa Fe left Hannah thankful they finally arrived in the small city. Weary from weeks of nightmares, she longed for a respite from traveling. The sense of foreboding stayed with her ever since Mr. Richmond's story of the beheaded Indian woman. Then, when General Carleton mentioned the savage attacks of the Apaches at supper earlier in the week, she grew even more fearful. She could not shake the feeling that something catastrophic was going to happen.

Why did they ever leave a safe and peaceful home? *Thomas.* Oh, if only he had not robbed that bank! She would be safe and happy back in Ohio, working by Drew's side in his clinic.

No, instead, she travelled uncivilized lands—under the constant threat of attack from wild animals or wild men. Starvation, something she had not thought possible until passing through Trinidad, piled on to her lengthening list of fears. What of the Confederate troops rumored in the western territories? Would they pose a threat to her?

Hannah shifted in the wagon seat, scolding herself for such sorrowful thoughts. Glancing at Drew, he seemed oblivious to her darkened mood.

As they wound down the mountain into the valley of Santa Fe, she pushed her fear aside for the time being. Despite the dangers and fears of this journey, she never tired of the varied landscapes and structures. As they neared town, she counted at least six tall churches, all magnificent in size and with noticeable crosses on their rectangular spires. They weren't really spires, not like the churches back home. They were more like towers. The light color of the church exteriors provided a stark contrast against the bright blue sky. Numerous flat roofed adobe houses littered the streets. Unlike the plank wood houses from back home, these were made with bricks of straw and mud. None stood more than one level. Several houses left their doors propped open. When she looked inside, those houses were packed with a large number of people sitting on the floor. She wondered if the houses were typically so full.

As the wagon train continued through town, many of the freighters headed directly for the town plaza, presumably the center of commerce. This was their final destination culminating in the sale of all their wares and goods.

The wagon train camped on the western outskirts of town close to the river. Tonight, they would make supper and chat around the campfire. Then tomorrow the routine of camp would begin again with laundry and such. Not waiting for Drew's assistance, Hannah jumped down from the wagon eager to be free from the wretched seat. Stretching her arms high over her head, she tried to work out the stiffness of muscles long inactive.

Some days the endless journey really chafed her nerves. They left Cincinnati over two months ago. They covered only a few more miles in the last two months as what they covered by steamboat in just those first few days. Wagon travel was indeed agonizingly slow. She hoped they would not be delayed in Santa Fe for too long. She was more than ready to settle in her new home even if it might be teeming with Apaches.

She rooted through the crate where she kept their pans and utensils for cooking on the trail. While she had other items stowed for when they finally found a home, she kept things simple like Betty showed her. Tonight they had fresh beef provided by some generous locals. She savored the long forgotten aroma of beef steaks sizzling in the pan. While she enjoyed the venison, buffalo, and other game eaten along the way, there was nothing like the familiar flavor of beef. Feeling ambitious, Hannah decided to mix up some biscuits and gravy. Perhaps keeping her hands busy would help her forget her fears.

"Smells delicious," Drew said as he came up behind her and put his arms around her. When was the last time he did that? Was it in Ohio? She leaned back against his chest, missing his nearness.

He kissed her neck and lightening shot through her limbs, improving her mood. He settled his chin on her shoulder still holding her close. Oh she longed for the privacy to succumb to the thoughts running through her head. Instead, she pulled away, aware of the constant watch of their fellow travelers. Kissing him on the cheek she shooed him away, but not before she caught his roguish grin.

In addition to her fears and the overwhelming length of the journey, the complete lack of privacy vexed her. The prying eyes of their companions never closed. Since they camped with the wagons providing a perimeter around the people, every conversation and action was scrutinized—and often whispered around the circle. Intimacy between a husband and wife seemed impossible. She wondered if any of the other married couples found it difficult, although there were very few couples in their wagon train.

Grumbling to herself, Hannah dished up the completed meal, the earlier embrace of her husband forgotten. Sitting near Betty and Paul, the foursome bowed their heads for Paul's blessing before eating the mouth-watering beef.

"Have either of you heard how long we will remain in Santa Fe before moving on our way?" Betty asked Paul and Drew.

They both shook their heads.

"I'm not certain how much farther we have to go before we get to the Arizona Territory either," Paul said.

"Do you think there is any possibility we might be there by Christmas?" Hannah asked

"Not sure. I'm certain the wagon master will be around in the next day or so to give us an update. We should be here for at least a few days," Drew said.

Hannah ate the rest of her food in silence as Drew and Paul speculated about their arrival date.

By the time they finished their meal, fast-paced rambunctious music filled the air. Hannah found herself tapping her foot to the beat as she sat around the fire with her husband and friends. Lieutenant Harrison joined them shortly after sunset.

Drew asked, "Where is that music coming from?"

Lieutenant Harrison replied, "The locals have a custom they call a *fandango*, or dance. Almost nightly, they gather at a *sala*, or dancing hall." He pointed towards the building nearby as several uniformed men ducked inside. "It is a relatively harmless form of entertainment."

"Come on," Drew said, his eyes sparkling with excitement as he grasped Hannah's hand. They followed the growing throng of travelers pouring into the *sala*.

Contrary to her husband's sense of adventure, Hannah felt more concerned than excited as they entered the long and narrow building. The room was lined with benches along every wall, except for the far side along one of the narrow walls where the stage held musicians. Velvety fabric covered the walls up to the top of Drew's head. Candles, ornate iron crucifixes, and gold framed pictures of saints adorned the walls. The bare dirt floor whirled dust around her ankles as the dancers waltzed down the center of the hall.

Drew led her to one of the benches on the long side of the *sala*, where she watched the diverse group of people gathering in the room. Men and women from every race and station of life participated. The dancers lined up, men on one side and women on the other. One obviously wealthy woman was dressed in a flowing lavender silk gown with large gold necklaces decorating her neck. She wore enough rings for every finger on each of her hands—each ring contained some sort of precious ruby, diamond, or emerald. In her hair was the most exquisite pearl comb. This woman partnered with a short local Mexican dressed in an open cotton shirt and leather trousers. His bare feet further contrasted the difference in class and clothing. Every dancing couple was similarly mismatched, such as the army officer paired with an old peasant woman.

The music was different from what Hannah remembered at the old barn dances and socials back home. A lively short and stout man on the stage picked out an energetic tune on a small *guitarra*. The *tombé*, a small drum, provided the steady beat. The fiddler was very tall and thin, with short, dark black hair slicked back from his brown skin. A thick black moustache hid his upper lip and wide dark eyebrows provided a strong line above his dark brown eyes. The ruffles on his sleeves bounced in time with each lively stroke of the bow against the fiddle strings.

The energy of this odd collection of people became contagious. More Americans joined in the revelry. The wagon master picked a lovely Mexican gal with a *cigarritos* dangling from her brightly painted lips. Most of the local men held a cigar or drink in one hand and a dance partner in the other. Even more scandalous were the

146

local women, many smoking *cigarritos* or gulping their champagne. After a few waltzes, the far end of the dance floor became obscured from the smoke and the dust kicked up by dancing.

Despite the unusual pairing of couples, everyone seemed well behaved. There seemed to be a general understanding and respect among the participants. The dancers kept arms and hands in appropriate places. Hannah overheard Lieutenant Harrison say that the *fandango* was simply meant to be entertaining. Most attendees only wanted to dance. Even the children joined in the fun. One adorable little girl, not more than six or seven years old, with dark curly tresses danced with the priest.

Turning towards Drew, she tried not to breathe too deeply of the dust and smoke. He bobbed his hand up and down against his leg keeping beat with the drum. When he looked at her, his eyes shimmered, free from the worried look he carried since they started west. She smiled. He nodded his head towards her, causing her focus to shift forward again.

A young boy of ten or so, stopped in front of her. He held out his hand towards Hannah, indicating he wanted to dance. She grew nervous, uncertain as to whether or not it would be considered proper.

"You should dance with him," Lieutenant Harrison said, sitting next to Drew. "It is considered impolite to refuse anyone requesting a dance."

Hannah glanced at Drew almost seeking permission. With a smile on his face, he nodded, giving her the courage to proceed. She was quickly swept into the crowd of dancers whirling about the dance floor. The music was jovial and one could not keep from becoming festive. As the song concluded, the young boy, with a huge grin on his face mumbled "gracias señora" before running off the dance floor into the haze.

She looked around frantically searching for Drew. She lost sight of him during the dance. Dancers moved about her, one pair bumped into her nearly knocking her on the ground. Suddenly the weariness of the journey hit her and her eyes began to water.

Chapter 14

Drew watched Hannah as she danced with the young boy, swirling about the room with a smile on her face. She seemed to be having a good time. The dust from the dirt floor and the *cigarritos* smoke grew thicker, but he kept his wife in sight, should she need rescued.

A smile teased the corners of his lips. Sometime during the last month, things seemed to improve between them, despite Hannah's tiredness. She smiled at him. The sharpness that lingered under every word over the past months vanished. Ever since the near miss at Devil's Gate. His heart lurched with the memory. For a few minutes he thought she might fall off the wagon, down over the edge into the canyon far below. Since then, he could hardly wait for a moment alone each day to wrap her in his arms or shower her with kisses.

As the song came to an end, Hannah looked around agitatedly. The smile on her face faded and the slump returned to her shoulders. Standing, Drew pushed through the crowd and grasped her hand. She looked near tears. He led her from the *sala* to a quieter area nearby. He placed one hand on the small of her back then clasped her hand with his other hand. Stepping forward, he led her in a brief waltz in the fresh air of the outdoors to the tune of the strange music echoing from the dance hall. When the song ended, he brought Hannah close, brushing a light kiss across her lips. He was rewarded with her lovely smile.

"You, dear wife, are amazing." He wanted to say more—to tell her how much her willingness to move clear across the country meant to him—but his own guilt blocked the words from forming.

He continued to hold her close for some time, swaying back and forth, not really keeping time with the music. He missed just holding his wife, resting her head over his heart. He missed a great deal about their life in Ohio. The routine of daily life without fear of danger. The warm bed shared at night. The privacy. Perhaps tomorrow he would find a way to get some time alone with her, apart from the crowded camp.

The next morning came sooner than expected. The noise from the dance hall increased in volume throughout the night keeping Drew from a peaceful sleep. As their neighbors returned to camp, many stumbled and tripped making more noise. He worried that one might lose their way and end up in his tent, so he stirred at every sound.

The smell of flapjacks grilling motivated him to rise. Hannah already started breakfast. He could hear her talking with Betty about the events of last night. Exiting the tent, he moved next to her and gave her a quick peck on the cheek.

"After breakfast, the wagon master said we would have the day to relax," Hannah said.

"I'm assuming you want to take a bath, Mrs. Anderson?" Drew teased.

"Oh, Mr. Anderson, don't think you will be skipping by without one, too," she shot back quickly, her smile giving away her lightheartedness. He smiled back as he turned to go check on the stock. It had been a long time since his wife teased him. He forgot how much he missed it.

Drew welcomed the idea of a bath. He could not recall the last time he had a bath. What a luxury to bathe as often as he desired— one he took for granted back in Ohio. Along the trail, washing up two consecutive mornings seemed a luxury. A bath was out of the question. But, since they camped near the river, he would gladly fill the water barrels and roll them up the bank so he and Hannah could indulge.

His mind began to wander as he made sure the oxen had plenty of food and water. How was Hannah really doing? The fear in her eyes last night at the *sala* had little to do with losing sight of him. There was something much worse troubling her, and had been for some time now. He knew this trip was hard on her—probably harder than she let show. Was this whole venture a mistake? Should he have done as she suggested and settled in Indiana instead?

No matter, they had come much too far to turn around now.

Perhaps they should go to Granite Creek, instead of La Paz. Paul and Betty would be there. A fort would be located nearby according to Harrison. The government seemed likely to set up the capital there.

Mulling over the idea, Drew recalled all of the things discussed over the meals with the governor. The place sounded far more picturesque than La Paz. Tall pines and junipers. Rivers and creeks. Several industries besides mining. A place like that would grow quickly.

Being deep in the wilderness, any medical care he could provide would be so much better than a complete lack of care. He could barter his services for goods. If there were several hundred men, it might mean sparse work at first, but over time as new settlers arrived, he would have more work. Maybe he could even help with animals.

"You seem deep in thought for such an early morning," remarked Lieutenant Harrison as he hobbled his horse with the others.

"Just thinking about how hard this trip has been, especially on my wife."

"Mrs. Anderson? She appears very confident and capable of dealing with the duties of a woman on the trail."

Wanting to shift the focus away from such personal discussions, Drew asked, "How much longer before we reach the Arizona Territory?"

"We are more than a week from Fort Wingate, which is last stop in New Mexico. Much of it depends on the weather and the Indians. From Fort Wingate, we expect the trip to take another four to six weeks."

"That will put us there around the beginning of January, right?"

"Most likely we will stop for a few days at Fort Wingate before heading out again, but it is possible we will be there by the beginning of the year," Harrison said.

"Might I ask a favor?" Drew hesitated, wishing he had thought through his forthcoming words more carefully. "You see... That is..." He stumbled to a halt. Perhaps it was ludicrous to ask the lieutenant to teach him how to shoot a gun. He was embarrassed to admit he had yet to learn.

"Drew, it would please me greatly to be able to help you with whatever you are about to ask. I can never repay you for saving my life," Harrison said.

"I thought you might be able to teach me to shoot my rifle," Drew said looking off into the distance. "We left in such a hurry, I had no opportunity to learn. I purchased extra ammunition with the intention of practicing, but…"

Harrison's astonished look further embarrassed Drew. But, he spoke kindly, "I don't suppose I would have thought a doctor would be particularly handy with a gun, given your nature to save lives rather than take them. Let's meet tomorrow morning for your first lesson."

Drew nodded, relieved that he would not be required to call upon Hannah's skill should they encounter trouble.

After Lieutenant Harrison left, Drew thought back to what he said about the rest of the journey. *Six more weeks. Maybe longer if we run into any trouble.* Reality dawned on him. They were just over half way to their destination. Dejected, he sat down near the camp fire, just as Hannah dished up the meal. He was unable to push aside the regret and guilt storming in his mind.

Sensing her husband's troubled mood, Hannah gave him an inquisitive look as she handed him a plate. The meal passed in silence.

Immediately following the meal, Drew stood and grabbed the water barrel, heading for the stream before Hannah could ask questions. Resigning herself to finding out what was troubling him later, she quickly cleaned up the breakfast dishes. She dug the tub out of the wagon and placed it in the tent. Then she made sure the fire was still stoked so she could heat the water. With the temperatures so cool, she would need to make sure the water was nice and hot.

Drew rolled the barrel back into camp next to their fire. The process of heating the water bucket-full by bucket-full took a fair amount of time. Hannah bathed first taking time to wash her hair. It felt so good to be clean. As she dried her hair by the fire, he took his turn. When he finished she was still drying her hair by the fire. He made quick work of emptying the tub and stowing it back in its proper place, before joining her by the fire.

His gaze was intense as he studied her. Hannah smiled, waiting to see if he would speak of his concerns, whatever they may be.

"The wagon master says that the Indians are calm right now and we can go outside the city for a short distance. I thought it might be nice to find a scenic lookout," Drew said.

Delight filled Hannah. Time away from the noise of camp and gossiping tongues was rare. What a treat to get time alone! She quickly gathered a few blankets and the canteens of water while Drew ensured the rifle was loaded.

They walked about a hundred yards up the slope of the closest hill before stopping. Drew spread out the blanket on the ground and helped her settle into a nice spot. The view was incredible. Looking towards the west, they could see green scrub brush and trees covering the mountains rising up from the fertile valley below. Several minutes went by before either spoke. They were content to soak in the view and revel in the peaceful silence.

"Do you regret leaving Ohio?" Drew asked.

The question came without warning, sharply breaking the serenity. Hannah took a minute to gather her thoughts before answering, "You know I didn't want to leave. I wish we could have stayed. But, I see now that we had to."

"Are you still angry with me?"

Staring at her clasped hands, she hesitated. The sad look on his face sliced her heart. "Not anymore." The guilt welled up. "I know I was hard on you—angry for much too long. I'm sorry, Drew. I was so disappointed that we had to leave. I thought I knew best. I was wrong."

"I feel I have failed you by bringing you on this arduous trip," he whispered. He studied his hands, though she wished he would look at her instead.

"You haven't failed me. Why would you say such a thing?"

"It's my fault we had to leave. I could have tried harder to change the opinions of the townsfolk. Perhaps if we had stayed for Thomas's trial, they would have seen we bore no responsibility in the situation.

"Instead, I brought you from Ohio, far from the land you loved.

And you have been forced to work harder than ever before, including driving the wagon—forsaking all comfort. All because I did not stand up to the townsfolk, you have suffered."

Her heart broke at the guilt he heaped upon himself. She refused to let him continue doing so. "None of that is your fault. You are a good man, a God-fearing man who desires nothing more than providing the best he can for his family. Right now that family is just the two of us, but one day it'll be more."

She paused, breathing deeply of the cool clear air. "I would go anywhere in the world with you. I love you. You are a part of me."

Drew turned to look at her. She hoped he saw the conviction and sincerity in her eyes. She could see he still wrestled with guilt. "But this trip has been difficult. Now, we are headed to an unknown land with unknown dangers. I couldn't bear it if my decision results in you being harmed."

"Yes, this trip has been hard. We've both learned things we wouldn't have given thought to a year ago. I learned to cook over an open fire built with buffalo chips. We learned to go days without water praying for God to send relief. We spent days climbing that never-ending mountain back in Colorado. I was so sore from sitting in that wagon seat I thought I might not be able to walk. But none of that is important. It is just a step along the way. You and I are together, heading toward our new home in the Arizona Territory. True, it might be dangerous. But once we arrive, we will build a new home. You'll start practicing medicine again, and we will raise our family there. It'll be home because we will be there together."

Scooting closer, he put his arm around her, bringing her head to rest on his chest. Looking down at her he whispered, "Thank you, dear wife. I needed that."

Perhaps she should tell him about her own fears and the nightmares. Turning her face up towards Drew, she tried to gauge what his response would be. Would he feel more guilt if she told him? Probably. She would, for his sake, keep those deep fears to herself.

"How would you feel about settling in Granite Creek, instead of La Paz?" he asked.

A smile exploded followed by a giggle of excitement. "I would love it!"

Turning to face her, Drew searched her eyes. "Truly?"

"Truly. I think it'll be a wonderful place to live and raise our children."

"Then that is where we will go."

His eyes continued searching hers. As his smile faded slightly, Hannah shivered—not from the cooling air—but from the look of passion in his eyes. Her breath caught as she realized how much she missed her husband. He lowered his lips to hers and she could not contain her own longing. As his kiss deepened, she responded with all of her heart. She lodged her fingers in his hair as he began to explore her body with his hands. Knowing where this was leading, she thought for a brief moment to pull back. As quickly as the thought came, it left and she surrendered herself to her husband.

As the moment passed, Hannah fought to catch her breath. Heat came to her face as she realized with a little embarrassment that they were on a hill in the middle of the New Mexico territory. She could hear Drew's ragged breathing settle as he released a satisfied sigh. She sat up, fixing her appearance before standing and suggesting they should head back to camp.

Hannah gathered their things as Drew shouldered the riffle. He grasped her hand and held it until they neared their wagon. She could not help grinning. She loved this man. As they deposited their things in the camp, she saw Betty's expression. The woman acted almost like she knew. Feeling heat rise to her cheeks, Hannah quickly started dinner turning away from Betty's view.

The bliss of the intimate moments with her husband faded much too soon as the image of his headless body from her nightmares returned to haunt her. What would she do if she lost Drew?

Chapter 15

Granite Creek, Arizona Territory

November 15, 1863

Will and his men were finally at their destination.

Just north of the Granite Creek area, he spotted a section of rolling hills. The green and brown of pine trees dotted the foothills of the granite-like stony mountains. Nestled in the valley below, a clear blue lake spread out nearly half a mile long. The grass was everywhere—on the forest floor, in the valley, sloping up the mountains. This was better than he dreamed.

His heart picked up pace and he sat taller in his saddle as his eyes quickly scanned the valley floor for any sign of structures or settlement. Seeing none, Will's hopes began to soar. Perhaps this perfect piece of land sat waiting for him to stake his claim. He smiled, unable to contain his excitement.

Leaving the herd and the bulk of the men back in the valley, Will and Ben scouted ahead to find the Walker settlement a few miles south and slightly to the west. When they rode into the cluster of tents, broken up by one log cabin, they were greeted warmly by the residents. After spending some time getting to know the Walker Party, Will and Ben set up camp for the night.

As Will stretched out on his bedding, he looked up at the star filled sky. He remembered the night back in Texas that he stood propped against the corral talking to Julia. He wondered then if the stars would be different in the Arizona Territory. They seemed just as brilliant tonight here in his new home as they had that night.

Rolling onto his side, his mind raced with thoughts and plans and dreams. Tomorrow he would have his land surveyed and file his claim to that glorious piece of property. He felt humbled that God smiled upon him to let him have such a beautiful new home. It far exceeded any expectation he had.

And the grass—it was everywhere! It was on the rolling hills, under the canopy of tall pines, and sprinkled on lower slopes of the mountains. The grass was an excellent variety well suited for the cattle and other livestock, though the horses still required feed.

The property he chose had plenty of timber for building the bunkhouse, barn, and eventually a cabin for himself. The lake meant a ready supply of fresh water until a drinking well could be dug. If he had the land memorized already, he would have been tempted to start drawing out plans by the light of the fire. Instead, Will tried to shut off his excitement to get some sleep. Morning would be here soon enough.

The next morning Will and Ben met with the land officer, Bob Groom. Groom and his associate followed them back to the property. Once they completed the survey, Groom agreed to hold the paperwork until the official land office was established. Will thanked the men and wished them well.

"Mighty fine piece of land you picked for yourself. Your pa would be proud," Ben said, slapping the younger man on the shoulder. "I'll go tell the men this is our new home and leave you to your planning."

Will found a spot near the lake. Sitting down, leaning against a tree, he looked out over his land. Digging through his saddle bags, he found a piece of paper and pencil. He started to sketch out where he would put his house, the bunkhouse, and a barn. His first priority was the bunkhouse. He could stay there for the time being—probably through the winter. He knew his father liked to keep some distance between him and his men, but it seemed foolish to Will to build a house for himself at this point.

That aside, he couldn't keep himself from dreaming of what that house would look like. He would place it so the back faced the lake. Maybe he would even put a porch on the back, where he could sit and rock and watch the sunset over the mountains. The space between the house and lake would be a great place for children to play.

Ha! Children. Where had that thought come from? There is not a woman within one hundred miles, and here he was dreaming of family and children.

It's not that he didn't want to marry. At twenty-nine, he just never made it a priority. Perhaps, deep down he always knew he would not be at the Star C forever. Of course, he didn't know Reuben would get the ranch or that his father would pass away so young. He always dreamed of starting his own ranch, even discussed it with his father on more than one occasion. Oddly, the way things turned out, it was as if his father nudged him in that direction with the terms of his will. But, the dream of starting his own ranch and the work it would entail, had it been enough to stop him for looking for a wife?

He shook off such thoughts, though a hint of loneliness took root. Not much sense on dwelling on such things now, especially when there was no possibility of changing the situation anytime soon. Certainly, when the time was right, he would know it and could think on it then.

Tomorrow he would pick which men would be on the crew to build the bunkhouse and then they would get started. Standing, he brushed the bits of grass from his jeans and whistled for Jackson to come. He led the horse over to the camp Snake and the others set up a few days ago.

"Congratulations, Boss," Snake said as Will removed the saddle from his stallion. "I hear this lovely piece of land is all yours."

"Thanks, Snake. Be sure to feed the boys well. Tomorrow, barring any bad weather, we start on the bunkhouse."

Snake let out a whelp for joy and continued banging pots and pans around. Within a half hour he presented a tasty supper of beans, biscuits, and beef steak. Each of the cowboys shoved their way to the front of the line with their tin plates. Will waited for his men to be served before holding out his plate. Not that Snake was not a good cook, but he would be thankful when they could get more variety to the meals.

"No more sitting on a horse all day and night!" Jed exclaimed.

"You're still a cowboy," Hawk teased, nudging Jed in the arm. "Last I heard, cowboys sit on a horse most days."

Jed rolled his eyes. "You know what I mean."

"Don't think it'll be easy for a while yet," Whitten said dolefully. "Case you haven't noticed, there ain't no bunkhouse sittin' around waitin' for us."

"Yeah," Owens butted in. "Who do you think is gonna' build all that?"

"Might be griping about strippin' one too many logs—longing for that saddle in a few days," Ben added, with a teasing smile.

"I'll take what I can git. That drive was 'bout four times as long as any other," Jed said. "I'll just be glad to stay in one place for a bit."

"Me, too," Hawk agreed. "It's nice to be home."

Murmurs of agreement echoed Hawk's sentiment.

Sitting down next to Ben, Will shared his plans. They discussed the best way to start clearing the land and where each of the buildings would be constructed. They would keep the herd close to allow them better control with a smaller number of men, leaving two or three in charge of the herd. The rest of the men would help fell, strip, and sand the logs for the buildings.

As the sky grew dark, a feeling of contentment settled over Will. He had his ranch at last.

The next morning, several members of the Walker Party came to help Will build the bunkhouse. They stayed for several days. By the time they left, Will and his men started the barn, which he hoped to have finished by the end of the week.

The labor was difficult, but the weather was perfect. The bright sun during the day took the edge off the cool temperatures. At night, the fire in the bunkhouse kept them warm. While some days white puffy clouds floated across the blue azure sky, Will had yet to see any rain or snow in the weeks since arriving in the territory.

Will stretched out the sore muscles of his back. Long months in the saddle on the trail had not prepared him for the strenuous labor of chopping wood, stripping logs, sanding, and sawing. After two weeks of this, he thought his body would adjust, but he was sore nonetheless. Purchasing the ticking in Santa Fe had been a good decision, one his muscles thanked him for nightly as he fell to sleep on his bunk.

Looking up from the log he was sanding, Will scanned the horizon and mountain slope. At night, firelight dotted the hillside. Then, at random moments during the day, he felt like they were being watched. Seeing nothing unusual, he returned his focus to the log.

Will could not believe he had his own ranch. Would his father be proud, as Ben suggested?

A wave of homesickness washed over him. He missed his father and his counsel, though he seemed to be managing well on his own so far. Still, he wished he could talk over his plans with his father. What would he think about Will's ideas and dreams for Colter Ranch? Would his father see something Will missed? Would he have suggestions on the best way to make those dreams a reality?

He sighed, brushing the sweat from his forehead. None of that mattered. He was on his own. He had to trust in his decisions now. No more second guessing. No more seeking his father's counsel. Colter Ranch would be the product of his choices, whether wise or foolish.

Will's excitement grew as he thought about all of the opportunities this land provided. Besides being able to support a herd much larger than his current one, this land would be perfect for the horse breeding business he dreamed of starting. With a lack of readily available horseflesh and a growing population, he would be able to easily sell horses to new settlers, and perhaps even the army. Of course, breeding horses meant he would have plenty of quality animals for his own use.

Will's stomach growled, bringing him back to reality. Must be time for supper. No sooner than the thought entered his mind did Snake ring the bell. Wiping the sweat from his brow, Will washed up outside the bunkhouse. A few days ago, someone threw together a crude table with benches on either side. It was barely big enough for the dozen broad-shouldered men crammed around it, but it was better than sitting on the floor. Perhaps he could make two chairs for each end to give them a little more space. Of course with several of them back caring for the cattle, it might not be an issue.

After the men gathered around the table, Will said grace. Even though some of the men didn't like the custom, they knew better than to grumble. He, on the other hand, would never tire of thanking God for all that He provided.

As soon as grace was done, the teasing began.

"You better pick up the pace out there Owens, otherwise

Covington's gonna beat you today," Jed said. The men made a competition out of who could prepare the most logs each day.

"My old bones don't move as fast as you kids," Owens shot back.

"Old! Ha! I'd hardly use your nineteen years as an excuse. You're just slow," Snake retorted, the oldest of the group besides Ben and Will.

"I suppose now that you have a warm cozy bunk to sleep in that you think you can just slack off," the normally shy Covington piped up, jabbing Owens in the ribs.

"Hey, no fair injuring the competition," Owens feigned injury grabbing his ribs.

Will enjoyed the friendly banter of the men. They had certainly worked out a lot of their differences. Hawk and Jed were now like brothers. Months ago, he would have put his money on Jed killing the young half-Indian, but now they had a strong friendship. Whenever one was riding flank, the other took the drag position at the back of the herd, so they could converse when the herd settled.

Owens and Whitten seemed to get along. When one was riding point in front of the herd, the other was out-riding, looking for strays. In the evenings, the two would convince Snake to pick up a game of poker.

The four Mexican *vaqueros* seemed inseparable as well. That could be because some of them still spoke little English. But that didn't stop them from joining in the joking.

At the next bite, Will was reminded of the Mexicans' good natured pranks, as fire burned through his mouth. He willed his eyes not to water, but it was too late. The heat was insatiable.

"Pedro, you got the boss today," Miguel stated with his thick accent, nodding in Will's direction.

All eyes turned to Will. He reached for some water, downed it and stole Whitten's water as well. It had been much funnier when it wasn't his mouth on fire. Snake tossed him a biscuit and he hoped the blandness would counteract the heat. He could see the men were uncertain if it was acceptable to laugh at the daily hot pepper joke when it was their boss suffering. Ben couldn't control himself. He was laughing hysterically. That must have been all the encouragement the rest of them needed for they soon joined in. The burning gradually subsided and Will laughed at the clever prank.

"Good one, Pedro," Will said slapping the man on the back. He wanted to make sure they knew it was okay to have a good time, even if it was at his expense. Too much of life was serious, as his father always told him. Laughter was rare and should be encouraged.

"I think I'd be volunteering for night duty, if I were you, Pedro," Whitten said. "Don't think I'd want to be on the other side of Boss's scheming mind."

Another round of laughter filled the room.

Following supper, Will took out his guitar and strummed out the notes that danced in his head since setting foot on this new land. He found such peace and calm here, and those feelings came through the music he composed. He already felt like this place was home in a way that Texas never was. He loved this new land with its strange white boulders and miles of grassland.

Perhaps some of the peace came because his brother wasn't here. He didn't miss the constant tension with Reuben. What a blessing to be far from his brother's harassment and condescending attitude.

Then again, maybe the peace was coming from a stronger connection with his heavenly father because of this magnificent land. No matter where the peace was coming from, he hoped it would last a good long time. It refreshed his soul as never before.

As the cowboys around him grew weary and turned in for the night, Will put his guitar away. Stretching out on the bunk, he felt his own eyes get droopy.

Sometime during the night, Will woke with a start. Sitting up suddenly, he hit his head on the bunk above him. What had he heard? Rubbing his forehead, he waited for the sound to register. Gunshots! Grabbing his big fifty rifle, he looked through one of the small cutout slits in the wall. The slit was not more than a few inches wide and tall, but it was enough to aim a rifle and defend his land. Then he heard the blood piercing scream of the Apaches. Other men jumped up armed and ready. Peering through one of the slits, the full moon illuminated the corral rather well. Seeing none of his men were in the line of fire, Will motioned the cowboys in the bunkhouse over to the west wall. They began firing at the Apache bandits.

"I count about ten Indians," Ben shouted over the rapid rifle fire. "They have the cattle corral open and are leading the herd out." Pedro and his crew only had part of the herd in the field tonight, the rest were in the corral—an easy target for the thieves.

"Whitten, Owens, can you make it to the horses if we give you cover fire?" Will asked.

"Sure thing, Boss," both men answered.

"First priority is securing the herd."

The cabin filled with the smoke of spent gunpowder as Will and Ben provided cover fire. Though few of their shots connected with the Apache thieves, they were able to distract them enough for Whitten and Owens to make it safely to the barn. They mounted bareback and bridle free since there was no time to saddle the horses. Owens aimed his revolver at the Indian holding the gate open. The shot connected and propelled the raider into the path of the frantic cattle crushing him under their weight. Owens, now having control of the gate, swung it closed. The bulk of the herd was secure. Whitten rode out toward Pedro, Miguel, Diego, and Raul to round up the remaining cattle.

Will and Ben darted from the safety of the bunkhouse, shooting in the direction of the now retreating Apaches. Hearing more than just horse hoof beats, Will knew he lost some cattle in the confrontation. Hopefully that was all they lost.

"Whitten, did you see how many they got away with?" Ben asked.

"I'd say about twenty head, no more," Whitten replied. "Doesn't look like any of the new breeders are gone. None of the horses are missing either."

Twenty head. Not bad considering they could have gotten a whole lot more. The full moon had been his ally tonight, allowing the night herders to spot trouble and sound the alarm quickly.

Will asked Whitten to stand guard tonight near the stables. The Indians had been bold enough to ride right into the heart of the ranch and Will was not taking any more chances. Starting tonight, he would post someone near the stables or outside the bunkhouse in addition to the men in the field with the cattle. Again he was starting to feel they were being stretched thin. Tomorrow they should be able to finish up the barn then they could concentrate on ranching—and their own safety.

Chapter 16

Drew's palms grew sweaty as he concentrated on the target before him. *This was a bad idea. I can't shoot a gun.*

"Hold steady," Harrison reminded him, "and look through the site. When you've got your mark lined up, just pull the trigger."

With jerky movements, Drew tried to line up the target. It always seemed to move more than he wanted it to as he adjusted his position. Sighing in frustration, he lost the target completely—and it was a stationary target.

"Patience," Harrison encouraged. "Don't let your frustration get the best of you."

"It shows that much?"

Harrison let out a deep belly laugh. "Yes. Tell me, how do you keep steady when you remove a bullet from a man's gut?"

Drew smirked, lowering the rifle to his side without taking the shot. That was a hard question. How did he keep a steady hand in surgery? "Practice I suppose," he admitted, remembering how shaky and nervous he had been the first few times he operated on someone.

"Well, that's how you're going to learn how to shoot," Harrison said. Picking up the rifle, he thrust it towards Drew.

Slumping his shoulders, he took the rifle. This seemed far more difficult than medical school.

"What's that?" Harrison mock scolded. "Sagging shoulders is horrible form."

Drew straightened his back and shot his friend a woeful look.

"You still want to go through with this, right?"

He wanted to back out. He couldn't shoot a gun and he couldn't take a life. Could he?

Grabbing him by the shoulders, Harrison gave him a shake. "What will you do if Mrs. Anderson needs you to protect her from the Navajo? Will you slump your shoulders in defeat then? Let her fend for herself?"

Remorse lodged in his throat as he remembered his motivation for asking Harrison this favor. "Of course not. I will give it my best attempt."

Raising the rifle to his shoulder, Drew closed his eyes. Slowly he opened them, looking through the site. Seeing the target he squeezed the trigger. The gun fired, jamming hard against his shoulder, almost causing him to drop the weapon.

"You did it!" Harrison exclaimed.

Rubbing his sore shoulder, Drew propped the rifle against a nearby tree. He walked toward the target, amazed that he actually hit it, though not exactly in the spot he expected. Perhaps he would do well enough in an emergency—just as long as he didn't think about his target being a man.

Maybe this wilderness living was toughening him up. Within the last month, he finally felt comfortable around the oxen. He was no longer the last one ready when the wagon train pulled out. His arms were bulking up, probably from heaving all those full water barrels into the back of the wagon.

Even though he felt more at ease, he still missed doctoring. He would be more than happy to settle down in Granite Creek and start living a normal life again. He would build a quaint house with an attached clinic. Paul already agreed to help him with the furniture. Hannah would have her kitchen, likely smaller than before, but he was certain she would be happy in it.

Thanking Harrison for the lesson, Drew headed back to camp. Turning his face towards the sun, he closed his eyes. An image of a small log cabin filled his vision. Hannah smiled at him, a little boy propped on her hip. Bounding in from outside was a little girl, perhaps a bit older than the boy. She had the same lovely deep blue eyes as her mother. They all smiled at him, love bursting forth.

Opening his eyes, he looked at the circle of wagons. The beautiful image faded too quickly, followed by a rush of disappointment. He never shared with Hannah how incredibly sad he was that they had no children yet. He didn't want her to feel worse than she already did. He knew she thought about it often. The way she would gaze longingly off at nothing in particular. Or the way she followed the movements of each of the children on the wagon train.

She would make a wonderful mother with her kind heart and her eagerness to take care of others' needs. He remembered the way she would take time to teach the young children that came into the clinic. She always spoke to them in a way they understood, easing their fears of what Drew was doing to set their broken arms or stitch their gashed foreheads.

A smile erupted from the love overflowing his heart. Hannah truly was an amazing woman and he loved her dearly.

Chapter 17

Colter Ranch

December 25, 1863

Christmas morning dawned cold and breezy. The snow from yesterday already melted away, leaving a light layer of moisture over the land. Will woke early and silently slipped out of the bunkhouse so as not to disturb the other men. In the stable, Will began brushing down his horse, Jackson, to ready him for an early morning ride. The night herders still covered for the next few hours, so Will took his time. As he cared for his horse, his mind began to reflect on the changes over the last year. For some reason, he always found himself in a pensive mood on this holiday.

He thought back to last Christmas—the last one with his father. The family gathered in the morning for the reading of the Christmas story. Then Mary and Julia set about the work of preparing a feast. Midday, the cowboys drove the cattle into the corral and joined the family for dinner in the ranch house. It was the only day of the year that the hired hands and the family dined together, breaking down the formality his father carefully maintained throughout the rest of the year. In the evening, Father, Julia, Mary, and the children piled into the wagon, while Will and Reuben rode on horseback into town for the Christmas service. Following the service, back at the ranch house, the family gathered around the fireplace and exchanged gifts.

A wave of homesickness washed over Will as he realized this year would be far different. There would be no church services to attend, no gifts to exchange, no family to share the day. He wondered how Julia was faring under Reuben's care. Would Reuben even permit the family to attend the church he so despised? As thoughts of his sister filled his mind, Will felt a pang of unexplained guilt. He hadn't wanted to leave her behind with Reuben, but what choice did he have? He could not go against his father's will. Truly, what kind of life would Julia have on Colter Ranch in the middle of the wilderness where they were always under the threat of Indian attacks? No, his father had been right to assign Julia's care to Reuben.

Knowing that did not make it any easier to go through the holiday without his family. He and Julia had always been close. And he loved to find ways to surprise her with an unexpected gift for the day. This year, there would be no gifts exchanged. He was not certain she had even received any of his letters, as mail service was mostly non-existent. That would hopefully change with the arrival of the army last week as they established Fort Whipple.

Sighing, Will decided to make the best he could of the day. Later, when all the men gathered to share their version of a feast, he would read the Christmas story, the only tradition he could continue. For him, the story was not about tradition. He loved reading it and being reminded of God's amazing miracle, that He sent his only son to the earth as a baby for him, Will Colter. How amazing was his God's love?

A shuffling noise sounded behind him. When Will turned, he faced Jed.

"Boss," Jed started, "I...um...wanted to ask you something."

Calmly Will nodded, encouraging him to continue.

"Remember back in New Mexico when you said that my family dying wasn't my fault."

"Yeah."

"How can you be so sure?"

Will hesitated. The question deserved an answer, but he had none ready.

"I mean, you said that God doesn't blame me. How do you know that?"

Lord, give me wisdom. He swallowed hard, hoping he would say the right thing to help Jed and not turn him away. "It is not His nature to blame us for things beyond our control. You could not have changed anything that happened with your family, no matter how much you want to."

Jed kicked at some dirt on the floor. "You seem to know a lot about God. Could you ask him to let my family know that I—" his voice cracked, "I miss them and I love them."

"We could both ask Him now."

"Naw. I'm sure he don't want to hear from some messed up cowboy. It's better if you just ask."

Will laughed. "By your definition, I don't think I can."

"What do you mean?"

"I'm a pretty messed up cowboy, too."

Jed's brow furrowed in confusion and surprise. "Why do you say that, Boss? You're one of the most decent, kindest men I know."

"I wasn't always so decent or kind," Will confessed. "Much of my life I've been ill-tempered, ready to jump into a fight at any moment—especially if it was with my brother. I've done a lot of bad things. Things I wish I could take back. Things I wish I hadn't done."

"But, you're a good man," Jed defended.

"Not without Jesus, I'm not. I make all kinds of mistakes." Will felt at a loss to explain things clearly. "It's just when I was a young man, I didn't care about anything or anyone. I almost lost my life on a cattle drive. After that, I realized what a fool I was. There was so much more to life than drinking and gambling and... Well, I finally understood what my father had been trying to tell me—that Jesus loved me and that I didn't have to carry around my guilt anymore."

Jed looked at him intensely. "I don't think he loves me."

Will's heart hurt for the young man, that he would really believe that. "Remember when that rattler almost bit you?"

Nodding, Jed broke eye contact, suddenly shy.

"If Hawk hadn't shot it, it would have bit you on the neck. There would have been nothing that we could have done to save you."

He paused, letting the words sink in. "I think God spared your life. He wasn't ready for you to die. He spared you because he loves you."

"Then he didn't love my family, because he didn't spare them!" Anger hardened Jed's stance.

Placing his hand on Jed's shoulder, Will countered his argument, "God loved my father, but he let him die this summer anyway. We all die. We all have a time. Just because God doesn't act, doesn't mean he loves someone less. I'm just saying that evidence of his love is shown in your life. He led you to the Star C, gave you a good job, surrounded you with friends that care about you. You're right, you've suffered—more than most. But, he never left you alone. He was always looking out for you. That, to my way of thinking, is what love is all about."

Jed seemed to consider Will's words. For several minutes, both were silent.

Finally, Jed spoke, "Will you still ask him? Will you ask him to make sure my family knows I love them? I just want them to know that."

"They know, son. They know. But, I'll ask him anyway."

A brief smile darted across Jed's face before being swallowed by sadness. "Thanks, Boss," he added before running from the barn.

Lord, I promised Jed. Please let his family know that he loved them. Still does. And, Lord, keep working on his heart. Help him to know that you love him.

Placing the saddle on Jackson's back, Will cinched up the straps and led the horse outside, his former homesickness vanished. Mounting with ease, Will nudged him into a gentle lope out to where the night herders managed the cattle. Over the past month, the night shift was comprised of the four Mexicans in his employ. Will had not planned it that way, but the men seemed to enjoy the camaraderie and after several days volunteering together, Will gave in.

"Feliz Navidad, Boss," Pedro greeted when Will pulled up next to him.

"Feliz Navidad, Pedro," Will answered. "Any trouble?"

"No, Boss. No sign of any Indian campfires for weeks now. Herd has been peaceful, enjoying their favorite grass."

Will chuckled. Pedro often told him how much the longhorns liked the Arizona grass better than the Texas grass. Will wasn't sure how the *vaqueros* knew such a thing, but found the idea humorous.

Will turned his horse back toward the lake, where he stopped and gazed over it. By this time next year, he would have the ranch house up. He longed for some privacy as he was beginning to feel cramped in the bunkhouse. He knew it was awkward for the men, too. While hanging around the boss on the trail was fine, doing so at home was another matter. Maybe he would get the house built early next year. And this is where it would go. On the slight rise overlooking this glorious lake.

He liked it here, in his new home, despite the concern of Indians and cattle thieves. The land was so incredible and peaceful. He felt like he belonged here, like he was destined to live here. He knew what his father would say to that. He would say that as long as Will set his heart upon God, He would lead his path. Will believed that was exactly what happened.

"Awful quiet this morning," Ben said, pulling Will from his thoughts.

"Yup."

"Don't you worry, we'll get yer house built soon," Ben replied. After working side by side for so many years, Ben easily read him. "When that wagon train gets here, maybe we can hire a few folks to help."

When the army arrived last week, Will and Ben made the trek north, about twenty miles, to meet them. They learned that the governor's party was expected in a few weeks and with them was a wagon train of some fifty or so settlers, or maybe that was the number of wagons. Either way, there would be a large influx of people soon. Ben was right, he could hire a few men to build the house and pay them in beef, which they would likely be eager to receive after months on the trail.

"Quite a different day than last year, huh?" Will commented.

"Yup," Ben responded. "Much has changed, but we'll make a festive day of it."

"You headed out to relieve the four amigos?" Will asked, referring to the group's new nickname.

"Yup. Covington, Jed, Hawk, Owens, and me will keep the herd out for a few more hours before we bring 'em into the corral."

Will nodded his approval, then watched as Ben rode off. Feeling the bite of the cold breeze, Will trotted Jackson back to the stable. When he finished rubbing down the stallion, he made his way back to the bunkhouse.

Snake had somehow enlisted Whitten's help in preparing the meal. Snake barked out orders, while Whitten jumped to comply. Seeing the two in action, Will wondered how the meal might turn out. Whitten did not impress him as someone skilled in cooking. Hopefully Snake was a good teacher. Either way, it would be tricky pulling off a big meal cooking over the hearth fire. There would be no stove until the ranch house was built. He had ordered it while in

Santa Fe and expected it to arrive with the governor's party.

Grabbing the coffee pot from the hearth, Will poured himself a cup of lukewarm coffee. Not the best, but it would do. In a few minutes, the four amigos filed into the bunkhouse, speaking rapidly in their native tongue, animated eyes dancing with excitement. Snake looked up glaring at the interruption, but the men didn't seem to notice. Taking seats around the table, they kept up the lively conversation. Will took a seat in one of the chairs he made, pulling a well-worn book from under his bed.

A few hours later, as promised, Ben returned with Covington, Owens, Jed, and Hawk following closely behind. Clusters of men formed around activities they enjoyed. Owens and Covington taught Jed and Hawk some new card game. Ben grabbed a book and sat in a corner, far from the noise, with a contented look on his face.

Snake didn't stop moving for a second, until he had an amazing spread of food laid out mid-afternoon. There were beef steaks, mashed potatoes instead of the usual fried potatoes, beans, gravy, biscuits, and Will thought he spied some cookies for dessert. The man out did himself. Following grace, the men dug in, passing bowls between dishing out greedy helpings.

After the meal, Will read the Christmas story. While not all of his men shared his beliefs, they listened respectfully. Jed and Hawk both seemed particularly interested in the story. He wondered if this was the first time they heard it. Pulling his guitar from its hiding place beneath his bunk, he opened the case and tuned the instrument. He picked out the notes to his favorite Christmas songs and was pleasantly surprised when most of the men joined in the singing. Pedro, Raul, Diego, and Miguel sang in Spanish while the rest sang in English. It gave Will goose bumps to hear the music this way.

The evening wore on and the men began to retire for the night. As Will stretched out in his bunk, he thanked God for a wonderful day and for his many blessings.

Stretching as she rose for Christmas morning, Hannah quickly donned her coat. The chill in the air filtered through the thin canvas walls of their tent. She smiled, relieved to get a break from traveling on this most blessed day. Last night, just before sunset, the wagons set up camp in this rather nondescript unnamed part of the Arizona Territory.

Exiting the tent she walked the short distance to the blazing fire Paul started. Since leaving Fort Wingate, the landscape became flat again and firewood was scarce. In order to conserve wood, she and Drew were sharing fires with the Lancaster's.

After breakfast was served and consumed, the settlers gathered in the center of camp for a Christmas service. Reverend Read led them in the reading of the Christmas story followed by a rather long sermon. Someone had a guitar and led the group in singing carol after carol. It was a lovely way to celebrate in the midst of the wilderness with harmonic music floating across the air.

Following the morning celebration, Hannah and Drew returned to the warmth of their shared fire. Joy filled Hannah. Christmas was her favorite day of the year—the day her savior entered the world. Although spending the day in a chilly wind huddled around a camp fire was so different from past years, nothing dampened her spirits today. Drew was at her side. Friends shared the fire. As much as she would rather be in a cozy home sitting in front of the fireplace, she gave up reminiscing about past Christmases long ago. She determined to take each year as it came. There was too much pain in looking back.

"My aren't you glowing today," Betty commented as Hannah joined her.

"I'm happy," Hannah replied, nearly giddy.

"In just a few more weeks, we should arrive in our new home. I can hardly wait. Can you imagine what it will look like?" Betty asked.

"You don't think it will be flat and endless like here?"

"Oh, no, dear. I know for sure there are mountains and valleys," Betty replied. "All of the mining is being done in the creeks and rivers in the area. I bet it is just beautiful."

Hannah thought it would be beautiful simply because they would never have to leave again. "I'll be happy to have a home and not have to ride in a wagon for hours on end every day."

"Oh, and to have a place dedicated for washing and cooking.

Won't that just be grand?"

"And some privacy, not that I don't enjoy good neighbors," Hannah said laying a hand on Betty's arm.

"I completely understand, dear."

The conversation lagged and Hannah gazed into the fire. They were so close. Soon, very soon, they would be in their new home and this difficult journey would come to a close. Drew would be back in his own clinic, and she would eagerly fall into the routine of assisting him. She sighed. She longed to be there already.

As Hannah's gaze lifted from the fire, Drew motioned for her to join him in the wagon. Saying her goodbyes to Betty, she followed quickly.

"Is something wrong?" concerned filled her voice at his unusual behavior.

Instead of answering, he pulled her to him and kissed her passionately. She melted into his arms and responded in kind. After a moment, Drew pulled away leaving Hannah breathless.

Confused by his spontaneity, she asked, "What was that for?"

"Because I love you so much, Mrs. Anderson," he said with a twinkle in his eye and a smile on his lips. "And I thought you might need some warming up on this cold Christmas Day."

"Drew!" She feigned shock, swatting him with her hand.

The smile faded from his lips, his face grew serious, and his voice husky. "Hannah, I love you so much. I don't know what I would do without you."

The sudden change in his demeanor set her on edge, causing her to wonder, yet again, what was wrong.

He held her gaze for the longest time, running his fingers through her hair, knocking the pins loose. He made no further move as she thought he might. Instead, he looked deep into her eyes, almost as if it were the last time he would see her.

"What's wrong?" she pleaded as her fear returned. He was acting so strangely.

Drew hesitated before answering, "I'm not certain." He glanced away, studying the canvas of the wagon as it protected them from the cold. "I have been rather unsettled the last few days."

Hannah remembered her nightmares. Maybe he had a similar dream about her. But it was just a dream, wasn't it? Nothing more.

Fear began choking her heart. Needing reassurance, she pressed her lips to his, kissing him softly.

He pulled away again, breaking the sweetness of the moment.

"I could not bear to lose you, Hannah," he said as he rested his forehead against hers.

Fear overwhelmed her, keeping words from forming. She could not bear to live without him either. She lost so many that were dear to her—and Drew was the dearest of all.

Chapter 18

A few days after Christmas, the governor's party arrived at the designated watering hole called Navajo Springs. The weather grew unpleasant, with blowing snow swirling about them. While Hannah wished they would press on, the government officials decided to stop and hold a brief inauguration ceremony. Huddled in a blanket, she stood close to Drew for warmth. Each breath of chilly air pricked her lungs.

"Just think," Drew whispered in her ear, "we are here for the inauguration of the first government officials of the territory. Look around. There are only a few of us that will ever know this story first hand."

His eyes glowed with excitement. She wished she was as excited as he. Instead, she shivered and longed for the shelter of the wagon.

"Memorize every detail so we can tell our children."

The mention of children reminded her of her bareness again, making it difficult to pay attention to the details of the ceremony. She hoped once they settled in Granite Creek she would finally be able to give Drew the family they both longed for. Realizing the ceremony started, she forced herself to listen.

Reverend Read opened the ceremony with one of his long formal prayers, so different from the way Hannah talked with God. Then, one of the judges swore in Governor Goodwin, Secretary McCormick, and others. After everyone was sworn in, Secretary McCormick stood and read the Governor's Proclamation. Odd that the secretary should read it instead of the governor himself, Hannah thought.

Secretary McCormick continued reading with great animation. He announced a census that would take place in the coming months, outlined the judicial districts that would be formed, and mentioned a forthcoming election for members of the legislature. He confirmed that the seat of government would be located near Fort Whipple. Then, for some length of time, he read the governor's plan for making the territory safe for settlers, at great expense to the natives, using such strong language such as "extermination."

Hannah barely felt her feet, for the temperature continued to drop. Just when she thought she might return to the wagon, Secretary McCormick waved the Union flag and cut the ceremony short. Shivering uncontrollably, she accepted Drew's assistance back onto the wagon seat. The Arizona Territory now had an official government in the middle of a cold and dreary snow storm.

The rest of the journey for the day, she spent huddled under layers of clothes, coats, and a blanket on the seat next to her husband. Did the governor really plan to kill all of the natives? Was it a matter of survival? Would she and Drew not be safe unless the Indians were all killed? It seemed rather extreme to her, but then women had no mind for politics—at least that is what she had been taught all her life.

The image of the floating woman's head returned from her nightmares. This wilderness held frightening dangers, threatening to rob her of any security she felt. She pleaded with God that she and Drew would be safe in the small settlement that would become their new home.

Home. It was almost within reach. Just a few more weeks away.

Miles of flat, treeless terrain stretched before them. The dark clouds hanging low in the sky continued pouring out a steady stream of snow. By the time the wagon train stopped for the night, the cold crumbled Hannah to exhaustion. Though she longed for a fire, she did not put up a fight when Drew asked her to conserve their wood and prepare a cold meal instead. For days, they had seen no trees or wood for fire. Unlike the prairies, there were no buffalo chips to act as a substitute. The only wood they had for fire was what little remained from their stay at Fort Wingate.

Since the snow still fell at a rapid pace, they ate the meal under the protection of the covered wagon. Winter days in Ohio had been this cold, but there she had the advantage of a warm house and glowing fire to comfort her. Here, on the open desert plains, the wind howled and snow swirled relentlessly. The most comfort she could hope to find was wrapped in her husband's arms as they shivered together under the weight of layers of blankets and clothing. What happened to the moderate climate reported in that Santa Fe newspaper?

After a quick cold breakfast, the team lurched forward creating the familiar sway of progress. It had been over a month since they left Santa Fe. Again the weariness of the trip weighed on Hannah. Cold and frustrated, she kept to herself. It took too much energy to stay warm, much less talk.

There was nothing about this forsaken frigid desert that she found to be comforting. She longed for the cozy nights by the fireplace in the parlor of their home. She missed waking up in the morning and walking to kitchen to prepare breakfast, where everything was in order and simple. Here, everything grew more difficult, rather than easier the farther they traveled from home. Tears pooled in her eyes and she tried to hold them back, lest they freeze on her rosy wind-kissed cheeks. Since leaving Fort Wingate, she had yet to do laundry. It took too much firewood. Back home, she had the luxury of doing laundry several times a week if needed. She never thought about how blessed they had been in Ohio. Now she guiltily acknowledged how much she had taken for granted.

Several days passed in a similar icy blur. Each task was completed slowly and deliberately in the howling wind. Day after day, Hannah could not think past how chilled she was. There was nothing, save their wagon, to block the wind. Even after snow stopped falling from the sky, they were still pelted with snow being picked up by the wind. Would this misery ever end?

The next morning, the sun finally peeked through the heavy snow laden clouds. The respite from the weather gave Hannah an opportunity to bank a small fire. As she started making breakfast, she suddenly felt very ill. The flapjack she flipped mimicked the motion of her stomach. Leaving it, she quickly ran to the outside of the wagon corral and lost the contents of her stomach. She stood there a moment, taking a few deep breaths. When she thought it passed, she started to walk back toward the cook fire. No sooner had she taken another step and she felt the bile rise again. Heaving, she doubled over. She could smell the flapjack burning from here and it caused her to gag again. If suffering through the cold was not bad enough, now she had to endure sickness.

"Hannah!" Betty called running to her side.

"Here," she managed to weakly reply.

"Oh dear! Here, brace yourself against the wagon and rest a moment. I'll go get some water."

Betty rushed back to the campfire and removed the flapjack from the heat. The burning smell dissipated by the time she returned with the water.

"Slow sips," she admonished when Hannah tried to gulp the water. Placing her wrist on Hannah's forehead she concluded Hannah did not have a fever. "How long have you been feeling ill?"

"It just came on suddenly this morning," Hannah said, her voice frail. She wanted to collapse on the ground. Betty's sturdy arm around her waist steadied her.

"Why don't you lie down and I'll see that your husband is fed."

The world spun as Betty helped her into the wagon, making sure she was covered with warm blankets.

Drew returned and Hannah could hear Betty's muted voice explaining what happened. In seconds he was at her side, as both a worried husband and a confident doctor.

"How long have you felt ill?" Drew frowned.

"Just this morning."

He repeated the steps Betty already took, ensuring that she had no fever. He placed his hands on her abdomen and asked her if she felt any pain when he pressed in different areas. Hannah felt fine— except she was going to be sick again. She sat up quickly and managed to lean over the side of the wagon just in time. Worry etched deep lines in Drew's forehead. She had seen this look before, usually when he was not certain what was wrong. Of course, he was probably worrying too much since it was his wife who was ill.

"Let me make you some tea to settle your stomach," Drew offered. "I could give you some laudanum, but that is probably unnecessary. I think you should just rest in the wagon today."

Lying back down, Hannah pulled blankets to her chin. When the tea finished steeping, Drew propped her up so she could drink. After the soothing liquid was gone, he pushed her hair back from her face and kissed her forehead.

"Get some rest," he said, the worried look still wrinkling his brow.

Hannah did as she was told. Although she faded in and out of sleep in the morning, she was much improved when the wagon train stopped for dinner. When Drew pulled the wagon to a stop, she appeared through the opening. Still feeling slightly dizzy, she waited for Drew to help her down.

"Your color looks much better. How's your appetite?" he asked.

Her stomach growled, answering for her.

She set about making a quick meal for them, of which she ate a double portion. In the afternoon, she sat on the wagon seat next to Drew despite the cold air. As the day wore on, the queasiness dissipated and she felt better.

Looking at the scenery around her, Hannah soaked in the beauty, letting it lift her downtrodden spirit. A few multi-colored mountains rose to the north, jutting from the flat valley floor below. Painted in pinks, reds, oranges, rust, and gray, the mountains had bands of colors stacked one on top of the other. For miles the vibrant colors danced in the sunlight, contrasted sharply by the pure blue sky. Snow capped the upper most peaks, while shadows obscured the crevices. She stared mesmerized until the scene faded in the distance behind them, leaving a momentary serenity covering her.

Sighing, she watched as the endless flat desert dominated the landscape once again. She wondered what caused her bout of sickness that morning. Perhaps she had taken ill due to the numerous days of unending cold. Deciding to think on it no more, she gave in to the soothing rocking of the wagon.

Over the next several days, Hannah continued to waver between heaving in the morning and being famished in the evening. What was wrong with her? Did she have some sort of weird sickness that only attacked her in the morning? She was growing concerned, but surely Drew would be able to tell her what was wrong? Or perhaps he already knew and she was dying? In that case, she was certain she did not want to know.

The governor's expedition had been stranded in the San Francisco Mountains for several days following the new year. A blizzard struck without warning, dumping more than a foot of snow on the chilled travelers. For days, Drew huddled next to his wife, not leaving the minimal shelter of their wagon. The conditions outside were so harsh that neither he nor Hannah braved the weather except when it was absolutely necessary. Unfortunately, necessity was more frequent than he hoped, as Hannah continued to be sick each morning.

"Drew," Hannah's weak voice whispered next to him.

The lamenting tone sent him into motion. He hopped out onto the springboard seat and waited for his wife to follow. Then he jumped down, reaching up to ease her onto the soft blanket of snow. When her feet touched the ground, she swayed, leaning on him heavily for support. Placing his arm around her waist, he helped her hobble a few feet from the wagon. Dropping to her knees, she doubled over, retching violently.

His breath caught in his throat. She had been so sick and weak and cold. Kneeling in the snow was not wise, but she had no strength to stand. Rubbing her back, he waited at her side while her stomach settled. For nearly twenty minutes she sat there, wavering between shivering and retching. He could not even offer her some tea, as they were completely out of firewood.

At last, she nodded that she was ready to return to the wagon. After he lifted her to the seat, she waited until he climbed up and could help her back inside.

The bottom half of her dress was soaked. "Do you have another dress you can change into?"

She nodded. With slow movements, he helped her change out of the wet green calico into the pale blue one—his favorite. Relieved that her underskirts and bloomers were not soaked through, Drew wrapped his wife under layers of blankets. Chills shook her body. Rubbing her arms and legs vigorously, he tried to help speed up the warming process.

When she finally fell back asleep, he remained only a few minutes before leaving. He had to get some firewood. She needed a hot fire and some calming tea.

A circle of men stood in the center of camp.

"Looks like the sky is clear today," Eli Jacobs said. "Most of the men should head up into the mountain to hunt elk or some other game. You, you, and you," he said pointing to a few of the governor's men and Drew, "will lead the young boys in searching for firewood. We need to gather enough for several days."

When Eli finished, the men split up for their various tasks.

On his third trip back up the mountain, Drew took in the beauty. Peaks rose high above burdened with heavy snow. Aspen and pine trees poked through the blanket of white, offering some variation. As he climbed further up the mountain with some of the governor's men, he turned and looked back down at the valley below.

The wagons were in their typical circle formation, with the campsites on the inside of the circle. There was little activity at the camp, as most of the travelers were bundled inside their wagons trying to keep warm. They ran out of firewood days ago and were grateful the snow stopped. Turning his focus back to the task at hand, Drew picked up several nice sized branches from the ground. It would be difficult to burn while wet from the snow, but it was better than no fire at all.

As he worked he thought of Hannah. She was not doing well and he could not think how to best help her. Thinking through the symptoms might help. Each morning she would wake and before she could finish preparing breakfast, she would run aside and lose the contents of her stomach. By dinner time she would start to feel better and managed to eat at least one meal. His doctor instincts told him something was definitely wrong, but...

Why didn't he think of it before! She must be pregnant. He thought for a moment and calculated how long since they were in Santa Fe. It was six or seven weeks ago. Yes, this was definitely morning sickness. He would ask her when he returned to camp, but he was certain she was with child.

Relief that it was not something more serious filled him, quickly followed by joy—overflowing and overwhelming. He was going to be a father! At last! He wanted to shout and dance and share his news with everyone.

Drew's excitement rose. If it was a boy, he would teach him how to fish, if there were fish in the Hassayampa River. If it was a girl, he would spoil her so much. He hoped she would be as beautiful as her mother. What names would they choose? Maybe Alexander after his father?

He remembered the brief image of his mind from weeks ago—the one where he saw Hannah with a toddler balanced on her hip. The picture held new meaning now, for it would soon be reality. He would have that son or daughter.

Thank you, Lord, for this long awaited child. Please let him grow to be healthy and strong. Keep Hannah safe and strong. He felt like dancing, as he continued to search for fuel.

Drew saw Lieutenant Harrison off in the distance to his right higher up the mountain. He was with the group of men hunting elk to feed the settlers. Since Harrison taught him how to shoot at Fort Wingate, Drew improved considerably, though not enough to join the hunting party. He changed direction away from Harrison to keep a safe distance from the hunters. Shots rang out, echoing off the mountain walls, as he reached a clearing. Someone must have hit their mark.

Soon the eerie quiet of the mountain turned to a low rumbling growing louder and more ominous by the second. Drew's heart started pounding in reaction to the unnatural sound. He saw drifts of snow start to give way beneath him as he realized the danger. Looking up the mountain as he started to run, he knew it was too late. His feet started slipping from beneath him, unable to gain traction.

The wall of snow hit him full impact mid-stride, knocking the wind from his lungs. He was up then down, tumbling over, being tossed around by the force and helpless to make it stop. His leg struck something, a rock or perhaps a tree. The pain that shot through his body was fierce agony. Drew felt his body being carried away out of his control. He knew he was not going to get out of this without help. Panic seized him. Was he going to die on this mountain?

Then without warning, the motion ended abruptly. Drew felt the heavy weight of snow crushing his chest. He tried to open his eyes, but he could not. Everything was icy and cold and confining all around him. His throbbing leg became numb. He willed his arms to move but they were pinned underneath a heavy, immovable weight. He tried to take a breath, but no air refilled his desperate lungs.

The impossibility of the situation hit him full force as the lightheadedness clouded his thoughts. *Lord, please take care of Hannah and our child.* All went black.

Chapter 19

Lieutenant Joshua Harrison could not believe he just witnessed the death of his dear friend, Drew. One moment, he saw him gathering wood in the clearing. Rifle fire from further up the mountain reverberated loudly through the forest. He saw the avalanche start, just seconds before he heard the deep rumbling. Before he could blink, or even call out for his friend, the snow engulfed Drew in a mighty white wave.

Once the snow settled, he ran toward the last spot he saw his friend, hoping against fear that there might be some way to rescue him. As he got closer and closer, all hope faded. There was no way to tell how far Drew had been swept away or how deeply he was buried. He could dig for days and never find him. The aftermath of the avalanche spread over several hundred yards. Standing atop it, he realized his vantage point was at least six to ten feet higher than it had been before, without climbing in elevation. Falling to his knees he prayed if there was a way, that God would spare his friend.

The tears falling from his eyes froze before covering much distance down his face. He already knew the answer—the man who saved his life just lost his own.

Images of Drew's kind face filled his vision. The laughter as Joshua made some joke. The sincere concern when he changed Joshua's bandages. The hidden moments Joshua let him think he was sleeping, as the doctor prayed over his wound. The courage and fear that filled Drew's eyes when he tried to teach him to shoot a rifle. The deep conviction when he spoke of matters of his faith. All of these things would be just memories of a friendship cut too short.

Joshua was not sure how long he knelt there before Bixley's hand on his shoulder stirred him. One look at the sergeant told him he also witnessed the terrifying scene and had come to the same conclusion. Standing, Joshua led the way back down the mountain. Both men remained silent in reverence for the fallen doctor.

With strong determination, Joshua entered the inner circle of the wagon train. How does one deliver the news to his best friend's wife that she is now a widow?

Hannah heard the shot and assumed the hunting party took victory. She smiled at the thought of how good fresh meat would taste, now that she seemed to be regaining her appetite. Hopefully Drew would be back with some firewood soon. She was tired of the constant freezing and longed for the warmth of a fire.

Then, hearing a terrifying thunderous sound, she hurried out of the wagon and looked towards the mountain, placing her hand above her eyes to shield them from the brightness of the sun reflecting off the snow. A giant swell of snow was coursing down the side of the peaks, swallowing everything in its path. Her heart leaped to her throat. Drew was out there and could be in danger!

As quickly as the avalanche started, it faded away long before threatening the camp.

She wasn't sure how long they all stared at the mountain before some men grabbed shovels and headed toward a different group of men coming down. The men coming down did not even stop to converse. They were walking with purpose—straight for her. Her heart lodged in her throat. The man leading the way was Lieutenant Harrison. His face was pale and his blue eyes had lost their laughter. His gaze connected with hers for the briefest moment, then quickly darted away. He stopped directly in front of her. Looking up, Hannah felt the breath rush from her lungs in fearful anticipation.

"Mrs. Anderson," he stated, reaching for her hands. "Hannah, I'm sorry, but—" His voice caught as she numbly tried to pull her hands back. Tightening his hold and regaining his control, he finished, "Drew was directly in the path. There is no possibility of survival."

Hannah heard a loud shrieking wail pierce the silence with heart rending grief. As her knees started to buckle, she realized the sound had come from her. She barely felt Lieutenant Harrison grasp her arms to keep her from falling. Sobs poured forth. Wailing erupted from the depths of her soul. Her body shook uncontrollably. He could not be gone. He was her love, her life. *God, how could you take him? I love him so. I need him. I cannot possibly live without him. He is a part of me. Why?*

Joshua steadied Hannah and allowed her to cling to him as if her life depended on it—her grip powerful and cutting into his arm. He was aware of the growing crowd and their questions, but he knew he needed to get Hannah to calm down. The broken shrieking sounds erupting from this formerly quiet, gentile woman, shredded his already broken heart.

Leading her to the wagon, he helped her climb up on the seat, then he sat next to her. Not knowing what else to do, he placed his arms around her. He hoped his compassion would give her some comfort. Silently he prayed for her, that God would not leave her and that she would be able to heal from this dreadful blow, for he was certain it was just that. Many times he witnessed hints of the deep abiding love shared between Drew and Hannah. How does one go on after losing someone so intertwined?

After a while, Mrs. Lancaster came by with some water, her eyes red-rimmed as well. Hannah was still crying but not with the same force. Climbing up next to Hannah, Mrs. Lancaster wrapped her in a warm embrace, freeing Joshua from his duty. Her eyes said that it was alright for him to leave Hannah in her care.

Stiffly he retreated from the wagon, headed towards his tent. Joshua fought the raw emotion that welled within him. Drew was gone. Not only did he save Joshua's life when he suffered from that bullet wound, but Drew also led him to the one who saved his soul. He answered all of Joshua's questions about God, no matter how silly or insignificant they seemed—questions that dogged him for years. And in the process, the two men became fast friends. Joshua taught Drew how to shoot a rifle, how to watch the sky for signs of approaching weather, how to watch the area around him for danger. But, it had not been enough to keep him from such an awful death.

What would become of Hannah? Who would drive her wagon the rest of the way to Granite Creek? What would she do to survive in this wilderness?

As he neared his tent, Sergeant Bixley approached. "Lieutenant Harrison, Major Willis is asking for you."

Numbly, Joshua walked towards the major's tent. He noticed the hunting party returned and butchered several elk. Food that cost him his friend's life, he thought bitterly. Fires were now blazing. They would have both the heat and food they needed. Yet, the thought did not bring him much comfort.

Stepping into the major's tent, he cleared his throat. "Sir?"

"Lieutenant, sit down. Fill me in on what happened," requested the major. Joshua—the lieutenant—recounted the story emotionlessly with the practiced ease of an experienced officer. In truth, he was thankful for his military training in moments like these, for Joshua—the man—would not be quite so composed. After finishing his report, he requested permission to leave. The major dismissed him, but Joshua hesitated.

"Is there something else, Lieutenant Harrison?" the major asked.

"Yes sir." Joshua paused as the thought from mere seconds ago fell from his lips. "With your permission, sir, I would like to drive Mrs. Anderson's team for the remainder of the journey. I feel it is my duty to see her safely to her destination." It was the least he could do for the man he owed his own life.

"Harrison, this is most irregular," sputtered Major Willis. "But, I will agree to it. Have Sergeant Bixley provide me with the daily reports. He can also keep watch over your men until we reach Fort Whipple. At that time, I will expect you to return to your duties."

"Thank you, sir," Joshua replied this time leaving the tent when dismissed. With determined steps, he headed back towards Hannah's wagon. He would do everything he could for Drew's wife, no matter the cost.

Sometime during the night, Hannah woke with a start. Momentarily forgetting what happened, she bolted upright. As the fog of sleep began to lift, everything came back in heavy, undaunted grief. Drew was dead. She was alone. God had forsaken her. Tears began to fall again. Her head hurt from all the crying and her eyelids felt heavy. Irritably, she frantically swiped at the tears wishing she could make them stop.

How could you! Her heart screamed in anger at God. How could a loving God lead them to a new land, only to leave her a widow on the doorstep of their new life? This journey was supposed to bring hope—a new life. Instead, it brought death. Drew's death. The death of her heart, her only true love. There was no life without her beloved Drew. *What kind of God are you?*

Realizing her fists were balled so tightly that her nails dug into her palms, she shifted her position and released her grip. Her stomach growled. She could not remember the last time she ate. Quietly moving about, she stepped off the wagon to stand by the dying campfire—that matched the dimness of her heart.

When she looked up, even in the deep shadows of night, she realized they were not camped in the same place. Frightened she looked around. The light of the moon reflected on the snowcapped mountains, which were further away than she remembered them. Where was she?

She wished she would have known they were leaving. Had the men from the wagon train found Drew's body? Was he given a proper burial? Or would his grave be unmarked, melting away as winter turned to spring? The morbid thought brought a fresh wave of tears.

Hearing someone stir in the tent pitched next to her, Hannah froze in place. Why was there a tent next to their wagon? *Her wagon. There is no more us.* Her mind reminded her again of her widowhood. Seeing nothing was where *she* left it, she climbed back into the wagon. Sitting stiffly, she pulled the blanket around her and crossed her arms in defiance. Her anger boiled over. She wanted to scream.

"Hannah," she heard her name being whispered as the weight of someone's step shifted the wagon to one side. Hope grew within her. Was it Drew? Was this all a bad dream? Was he really here?

Just as she parted her lips to speak his name, reality killed her heart. The man's head poking through the opening of the wagon cover looked familiar, but it was not her beloved. As he spoke her name a second time, she recognized the voice. Since when had Lieutenant Harrison started calling her by her first name? And what was he doing here?

"I heard you stirring. Can I get you anything? Are you alright? You must be thirsty, let me get you some water," he whispered in rapid succession. She felt the wagon shift weight twice more, likely him getting down and then back up again.

"Here," he said.

She took the offered cup of water and chugged it in the most un-ladylike manner, swiping away the dribbles with the back of her hand.

Still leaning into the wagon from the springboard seat, Lieutenant Harrison said, "We've been so worried about you. You have been impossible to stir for two days now. Even with all the swaying and lurching of the wagon, you have not moved in the slightest." His concern was evident.

She said nothing. She was still too angry. And she really did not care if anyone was concerned or not. Her husband was gone and her life was over. They could just stop her wagon by the side of the road and leave her here to die. It mattered little to her. In fact, it did not matter at all.

"Would you like something to eat?" the lieutenant asked. "I can find the bread Mrs. Lancaster set aside for you. Or I can see if I can find some dried beef. Do you have a preference?"

Hannah did not make any noise or acknowledge him in any way. She didn't care if she ever ate again. Her Drew was gone.

She startled when the lieutenant touched her shoulder softly.

"Hannah, you have to eat something. If not for you, then for the baby."

His comment angered her further. She grabbed his hand and threw it from her shoulder before spewing forth words coated in bitterness. "What baby? I don't have a baby. What are you talking about?" Was she losing her mind?

"Mrs. Lancaster said you were…um…with child and that if you moved so much as an inch I should ensure you ate."

The truth hit her, almost physically knocking her back as she suddenly realized she *was* with child. That explained the nausea for the past few weeks. She placed her hand on her stomach, tears streaming down her face again. This was not the picture of family she longed for. This was Drew's child. He was supposed to be here, at her side, to raise this child with her. Family was not a widow in a wilderness raising her child alone. But, she would do what she could for her child, her last living link to her treasured Drew.

Barely audible, she whispered, "Some bread would be nice." Needing little encouragement the lieutenant quickly offered her a small meal of bread, dried beef, and more water.

Still sitting in the dark wagon, she nibbled slowly. The lieutenant remained on the wagon seat as she ate, not attempting further conversation. Only when she finished eating and was once again settled down to sleep did he return to his tent.

As sunlight filtered through the opening of the wagon cover, Hannah woke. The wagon was already swaying. Curious as to who was driving the wagon, she moved so she could see out the narrow opening. It was Lieutenant Harrison! *Shouldn't he be with the cavalry? What was he doing?*

Though she wanted to stay abed all day and forget the tragedy consuming her thoughts, an urgent need to relieve herself spurred her forward. She climbed through the opening and took a seat next to the lieutenant.

"How are you this morning?" he asked.

Clearing her throat, she lied, "Fine." She would never be fine again.

"Good."

"Might we pull over for a minute?"

Hannah's expression must have shown the urgency, because Lieutenant Harrison did not hesitate to comply. She walked a short distance to a shrub to provide herself some privacy. She did not delay in returning to the wagon.

Once back on board, Harrison seemed eager to get moving again. She noticed his face was flush.

"Are you feeling well?" she asked, sitting stiffly at the far end of the seat.

"Fine," was his curt reply.

Her concern quickly vanished as a new wave of grief spilled into her heart. Staring at the back end of the wagon in front of them, she felt despondent. What would she do on her own? Would the aching never cease? How could she provide for herself and a little one? Drew was really gone, never to see his son or daughter born.

The home they were going to build in the Granite Creek settlement would never rise. The clinic he would run would never exist. Their child would grow up without a father. Oh, how he would have loved their child!

Instead of seeing the hopeful future Drew painted for her, she saw nothingness, blankness, death.

She became so consumed with her thoughts that she forgot Lieutenant Harrison was even there. She startled when he spoke.

"We should be stopping shortly for the midday meal. Mrs. Lancaster is most eager to see for herself how you are doing. She insists that she will take care of preparing the meal for you."

Hannah nodded numbly. Looking around as the wagon pulled into camp formation, she realized there was no snow on the ground and the temperature warmed considerably. How far had they traveled since... The accident?

Lieutenant Harrison set the brake on the wagon before circling around to her side. She let him help her down, too empty to manage the simple task on her own. Then he pulled a crate from the wagon and directed Hannah to sit there. She looked longing back towards the mountains far off in the distance—Drew's final resting place.

As she sat, she stared at her fingernails, keenly aware of how chipped and uneven they were. Strange how the oddest thing brought some sense of normalcy. Clasping her hands together, she let her gaze drift to the ground. Tall grass hid her feet and brushed against the long skirt of her calico dress. The soft blue color had been Drew's favorite, she thought as she unclasped her hands and brushed the dust from the dress.

Blue. As a widow, she should be wearing black. But, she did not own any black. And she was in the middle of a vastly unpopulated wilderness. Where would she find black cloth or black dye? And did she really want to destroy the dress that would always remind her of him?

Betty bounded over to where Hannah sat. Wrapping her in a motherly embrace, Betty said nothing. The gentleness of the action brought forth more tears. Hannah soaked in the compassion from the older woman as Betty stroked her hair and whispered words of love until Hannah calmed.

"You sit right there," ordered Betty as she started preparing the meal. "I know you are dealing with a lot, dear, but we need to come up with a plan for you once we arrive at Granite Creek. You are welcome to help Paul and me with the boardinghouse. We will likely have more than we can handle on our own."

Now that someone else made mention of moving on with her life, Hannah refused to talk about it. There was no life without Drew. As she looked away, she was reminded of the way his face lit up when he teased her. His serious nature when treating patients was always followed by a kind soft voice, setting their minds at ease. She loved the way her heart would jump just at the sight of him coming into her kitchen from the clinic.

Those times were gone, left thousands of miles behind—locked away in some other lifetime. Buried under ten feet of snow.

She knew she should respond to Betty, but words would not come. She turned her face back to the older woman. With her eyes she begged the discussion to end. It was too painful to consider her future when she could not see beyond today. Betty must have read her expression, for she did not press the issue.

The next week passed in the familiar routine of the trail, only under a heavy shroud of grief. Hannah forced herself daily to gather firewood and prepare meals, hoping the routine action would pacify the ravenous pain chewing up her heart. Each day she looked forward to the time Lieutenant Harrison checked in with his commanding officer. For those few minutes she could feel the full depth of her agony without having to pretend she was fine. Then, when he returned, she would carefully put on her mask of hollowness and silence.

After the evening meal each night, Hannah and Lieutenant

Harrison sat around the fire with Betty and Paul. It should have been Drew there by her side. Some nights Betty started singing hymns with Paul and the lieutenant joining in. Hannah remained silent and distant, closing off her heart from everyone. She could not praise a God who would abandon her. Other nights, her friends would converse with her, trying to get her to decide where she would live and what she would do once they arrived in Granite Creek. But, Hannah would not respond.

While physically present, her heart was not. It was buried on that snowcapped mountain with her beloved. There was no funeral, no burial, no grave. She would never see him again, nor be able to visit his grave. Her Drew was forever gone.

Chapter 20

Fort Whipple, Arizona Territory
January 22, 1864

Since joining the California Volunteers, Lieutenant Joshua Harrison had seen numerous forts throughout the western territories in varying stages of permanency. Fort Whipple was probably the most primitive—just a large gathering of tents clustered together. Not a single permanent structure had been built in the month since the army established the fort. On one side of the camp, there were several corrals for the horses, oxen, cattle, and other livestock needed to support the military. Somewhere he even heard the clucking of chickens, probably hens to provide eggs for the large group of hungry soldiers.

The soldiers already occupying the fort formed precise lines as the governor and his party pulled to a stop. Joshua helped Hannah down from the wagon as the government officials made their way to a crudely constructed stage. Staying on the edge of the crowd, Joshua watched as the soldiers offered up an eighteen gun salute for the new governor. Then Major Willis spoke briefly, followed by the governor.

While the government officials announced their headquarters with the military at the fort for the next few months, the rest of the civilians continued into the town roughly twenty-five miles south. On horseback, the trip could be made in one day, but traveling in heavy laden wagons pulled by oxen and mules, the settlers should arrive in two.

When the brief celebration concluded, Joshua found a flat area to set up the tent for Hannah. The cavalry, of which he was still a member, was stationed here and here he would have to remain. And he wanted to keep Hannah close.

He and Mrs. Lancaster heatedly discussed what to do with Hannah this morning. While Mrs. Lancaster thought she would be better off working with her at the boardinghouse, Joshua disagreed. He thought Hannah should remain with him, where he could offer her protection. Hannah said nothing, resigned to let others decide her fate. In the end, Paul suggested to his mother that they get the boardinghouse set up first and let Joshua care for her. Then, perhaps once they were settled, they would see if she wished to join them.

After depositing Hannah with her belongings in her tent, Joshua sought out the supply officer. She would have no use for either her husband's medical supplies or the wagon and team. With her current state of mind, he saw no reason to involve her in disposing of these things. The supply officer eagerly purchased the medical supplies, wagon, and team for the army. Pocketing the cash, Joshua headed towards the mess hall.

Upon nearing the mess tent, he saw the long line of hungry men waiting for their turn to be served. Skipping ahead to peer into the tent, he saw there were but two lonely Mexican women frantically dishing up food for the hungry crowd. He spoke with the man in charge of the kitchen to secure a position for Hannah. She would probably not be pleased, but he also did not think she would refuse the position. Deciding dried beef and leftover bread would be meal enough, he left.

After checking in with the major, Joshua walked back towards Hannah's tent. As he suspected, the major ordered him to report back to his post with the cavalry tomorrow morning. Good thing he already made arrangements for Hannah's supplies and secured her a position as cook, for he would have limited time to care for her after today.

"Hannah," Joshua called to announce his presence outside her tent. With her acknowledgement, he entered, briefly realizing the impropriety of a single man entering a now single woman's tent. He tied back one side at the entrance leaving it open. With some embarrassment, it dawned on him how many of his actions in taking over her care slightly crossed the lines of proper society.

Having pondered what he was about to say for days, did not make the task any easier. Joshua nervously shifted his feet, kicking up little puffs of dust. The hollow look in her eyes furthered his resolve to say what he came to say. "I would like to discuss your future." When she parted her lips he stopped her before she could protest. "Wait, hear me out."

Hannah nodded and Joshua continued, "I know that you are still grieving your husband's death and what I am about to ask is unusual, but I think it is for the best. I would like you to marry me," he stated with the precision and authority he used to command his troops.

Seeing her brows furrow, Joshua realized he was making a mess of this. Of course she was not one of his men he could order around. He quickly softened his approach. "Would you like to marry me? I could provide safety for you and your child. I cannot promise to replace the husband you loved dearly, but I can promise to see to your needs. I would always treat you with the respect you deserve and I would care for your child as my own."

He swallowed as the silence stretched, wondering if he just made a grave error.

The words hung between them. Hannah was stunned and mortified. Did she hear the lieutenant correctly? Did he just ask her to marry him? Had he taken leave of his senses? Anger at the preposterous nature of his request rose from within her. She tamped it down, not wanting to disrespect him for an obviously difficult gesture.

Not knowing what else to say, she said, "But I don't even know your first name." She needed some time to think this through.

"Joshua," he replied, as if that would somehow make his request less absurd.

As the shock wore off, she knew she could not possibly accept his proposal. Drew had been gone but a few weeks. Her heart was still broken. She could not be with another man, even in name only. She would do what she needed to do to care for her child alone. Quietly, calmly she answered, "I cannot marry you."

"But you need someone who can care for you. Your child will need a father."

His persistence pulled Hannah from the numb stated she lived in for weeks, stirring the raw mix of emotions to boiling.

"My child has a father and he is dead! You cannot replace

Drew. No one can fill the emptiness I feel. You have no right to come in here and start ordering me around like one of your men." She stood, moving closer to the lieutenant. Poking her finger into his chest, she confronted him with full force of the rage churning within her. "You have taken control of my life since the moment my husband was buried on that mountain. You have ushered me from place to place like cattle, telling me when I should do what."

"Hannah, I am not suggesting you marry me so I can command you," he answered calmly, appearing unaffected by her tirade. "I just think life is going to be difficult for you on your own. I wanted to offer you protection."

"Why would you want to take on such a responsibility that is not yours to bear?"

"Because, God asks us to care for the widows and orphans. I have the means to do that for you."

"I do not care what God asks you to do! He has abandoned me. If he wanted to care for me, he would not have taken Drew!"

He took her shaky hands in his. The kind act deflated her gusto and she slumped her shoulders forward, barely holding the tears at bay.

"God has not abandoned you." The lieutenant's voice softened as he spoke. "He brought Mrs. Lancaster and me alongside you when you were consumed with grief. He cares for you and he will never leave you."

Hannah refused to believe what he was saying was true. God took Drew away. How could He love her?

Lieutenant Harrison knelt before her, still holding her hands. "If you don't want to marry me, you don't have to. I simply wanted to make the offer to relieve some of the burden you will face."

She probably should accept his offer. What would happen to her, a single woman on her own? How would she provide for herself, for her unborn child? When her father died and she needed to decide what to do with the farm, her aunt reminded her that men were better at reasoning through an emotional situation. Her uncle had made the best decision for her then. Perhaps Lieutenant Harrison was seeing this situation rationally. Perhaps she should listen to him.

Yet, the grief was too new, too raw. Drew had only been gone a few weeks. How could she possibly commit her life to someone else? And only to satisfy her need for security. It was not fair to her, her unborn child, or to the lieutenant.

Withdrawing her hands from his, she clasped them in front of her. Squaring her shoulders, she replied, "I can't. I just can't."

Lieutenant Harrison rose. His stoic face revealed nothing. He reached into his pocket and handed her some money. "This was from the sale of the medical supplies, wagon, and team. I was able to get a fair price from the supply officer."

"Thank you," she whispered, shamed by her earlier anger in the light of his compassion.

"I also spoke with the head man in charge of the mess tent. He needs another cook and you may have the job in exchange for free meals and a meager wage. He could use your help as early as tomorrow morning." After giving her directions on where to report, he strode over to the tent entrance.

"If you change your mind, Hannah, the offer still stands."

"Thank you, Lieutenant. I am grateful for a friend such as you."

Nodding, he left, leaving Hannah to wonder if she made the right decision.

Chop the onions. Cube the beef. Prepare a stew to feed nearly a hundred hungry men. Add some salt. Lift the heavy pot over the fire. Stir. Don't think about anything other than the task at hand. If you think, you will remember you are alone.

Stir. Watch the swirls of savory stew circle round the pot.

With deliberate thought, Hannah focused on her new job at the mess tent. She repeated the mantra of intentional thought daily. And for the past two weeks, it served her well, allowing her to get through the days without thinking of Drew and without crying. Only in the stillness of the late evening did she think of him, her love. Then, she cried until exhaustion swept her under its warm embrace.

No, she was doing it again. Letting her mind drift back to him. His blue eyes. His long gentle fingers.

Stop!

Get the coffee beans. Grind the coffee beans. Start the coffee.

Keep thinking about the little things, the mundane.

Hannah looked up from the third pot of coffee she started as the men filed in to the mess tent for their midday meal. The meals quickly became her favorite part of the day. It was much easier to keep her thoughts and emotions under control when she was serving the men.

She pasted on a smile that she did not feel, before taking her place behind the large pot of hearty stew. Hannah smiled at the first young man in line as she took his plate. She mindlessly asked how he was doing and listened to his chatter until the man behind him thrust forth his plate. Most of the men talked to her as she dished up their food, most likely eager for attention from a woman.

Within days of being at the fort, Hannah understood why these men longed for female attention. There simply were very few women around. Besides herself, there was the post doctor's wife, the two Mexican women working in the mess tent, and a laundress. Five women versus nearly a hundred men. And from what she heard of town, Betty Lancaster was the only woman there.

So at each meal, whether or not Hannah felt like smiling, she did. In some strange way, just listening to these men helped heal some of her loneliness. They told stories of family back home, for many left their families in California. Others told stories of loved ones lost along the way. Some even tried to propose to Hannah once they found out she was a widow—at least until Lieutenant Harrison stepped in. She was not sure exactly how he did it, but one day the proposals just stopped.

Lieutenant Harrison. Since his awkward proposal, Hannah saw him but once in the past two weeks. Either he gave up eating altogether, or he was away from the fort. Though she wished he would have said something, she knew he owed her no explanation of his whereabouts. He offered his protection through marriage, and she refused him. She had no right to place any demands on him.

Yet, it would have helped her loneliness to know she had at least one friend here.

But, his absence doubled her doubt about her refusal. Perhaps Lieutenant Harrison was right. How could she care for a baby and work long hours at the mess tent? She barely had energy to care for herself at the end of each day. How could she care for a child, too?

Several times Hannah considered running to the lieutenant begging for his forgiveness, hoping to see if he would still have her. Then a memory of Drew would sear her heart and strengthen her resolve. It would be foolish to rush into anything now. Perhaps, in time, she would figure out what was truly best for her and her child.

Chapter 21

Colter Ranch

February 22, 1864

Will woke to the aroma of bacon already being fried. Stretching out his sore muscles, he took his time getting out of bed. Yesterday, he and several of the men finished a small cabin for his new cook, Rosa. He put off hiring someone to cook and do laundry for several months now. He finally hired the young half-Mexican half-Apache woman when Snake could no longer juggle cowboy duties with cooking duties. He really needed the man working with the cattle and managing the butchering.

At the beginning of the month, Will hired several men from the recently arrived wagon train to help build the ranch house. Most of the men agreed to work in exchange for fresh beef, which Will readily supplied. With so many men working together, the ranch house was completed in two days. He moved in immediately, more than ready for the solitude of his own house.

Sitting down at the table, alone, he lowered his head to say grace. When he finished, Rosa shoved the full plate in front of him with a curt, "Eat." Her three favorite words were eat, sit, and shoo. When she was satisfied he did not need anything else, she carried the prepared food across the lawn to the bunkhouse.

The first weeks in his house were wonderful. Peaceful quiet surrounded him each day. He was not on guard, constantly concerned for the image he projected to his men. Instead he could truly relax. Back in Texas, he craved the hour of solitude in his room before retiring each night. It never seemed long enough. But here, day after day, hour after endless hour of complete silence, Will felt lonely.

At first he tried to fill the silence with music from his guitar. Then he would read his Bible or another book. Then he would write letters to his sister. But after a few nights of the same, he grew bored.

He added small chores to the routine, like fixing bridles and saddles. But nothing staved off the loneliness.

The sound of shuffling feet drew his attention to the doorway.

"Who do you want to ride into Fort Whipple with you this morning?" Ben asked.

Will finished his last bite before answering, "I'll take Jed and Covington."

"I'll have 'em bring Jackson up in a few minutes then."

As Will took one last chug of his coffee, he pushed away from the table, trying to push away the loneliness as well.

The men were waiting for him out front as promised. Mounting his steed, Will led the way north to Fort Whipple. Last month, shortly after Governor Goodwin arrived, Will met with the supply officer at the fort to see if they would be interested in purchasing some beef cattle from Colter Ranch. He took a few head to show the supply officer the quality and the officer purchased them on the spot. He asked Will to come back in a few weeks to discuss a contract.

Pulling into Fort Whipple a few hours later, the three men rounded the steers into a corral. Will left Jed and Covington instructions to stay with the animals until he completed his discussion with the purchaser. The supply officer, glad to see Will, quickly concluded the negotiations. He was pleased the army agreed to purchase one hundred head to be delivered every month. With the army contract and the contract with several establishments in town, Will would not need to drive more than a few hundred longhorns across the Indian infested wilderness to the California market. Perhaps, in time, he would have no need to drive cattle to California at all.

Gathering his men, they headed to the mess tent to get some food before making the trek back to the ranch. Beans, potatoes, and beef steak were the perfect solution to hungry bellies.

As they progressed their way through the line Will scanned the tent, a habit from years of scanning the horizon while working with the cattle. His eyes stopped abruptly on the lovely young white woman chatting jovially with an officer as she dished up his food. His heart beat faster at the sight of her. Her hair was the most interesting shade of blonde with touches of red. Even from this distance, he could see her eyes were as blue as the vast Arizona sky.

Her ivory skin looked soft. What would it be like to touch her?

Snickers from Covington and Jed roused Will from his overt interest. Embarrassed for acting like a school boy, Will chided himself, feeling heat rise to his face. It had been a long time since he laid eyes on a young beautiful white woman. That must be why she was affecting him so.

In a few more steps he and his men would be standing directly in front of her. Though he tried not to stare, he couldn't help it. Her pert lips stretched thin in a smile that did not quite make it to her eyes. Her voice sounded light and sweet, like an angel. He tried to take in all of her lovely features, but most were blocked by the line of men in front of him.

Suddenly, the woman yelped in pain. She doubled over clutching her stomach. Will jerked forward slightly, ready to lend aid. In a moment the pain subsided and she stood straight again, her face still rather pale. His eyes moved to where one hand lingered over the swell of her stomach. It was then Will noticed she was with child. He felt twice as foolish for his earlier thoughts, realizing she was probably married to that young officer he saw earlier.

The young officer rushed to her side. "Hannah, are you alright?"

"I'm fine, Harrison," she answered with a heavy breath. "I'll go lie down after I finish serving these men."

The man named Harrison hesitated then returned to his half eaten meal.

Seeing it was his turn to be served, Will held out his plate. "Ma'am," he said with a nod as she lifted the ladle of beans toward his plate. Before tilting the ladle to the side to deposit food on his plate, her eyes grew wide and she doubled over again. The ladle slipped from her hand landing on the ground with a soft thud. Instinctively, Will let his plate fall to the ground as he caught her around the waist. Covington was right there with him. Jed was about to take off for the post doctor when Harrison took the woman in his arms and ran out—but not before Will noticed the blood staining her dress.

It was few minutes before the men in the mess tent returned their attention to their meal. Will picked up his plate, dusting off the bits of dirt. One of the Mexican women jumped in to serve the remaining men. As they found their way to a table, Will offered up a brief prayer for the woman, certain she could use it.

Hannah's screams sent fear crawling down Joshua's spine as he swept her into his arms. Frantic, he ran to Dr. Murphy's tent, shouting for Mrs. Murphy to ready a bed. It was when he gently laid Hannah on the bed that he saw it. Her dress was covered in blood.

She screamed fiercely, barely able to catch her breath between bursts of pain. Hannah clutched his hand, the pressure of her grip strong. Not knowing what else to do, Joshua stood by her side. She looked up at him with eyes full of fear. "It's too soon," she panted, almost as if asking him to make it stop. How he wished he could.

Dr. Murphy quickly assessed the situation and enlisted the aid of his wife. Mrs. Murphy produced a stack of towels and bandages, before retrieving some water. The doctor turned and asked Joshua, "When is she due?"

Joshua shook his head. He had no idea. It was not something they discussed.

The doctor muttered something, then Mrs. Murphy ushered Joshua outside. Not wanting to go far in case Hannah needed him, he took a seat on the ground just outside of the medical tent. The screams seemed to last forever. He lowered his head to his hands, lifting prayers heavenward. He was certain there was no hope for the child, but he prayed for Hannah, for her life.

His heart broke for the overwhelming grief she faced these last few months. First the loss of her husband. Now… He did not want to think how deeply she would grieve if she lost this child, too. He knew how it would affect him if it was his child.

Sometime around eleven at night, Mrs. Murphy laid a hand on his shoulder. "I'm sorry, but the baby did not survive," she said. "Your wife is resting, but you may see her now."

He was too concerned for Hannah's safety to correct the doctor's wife, though he wished what she said was true. Jumping up quickly, the numbness in his legs slowed him. Shaking each leg to get the blood flowing, he passed through the curtain. The sight of Hannah's frail form brought a groan from his lips. Her skin was gray and her eyes appeared sunken. Perspiration dotted her forehead. Her hair had fallen loose of the normally neat chignon. Instead, it was a tangled mess—yet beautiful. Reaching over, he gently rested his hand on her head praying for the Lord to heal her. She did not stir at his touch.

Not wanting to leave, he took the seat next to her and kept his hand over hers. When did she become so important to him? He wondered as a fierce protectiveness flooded his heart. He wanted to shield her from this pain. He wanted to make life better for her. Keep her from harm.

Mrs. Murphy was at his side again speaking softly. Judging by the crick in his neck, Joshua must have fallen asleep in the chair.

As dawn lit the tent, he shot to his feet. He missed his scheduled report to the major! If he did not leave now, he would have to report for his morning duties unshaven and in yesterday's uniform. He rushed back to his tent after letting the doctor's wife know he would return later to check on Hannah, hoping he would be in less trouble than he thought.

Chapter 22

Hannah tried to move, but her limbs felt like giant logs, stiff and nearly impossible to lift. She saw a kindly woman grab a wet cloth before turning to face her.

As she mopped Hannah's forehead, she said, "Glad to see you are awake. Your husband will be greatly relieved."

Confused, Hannah asked, "Drew?"

The woman paused, looking perplexed. "Joshua," she offered before introducing herself as Mrs. Murphy, the post doctor's wife. "But you may call me Martha."

Martha helped Hannah sit up and drink some water. Absently, she placed her hand on her stomach. Her eyes grew wide when she no longer felt the bulge of pregnancy. What happened to her baby?

Martha placed a calming hand on her shoulder. With soft words she said, "I'm so sorry, Hannah, but the baby was lost."

Tears welled in Hannah's eyes as she sank back down into the bed. Her last connection to Drew was gone, ripping a new and deep cut into her heart. She truly had nothing left of her beloved. God had finally taken everything she held dear. Her mother. Her father. Her home. Her husband. Her child.

What kind of horrid deity could be so cruel, so heartless? Why could he not leave her alone or leave her with some hope? Why did he have to strip her of everything, leaving her an orphaned, homeless, widowed woman?

She would never trust him again. Never.

Sometime later, Hannah woke again. She heard soft voices nearby. It sounded like Lieutenant Harrison and the doctor's wife.

"Mrs. Murphy, although Hannah is very dear to me, she is not my wife."

Hannah breathed a sigh of relief. When Martha mentioned her husband the last time she woke, Hannah went from hope to despair in a few short seconds. Thankfully the lieutenant was setting Martha straight.

Joshua's voice continued, "Her husband died in the mountains shortly before our party arrived at the fort. He was my friend and I have taken it upon myself to see she is cared for."

"I see." Martha's voice sounded unconvinced.

"May I see her?"

The curtain parted and his gaze connected with hers. Hannah saw something more than concern in Lieutenant Harrison's eyes before he could mask it. He sat in the chair next to her taking her hand. She did not pull away, for she truly needed a friend right now—someone to lean on. Tears threatened to form, yet again, until Hannah looked away.

"Dr. Murphy says you will need to rest for several weeks," his voice was soft as he spoke. "I have taken the liberty of arranging for your care, so you need not worry about rushing back to work at the mess tent."

"Thank you, Lieutenant," Hannah replied.

"I am so sorry, Hannah." The compassion in his voice nearly undid her. His fingers gently ran across her knuckles, breaking down her resolve.

"Please don't. I don't want to remember all God has stripped from me," she whispered as rivulets moistened her face. She pulled her hand from his and absently brushed the blanket covering her empty womb. Looking away, she said coldly, "I'm tired and would like to rest now."

He stood without a word. Leaning over he placed a kiss on her forehead. As he straightened and turned to walk back through the curtain, she noticed a slight slump to his shoulders. Had she wounded him by her need for privacy?

She closed her eyes and let the healing sleep work.

"Hannah," Martha said, her voice sounding far off.

Hannah blinked several times trying to get the fog to lift. When her eyes opened fully, Martha stood by her side.

"I brought you some broth," she said, instructing Hannah to lean forward. She propped several pillows behind her until she sat up enough to eat.

"Joshua stopped by again this morning," Martha stated as she lifted the spoon to Hannah's lips.

She took the sip of salty liquid and swallowed. She glanced away, hoping to avoid showing any interest in the conversation. All she wanted to do was sleep forever. To be reunited with her beloved Drew and her miscarried child. She did not even know if her child had been a boy or a girl. They buried it before she could see.

"Here," Martha said to get her attention for the next sip of broth. Returning to her previous conversation, she said, "He wanted me to tell you he would be out with the governor's men again for the next several weeks."

Again, Hannah swallowed the broth, not commenting.

Lifting the spoon, Martha said, "That young man seems quite concerned about your wellbeing. Said he even tried to get assigned some duties close by so he could keep an eye on you."

Sip. Swallow. Silence.

"But, Major Willis refused his request."

Why did Joshua insist on butting in? Hannah thought. Couldn't he just leave her in peace? Leave her to her dark mood?

"What's that frown for?" Martha asked after the next sip slithered down her throat.

When Hannah remained silent, Martha did not press her further.

"Anyway, Joshua said he would come back to see you just as soon as he could."

At the next spoonful, Hannah shook her head. "No more," she said, referring to both the conversation and the broth. Shutting her eyes, she hoped Martha would assume she needed rest.

Sometime in the middle of the night, Hannah sat up, wide

awake. She stared up at the ceiling begging for sleep to return. She could not handle the thoughts that were waiting on the edge of her consciousness. She did not want to remember she was alone, abandoned.

Sobs escaped from the captivity of her throat. She could control them no longer. She cried for Drew. She cried for her dead child. She cried for the loss of her dreams of a new life in this wild territory with her beloved. She cried for the past loss of her mother and of her father. She cried for her lost relationship with her savior.

She was so cold, so lonely, so desperate.

She had no one. Not God. Not family. Not her husband. Not her friends. She was utterly alone.

A light flickered on and approached closer, illuminating Martha.

"Oh, Hannah," she exclaimed as she set the lamp on the stand next to Hannah's bed. Then she took Hannah in her arms and rocked her back and forth. "There, there. Let it all out."

She sobbed for what seemed like hours. Martha said nothing. She did not try to offer any advice or convince Hannah that God still cared. She didn't recite verses about how everything would work out. Instead, she just held Hannah until, at last, the tears dried up.

Sniffling, Hannah took the handkerchief Martha handed her. She blew her nose and wiped her eyes. Then she lay back against the soft bed, letting sleep take over once again.

Finally, four weeks later, Dr. Murphy pronounced Hannah fit enough to return home to her own tent. She was cleared to work for part of the day with the strong admonition that if she felt tired, she should rest. The man who ran the mess tent was eager to have her return under any condition. The constant flow of government men in addition to feeding the army was more than they could handle without Hannah.

Days became filled with routine again. She slept past the morning meal, still physically recovering. Then midmorning she would wake, dress, and head to the mess tent. Hannah prepared the midday meal then helped serve it, before retiring back to her tent for rest. The other two women prepared the evening meal, but Hannah returned to help serve. As her strength increased, she increased her responsibilities.

This particular day, a Sunday, Hannah rushed from the mess tent to Charles and Martha Murphy's tent. Since returning to work, she reserved Sunday afternoons for the couple who became dear friends. Though she was far from forgiving God for destroying her life, she felt comfort in spending the afternoon with the Murphy's.

"Knock, knock," she said as she poked her head into their tent.

"Hannah, come on in," Dr. Charles Murphy greeted.

Martha gave her a warm embrace, then motioned her to a seat. "How have you been?"

"Tired," Hannah said, smiling.

"Shall we get started?" Charles asked, opening his Bible.

Hannah inwardly cringed, as she had every week, not ready to let go of her anger. Yet, each week she returned. She did not understand her own reasoning for coming back.

Soon Charles' deep bass voice filled the room as he read a passage of scripture. Over and over it seemed the passages Charles picked talked of God's enduring love and faithfulness. The more she listened the more she let go of some of her distrust.

Following today's reading Charles excused himself, giving Hannah and Martha some time alone. Martha appeared a bit nervous, shifting in her chair.

"Hannah," she said, "I just wanted to let you know that you are not alone in your loss."

Hannah sharply sucked in air through her nose.

Before she could respond, Martha continued, "I, too, have lost not one, but three children." Martha broke eye contact and fiddled with the handkerchief clutched in her hand. "My first child miscarried, much like what you experienced." Tears formed in the corner of her eyes, but held without spilling over. "Then, my second child, a son... He died of whooping cough as an infant. Sad, isn't it, that a doctor can work to save the lives of so many, but loses his own son?"

Martha's voice broke and the tears flowed. "It was so hard when he died. Charles blamed himself for the longest time. And I became bitter. I guess I blamed him, too. I mean, he was a doctor and had cured hundreds of infants with whooping cough with success. All except our son."

Martha sniffed and dabbed at her eyes. Hannah sat ramrod straight listening intently to the tale. Who would have ever known, looking at Martha today, that she had faced such insurmountable loss?

"Then, when our third child was born, Lilly, both Charles and I were overjoyed. She was such a precious little girl. We loved her dearly. When she was three years old... She got the measles. Charles and I tended her day and night. Then one day the fever broke... It appeared she was on the mend..."

A sob caught in Martha's throat. "The next morning, when I went to check on her, she was gone."

Tears came to Hannah's eyes. Martha stood and wrapped her arms around Hannah. They both cried, letting some of the sorrow flee from their broken motherly hearts.

After several minutes, Martha stepped back. Grasping Hannah's hands in hers, she said, "I tell you these things, not for your pity, but to help you understand that you are not alone in your grief. You have a sister here before you that has walked a most sorrowful journey and survived."

Looking her straight in the eyes, Martha said again, "You are not alone."

Hannah nodded numbly, not quite ready to let that truth fully sink in.

Martha released her hands. Dabbing her eyes, she said, "If you ever want to talk to me about any of the heartache you are going through, please know that I am here for you."

Hannah nodded, trying to remain detached. "I better get back. It's past time to start supper preparations."

Martha smiled. "Go with God."

The words echoed in her mind as she walked back to the mess tent. By the time she arrived, the two Mexican women already had the meal well under way. They assured her that they could cover things for tonight, sending her back to her tent.

Laying down on her bed, she thought of all that Martha said. Though Martha had not lost her husband, she had lost three children. Surely her grief equaled that of Hannah's. Yet, here she was, however many years later, a sweet compassionate woman—not a hint of grief present.

Hannah wondered if she might heal so well from this burden of grief. How long would it take?

Joshua was disappointed when he returned to Fort Whipple, only to be sent out again with fresh horses. He and his men spent the better part of the month escorting the governor on his tour of the territory. When they returned to the fort this morning, he thought Major Willis would give them several days off, but instead he immediately gave him a new assignment.

The gentle lope of his horse calmed Joshua's earlier anger at Major Willis. He hoped to check on Hannah before departing again, but the major only gave him enough time to change into a fresh uniform and gather a few supplies for the next week. There was no time to find Hannah, much less have a meaningful conversation.

When he left over a month ago, she was still recovering from the loss of her baby. It pained him to leave her in such a state, but his first duty was to the army and not to the wife of his lost friend. However, Joshua found it impossible to think of her as Drew's wife any longer. Despite how ill-conceived his proposal had been, in the weeks away from her, he wished she had agreed to become his wife. He missed her and thought of her often.

Nonetheless, there was little he could do about any of that now. He and his men were out on patrol for the next several weeks, escorting the military mail between Fort Whipple and Fort Wingate in New Mexico. Like always, Joshua would place his focus on his work, placing his life on hold for another time.

Chapter 23

Arizona Territory

March 29, 1864

Will, Ben, and several other hands rode into town. Lieutenant Colonel King Woolsey called a meeting of the area miners, ranchers, and other settlers following the recent Apache attacks. Three Americans and five Mexicans had been killed a few days ago, this coming closely on the heels of a cowboy's brutal murder in town. All the deaths were being attributed to the savage Apaches.

Listening carefully, Will found Woolsey to be a charismatic fellow. He rallied the men with his talk of revenge. When he stated that the only good Indian was a dead one, the crowd cheered. The Apaches had been terrorizing the citizens of central Arizona for months now and the latest attacks stirred their anger. They wanted blood for blood. Woolsey was there to meet that need.

Will was concerned both by the Indian raids and by the blood thirsty settlers. While he longed for a more peaceful resolution, he knew it was unlikely to come without loss of life first. Pushing aside his own opinion on the matter, he had a duty as a local rancher to assist in tracking down the offending savages.

By the end of the day, Woolsey amassed one hundred volunteers comprised of the ranchers, miners, friendly Maricopa Indians, Mexicans, and townsfolk. Will, Ben Shepherd, Pedro Morales, and Sam Whitten represented Colter Ranch. The group of Arizona Volunteers followed Lieutenant Colonel Woolsey's direction and set off in pursuit of the Apaches.

On the third night of their pursuit, Woolsey announced they would continue marching through the night. He divided the men into three companies. Will and his hands were part of the company that moved down the center of the nearby Squaw Canyon. Within two days, the B Company spotted the band of Apaches.

Charging with the rest of the men, Will loaded his rifle and fired at the Indians. Ben was to his left taking similar action. On the other side of Ben, Whitten and Pedro joined the fight. Smoke from the weapons fire permeated the air. The war cries of the Apaches echoed off the canyon walls as Will and his men advanced.

As they pressed further into the canyon, the Apaches fled directly into the path of one of the other companies. Caught between the canyon walls and two companies, the Indians were at a disadvantage. Whitten hit one of the Apaches in the leg as he dove for cover. Both Pedro and Ben hit one Indian each killing them on contact. As the Indians began to scatter, several more were shot down by. The battle lasted a half hour before a large number of the Apaches found escape. Will counted at least fourteen dead and several more injured.

Not to be easily deterred, Woolsey sent a few men off to rendezvous with the remaining company, while the rest of the men pursued the fleeing savages for a few more days. The volunteers' provisions were running low, so they finally gave up chasing the Indians and returned home.

Riding over the mountain towards home, Will thought of what they had done. He found it a difficult experience to forget. He knew that as long as the Apache attacks were left unanswered, the settlers would never be safe. Yet, General Carleton's "extermination" order and Woolsey's blood thirst for the Apaches seemed extreme. There was no perfect solution. If both sides refused to meet halfway, the killing would continue until one side came out the victor. He suspected in the end the Apaches would be the ones to suffer the most.

One thing Will knew for certain, he would keep his focus on ranching. No longer would he participate in Woolsey's raids, nor would he fight the Apaches except in self-defense. He had no taste for killing.

Chapter 24

Fort Whipple

May 16, 1864

Hannah reached up to wipe the sweat from her brow. Though the temperature was pleasant, the sun beat down on her and the two Mexican women from the mess tent as they packed crates of food and supplies.

Upon the governor's return from Tucson, he announced the Granite Creek area would become the official territorial capital, to be named at a town meeting at the end of the month. Since the military provided protection for the settlers, Major Willis ordered the temporary fort moved to just one mile northeast of the town, instead of the current twenty-five miles. The entire fort was a flurry of chaotic activity.

For the past few days, Hannah and her coworkers prepared extra bread and other cold fare for the soldiers, cavalry, and civilians to pack on the two day move. The midday meal today would be the last hot meal prepared until they unpacked at the new fort location.

Stirring the beans over the fire, Hannah looked around at the emptying mess tent. Several soldiers made quick work of loading the crude tables and benches into one of the two wagons designated for the mess hall. Hannah doubted they would be able to fit all the furniture, tents, supplies, food, and dishes into only two wagons. Hopefully these men were very skilled at packing a wagon to overflowing.

Right on schedule, men formed a line for the midday meal. Hannah left the other two women to continue their packing while she went about serving the men. She instructed the hungry patrons to grab their own coffee—it would be self-service today—while she heaped food onto waiting plates. She kept her chatter with the men to a minimum, hoping to speed the line along. Since the furniture was packed, most of the men stood to scarf down the simple meal. After an hour, everyone was served and the tent cleared out.

Two men started dismantling the tent from around them, stealing the last of the cool shade. The rest of the packing would be done in the bright afternoon sun. Hannah ran her dress sleeve across her forehead, mopping up the newly formed beads of sweat. Oh, for a gentle breeze!

As the sun faded from the sky, Hannah took one last look around the mess tent area. Two overloaded wagons were the only thing in sight.

Having worked most of the day preparing the mess operations for the move, Hannah worked late into the evening on her own things. She secured the remaining crates and trunks of her belongings. She left a few small items she needed for the morning in her carpet bag. Besides the bag, her bedroll, and tent, everything was loaded and ready to go.

The next day, shortly after the morning meal, the last items were loaded and the fort became mobile. Hannah always thought of a fort as a stationary post until now. The cavalry split into two groups, one leading the train of wagons, the other bringing up the rear. Most of the civilian wagons were interspersed with military supply wagons, while many of the soldiers walked the twenty-five miles on foot.

For the first time since arriving in the Arizona Territory, she soaked in its beauty. The sky was wide and deep azure blue before them. The wagons jostled over rolling grassy hills skirting the forests of tall pine trees. The mountains to the southwest had odd rocky, almost boulder-like shapes peeking out between the trees. Hannah had never seen such chalky gray-white mountains before. The color sharply contrasted against the brightness of the sky and the dark green pines, causing her to squint at the sight. The dry air carried a heavy fragrance of pine. As the sun dropped behind the mountains, deep reds and streaks of light made a beautifully colored back drop for the now shadowed rocks.

As the wagon pulled to a stop, Hannah climbed down. Walking around to the back, she dug around in her carpet bag for some paper, and took off towards the forest. The edge of the forest nearest the campsite offered sparse cover, so she walked several more yards until coming to a boulder. She crouched down, quickly taking care of business. When she stood and smoothed out the skirt of her dress, she caught movement out of the corner of her eye. Taking a cautious step, she looked around the forest in the dimming light. Not seeing what caught her attention earlier, she turned back towards camp.

Stopping short, she let out a high pitched scream with all her might.

Joshua finished unsaddling his horse when he heard a woman's terrified scream. Dropping the saddle to the ground, he grabbed both his carbine and Dragoon revolver. Then he took off, with Bixley close by his side, towards the screams still echoing through the air. Dodging the tall ponderosa pines, he skirted a large boulder and that is when he saw her.

Hannah knelt on the ground, screaming like she was touched. She had her hands over her eyes so she didn't see him approach. Joshua looked around to find the source of her fear, but only saw the two Pima guides for the army standing nearby. They must have come running to lend aid. Bixley walked over to question the two Pima guides as Joshua knelt beside the hysterical woman.

"Hannah," Joshua said as he gently laid a hand on her shoulder.

She tensed and shrunk from his touch before dropping her hands to her sides.

"Whatever is the matter?"

Her face was pale and her breath came in short puffs. Slowly she turned her head towards him. The fear in her eyes scared him enough that he took another look around to make sure they were safe. Seeing nothing, he looked back into those beautiful blue eyes.

As he lifted his hand to push a strand of hair from her face, Joshua said, "Tell me what has you so frightened."

Her eyes darted away towards Bixley. Instantly she tensed. "Those Indians…"

"Those are the army's Pima guides. Is that what frightened you?" Joshua said as he wiped the tears from her cheek with his thumb.

She nodded.

"They are quite harmless. Good friends."

"I thought they were Apaches," she said as Joshua helped her to her feet.

Her foot caught on a rock and she lost her balance, falling towards him. Instinct propelled his arms forward, around her, to steady her. She was so close he could smell the sweet fragrance of her hair. Unwilling to let go, Joshua held her close. His breathing went shallow and his heart picked up pace. What would it be like to kiss her? He thought as he parted his lips.

"Everything okay, Lieutenant?" Bixley asked, breaking the spell.

Joshua let go of her slowly, knowing Bixley would probably rile him for his behavior later.

Clearing his throat, he said to Hannah, "Come meet our Pima guides." She followed to his right, slightly behind as if still uncertain these Indians could be trusted. Joshua introduced her to the guides and after a brief explanation of the misunderstanding, everyone seemed more at ease.

Offering her his arm, Joshua led her back to camp, notably aware of her light touch on his arm. He performed similar gentlemanly acts numerous times with her. Why were his senses suddenly in tune with her every breath?

He stopped at the campfire near the mess wagon. When Hannah let go of his arm to retrieve her bedroll, he suddenly felt her absence. Joshua watched as she settled by the fire. Longing filled his heart as he stood there, realizing just how much he would like to keep her close. Perhaps he should reiterate his proposal from a few months ago.

On Sunday afternoon, Hannah tapped her foot impatiently as the last few men filtered into the mess tent at the new fort location for the midday meal. She could barely contain her excitement. She and Martha were going to visit Betty this afternoon on her half day off— which would start just as soon as these last few men were served.

She hurried back to her tent to clean up. Checking her appearance in the mirror, she looked as tired as she felt. Months of living in a tent added to her frustration. It would be so good to have a home again.

Hannah squared her shoulders, trying to think on better things, as she exited her tent. Martha stood waiting a few feet away, with Lieutenant Harrison and two men astride their cavalry horses. When she mentioned to the lieutenant the planned visit to town, he insisted that he accompany the ladies. Later she learned that Major Willis wanted all civilians escorted on any trips to town, despite the short one mile distance.

After greeting the lieutenant and Martha, Hannah waited as Lieutenant Harrison helped Martha into the wagon. Then, grasping her waist, he lifted her up to the seat. Taking the small spot next to Hannah, the lieutenant released the brake and started the wagon in motion.

Hannah surveyed the sights from her spot on the hard springboard seat sandwiched between Martha and the lieutenant. She had an image in her mind of what she thought the town would look like, but reality seemed more primitive than she imagined. In the center of town, there was a large square, what she would call a city block back in Cincinnati. The square included a smattering of log cabin structures, tents, and covered wagons. A clearly defined road outlined the edges of the square. The road was wide allowing enough room for a wagon to stop on one side and still allow two wagons to pass in opposite directions. On the other side of the wide perimeter road, there were more log cabins, tents, and covered wagons. Before arriving at the boardinghouse, Hannah had counted at least six semi-permanent structures, far fewer than she presumed.

Lieutenant Harrison turned the wagon down one of the streets bordering the town square before stopping in front of one of the log cabin structures. A simple painted sign announced "Lancaster's Boardinghouse." Lieutenant Harrison jumped down from the wagon. Before he turned to help her down, she exited from the other side behind an excited Martha.

"Hannah!" Betty's cheerful greeting reached her ears before the woman stepped from the doorway. Betty engulfed her in a firm embrace and Hannah savored the comforting action.

"This must be Mrs. Murphy," Betty said as she released Hannah.

"Betty, pleased to meet you," Martha said as she was engulfed in an equally warm hug. "Please, call me Martha."

"Come, dears," Betty said, leading her visitors into the dining hall. "We'll take our tea back in the kitchen."

As Hannah followed behind Betty, she studied the room. There were three rows of long tables with benches on both sides. It looked like the room could serve roughly thirty men, with ten or so at each table. Walking through the entrance to the kitchen, a wall stood immediately to the right. Straight ahead, along the back wall, there was a door. Betty propped it open to allow the fresh May air to fill the room. Next to the door was a fire fueled stove. On the wall opposite the stove was a table big enough to fit four people. The final wall was lined with shelves, acting as a pantry and dish storage.

"A real stove." Hannah sighed in admiration. She had not laid eyes on a real stove since leaving the clinic back in Ohio almost nine months ago. The memory threatened to spill gloom on a pleasant visit, so she forced her attention back to her friends.

Grabbing three mugs from a shelf, Betty poured tea for the three ladies. "Please sit," she said motioning towards the table.

As she took her seat, Hannah noticed another door off of the kitchen next to the open back door. That must lead to their private rooms or a storage area.

"This place is amazing. How did you and Paul build all of this so quickly?" Hannah asked.

"Well, we hired some of the miners and ranchers looking for extra cash. We have two bunkhouses out back where the men board. Each one can hold up to ten men, maybe more when we need to pack them in. The bunkhouses each have a small room where the men can wash up. Besides the outhouses, we also have a very small barn, if you want to call it that. That's where we house Gerdie and a few chickens. Gerdie's the milk goat. The small corral next to it will fit a horse or two and it gives Gerdie a place to stretch her legs."

"How many boarders do you have now? What do they do for a living?" Martha asked, lifting the steaming cup to her lips.

"Right now we have twelve men. Most are miners. A few of those government men stay here from time to time."

"How do you feed so many between you and Paul?" Hannah asked.

"Honestly, I could use some help. If I only had to worry about cooking, I could probably handle it. But with three meals a day, laundry, and cleaning, I've got my hands full. Paul doesn't get out to the mine as much as he'd like since most days he's stuck here helping me clean. He never complains about it but I know he would like me to find some help."

"I know how hard it can be just to feed a large group of men," Hannah sympathized.

"Mornings are the most difficult since I am often preparing packed lunches for the miners in addition to breakfast. The afternoon is when I get the cleaning done while they are off at the mines. Then, as soon as that's done, I'm working on supper."

"Do you serve meals for men who don't board here?" Martha asked.

"Yes. We have separate rates for individual meals. Most anyone who comes into town these days comes in for dinner. We often are left with some patrons standing, waiting for someone else to vacate a seat."

"Well, sounds like you *are* busy!" Hannah said.

"You are looking real good, Hannah. How have you been doing at that fort?" Betty asked.

Hannah started sharing about the routine of daily life at the fort, but before long Betty steered the conversation towards a more personal vein.

Looking into Hannah's eyes, Betty said, "I was so sorry to hear about the loss of your baby. I wish I could have been there for you through such a difficult time, dear."

The softness and compassion in Betty's tone broke down the barriers she had carefully erected around her heart. Tears streamed down her face.

"It was so hard to lose the baby..." She choked on a sob. "Especially with Drew gone. The baby was... my last connection to him."

Martha grasped Hannah's hand as Betty pulled her into a motherly hug. For several minutes, she let herself be comforted from her sorrow by her caring friends. When her tears finally stopped, Betty took the seat next to her.

"Dear, I know it is hard right now. But, I promise it will get easier with time."

Hannah nodded, wiping her face with her handkerchief. When she drained the last of her tea, Betty stood to refill it.

"Hannah," Martha said, "You should really think about moving into town and working with Betty."

Betty nearly dropped the teapot as she whirled around to look at Martha with a stunned expression. Hannah was certain her face mirrored the same surprise. What made Martha think of such a thing?

"Well, don't look so shocked," Martha said, looking from Hannah to Betty. "It makes perfect sense for both of you. Betty needs the help and the company would be good for you, Hannah. It doesn't sound like you would be working any harder than you do now."

"She's right. I would love to have you work for me," Betty agreed, excitement sparkling in her eyes. "I can pay you a decent wage beyond room and board." Taking on a look of mischief, she said, "We may have to boot Paul out to the bunkhouse, but I don't think he would mind, especially if it meant he could spend time working his placer mine."

Hannah thought for a moment. She was lonely at the fort. Besides Martha, the only ladies were her Mexican coworkers who spoke little English. She and Martha were always so busy they rarely had time to socialize. If she worked for Betty, she would be in town. And she would be near Betty, the woman who was like a mother to her. She would live in a building. Cook over a real stove. Stop living out of crates. Of course, Martha was right. Both she and Betty needed this arrangement.

"I'll do it. How soon do you need me?"

"Tomorrow would be just fine."

Martha beamed, obviously pleased to have orchestrated the entire thing.

Chapter 25

Once back at the fort, Hannah asked Joshua to walk with her for a moment. Looking forward to some time alone with her, he quickly agreed. He offered his arm then led her along the outer perimeter of the fort.

"Lieutenant," she started. Joshua really wished she would call him by his given name, but decided not to press the issue tonight. "I'm going to move into town."

At first Joshua thought he didn't hear her right. Stopping, he turned towards her. The pink tint to her cheeks and the brightness lighting her eyes showed her excitement. Why would she be moving to town? "When?"

"If possible, I would like to move tomorrow. I am going to work for Betty at the boardinghouse. She really needs the help."

Turning pensive for a moment Joshua said nothing. If she moved to town, he would rarely see her, as his duties kept him either at the fort or on patrol. She sounded so confident and sure of her decision. And he knew she and Betty were close friends. But that did not keep his heart from pricking at the thought of being separated from her. For just a brief moment he considered asking her to marry him again, but discounted the idea as being desperate.

"Lieutenant?" Hannah asked, stirring him from his thoughts.

"I beg your pardon," he replied. "My mind was elsewhere. What did you say?"

"Would you be able to help me move?"

Another twist drove the knife a little deeper. How could he convince her to stay? Should he?

As much as he wanted to keep her near, he would do anything for her. "Of course. I'll speak with the major first thing in the morning. I'm sure he will be agreeable, after all, we are here to help protect the citizens."

Leading her back to her tent, he bid her good evening, resisting every temptation to confess his feelings and convince her to stay. One thing was certain, he would greatly miss the lovely Hannah Anderson.

Morning dawned. Hannah still could not believe the quick decision she made yesterday about moving to town—yet it felt right. Nothing about her life in the Arizona Territory turned out the way she dreamed. Drew always made decisions for them, though he sought her opinion. Since losing him, she let others, mainly Joshua Harrison, fill that role. But, she was a widow, with no one seeing to her care. She needed to take charge of her own life now. So, she made her first decision, one she hoped would prove to be a good one.

Walking towards the mess tent, she dreaded telling the manager she was leaving, especially after he treated her so well and gave her the job sight unseen. Walking around to the back of the tent, Hannah greeted her two coworkers before spotting her manager. She took a deep breath and walked in his direction.

After a brief conversation, the manager told her he was thankful for her great work over the past months. If things didn't work out in town, he would gladly have her back. While comforted by his offer, she felt confident she would not be back.

As she walked back to her tent, Lieutenant Harrison already started loading her things into a wagon. He smiled as she approached before lifting the last trunk into the sparsely filled wagon. Then he turned and helped her up to the seat, climbing next to her.

The old familiar sway of the wagon seemed almost comforting to her, calming her nervousness about the move. Joshua must have sensed her mood, for he said nothing during the short trip to town, an odd silence from the man who conversed so easily with her.

As they turned down the street in front of Lancaster's Boardinghouse, Betty waved a greeting. Hannah smiled and waved in return. Paul stepped out from the dining hall as Joshua pulled the wagon to a stop.

Hannah sighed. This was her new home.

"You can pull the wagon around to the side door," Paul said, indicating a separate door to the personal living quarters on the outside of the building.

Once Joshua stopped the wagon in the designated area, Paul helped Hannah down.

"Ma had me clear my stuff out this morning, so the place is all ready for you," he said. "Go in and take a look around. The lieutenant and I will bring in your things."

Hannah stepped into the small living quarters, giving her eyes a minute to adjust to the dimmer light. Only one window graced the room, allowing light to filter in from the town square. Next to the door she entered, sat two chairs and a small table. A wood heating stove stood near the center of the room, to allow for maximum heat in the winter. The rest of the space was sectioned off by two curtains strung on a line across the length of the room. She passed through the curtain and quickly discovered a bed and small dresser penned in by another curtain. Lifting back the edge, she saw another bed and small dresser, with a few items scattered on the top. A Bible lay on the corner closest to the bed. That must be Betty's room.

A clearing of a throat behind her caused Hannah to jump back, dropping the curtain closed.

"Where do you want this?" Joshua said. When had she stopped thinking of him as the lieutenant?

As he looked around the small bedroom of sorts, his face flushed when his gaze reconnected with hers. She felt a similar heat touch her cheeks as she realized he was standing in her room. Why should such a simple act cause such a reaction?

He shuffled his feet, stirring Hannah from her confusing thoughts. Pointing toward the foot of the bed, she barely squeaked out a "There." She was acting like a silly buffoon.

Slowly Joshua slid the trunk from his shoulder. Once it was safely on the ground, Hannah caught him rubbing his shoulder. Heat rose to her cheeks again as she realized she kept him waiting too long.

Paul bounded into the room with the last of her things and deposited them on the floor in a pile as Betty bustled into the room.

Looking at Joshua, she said, "Dear, won't you join us for dinner before you return to the fort?"

"Certainly. Lead the way."

Betty took them through the door between the living quarters and the kitchen, before leading them back into the dining hall. Two patrons sat at the middle table, so Betty led them to the table closest to the kitchen. Once Hannah and Joshua were seated, Betty and Paul brought in coffee and food for all four of them.

After a quick prayer, Paul said, "Hannah, you have no idea how glad I was to hear you were coming. Ma is working far too hard and I was getting worried about her."

"Nonsense," Betty replied, swatting at her son's arm. "I am just fine."

"Don't let her fool you. She needs the help." At his mother's glare, he said, "What? I've seen the way you fall into bed exhausted each night."

"You make it sound like I'm ready to go to glory," Betty teased her son. Taking a more serious tone, she turned to Hannah, "But, I am grateful for the company." Betty winked, "It will make laundry go so much faster with someone to talk to."

Hannah laughed. She forgot just how much she missed the dynamic mother and son.

Glancing over at Joshua she saw him jerk his head away suddenly, as if the corner of the room held something that warranted his concentrated attention. He was acting so odd today.

As Hannah finished her last bite, Betty stood. When Hannah started to rise, Betty said, "You just sit, dear. Soon enough you'll be on your feet all hours of the day. Paul and I will take care of this." She motioned her arm over the dishes Paul stacked neatly into a pile.

When mother and son retreated to the kitchen, Hannah looked over at Joshua again. His gaze bore through her. She supposed this would be the last time she would see him for a while.

Joshua looked over at Hannah, her blue eyes shimmering in the light from the oil lamp on the table. The impulse to reach for her hand was strong, but he kept his palms flat on the table in front of him. Clearly she had something to say, but remained silent for a few breaths.

"Joshua," she started. His heart soared. She finally used his given name. "Thank you for everything... Not just for today, but for..."

Holding up his hand he stopped her. "There is no need to thank me for that," he said, knowing she was about to thank him for taking care of her after Drew's death. He would have done anything he could for Drew. The look in her eyes told him he read her correctly.

Not wanting to part without some assurance of seeing her again, he said, "I hope that you might allow me to visit from time to time. I've come to treasure your friendship and will miss it." He inwardly kicked himself as he stood, knowing that she had become so much more than a friend to him.

Hannah stood and followed him outside. "I would welcome your company, for you, too, are a treasured friend."

Before he knew what happened, she gave him a quick kiss on the check. Then she turned and was gone. Unconsciously, he rubbed the spot her lips had touched, astonished at how deeply he was affected by the innocent action. He needed to find an excuse to get back to town often.

After saying her farewells to Joshua, Hannah searched for Betty. She found her friend in the back hanging sheets on the clothesline. Lifting the next one from the basket, Hannah pinned it on the line.

"That young man is smitten with you," Betty stated matter-of-factly.

Confused, Hannah asked, "What young man?"

"The lieutenant."

"That could not possibly be."

Betty snorted, apparently not agreeing with her assessment. Changing the subject, Betty said, "After we finish hanging the laundry, I'd like your help cleaning the washroom in 'Gold Rush'."

At Hannah's raised eyebrows, Betty explained, "'Gold Rush' is the north bunkhouse and 'Mother Lode' is the south bunkhouse. The men thought it would be funny to name them. I didn't see any harm in it, so the names stuck."

She smiled at the names, obviously the idea of a miner. Betty led her to Gold Rush and showed her what to clean.

Once that task was done, they started supper in the kitchen. Betty cut up the fixings for venison stew, while Hannah started the biscuits. As they worked, Betty explained the routine. Any man who wanted a packed lunch for the next day was to let her know at supper the night before. In the morning, they rose early to make the packed lunches, and then prepared breakfast. On rotating days, they laundered the bedding in the bunkhouses, washing only a few per day. They cleaned the washrooms on alternating days, so tomorrow they would clean the Mother Lode. The men were responsible for hauling their own water for bathing. If they wanted hot water, they could request it in advance and it cost extra. Any clothing they wanted laundered was to be placed in a designated area on their bunk. Anything else would be left alone. Wash days were Wednesday and Saturday. During those days, they did not launder sheets.

The men were expected to be clean when they showed up in the dining hall. There was to be no swearing, spitting, or drinking in the dining hall. What the men did in the bunkhouses was up to them, but Betty demanded they keep it civil. Paul hauled all of the water for cooking and cleaning from the town well. Having listened carefully to the long list of tasks, Hannah was astonished Betty managed to get it all done.

"One last thing, dear," Betty said, turning to look Hannah straight in the eye. "I will not tolerate any untoward behavior from these men. If any of them even so much as look at you funny, you tell Paul and he will take care of it. Many of these men ain't seen a young woman for a good long time, much less a real beauty like you. You remember what I said—be sure to let Paul know right away if you have any concerns."

Shortly after the admonition was issued, noise drifted in from the dining hall. The men began to gather with eager anticipation for their evening meal. Hannah pulled the last of the biscuits from the oven, still a little giddy over using a real stove. Betty dished up bowls of the stew and instructed Hannah to place the biscuits in three large serving baskets, one for each table.

Paul appeared from nowhere and began carrying the bowls out

four at a time, skillfully balancing them on his arms. Betty pointed at the biscuit filled baskets and gently prodded Hannah into the dining hall. The second she stepped over the threshold, all conversation stopped and every eye was on her. Heat rushed to her face and she wanted to turn and run. Taking a step back, she was blocked by Betty.

Seeing the situation was a bit uncomfortable, Betty stepped around her. "This is Mrs. Anderson. She works for me and you will be treating her respectfully, you got that? Now, please show her what fine manners your mamas taught you." She nudged Hannah further into the room.

"Howdy, Mrs. Anderson," several men said as she neared the first table. When she set the biscuit laden baskets on the table, they politely said, "Thank you, Mrs. Anderson." It was evident Betty was easily able to control the large group of men. Hannah retreated to the kitchen and Betty asked her to help serve the remaining bowls. She suggested Hannah take only as many as she could comfortably carry.

When the men finished eating, they handed their dishes down to one end, stacking them on top of each other. Paul took the stacks into the kitchen for cleaning while Hannah went around the room for the count of boxed lunches. The process took longer than expected, because the men were inquisitive about the new arrival.

"Where you from?" one short balding man asked.

Looking to the kitchen doorway, she saw Betty nod. She answered that question, as well as several more. By the time she had the list of lunches, she supposed they knew half of her life story. The men thanked her for a wonderful meal as they made their way out of the dining hall.

"You did real good, Hannah," Paul reassured her.

"Yes you did," Betty agreed. "Letting the men get to know you like that is a good thing. They will see you as a person, not just a pretty face. And, you'll find out when you get to know them, most of them are real lonely and are just looking for someone to talk to. They really are a harmless bunch."

Once the dishes were cleaned and stowed away, Hannah and Betty crossed into the personal quarters from the kitchen doorway. Betty showed her the dead bolt for both doors, stating that one could never be too careful. Exhausted, the two women retired to their beds.

Hannah's mind raced as she reviewed all of the events of the day. For the first night in ages, she did not think about Drew and fell asleep tear-free.

Chapter 26

Colter Ranch

May 29, 1864

Will grabbed a change of clothes and stuffed them into his saddle bags. Slinging his holster around his waist, he fastened the belt buckle. He checked the ammunition then placed the revolver in the holster. Too much Indian activity lately to risk being unprepared for the trip to town. Resting his saddle bags on his shoulder, he swiped the egg sandwich Rosa made from the plate on his table.

Closing the door behind him, he chomped down on a bite of the sandwich before settling the saddle bags on Jackson's rump. One handed, he mounted the stallion and *hupped* him into motion. As he moved the horse forward, he finished off the last of his breakfast. Ben followed behind on his mare, trailed by Covington and Whitten in the wagon.

When Bob Groom rode out to the ranch last week, Will had been surprised to see him. Other than occasionally running into him in town, he hadn't seen Groom since he surveyed his land last fall. Bob stayed for dinner, relaying a great deal of information about the changes in town. He told Will about the town meeting scheduled for tomorrow night. The plan was to name the town and go over some other business. Bob suggested that he attend.

It was a great opportunity to get to know more of his neighbors. Other than a few men at the fort, Lancasters, and the men from the Walker Party, he didn't know very many people in the area. With the town officially organizing, many people from all over the area should be there.

Making some new friends might help with his loneliness, too. More so in the last few months in the empty ranch house. The quiet evenings long ago became too quiet. The more time he spent there alone, the more he longed for a wife and children. He supposed it was the next natural progression in his life.

He would turn thirty soon. His father had been married for ten years at this age and was already raising two sons. Here Will was, building up his ranching business in his brand new home, alone. He should be content.

But he wasn't. He wanted the companionship of a wife. Pretty crazy idea when he'd only seen one or two women since arriving in the territory.

Will grunted. There was little hope of finding a wife here. At least not right now. Perhaps when more settlers moved to the area. Then again, perhaps he should just leave it in God's hands—since it would take a miracle to send him a wife in this wild territory. No single woman would venture here on her own. It would be too dangerous.

Maybe he should write to his sister to see if she knew of a young woman that would be willing to move to the Arizona Territory. Lots of men found their wives that way. What harm would there be in doing that? At least then he would not be so lonely.

No. He didn't want to commit to marrying a woman sight unseen. How would he know if she shared the same faith or cared to live in the wilderness? How would he even know if he liked her?

Breathing deeply, the fresh pine-scented air cleared his mind. Will focused his attention back on the road. He was starting to lag behind the wagon and needed to remain alert in case of danger. He must have been day-dreaming longer than he thought, for they were pulling into town already.

Covington called the wagon to a stop in front of Don Manuel Yeserea's store. The log cabin was the largest building in town and it doubled as both living quarters and store for the young owner from Santa Fe. He came west last fall to set up the store, resupplying with monthly shipments from Santa Fe. Will entered the building to pay for the supplies and then left the work of loading to Ben, Covington, and Whitten before leading his horse to Lancaster's Boardinghouse.

After tying Jackson to one of the hitching posts, he entered the dining hall. It was the busiest he'd ever seen it. Looking around for an open seat, Will stopped short when he saw a young woman cross the threshold from the kitchen. She was beautiful—stunning— despite a slightly frazzled look. He stood stock still, following her every movement with his eyes as his heart rate quickened. She smiled as she laid a plate full of food before a diner.

A man behind him cleared his throat rather loudly, mobilizing Will's feet. He quickly took the nearest seat, making sure his new vantage point offered a good view of the lovely server. When she turned her face his direction he sucked in a breath of air. Her eyes were the bluest he had ever seen—except maybe once before—mesmerizing.

The man sitting next to him jabbed in him the ribs with his elbow. "Pretty thing, ain't she," he said and then introduced himself, "Name's John Boggs."

What was wrong with him? Ever since moving to this territory, he acted all brainless when he saw a pretty woman. Not that he'd seen many. Just that one at the fort and this one. She's probably married, too.

"Will Colter," he said shaking the man's hand.

"Just don't let Mrs. Lancaster see you gawking at the young lady like that. She might run you outta here."

Still watching the young woman closely, Will only paid John partial attention while he shared his background. Originally from Missouri, he came west to make his fortune in a nearby placer mine. He stayed at the boardinghouse and on most days was out mining. With the influx of people for the big meeting tomorrow, he decided to stay in town to get to know some folks. The man enjoyed talking, that was for sure.

The young woman arrived at their table and greeted John Boggs by name before turning toward Will. "Will you be dining with us, Mr. ...?" the young woman hesitated, one eyebrow lifted in question.

She was even more beautiful this close. Swallowing the sudden lump in his throat, Will managed to stammer out his name. "Colter. Will Colter."

Propping one hand on her hip, she asked, with an impatient tenor, "Will you be dining with us, Mr. Will Colter?"

Nodding was the only encouragement she needed. She told him the price for the meal, collected the money, and set the plate of food in front of him. As she moved on to the next customer, he stared after her.

"Her name is Mrs. Anderson," Boggs said. "She used to work at the fort serving chow for the soldiers."

Will nearly choked on a bite of his food at the news. He looked at her again and suddenly realized why she looked so familiar. She was the woman who collapsed in his arms. Wasn't she married to that officer? Why would she be working in town if that were the case?

"Where's her husband?" he blurted out the question.

"Oh, she don't have a husband, least not any more. Heard he was a doctor and he died in an avalanche in the San Francisco Mountains on the way here. They were part of the group that came west with the governor. There was some lieutenant that helped her get the rest of the way here, but I don't know nothing else 'bout him."

Boggs rambled on about other things while they ate, but Will barely heard a thing he was saying. Mrs. Anderson was unattached, and for some reason that pleased him. He continued to watch her as she moved about the room. She wore a simple green calico dress with an apron covering most of the ensemble. Her hair was pulled back into some twist at the base of her neck. She had a good rapport with the boarders, laughing at some of their jokes and congratulating them on their recent mining success. She was comfortable jumping into conversations while she refilled coffee or brought an extra helping of food.

Frowning, he shook his head as if to clear his thoughts. He needed to stop staring and start eating.

"Is there something wrong with your meal, Mr. Colter?" concern edged her voice as she refilled his coffee, pointing towards the barely touched plate of food before him.

Clearing his throat, he frantically searched for an excuse to put her at ease. "Nothing wrong, ma'am. Just listening to Mr. Boggs instead of eating."

Chuckling, Boggs replied, "Yeah, I am sure it was *me* that captured your interest."

Will's face heated as the truth came out. Ducking his head, he hoped Mrs. Anderson would not notice his flushed face.

"Well, I might suggest you make eating a priority, Mr. Colter, so we don't have to kick you out when it comes time to start supper," Mrs. Anderson replied, the humor coating her words. When he looked up again, she flashed him the most brilliant smile before scurrying back to the kitchen.

Picking up his spoon, he started shoveling the food in, not wanting to disappoint Mrs. Anderson again. As Mr. Boggs excused himself, Will noticed he was the only customer remaining.

"Will!" Betty exclaimed as she bustled his direction. "A bit early to be bringing in more beef. Are you here for the meeting?"

As she sat down across from him, he nodded. "Yes. I was hoping you might have a bunk for me for a few days."

"Dear, we are filling up pretty fast, but we should have one left in Mother Lode." Turning her head toward the kitchen, she yelled, "Hannah! Leave those dishes and come in here. I want you to meet someone."

Hannah. The name was as lovely as its owner, Will thought.

Wiping her hands on her apron, Mrs. Anderson moved to Betty's side. A wry smile played on her adorable lips. She found this amusing.

"Have you met Mr. Colter?" Betty asked.

"I see you *were* planning on staying in the hall until supper," Mrs. Anderson giggled, eyeing his half-eaten meal.

Betty smiled. "Will is the rancher I was telling you about—the one that supplies all of our beef."

"Pleased to meet you, Mr. Colter. Again."

"Likewise," Will said.

Betty raised her eyebrows, as if she just thought of the cleverest idea. "He is in town for the meeting. Will you show him to the empty bunk in Mother Lode?"

Mrs. Anderson motioned toward the front door. "This way, Mr. Colter."

He stood and followed behind her as she led the way. Since her back faced him, he allowed his eyes to travel the length of her form. She was about the same height as his sister, just the right height for him to drape his arm around her shoulders. The strings of the apron formed a bow accenting her tiny waist and drawing his attention to the alluring sway of her hips. His mouth went dry at the unbidden thoughts aroused by his perusal. Chasing those thoughts from his mind, Will forced himself to look at the ground rather than notice any of her other pleasing features. He was acting like a buck, not a grown man. What was wrong with him?

She knocked on the door and called out a greeting before entering the Mother Lode bunkhouse. Walking down the line of bunks she stopped before one at the back. "This is the last one left, Mr. Colter. I hope this will do."

He nodded, unable to speak.

"This is the wash room area," she said, leading him to a small side room with a basin and pitcher of water.

Leading him back through the front door, she circled around the bunkhouse. "There should be one stall left in the stable for your horse. You'll have to feed and water him. And, over there," Mrs. Anderson said, pointing to a small building, "is the necessary."

When she turned to face him, Will realized he had been following too closely. She was mere inches from his chest. Swallowing hard, he took an involuntary step backwards as she craned her head to make eye contact.

Clearing her throat as pink flushed her cheeks, she said, "Well, I'll let you get settled then."

"Ma'am," he managed a quick farewell before she nervously stepped around him.

Watching her head back to the dining hall, Will tried to get himself under control. Walking back to the front, he unhitched Jackson and led him back to the barn. Removing the saddle, Will set it aside. He found a brush and began smoothing his horse's coat.

Mrs. Anderson had been so close when she turned around. And he had been shocked by the strong impulse to kiss her. He only just met the woman. Knew very little about her. Yet, he was drawn to her. Wanted to be near her. Wanted to get to know more about her.

Once he finished brushing Jackson down, he pitched a few forkfuls of hay into the stall.

"Must be going loony," he muttered to his faithful steed. For there was no other reason to be reacting the way he was.

Hannah hurried back to the kitchen. The day was busier than they expected. With the town meeting tomorrow, many area ranchers arrived early and several of the men who typically left for the mines stayed in town. Normally for dinner they had only a handful of men to feed. Not today. Somewhere around forty she stopped counting. Her feet hurt from rushing around and she longed to sit and rest a few minutes, but these dishes would not wash themselves.

When Paul arrived to fill the wash basin, she had him leave the door propped open. The kitchen was still warm and she needed the fresh air. The unexpected rush of customers left both her and Betty scrambling to finish all their chores. She would have to manage dishes by herself.

She glanced out the back window as she scrubbed the plate in her hand. Betty pulled down the last of the dry bedding from the clothesline. On her way to Gold Mine, she paused, exchanging a few words with Mr. Colter. He nodded his head and touched the brim of his light tan hat as Betty entered the bunkhouse. It would take her the next thirty minutes or so to redress all of the beds with the clean linens. As soon as Betty was done with that chore, she and Hannah would need to start supper preparations.

The soreness in her neck prompted Hannah to rock it back and forth as she set the wet plate aside. Sighing, she started on the next plate, deciding she would wash several in a group before drying them.

"Need some help?" a deep masculine voice said from the doorway.

Startled, Hannah jumped, splashing a great deal of water down the front of her dress and apron. Looking down, she cringed at the soaked mess before turning to see Mr. Colter. He stood in the doorway, leaning against the frame with one leg casually slung over the other resting on the tip of his boot. His arms were crossed loosely across his chest. Again she was struck by his height—nearly a good foot taller than Drew. And those golden eyes.

Remembering her drenched clothing, she quickly turned back towards the dish pan. Heat flamed her cheeks and her embarrassment was complete.

His voice sounded closer as he said, "Betty thought you could use some help and suggested I make myself useful."

She laughed nervously, honestly thankful for the help. She might get a few minutes to rest after all. Nodding her head towards the towel on a hook, she handed him a wet plate. He took both towel and dish, making quick work of the task.

Feeling awkward in the silence, she picked up the conversation. "So, Mr. Colter, where do you hail from?"

He took the next plate. "Texas. Born and raised on a cattle ranch."

His short answer did nothing to help her feel more comfortable. With most of the boarders, a question like that would result in at least a ten minute answer. Not so with Mr. Colter.

Trying again, she asked, "How long have you been out west?"

"Since late last fall."

That's it? Four short words? What a conversationalist! Forcing the frustration from her voice, she kept her tone light, "What brought you here?"

Silence, except for the swishing of dish water, answered her. At least he could make an effort to answer, even if he found her boring. Glancing his direction, she caught him staring at her. Quickly his gaze darted away as he cleared his throat.

After several more dishes changed hands and just when Hannah thought he was not going to answer, Mr. Colter spoke. "After my father died, my older brother got the ranch back in Texas. He and I got along as well as Cain and Abel, him being more like Cain. My inheritance was half the herd, half the money, and half the breeding stock. All I needed was land and I would have myself a ranch."

Hannah almost stared in surprise—so many words strung all together coming from the quiet cowboy.

He continued, "My father talked about the Arizona Territory often during the spring before he passed. Thought it would be a good place to raise cattle. When my sister, Julia, was clearing out his things she found several letters about the territory. The letters were quite detailed about this area and included information on the best route to get here. I was surprised my father even received the letters, given that Texas sided with the Confederacy. But somehow those letters arrived and somehow they were discovered just when I had to make a decision."

He paused, setting the plate in his hand aside. Turning his head, his eyes connected with hers. "It might sound silly, but I knew this was where God wanted me."

The circumstances that led him here could hardly be described as anything less than Providence, as he suggested. "No, it doesn't sound silly."

"What about you?" he asked, taking the mug from her extended hand.

"I'm afraid my story is a sad one," she answered, handing over another of the never ending supply of dishes. "My husband was a doctor in Cincinnati, Ohio. His brother ran into trouble with the law that left us ostracized by the community, forcing us to leave for a new home where Drew could continue to provide for us. Drew learned about the Arizona Territory from the newspaper. We originally thought to settle in La Paz. But, on the way here Betty and Paul convinced us this would be a better area."

Hannah paused, staring at the mug in her hand. "Like you, Drew thought the Lord was directing us here, only he didn't know it would ultimately lead to his death." Her voice wavered on the last words and she stopped abruptly.

"I'm sorry for your loss," he said, taking the last mug from her hand.

Swiping at the lone tear trickling down her face, she added, "What is done is done. No amount of wishing or praying will change what happened."

The silence stretched. Hannah blinked several times rapidly, hoping to hold any further tears at bay.

Mr. Colter's voice was soft and compassionate when he spoke, "You must miss him."

The lump in her throat kept her from saying more than, "I do."

As she stared into the dish water, Drew's reflection appeared. She missed those blue eyes, the laughter, the teasing. The years in Ohio had been wonderful. She hated that he never made it to their new home to see this beautiful land of his dreams.

A scuff of Mr. Colter's boot against the wooden floor reminded her she was not alone. Sighing heavily she said, "Thank you for your help. I don't think I would have finished before supper otherwise." She smiled, letting the sad memories melt away.

"Any time, Mrs. Anderson," he said as he touched his hand to the tip of his cowboy hat. Turning, he left the way he came, quickly and quietly, leaving Hannah to wonder about he said.

Chapter 27

Hannah rolled onto her side, stuffing her arm underneath her pillow. Why could she not get what Mr. Colter said out of her head? How could he be so sure God led him here? Rolling onto her other side, she closed her eyes again, but her mind would not be still.

Did God lead her and Drew here? It was a question too painful to contemplate. Drew seemed to think so. But, if it was true, did it mean God planned to take Drew? Did He plan to leave Hannah here alone?

Flopping onto her back, Hannah sighed. Light barely colored the sky, spilling in through the window as shades of gray. Resigning herself to starting her day, she threw back the light cover and plopped her feet on the floor. Propping her elbows on her knees, she rubbed the sleep from her eyes before standing. Donning the gray work dress, fitting her sullen mood, Hannah quickly brushed out her long hair. Then she slipped on her shawl without taking time to pin her hair back.

Picking up her Bible, she quietly exited through to the kitchen. Opening the door to the outside, she took a seat on the bench Paul built next to the back of the building. She sat there silently for a moment gazing out across the town square. A gentle breeze tickled her face. She closed her eyes and soaked up the early morning sun.

Opening her eyes she placed her Bible on her lap, reluctant to open it. Since the baby died, she had not really been on speaking terms with God. She didn't understand why he would take her child and her husband. It was so hard to be left behind. Even though she spent most Sundays studying the Bible with Charles and Martha, she had yet to open the pages and seek him on her own. She wanted to believe that God had some good purpose, some meaning for the tragic way her life turned out. Yet, she was afraid to ask—to learn that there might have been no purpose at all.

Lord, if it was your hand leading us west, what purpose could you possibly have in taking Drew's life and leaving me behind? A lone tear trickled down her face. The breeze lifted strands of her loose hair, carrying them over her shoulder. Fragrant pine tickled her nose.

The stillness of the morning failed to answer her question. Perhaps it was one that needed answering over time.

She desperately wanted to find her way. Questions poured from the depth of her heart. Who was she apart from Drew? Was it possible that God had some purpose for her life—something more than just going through the motions like she had since Drew died? What did the future hold for her? Was it his purpose that she work at Lancaster's? For how long? Would she ever have a family of her own? Would it last more than a few fleeting breaths on the face of this earth?

Looking back down at the Bible laying in her lap, she opened it to the Psalms. Eyes darting across the words, she read several chapters. Over and over, one word stood out above the rest: refuge. And each time the word was mentioned, it was always in conjunction with the Lord being her refuge. Though none of her questions seemed to be answered, the one she had not asked was. She was not alone. She had a refuge, a shelter in God—a shelter from the questions, from the unknowns.

Lord, help me to seek you as my refuge. Help me to know you are with me. Guide me in the path you would have me pursue. Show me for what good thing you brought me here.

Will woke early, not used to the strange noises of so many boarders crammed into a small space. Longing for the quiet, he threw on a pair of jeans over his drawers. Not bothering with a shirt, he stepped from the bunkhouse towards the outhouse. When he headed back to the bunkhouse, something caught his eye. Ducking behind a tree, he glanced past it to see Mrs. Anderson seated on a bench behind the dining hall. Her face was obscured by her long strawberry blonde hair as her head was bowed. Annoyed with himself for not taking the time to put on his shirt, he waited behind the cover of the tree for her to go inside.

Minutes ticked by and still she remained with her focus intent on the book in her hand. The sound of pages being turned seemed loud in the early morning stillness. Afraid he would draw her attention if he darted back to the bunkhouse, he stood still. Such a private moment, and he was gawking at her, unable to take his eyes from her.

His pulse quickened the longer he stared. She was lovely, attractive. Something about her drew him in. A flash in his mind's eye painted a picture of her standing over the stove in his ranch house. She seemed like she could belong there. Inwardly sighing, he chided himself for such thoughts. It was clear from their conversation yesterday afternoon that she still grieved for her lost husband.

Patience, Will. In time he would find a wife and make a family. No need to spend too much time thinking about it and trying to fit every pretty, unattached woman into that picture.

Stifling a laugh, he thought back to what his mother had called him—brooding. She said he was always working his mind over every little aspect of life. Too much brooding, she said, was a bad thing, making a man put too much faith in his own judgment instead of seeking God. His mother was right. He needed to stop brooding over his loneliness and let things be what they would be.

Pushing away from the cover of the tree, he considered making a break for it when a commotion from the front of the dining hall drew her attention. As soon as she was inside, Will ran back to the bunkhouse. He donned his shirt and belted his revolver holster around his waist. As he ran toward the front of the dining hall, he hastily buttoned his shirt. Several other boarders in various stages of dress, guns in hand, followed him.

Two uniformed men carried a third into the dining hall. Mrs. Anderson instructed the men to place their wounded compatriot on one of the tables. Will stood by ready to lend aid, amazed by her ability to stay calm.

Hannah quickly recovered from the shock of three soldiers storming through the front door. One of the young men explained they were on patrol south of the town when they stumbled across a gang of Mexican cattle thieves. The altercation left one of the men with a gunshot wound in his leg. Having assisted Drew with similar patients, she squared her shoulders and took charge.

"What's your name?" she said in a calming voice to the injured man.

"Jensen, ma'am."

"Well, Jensen, we will have you fixed up shortly."

Looking around for someone to help, Hannah's eyes landed on Mr. Colter. Looking directly into his eyes, she asked, "Would you place your hand here to help with the bleeding, while I go get a few supplies?"

When he failed to move, she took his hands and placed them over the wound. Turning on her heel, she hurried back to her room. Opening her trunk, she dug around for Drew's medical tools—the few she kept—and some laudanum. Grabbing a ribbon from her dresser, she ran back into the dining hall.

As she leaned forward to study the man's injuries, her long loose hair fell over her shoulder. Feeling a little scattered, she secured her hair with the ribbon, despite her shaky hands.

By now, Betty arrived with a stack of towels and bandages of every kind. Mr. Colter still stood over Jensen, pressing his hands against the wound. His eyes connected with Hannah's, his kind look giving her courage. She nodded, instructing Mr. Colter to move aside as Betty handed her several bandages. She placed the bandages over the wound to soak up some of the blood, as she had done dozens of times at Drew's side.

A moment of fear and self-doubt threatened. She took a deep breath, letting it out slowly. She could do this.

Betty whispered near her ear, "I already sent one of the soldiers for Doc Murphy."

Relieved by the news, Hannah knew she would not have too long to wait for help.

Jensen groaned. When she looked at him, he seemed frightened. "You'll be just fine," she encouraged.

As Betty tied a tourniquet above the wound, Hannah poured a

dose of the laudanum. She lifted it to his lips. "This should help with the pain."

He swallowed.

Removing the first set of bandages, Hannah took a clean one to mop up more of the blood. Studying the injury carefully, she looked for the corresponding exit wound. Only finding the entry wound, she assumed the bullet must still be lodged in Jensen's leg.

Looking through Drew's instruments, she failed to find a scalpel. She would need something sharp to cut open the wound in order to fish out the bullet.

"I need a knife," she said and several were proffered. She took the one from Mr. Colter, testing the blade to make sure it was good and sharp. It was—as she expected from the experienced rancher.

"Mr. Colter, Mr. Boggs, please hold Jensen down." Turning her attention to the young man writhing in pain she said, "I need to get the bullet out and to do that, I will have to cut near the wound. This is going to hurt."

He nodded, though his eyes started to gloss over as she began. When Jensen jerked away, she glared at Mr. Colter. "I need him still."

Mr. Colter tightened his hold as she carefully made the cut with the large awkward knife. Having Betty assist, she was able to quickly locate and extract the bullet. She poured some whiskey over the wound to clean it. Either the pain intensified or the laudanum started working, for Jensen passed out. She adeptly threaded a needle and stitched up his leg as best she could. Then she wrapped the leg in bandages.

"Let's get him to one of the bunks to rest," Betty suggested.

Mr. Colter and Mr. Boggs, carried the young man the short distance to the Mother Lode, followed by Hannah and Betty. One of the miners cleared his things off his bunk, offering it up for the injured man. Betty stayed with Jensen and shooed Hannah and the rest of the men out of the room. Having no other place to go, many went back into the dining hall.

Hannah started cleaning up the dining table turned surgery. Even though there seemed to be a large amount of blood staining her hands and apron, she was certain Jensen would survive. She had seen men recover fully from worse.

Scrubbing the table with vigor, the reality of what she had just done set in. She just cut open a man's leg and removed a bullet! Feeling light-headed and queasy, she started to make her way out back. As she crossed the threshold from kitchen to grassy lawn, her legs buckled beneath her. Strong arms clasped her waist keeping her from falling to the ground. She felt herself being eased to the bench where she sat just moments ago in silence with the Lord. Her head still swam, so she closed her eyes and leaned her head back against the cabin wall. With the first deep breath through her nostrils, she smelled a light scent of horse and man. The second breath added pine to the mix. A gentle hand held hers, giving her strength. As she opened her eyes, Will Colter stood before her, keeping her steady.

As the events of the morning hit her full force, she felt the bile rise to her throat. Twisting her torso to the side of the bench, she leaned over and retched. With unsteady hands, she found a non-blood-stained corner of her apron and wiped her mouth. Taking deep breaths she managed to recover. Mr. Colter handed her a cup of water, which she sipped slowly until it was gone.

"You did good," Mr. Colter said with an encouraging smile. "Without your quick action, that young man might have died."

Hannah nodded numbly as her nerves began to settle.

"How did you know what to do?"

"I assisted my husband many times with similar wounds. This was the first time I've done that on my own." She managed a half smile.

Standing, Mr. Colter offered her his arm for support, leading her back to the kitchen. The fragrance of frying bacon filled the air, causing her stomach to flutter. Entering the dining hall she saw it had been set to rights. Men stood slowly removing their hats or placing one hand over their hearts. The admiration in their eyes was clear and Hannah was humbled.

Dr. Murphy arrived with several mounted cavalry men. Hannah directed him to the patient and stood by while he conducted an examination. He was obviously impressed with how well she took care of the young man, because he praised her efforts several times. Another group arrived from the fort with a wagon to transport Jensen back. Since he was still out cold, they decided it would be best to leave in short order.

It wasn't until after they left that she noticed Martha Murphy. "You look exhausted," Martha said. "Don't worry about fixing breakfast for these men. Betty and I will take care of it. I'll be here to help all day, so you lie down and rest for a while."

Hannah quickly complied, her energy drained.

Will still thought about the events of the morning as he sat down for supper in the dining hall. The image of Mrs. Anderson sitting on the bench, Bible in hand, kept coming to his mind. She seemed at peace this morning in that private moment. Private. That is what it should have been—not with him looking on.

Then, she transformed into this confident skilled woman, removing the bullet from a young man's leg. How could he be anything but impressed with this woman?

As if thoughts of her could conjure her presence, she entered the dining hall. Mrs. Anderson missed the morning meal, but made an appearance at dinner earlier in the day. Now here she was, looking beautiful as ever, filling up coffee mugs for the supper hour. Her color returned and she looked more refreshed as the day went on. He smiled as she filled his mug.

When she moved to the next patron, Will turned his attention to the conversations around him. The town meeting was scheduled for this evening. Speculation abounded. Excitement mounted as the men looked forward to what Bob Groom and the town leaders would say.

Shortly before seven, Will arrived at Don Manuel's store, the site selected for the town meeting. They squeezed together to make room for as many men as possible. Bob Groom led the meeting. After a few cursory comments, he announced the leaders selected a name for the new town. Prescott was the name chosen in honor of the famous historian and writer. He also confirmed the rumors that Prescott was now the official capital selected by the governor. A large round of applause followed.

When the crowd quieted, Van Smith joined Bob in the front. They recently completed a survey of the town site, mapping out lots which would be auctioned on the fifth of June. These two men would act as the land agents for the town and supervise the collection of funds from the auction. The money would be used for the town.

The townsmen were pleased with the information from the meeting. Many were already discussing which lots they would bid on. Being chosen as the capital meant the town would grow at a rapid pace. Following the meeting, the boardinghouse dining hall was open for refreshments and dessert. Many of meeting attendees lingered over the apple pie discussing the events of the day and plans for the future.

Will's mind kept drifting back to Mrs. Anderson. After eleven, Paul came around asking the men to move out so they could close and clean the dining hall. Will lingered a little longer and was just about to be the last out the door, when Mrs. Anderson's voice stopped him. He turned toward the sound, smile stretching across his face.

"Wait," she said. "Yesterday you said something about God directing you to the Arizona Territory. What did you mean?"

That certainly was not what Will expected. "That is not a quickly answered question, ma'am. Perhaps best left for another day."

"Do you believe God has plans for us?"

His heart slammed into his chest at her wording. She could not possibly mean "us" as in him and her. The thought warmed him and he felt his lips curl in a half smile.

"Yes, I do," he replied. Let her interpret that however she might, he thought, as he walked the short distance back to the bunkhouse.

The next morning, as soon as Hannah finished the breakfast dishes, she took off down the street towards Don Manuel's store. After patching up Jensen, she must have received half a dozen proposals yesterday afternoon before word circulated that she was a widow. It was time to do something about it.

Stepping into the dim log cabin, Hannah waited for her eyes to adjust to the light. The store was no more than a few rows of shelves containing various items, scattered in no particular order. The place was an eighth of the size of Francis' mercantile back in Ohio. Scanning the shelves, she looked for anything she could use to dye her clothing black.

Her boots clopped loudly on the wooden floor, drawing more attention to her presence than she would have liked, though there were only a few customers in the store. Making her way to the last isle of shelves, she sighed in frustration. There was nothing.

She walked to the counter where Don Manuel stood. "Excuse me, do you carry any black dye?"

"Got nothing like that here. What'd you need it for?" Don Manuel replied.

Nerves got the better of her. Any hope of a composed conversation died. "I am a widow," she blurted out, hoping the reason would be obvious.

"Well, if you want I can order it from Santa Fe, but it will probably be a few months before it gets in. And I'll need the money up front."

When he told her how much it would cost, Hannah choked. The price was insane.

"Don't mean to intrude, Mrs. Anderson," another customer said. When Hannah turned his direction, she recognized him as Captain Walker.

"I couldn't help but overhear," he said with a sympathetic smile on his lips. "It would be a shame to ruin such a pretty dress."

Hannah didn't know whether to be flattered or angry. "But, I'm a widow. I should be wearing black."

"Maybe back East. Or in the big cities in California. But you're in the West. Things are a mite different here. No one in this town expects you to wear black. Everyone knows the story of how you arrived here. No one questions that you are still in mourning."

Looking down at the floor, Hannah wanted to object. If that were true, why did so many men ask for her hand in the last day?

"Mrs. Anderson," Captain Walker continued, "Life in the West is different. A month seems like six, a year seems like three. Putting food on the table and staying alive are the priorities here. I know you womenfolk put a lot of importance on following the rules of society. But in a place as remote as this, there are more important things.

"I've traveled all over the territories. Ran into more widows than I'd like to count. Most aren't wearing black and most aren't waiting a year or more to get hitched again."

Hannah's head snapped up to see if Captain Walker was serious. He was.

"I certainly hope, for your sake, that when the right man—"

A crash of merchandise falling to the floor in the next aisle caused her to look that way. A light tan cowboy hat ducked below her line of sight in a flash.

Walker continued without missing a beat, "Comes along, you'll consider that some rules of society can be bent in the wilderness."

Stunned, Hannah could not think of a proper response.

"I don't mean any disrespect. Just making an observation," Captain Walker said before taking his leave.

Whether she wanted to or not, she may just have to take Captain Walker's unsolicited advice. She could not justify spending that much for dye. Maybe if she stopped wearing the light blue calico and stuck with her gray and green dresses it would be close enough. Without another word, she started out the door.

"He's right, ma'am," Will Colter's voice startled her.

"Pardon?"

Pushing away from the side of the cabin wall where he had been leaning, he said, "It'd be a shame to ruin such a pretty dress." Touching his fingers to the brim of his light tan hat, he bid her good day.

Chapter 28

Prescott

June 24, 1864

Since Will's last visit to the town, he thought of Hannah often. The more time he spent alone in the big, empty ranch house, the more he thought of her.

And he had the same argument in his head over and over. Should he try to get to know her better? Or was she still grieving the loss of her husband? On one hand, he could not deny she intrigued him. But, he wanted to respect her need to mourn. But, he really wanted to be near her.

A playful smile stretched across his lips as he remembered her shocked look when Captain Walker suggested she not worry about wearing widow's black. She seemed scandalized by the idea. He wondered if she took Walker's advice or not.

As Will neared the town he immediately noticed significant changes. Newly named streets and new buildings made the town almost unrecognizable from a month ago. The road he entered on was called Gurley Street. As he neared the center of the town, he saw a brand new building for the Arizona *Miner*, the semi-monthly newspaper, near Don Manuel's store. The building was the first of its kind—finished flat board planks, whitewashed and new. All of the other buildings more closely resembled log cabins of varying sizes and in varying stages of construction.

On Cortez Street, there were other buildings being erected near Lancaster's Boardinghouse. One looked like it might be a restaurant. Another, perhaps a store. On Montezuma Street, the street parallel to Cortez on the other side of the grassy town square stood a new saloon and several other temporary or unfinished buildings. The next street past Montezuma was Granite Street, near which construction had started on the Governor's Mansion.

The streets were wide, large enough to pass two wagons, with enough room left for wagons to be parked alongside the streets. Leaving the wagon in front of Lancaster's Boardinghouse, Owens and Whitten decided to check out the town's new digs—and most likely the saloon.

Will, on the other hand, was eager to see Hannah. Grabbing the first of several crates of smoked and preserved meat, he entered the dining hall. All was quiet—not even a sound from the kitchen. The back door was propped open. Peeking out, he didn't see anyone so he left the first crate on the table.

Surely the ladies were around somewhere. The clothesline in the back was empty, though a tub of clean water and soap waited nearby. First he checked the Mother Lode. Opening the door he listened for the slightest sound. Still no one. He pulled the door shut behind him and walked the few steps to the Gold Mine.

As he reached for the door handle, the door flew open and Hannah ran headlong into his chest showering him with a stack of dirty laundry. Instinct caused him to grab her upper arms, steadying her, and saving them both from toppling to the ground. The contact sent lightening up his arm. She was mere inches from him. She was wearing the light blue calico dress, not widow's black, he noted. As he looked down he swallowed hard at the sight of her lovely deep blue eyes looking into his. His gaze dropped to her soft, pink lips.

When Hannah opened the door with an armload of laundry, the last thing she expected was to crash into Will Colter. Tilting her head back, her gaze moved from the buttons on his shirt, up his neck to his golden brown eyes. His dark brown hair was crowned with his trusty cowboy hat. His jaw was strong and angular coming to a nice smooth chin. She didn't remember him being this handsome or tall. He was still holding her arms. Embarrassed, she felt the heat rush to her face before looking down at the laundry scattered on the ground.

"Hannah, is something wrong?" came Betty's voice from the bunkhouse. Catching sight of Will with Hannah in his arms, she broke into a wide grin.

Will abruptly released her, saying, "Sorry, ma'am," as he bent down to help pick up the laundry.

"I can get that," Hannah said lamely as she stooped to pick up the clothes, nearly bumping her head on his. She let out a nervous laugh. Taking a step backwards, she kneeled again, this time with a little more distance between her and Will.

"Will, so good to see you," the still grinning Betty said, mischief shading her voice.

"I'm here with the monthly supply of beef." Placing the last of the laundry in Hannah's arms, he added, "Pleasure to see you again, Mrs. Anderson." His gaze held hers, steady, unmoving.

Clearing her throat, she replied with a brief nod, "Mr. Colter."

"Hannah, dear, why don't you set that laundry over by the wash basin and then show Will where to put the supplies."

Still flustered, Hannah dropped the laundry in a pile, aware that Will followed close behind. Turning towards the front of the dining hall, she was careful not to accidently launch herself into his arms again. Her nervousness increased. She needed to get him talking. Otherwise, she might just keep thinking about his touch. "How are things at the ranch?"

"Good. We had a good breeding season this year. The cattle seem to like this Arizona weather as much as I do."

She laughed. "This weather is incredible. Not nearly the cold spells I was used to in Ohio. What is your ranch like?"

"It's northeast of here, nestled in a series of rolling hills near one of those granite looking mountains. I've never seen such bright white rock. Not too far from the ranch house is a small lake." His eyes lit with excitement as he described his home. "The bunkhouse is set farther to the east, near the barn."

"You have a ranch house built already? Tell me about it."

"It's a three room log cabin. I built out two bedrooms and then the large room has a cooking stove on one side and fireplace on the other. There's not much to it. Kinda empty."

Hannah picked up on the far away tenor of his voice. Loneliness? "Do you ever get lonely out there?"

His hesitation made Hannah think she was right. He was lonely.

Hefting one of the crates from the wagon, he said, "It can be at times. Mostly the boys and I are out taking care of the cattle so there's always someone around."

"Someone or some cow?" she teased as she led him through the dining hall to the kitchen.

He chuckled. "Probably more cow."

She directed him to put the crates on the table so she could unload them. Once they were empty, she found herself wishing for an excuse to keep him there.

"Would you care for some coffee?" she asked, directing him to sit at the table.

"Love some." Will's smile brightened his face. As she turned to warm the coffee, he asked, "How do you like working for Betty?"

"Oh, I like it a great deal. Betty and I became friends on the Santa Fe Trail, that's the route we took to get here. We traveled the entire length of the journey in the wagon in front of hers. She's the one who taught me how to cook over an open fire. I had never been without the luxury of a stove before, nor would I want to be again."

Pulling two mugs from the shelf, she filled them with coffee. "Sugar?"

Will shook his head. Drew had liked his coffee black, too.

Handing him the mug, she continued, "Betty is a real sweet woman. Almost like a mother."

"Was it hard to leave your mother?"

So many questions from the quiet man she met last month. Seems he could carry a conversation after all. She debated for a brief moment, under the guise of sipping her coffee, whether or not to tell him about her childhood. Last time she had so little to say that was not gloomy. This topic was no better.

Plunging ahead, she said, "My mother died in childbirth when I was twelve. We lived on a farm and after she died, my pa sent me to live with my aunt for a few years. I was almost fifteen before he brought me back to the farm. I never was sure why he sent me away for so long. Then, when I was eighteen my pa died. The doctor said it was his heart." Shaking away the sad memories, she finished, "Anyway, Betty is what I wished for in a mother and I love working with her."

Will's eyes were full of compassion as he listened to her story. "What did you do after your pa died?"

"I don't have any brothers or sisters, so the whole farm was left to me. I certainly couldn't run a farm by myself and there were crops in the field waiting to be harvested. My uncle advised me to sell the farm and with his help I got a good price. Then I moved into the city and worked at the mercantile until I married Drew. We never spent any of the money from the sale of the farm until we left for Arizona. It made the trip much easier."

She looked up from her coffee mug into his warm golden brown eyes. Suddenly feeling self-conscious about how much she was talking, she mumbled, "I'm sorry to go on so."

His smiled, sending waves of warmth over her.

Before he could respond, Betty bounded in through the back door. "Dear me, we better get started on dinner."

Hannah asked him, "Will you be staying for dinner?"

"I wouldn't miss it," he said as Betty rushed him out of the kitchen with a stern look and shake of her arm.

Mixing up the biscuit dough, Betty commented, "You two sure did talk for a while."

Hannah's cheeks flushed as she turned to grab items for the meal. One thing was for certain, she did enjoy talking to the man now that he found words to contribute.

After being kicked out of the kitchen, Will decided to take a stroll around town. He stopped by the Arizona *Miner* and picked up the latest edition from just a few days ago. Tucking it under his arm, he looked around the booming town. Paul Lancaster drew water from the well at the center of town. The well sat next to a large grassy section that was rumored to be reserved for a government building and town square. Odd how such a new town thought to reserve space for social gatherings.

Taking a seat in the shade, Will read the newspaper. An advertisement for Jackson's Boardinghouse on Montezuma Street caught his attention. The man was offering lower rates than Betty. Apparently, the establishment opened today. Seeing how busy Lancaster's was the last time he was in town, Will doubted the competition would hurt Betty's business.

The newspaper also mentioned the holiday celebrations planned for the fourth of July. He assumed the town would not have a celebration since it was so new. But, after today's visit, he saw the town had grown considerably and understood the desire for the festivities. He would plan to corral the cattle for the day, so he would only have to leave a few men at the ranch. They could use something fun to look forward to.

A shadow fell across the ground in front of him. When he looked up he saw Whitten and Owens shifting from foot to foot.

"Are we gonna get some grub before we go, Boss?" Owens asked. The man was always thinking about food.

Nodding his head, they walked to the dining hall at Lancaster's. The place was busier than he expected, since most of the miners usually ate their packed lunch at whatever creek they were mining. Will recognized several men from the town meeting last month including the journalist for the newspaper. Owens found a spot for the three of them to sit.

Hannah came around with coffee, and paused, looking at Will. "Who do we have here?"

"This is Daniel Owens and Sam Whitten. Boys, this is Mrs. Anderson."

"Pleased to meet you," she said with a smile.

As she continued on to the next group of men, Owens jabbed Will in the ribs. He said, rather loudly, "I can see why you've been insisting on making the deliveries, Boss."

Both Whitten and Owens chuckled heartily, having fun at Will's expense. Hannah glanced back over at them, her flushed face indicating she heard the teasing. Will just gave her a sheepish smile and shrugged. He wasn't sure but he thought she smiled back before going to the kitchen.

Arms loaded with plates of food, she made the rounds. "Mr. Hand, I was excited to read your article about the upcoming holiday. Mr. Binks, how is the Governor's Mansion coming along? Mr. Smith, in town for the day?"

Will watched amazed that she appeared to know everyone in the town by name and what business they pursued. No wonder Lancaster's was so busy. Then another thought occurred to him, one that he didn't like at all. With all of this attention, she would not remain unattached for long.

"Mr. Colter, Mr. Owens, Mr. Whitten. How long are you gentlemen in town for?" she asked, making direct eye contact with Will.

Whitten beat him to the punch. "We'll be heading back after the meal, although we'd rather stay and chat with you, pretty lady."

"So soon?" Hannah questioned, her expression giving away her disappointment.

"I'm afraid so," Will answered.

"Will we be seeing you on the Fourth?"

"Wouldn't miss it for anything," Will replied with a smile.

A few more men entered the dining hall, drawing Hannah's attention. As they took their seats, she quickly fetched them coffee and a meal. As she set a plate down in front of one man dressed in a rather expensive looking suit, he grabbed her wrist.

"You know, you are lovely," the man said, his eyes undisguised as they traveled her body. Will tensed at the man's disrespectful appraisal.

"If you ever get tired of just chatting with these men, you could make much more money in my saloon," the sleazy man said, letting his hand travel up her arm.

Will bolted to his feet, along with several other men.

"You know these men would much rather bed you than talk to you, as pretty as you are."

Will scrambled over the bench, moving towards the man. The sound of a rifle cocking stopped him from moving forward. Following the sound led him to the kitchen. Betty Lancaster stood, rifle braced against her shoulder and pointed at the repulsive saloon owner's chest.

"Trent Montgomery! You get your slimy hands off her!" Betty's voice silenced the room. "Or I'm gonna blow a hole through you."

"Now, now, Mrs. Lancaster, I didn't mean nothing by it," Trent said, lightly running his hand down Hannah's arm before placing it on the table. "Just want to make sure the girl knows she has options."

Paul entered from the kitchen. Quickly assessing the situation, he took the few steps towards Trent at a rapid pace. "She doesn't need options," Paul's deep voice boomed. "She's with family."

Then with no warning, the brawny Paul grabbed Trent by his shirt collar and hauled him to his feet. Shuffling him out the door, he shouted after him, "You and your kind are not welcome here!"

Turning back towards Hannah, Paul spoke with her softly for a few moments, leading her back to the kitchen. As Will took his seat to finish his meal, he heard many echoed murmurs about "that scum" Trent treating a decent woman that way. He agreed with many of the complaints and thought of several of his own.

Just as Will was getting his temper under control, several military men entered the establishment. One in particular looked familiar.

"Lieutenant Harrison!" Hannah exclaimed when he turned her way.

That's what Will thought. This was the lieutenant rumored to have taken care of her following her husband's death.

"Hannah," the young lieutenant greeted, taking her hand and placing a kiss on top of it.

Though the man treated her with the utmost respect, Will's jaw tightened in jealousy. He was far too friendly for Will's taste. The last bite of his food turned to lead as he tried to swallow it.

The young lieutenant certainly captured her attention, for she hurried to serve him and his men. Passing their empty plates down to the end, Will expected she would carry them to kitchen. Instead, she still stood near that Harrison fellow, deep in conversation. It was Paul who came to clear away the plates. The room was clearing out and Will knew his men wanted to be on their way, so he stood and headed out the door.

"Mr. Colter," Hannah called from the doorway as he untied his horse. "Thank you for the supplies."

"Ma'am," he acknowledged.

"We'll see you on the Fourth then," she said as they pulled away, giving Will a little hope that he might have made a lasting impression.

Joshua was pleased when Hannah lingered near the table he and his men occupied in the dining hall. In truth, he was hoping to steal a few minutes of her time, for that was all he had. As the other diners dispersed, Hannah surprisingly took a seat across from him.

"How have you been, Lieutenant?" she asked. "It has been quite some time since you have been by."

Was that disappointment in her voice? He dared only hope. "Please, Hannah, will you call me Joshua?"

She smiled as she nodded. "Joshua, then. How have you been?"

"Well," he answered. "We have been out patrolling the forests and rivers lately, making our protection known. I am pleased that our presence has provided safer conditions for many of the miners in the outlying areas."

"And you are staying safe?" Concern edged her voice.

"Of course. And you, how have you been?"

She laughed, such a light feminine sound. Joshua smiled as she answered, "Oh, you mean other than removing bullets from your soldiers in my free time?"

"I heard the tale. Jensen has recovered nicely and speaks of you with admiration."

She smiled. "Glad to hear he's doing well. I have been well. Working with Betty is very uplifting, most days."

He spoke of other news before the silence stretched between them. If his men were not sitting nearby, he would ask to visit on his next day off, whenever that might be. As it was, he may just settle for surprising her instead. Joshua hated to leave so soon.

"It was good seeing you again, Hannah," he said. "Sadly, I must take my leave. I am scheduled to report back to the major soon and we need to be on our way."

"Take care, Joshua," she said as he stood.

"You as well," he replied before leaving the dining hall. If nothing else, he hoped to see her for the Fourth of July celebration.

At the end of the day, Hannah settled her weary body down on her soft bed. As she turned down the light, she thought back on the day. Such unexpected encounters—one with the mysterious rancher, one with the sleazy saloon owner, and one with Joshua.

Her temper rose as she thought back to Trent Montgomery's

suggestion that she work at his saloon. The only way she would need that kind of money was if she decided to move back to Ohio.

Move back to Ohio. She had never once even considered it. But now that Drew was gone and she was on her own, she could move back. How would she get money for such a trip—for there was no way she would do what Trent Montgomery proposed. Then there would be the long months of traveling again. And she would have to take some sort of job on the wagon train back. What would she go back to? Working for Francis at the mercantile?

No. Going back to Ohio was not really an option. She was here. She had a good job with Betty, a roof over her head, food on her plate. She had friends—Betty, Martha, Joshua. Perhaps even Will Colter.

Heat rushed to her face at the thought of him and how she threw laundry on him this morning. And how warm his hands felt as he held her steady. She tried to ignore the fluttering of her heart. She had been affected by the tall rancher—more than she cared to admit—and the prospect of seeing him again soon at the upcoming celebration caused a smile to stretch across her lips.

Chapter 29

Prescott

July 3, 1864

Hannah greeted Martha as Paul helped her into the wagon. "Thank you for coming on such short notice," Hannah said, truly grateful Martha had not minded the last minute request for help. First thing this morning, Betty asked Hannah what she thought about making pies for tomorrow's celebration. She agreed and suggested they bring Martha to help.

"I welcome any chance to get together with you and Betty— even if you are putting me to work," Martha said, her laughter floating on the breeze.

They covered the distance from the fort to the creek in a matter of minutes. Paul set the brake on the wagon, then helped Martha and Hannah down. Each took a basket from the back of the wagon. Paul grabbed the rifle, balancing it against his shoulder, heading for the pecan trees first. Hannah and Martha stayed closer to the wagon, picking blackberries from the bushes.

The shuffling sound of miners sifting through the dirt carried downstream, accompanied by the occasional muffled voice. The breeze rustled the branches of the pecan, mulberry, and pine trees shading the banks of the gurgling creek. She and Martha worked alongside each other in companionable silence.

Plucking a plump blackberry from the bush, she popped it into her mouth. The sweetness slid over her tongue sparking anticipation for the pies these berries would become.

Hannah spent many of her morning devotional times recently contemplating what God might have planned for her future. Though circumstances forced that future to be without Drew, Hannah's heart still struggled with understanding what that really meant. Would she remain unmarried, working at the boardinghouse forever? Was there some other plan for her? If so, what did it look like? She still longed to be a wife and mother. But, how would that dream look without Drew? Was it wrong to still want those things?

She had no answers for her many questions, yet each day she felt like a little part of her became more prepared to hear those answers—whatever they may be.

Then, there were the unbidden thoughts of Will Colter adding confusion to her heart. Since his delivery a few weeks ago, Hannah caught herself often wondering what he was doing. She admitted, with some excitement, that he was part of the reason she spent hours in the evening working on a new brown calico dress for tomorrow's festivities. She wanted to impress him. Yet, she wondered if being drawn to him was somehow being unfaithful to Drew.

"I think your basket is as full as mine," Martha said, pulling Hannah from her thoughts.

She glanced down at both baskets of blackberries. There would be plenty for several pies. Smiling at Martha, she tried to hide her inner conflict. She turned and walked the few feet back to the wagon, depositing her basket in the back. Paul returned with a full basket of pecans as Martha slid hers into the wagon. Deciding they had plenty of both, the three returned to the boardinghouse.

Betty greeted them at the front door. "I decided to make dinner self-service. Anyone who wants to stop by today can grab some of the bread, cheese, and jerky from the table. All we have to do is check on the coffee."

Hannah carried her basket to the kitchen, where crusts covered the bottom of several pie tins. "I see you've got a head start."

"Of course, dear. I don't want to be up till the wee hours of the morning baking."

Hannah doubted they would be baking that late, especially with Betty's time saving dinner plan.

As she set out the ingredients for the berry pie filling, Betty and Martha started shelling the pecans.

"Looks like Mr. Barnard's hotel will finish in time for tomorrow," Betty said. "I walked over there briefly after you left. He said he still plans on providing all the food tomorrow as part of his grand opening."

"What's he serving?" Martha asked.

"Venison, chili, biscuits, and the like. Though he said he forgot about dessert. He was glad to hear of our plan."

"His place is the one with the sign 'Juniper House', right?" Martha asked.

Hannah replied, "Yes, it is. When he stopped in for supper last week, he seemed concerned about whether or not everything would come together, but it sounds like it has."

"Mr. Lount's and Mr. Noyles' saw mill made it possible for Mr. Barnard to build that hotel," Betty said. "Can you even image how long it would have taken without that steam powered machine spitting out planks so quickly?"

"I noticed on the way in to town how much has changed since I last visited," Martha said.

"Last week several new settlers arrived from California," Hannah said. "Most of them were related. Part of a big family."

"One man is going to build a boot and shoe store," Betty said. "Imagine new shoes readily available!"

"We barely even noticed the new restaurant that opened a few weeks ago," Hannah said. "With so many new settlers arriving, we still serve a packed dining hall, despite the competition of Jackson's Boardinghouse and the restaurant."

"I'm sure all of the eligible men have ulterior motives," Martha teased.

Hannah looked up from the pie she was filling. "Whatever do you mean?"

"Just that a beautiful, available woman does not go unnoticed."

Hannah rolled her eyes, drawing a smile from both Betty and Martha. Walking to the oven to check on her berry pie, she hoped the conversation would turn away from her. At least then she could put off her thoughts of this morning. Seeing the pie was done, she grabbed a towel and removed it from the oven.

The small kitchen workspace overflowed with their tasty creations, so Hannah picked up one of the cooled pies, to make room for the hot one. Taking a cooled pie in each hand, she entered the dining hall and set the pies on the far table. Martha and Betty followed Hannah's lead, clearing more space in the kitchen.

As supper time drew near, Paul took Martha back to the fort, so he could return in time to help serve the boarders. Once the boarders were served, Hannah pulled the last of the pies from the oven, setting them in the kitchen to cool. The aroma of pecan and berry pies overwhelmed any other scent, causing many of their customers to comment. Some tried to sneak a piece tonight, but Paul stood guard, ensuring them they would get a piece during the holiday festivities.

After finishing the supper dishes, Hannah went to her room and laid out the new brown calico dress for tomorrow. How fun it would be to have a day off to enjoy celebrating the country's birth and spending time with friends. It had been a long time since she celebrated anything.

As Will and his men neared the town, his anticipation grew. He looked forward to this day for weeks. He was determined to spend as much time as possible with Hannah today. He realized that if he wanted a chance to get to know her, he needed to act quickly. Though he hated thinking of winning her affection as a competition, it was. There were so few unattached women in the area for the large number of single men. Competition, especially for someone as comely as Hannah, would be tough. Hopefully his charm and quick action would give him a fighting chance. Hopefully.

"Wow!" exclaimed Hawk, pulling his horse to a stop.

"They have a stage and everything!" Jed echoed.

"Come on," Covington said, tying his horse to a hitching post. "Let's go see everything!"

As the three youngest men of his crew took off running around the square full of people, Will slid a bouquet of flowers from his saddle bags.

Ben, having noticed the flowers, teased Will. "Got yerself a special gal, huh? I knew I shouldn't have let you make those deliveries alone."

Heat rose to Will's face. He walked away quickly, hoping the rest of his men missed the jibe.

Scanning the crowd, he tried to find Hannah. An unexpected case of nerves assaulted him. What if he was wrong about the connection between them?

Taking a deep breath, he moved forward, rehearsing his speech for later. At some point, he would ask her to take a walk with him. Then he would ask her to visit the ranch in a few weeks. He hoped she would say yes. He really wanted her to see his beautiful property and it would be a perfect opportunity to get to know her away from the prying eyes of the competition.

Ben followed close behind him as he made his way across the lawn towards the back kitchen door of the boardinghouse.

"Will!" Betty hurried to greet him.

Eyeing the flowers in his hand she started to make some comment when Ben spoke. "You been holding out on me, Will. And who is this lovely lady?"

Pink colored Betty's cheeks. Will quickly introduced the two, wondering how he managed to never have done so before now.

As two of her boarders struggled to get a table out the door, Betty's attention shifted. "You be careful with those pies!"

Ben muttered to Will, "Please tell me, she ain't your special gal."

Shaking his head, Will chuckled.

"Good. Thought she was a mite old for ya. But not for me."

As Hannah slipped on her new dress, she heard Paul directing several men to carry the dining hall tables and benches outside. Betty's muffled voice from the other side of the wall reassured her that the pies would be safe. Taking extra care with her hair, she wove a matching brown ribbon into the chignon fastened at the base of her neck. Then she placed her bonnet on her head, tying a loose bow under her chin.

Stepping out the back door from the kitchen, Hannah saw many area ranchers were beginning to arrive. Some of the ranchers that lived down the mountains in the Peeples Valley area, arrived last night, setting up campsites on the edge of town. Searching the growing crowd for one particular rancher, she was disappointed not to see him yet. However, she spotted Martha Murphy waving to get her attention as the military personnel arrived from the fort.

"You look lovely. Is that a new dress?" Martha asked, greeting

Hannah with a hug.

"Oh, look, there's Joshua," Hannah said as she pointed to Lieutenant Harrison and his company of cavalry. They were starting the parade along Cortez Street. Hannah almost missed the inquisitive look that passed between Betty and Martha, as she led them to a better vantage point. The uniformed men always looked so dashing in parade formation.

Enamored by the parade, Hannah failed to see Will Colter as he approached with some of his men. "Hello, Han—Mrs. Anderson," Will said gently touching her elbow to get her attention.

She turned her attention to the tall rancher just as he thrust his hand forward. "For you," he said as she studied the small bouquet of bright yellow wildflowers. Letting her gaze float back up to his face, she warmed under his bright smile.

"Th...Thank you, Mr. Colter. That was very thoughtful," she replied accepting the gift, her grin equally as bright. *How sweet.*

Betty must have seen Will approach with the bouquet, for she held out a container with some water. Hannah placed the lovely blooms on the pie table close by.

The noise of the parade cut off any further conversation. Will motioned Hannah to stand next to him to watch. Taking her hand, he led her near the front to the best vantage point. The parade rounded the corner from Cortez onto Gurley Street, then down to Montezuma, effectively circling the crowd in the town square. Moving to the designated area, the army performed several drills for the spectators. When they finished, loud applause was their reward.

Mr. Barnard came forward to announce the food was ready, so the crowd began forming a line. Will offered his arm to Hannah which she accepted. Betty and Ben followed behind, as did Charles and Martha.

"Thank you again for the flowers," Hannah said. "They are lovely."

"Not as lovely as you," he replied with a tender expression.

Hannah blushed at the compliment. *First flowers, now compliments? What has gotten into Mr. Colter?* Seeking to shift the attention from her, she asked, "Is everyone from the ranch here with you?"

"Everyone except Pedro and Miguel. They volunteered to keep

an eye on things." They took a few steps forward in the line. Then, he turned and looked down into her eyes. "How have you been, Hannah?"

The direct question gave her a moment's pause, as did the fluttering of her stomach at his gaze. She looked away, suddenly self-conscious. "I've been well. The boardinghouse has been very busy. Betty, Martha, and I baked pie after pie yesterday." Glancing up at Will out of the corner of her eye, she teased, "I will certainly miss your help with dishes this evening."

Will chuckled. He had such a deep laugh and it lit up his whole face. "Who knows, you may get some extra help after all."

When they arrived at the buffet, each of them took a sampling of food. Will looked around for a place to sit. All of the tables from the boardinghouse were full. While any one of the men sitting there would likely give up their seat for a lady, he doubted if they would let him join her. Wanting to keep her at his side, he searched for another place. Seeing a shady spot on the grass he motioned her forward. "Will this be okay, or should I see if I can get a blanket for you?"

"This is perfect," Hannah answered, handing him her plate. She sat down on the ground and spread out her skirt.

Will handed down both plates as he took his place next to her. After taking his plate back, he hesitated. "Would you like me to say grace?" At her smile and nod, he said a quick prayer, not entirely aware of his own words as her nearness distracted him.

When he looked up from the prayer, his heart started beating faster. That shade of brown she wore made her eyes appear even deeper blue. The life reflected there drew him in.

"I didn't realize there were so many people in the area," Hannah said, stirring his thoughts from her appearance.

Looking around the crowd, Will agreed. He figured there were roughly three hundred men there. And there were about ten women—the most important one sitting next to him.

He turned his attention back to Hannah as he swallowed a bite of the venison. The dress she wore hugged her curves in a pleasing way, before narrowing at her waist. Will thought he could easily span that waist with his hands. Heat rose to his face with the thought. He quickly stuffed a biscuit in his mouth to shift his focus.

He was still contemplating his next move when an unexpected visitor arrived.

Will glared up at the officer whose shadow fell across his plate. What was he doing here? Before Will could think of some pleasant way to get the man to leave, Hannah looked up.

Her face lit up, as Will's heart sank.

"Joshua, please join us," Hannah said to the lieutenant. "Have you met Mr. Colter?"

As Hannah made the introductions the two men sized each other up. Will was disappointed to still be associated on a more formal basis while the young lieutenant was on a first name basis. He wasn't sure why, but it stuck in his craw. As they shook hands, Will gripped the man's hand firmly. He found himself feeling possessive and not the least bit happy with sharing Hannah's time. Harrison's shake was curt, adding to his air of military precision. Will could only wonder at what was going through his mind. Hannah appeared oblivious to the subtle tension between the two men.

Taking a seat on the other side of Hannah, Harrison launched into a conversation with her immediately. "Are you enjoying the celebration?"

"I loved the parade. Seeing the military drills really adds to the patriotism of the day," she answered, her eyes sparkling with excitement.

After Harrison directed another question to Hannah, seemingly ignoring Will, he began to feel like an outsider—and this was supposed to be his time with Hannah. As his jealousy started to rise, he stood, excusing himself with the pretense of wanting to watch the miner's rock picking competition. He walked over close enough to see, but not really seeing. Crossing his arms over his chest he knew he could not just leave her there alone with the lieutenant. Their obvious connection already put him at a disadvantage. If he had any hope of winning Hannah, he should march right back over there and steal her away. But, something held him back.

His mood must have been transparent to Betty as she

approached, for she said, "She doesn't love him, you know."

"Beg your pardon?" Will asked, caught off guard by her candor.

"Don't worry. She doesn't love Lieutenant Harrison," she confirmed before turning her attention back to the miners.

Will hoped that was true, but he had his doubts. He looked over at the two as they were deep in conversation. They had such a comfortable familiarity between them. She seemed genuinely delighted by the lieutenant's presence. Did she look like a woman in love? Did he even know what that looked like?

He thought of his parents who loved each other dearly. It was evident in every interaction. His father gave her hand a gentle squeeze as they gathered for supper each evening. His eyes would take on a different, softer look when he spoke to Will's mother and she reflected that same look. How does a man know when a woman is in love?

As she watched Will walk away, Hannah felt disappointed. He seemed to be warming up to her, but then his abrupt departure threw her off balance.

Nonetheless, she was here with Joshua, so she focused her attention on him. "What did you do before the war?"

"Back in '49, my family moved to California during the gold rush. I was twelve at the time. My father was always a shrewd man and, when he made his fortune, he invested it wisely in a freight company. In a few short years, he built the business into a successful enterprise. When I finished school at sixteen, I spent the first two years working different jobs at the freight company. Father sent me east to Georgia to attend university with my cousin."

Joshua paused, his eyes taking a faraway look. "I had a wonderful time getting into all manner of trouble with my cousin, but still managed to keep up with my studies. When I finished at the university, I returned to California to help my father run the company.

"When the war started, and California called for volunteers to serve throughout the West, I applied for a commission as an officer in the cavalry. It was approved and I joined the First Cavalry of the California Column."

"So, you joined in California at the onset of the war? How did you end up at Fort Larned?"

"The First Cavalry, once we were trained by one of the regulars, travelled all over the Arizona, New Mexico, Colorado, and Kansas territories. We fought in skirmishes in most of these territories.

"Once the governor's itinerary was finalized, General Carleton assigned the First Cavalry to escort his party safely to the Arizona Territory. Then we were to remain at Fort Whipple for the time being."

Hannah marveled at how much of the country Joshua had seen. When she first met him, she thought he might have been a regular, one of the men in the army prior to the war, for he seemed a natural cavalry man. But, she learned later that most men in service to the Union were volunteers, set to muster out by the end of the war and return to their former lives.

"Do you like your job?" she wondered aloud, glancing back towards Will. Betty said something to him and he looked her direction, then away.

"Most of the time. More so, since having found my faith," Joshua said. "That helps me let go of the horrific things I have seen. When I was first training under Captain Benjamin Davis, I instantly felt as if I was where I belonged. The discipline of the cavalry suited me well. I enjoy the strategy involved in planning and executing orders."

"What will you do once the war is over?"

"I have thought that if the army should still require men in the West that I might stay on. If that does not happen, then perhaps I will return to California and work for my father again."

Taking her hand, he looked into her eyes. "Of course, much of that will depend on the situation I find myself in, once the war is over."

Hannah swallowed. Something in the intensity of his look told her things might be changing between them.

Chapter 30

Still perplexed over the situation with Hannah, Will decided he would not give up without a fight. He strode to where she and Lieutenant Harrison were seated. Though irritated by the lieutenant's familiar hold on her hand, Will pasted on a smile and extended his hand. "Come watch the miner's competition with me. It's very entertaining."

Hannah smiled and took his hand. Inwardly, he rejoiced over the small victory. He helped her up and waited as she brushed bits of grass from her skirt. When he offered his arm, she took it. They arrived at the miner's competition just as it concluded, dashing his hopes momentarily.

Someone suggested a roping contest among the cowboys, unknowingly aiding Will's cause. Several men from the other area ranches lined up, next to Jed, Whitten, and Owens. Will pointed out his men to Hannah and could not help but notice her louder cheers for them as they dazzled the crowd with their lasso tricks.

Then Covington came up next to Will and Hannah. "Boss, you should go out there. You're the best roper in this whole territory," he bragged.

While Will was good with the rope and knew several fancy tricks, he doubted he was the best. He certainly didn't want to leave Hannah's side again, especially not to show off in front of the crowd. He pretended not to hear Covington's comment, until Hannah spoke.

"Go ahead, Mr. Colter," Hannah said.

Several others around them agreed so Will was obliged to take the stage. As he started forming the loop, he noticed Harrison and Covington flanked Hannah in the crowd. He sighed inwardly, thinking he lost her attention again. However, catching Hannah's gaze, he realized the opposite was true. Maybe showing off his rope skills would work to his advantage after all. He started with some easy twirling of the rope in front of him then progressed to more challenging moves. He finished with stepping into the loop while continuing its spinning up his body, until it was over his head.

Covington shouted out that he should take a volunteer to step into the loop. Agreeing, he waited to see who would come forward. Will had not expected Hannah to stumble forward, until he saw Betty and Martha's mischievous looks from behind her. If he didn't know better, he would have thought the two women were conspiring to help him.

Will took Hannah's hand and led her to the center of the stage, his heart racing. He explained that when he started twirling the rope near the ground, he wanted her to step into the center when he nodded. When she was ready, he started. Once she was inside the loop, he performed the same trick with her—moving the loop upward, overhead and back down again. He resisted the temptation to tighten the rope about her waist and pull her to him. The last thing he wanted to do was embarrass her.

The crowd applauded and cheered loudly. Will took Hannah's hand. While she curtsied, he bowed. She was breathtaking as her face glowed from the thrill of the experience. He wanted to take her in his arms and kiss her.

Instead, he directed Hannah back toward the crowd.

"That was amazing!" she exclaimed, followed by nervous laughter. "Where did you learn how to do that?"

"Growing up on a ranch can be kinda boring. It was a creative use of my time that kept me out of trouble and away from my brother."

"Mrs. Lancaster, how long do we have to wait for that delicious looking pie?" a short somewhat fleshy man asked, greedily rubbing his hands together.

Others followed suit, begging for dessert to be served, until Betty agreed. Enlisting Hannah and Mrs. Murphy's help, Betty started slicing the sweet treats. Again, Will was separated from Hannah. Taking his piece of pie, he found a spot in the shade to sit and wait for her to be free. The serving took longer than expected as every miner, rancher, and townsman wanted to chat with the lovely ladies.

Harrison appeared, taking a seat next to Will without invitation.

"What exactly are your intentions with Hannah?" the lieutenant asked, getting to his purpose immediately.

Clenching his jaw, Will did not take more than a second to respond, irritated by his brashness. "I might ask you the same question."

"Don't be coy with me, Colter. The roping trick was an interesting way to get her attention. I suppose you planned to have your men call you out so you could show off." The lieutenant's irritation sharpened his words.

"I planned nothing, other than a lovely afternoon with a lovely woman."

"I suggest you reconsider the rest of the afternoon."

Will did not like the Harrison's demands. "She seemed to enjoy my company today, Harrison. That got you on edge?"

"Tread lightly."

"Why? Do you have some sort of agreement or commitment to Mrs. Anderson?" Will challenged. "From where I sit, I doubt it, as she doesn't impress me as the type of woman to take a commitment lightly."

Harrison's lips formed a thin line as his brows drew together. "I have not spoken to her of my affections, yet. But I had planned to do so very soon. I would appreciate your bowing out."

The competitive spirit rose in Will. He had not planned to fight for Hannah, but he was not ready to step aside easily and see her coupled with this arrogant man. "While I find your confidence in the lady's presumed acceptance admirable," Will replied, purposefully finding the biggest words he could think of, "I propose we let her decide who she prefers."

Harrison bolted to his feet. For a brief moment, Will thought he might engage by throwing a punch. He did not. Instead, he turned back towards the cavalry as they gathered for the last presentation.

"Guess we've got a real competition going," Will muttered to himself as he searched the crowd for Hannah. He tried to push forward to catch sight of her, but to no avail. At least Harrison, as one of the mounted cavalry, would be busy with the final presentation.

After the grand finale, the crowd started to thin. Many men went to the saloon, while a few lingered about the town square. Will caught sight of Hannah, Betty, and Martha near the pie table, clearing the dishes away. The three ladies disappeared inside the boardinghouse.

Frowning, Will could not keep his disappointment from showing. He hoped to speak with Hannah before she returned to work but he was too late.

Paul filled the reservoir with water for the ladies then went to find a few men to help him bring the tables and benches back into the dining hall. While Hannah and Martha brought all of the boardinghouse's dishes in, Betty heated the water for the large dish washing chore.

Hannah could not stop smiling. Her cup was overflowing.

"You are positively radiant," Betty said. "You obviously had a good time, dear."

"I did. I can't remember the last time I had so much fun. Wasn't Will's roping fantastic?"

"Will?" teased Martha. "You mean Mr. Colter, right?"

Hannah felt the heat rise to her face.

"I couldn't help but notice you had one or two admirers today," Betty said.

She had an idea who Betty was talking about, but she wasn't sure she liked the direction of this conversation. Playing it off, she asked, "What do you mean?"

"Mr. Colter and Lieutenant Harrison were both enamored by your presence," Martha said with a dramatic flair.

Betty said, "Oh, I think they are more than just enamored. I think they are both in love with you, Hannah."

Her mouth suddenly felt dry. That was not possible. Was it?

"Oh, that lieutenant has been in love with you since you were at the fort," Martha said. "I don't think you will be single much longer. And to think, you've got a choice of two very handsome men."

The thought sobered Hannah. She wasn't sure if her friends were just teasing her or if they were serious. She didn't want to think about what would happen if what Betty said was true. Even though she was not wearing widow's black, she was still mourning her husband. Wasn't she?

"Dear, don't look so sad about it," Betty said as she started washing the dishes. "I know what you're thinking and you just leave that thought lie. Drew was a wonderful man, but he is gone now. It is okay to move on."

She was not ready for this discussion, despite her own confusing feelings. "But you haven't moved on. At least you haven't married again," Hannah said.

"Yes, that is true. But I am also not as young as you, nor as beautiful. And I have my son to take of me. As young as you are, you can look toward the future and see it with a man and with a house full of children. You do want a family, don't you?"

Both set of eyes were on her as she dried the next dish. "Yes, I do want a family. I thought that longing would go away after Drew died, but it hasn't. It has only gotten stronger."

"Then we must help you decide who you want to share that life with," Betty said, mischievous grin in place.

Martha stopped her short, "Now Betty, don't be interfering with Hannah's life. It's one thing to listen and help her see what she hasn't noticed, but don't you go plotting out her life for her. Her heart needs to decide on its own."

Betty pouted. "That doesn't mean we can't list the fine attributes of each man does it?"

Hannah covered her eyes, pretending to hide from Betty. Martha burst out giggling at her reaction. Betty couldn't pretend to be upset any longer and joined in the laughter. Before Hannah knew it, she was carried along in the swell. Soon none of them could remember what they were laughing about. Tears pooled in the corner of their eyes. Paul stuck his head in through the back door, took one look, cocked an eyebrow, and walked back out. His expression and subsequent quick exit brought another round of hysterics. It felt so good to laugh with her friends.

Once the dishes were clean, Hannah poured coffee for each of them. Then the ladies gathered around the kitchen table and continued their discussion.

"Hannah, you really should consider what we're saying," Martha said. "Even if you haven't given it much thought before."

"Yes, dear, we want you to be happy. Even though I love you

like a daughter, I don't expect you to keep working for me forever."

Hannah's heart turned upside down. She didn't know what to think. "I loved Drew so much. I don't think about him as much now, but I still miss him. The way I felt about him was different. I don't feel that way about either Will or Joshua."

"Love takes on a different shape with different people in our lives. The way you loved Drew will not be the same way in which you love your next husband," Betty said. A distant look shaded her eyes. "Before I met Henry, I loved another man. We were going to be married, but he was killed in a tragic accident weeks before our wedding. We had been so passionately and madly in love. I didn't think I would be able to breathe without him. But I grieved and I moved on. I wasn't the same girl when I met Henry. I had changed. What I wanted and needed changed. I loved Henry with all of my heart from very early on, but it was calmer, steadier, and settled."

"Weren't you attracted to Henry?" Hannah asked.

"Oh, don't get me wrong. We still had sparks flying. We couldn't keep our hands off of each other. I'm just saying it was different from my first love."

"Hannah, I think Betty is right, although I can't say from personal experience. Just think about it. Will and Joshua are not the same men as Drew. They have vastly different interests. Drew was a doctor. Will is a rancher. Joshua is a lieutenant in the army. Each man is unique in his own way."

"Yes. Drew was at ease around you and loved to tease you. He had an innate calmness in his spirit. He was fiercely protective of you," Betty said. "And he wanted to spend every waking moment at your side. The lieutenant, while he wants to care for you, can never be there as much as you might want. His first love is the army—well maybe God, then the army—then you. He respects you greatly, but would often be in a position to leave you on your own. Will, on the other hand, sees you as wife material, even if he doesn't quite know it yet. He admires your independence and desires your companion-ship. I'm sure he would care for you and protect you, just like the others, but he also understands that you can hold your own."

Hannah stared at the coffee mug in her hand. "What should I do?"

"Let God and time work its course," Martha advised.

Dr. Murphy appeared a moment later to take his wife back to Fort Whipple. The sun was hanging low in the sky and they would have barely enough daylight left to make it back. Hannah and Betty said their goodbyes, sad to have their friend leaving already.

Hannah needed to be alone with her thoughts, her mind churned over everything her friends said. As Betty retired to their private rooms, she stayed in the kitchen. The noise from the saloon filtered across the square. She hoped they wouldn't be rowdy too late into the night.

Did she love Will or Joshua? Could she love either of them?

Joshua was a dear friend. She enjoyed his company and sensed something different when they talked this afternoon. Hannah would be forever grateful for how he stepped into the darkest days of her life and carried her to safety. He was a very honorable man. He commanded the attention and loyalty of those around him. But did she love him?

What about Will? He was so quiet sometimes. She often felt like she had to pull the conversation from him. Yet, when he did speak at length, most of the time it was deep or profound. And he was ruggedly handsome. She remembered back in May how easily he spoke of God. She knew that was important to her, and it sounded like it was important to him.

A gentle knock on the open back door drew her attention. Will Colter stepped just over the threshold. She greeted him with a warm smile.

"Would you care to take a walk?" he asked.

Hannah felt her pulse quicken and her heart flutter. *It must be all that talk with Betty and Martha.* She stood, taking his offered arm. As they walked together in silence, she was more aware of him than before. He walked comfortably, with confidence. Where her hand rested lightly in the crook of his arm, she could feel the strength. This was a man that was used to hard work. She felt very safe with him.

"Hannah," Will started. "May I call you, Hannah?" he asked when he realized his mistake.

"Yes," she answered softly.

"Thank you for spending so much time with me today. I didn't mean to take you away from Mrs. Lancaster and Mrs. Murphy."

That's odd. Does he really think he took me away from them? "There's nothing to apologize for. I had a wonderful time."

The tinny music from the saloon carried across the square, filling the awkward silence.

"That berry pie was delicious. The best berry pie I've ever had," Will said.

Hannah got the feeling that he didn't want to talk about her baking skills. There was definitely something on his mind. Turning to face him, she looked up and asked, "What's wrong, Will?"

As Will looked down at her, his well-rehearsed speech dissolved on his tongue. The dimming light cast an almost angelic glow to her face. She was so close and the way she was looking at him was too much. He lowered his head and without warning gently kissed her. At first, he felt her body tense, but then she quickly gave into his kiss. When she put her arms around his neck, Will pulled her closer and deepened the kiss. She was so sweet. He could go on kissing her forever, savoring everything about her.

Unfamiliar feelings bubbled to the surface. He pulled away suddenly, needing to put some distance between them, frightened by the intensity of his feelings.

His voice husky, he said, "I'm sorry, I didn't mean to do that." *What kind of stupid thing was that to say?*

Turning away from him and towards the boardinghouse, Hannah said, "Your voice betrays you, Will." As he followed in stride next to her, she teased, "I don't think you are one bit sorry."

Embarrassed, Will searched for the words he wanted to say. "I *am* sorry—sorry that I did not ask your permission first." His heart was pounding loudly in his ears. He hoped he hadn't just ruined his chances with Hannah by being so brash.

They walked the remainder of the way back to the boardinghouse in silence. Stopping at the back door, Will turned to her, knowing this would be his last opportunity to ask her.

"Hannah, I was wondering if you would like to come see the ranch some time."

"I would love to."

His heart leaped within his chest. He flashed a grin before wishing her a good night.

"Good night, Will," she replied to his retreating back.

Once he was out of sight, she closed and locked the door. Leaning against it, Hannah took a deep breath to steady herself. She was shocked when Will kissed her and even more shocked at her own reaction to the kiss. The kiss was so blissful. She hadn't wanted it to end. When he pulled away abruptly, she thought she had done something wrong. But, even in the dimming light, she saw the unmistakable look of passion in his eyes.

Will was most definitely different than Drew. When she first met him, she thought Will was a bit too quiet. She recalled his short answers to many of her questions. But, as she got to know him better, she saw a deep, sensitive man who tried so hard to be the steady leader his men expected. And during the roping competition, she saw the fun and playful side of Will Colter.

Yes, Will was very different from Drew, but in the most pleasant ways.

Chapter 31

With nervous anticipation, Hannah dressed in her green calico dress. She liked the way the green of the dress brought out the reddish highlights of her hair. She wanted to look her best for the picnic outing at Will's ranch. Before he left town two weeks ago, he suggested today for the visit. The last two weeks seemed to drag on. Hannah could hardly wait to see him again—especially after that kiss. Countless times she fell asleep to the memory, savoring each nuance, and eagerly looking forward to the next. Checking her appearance in the gilded handheld mirror, Hannah blushed, pleased with the reflection.

The morning breakfast routine was the only thing standing between Hannah and the picnic. Will should be here any minute now, she thought as she set plate after plate before hungry boarders. Returning to the kitchen, Hannah took the refilled coffee pot from Betty with shaky hands as her excitement grew.

As she finished refilling the last mug, Will Colter entered the dining hall. He was dressed in a blue cotton button down shirt and jeans that hugged his muscular thighs. The light tan cowboy hat brought out the gold flecks in his eyes. His hair, mostly hidden by the hat, curled over the collar of his shirt, tempting Hannah's fingers. He stood still, near the entry with two young cowboys on either side.

When his gaze connected with hers, she smiled giddily. Hannah covered the distance between them. "Will, please have a seat. Would you like some coffee?"

Before answering her question, Will took her hand in his rough one. Lifting her hand to his lips, he pressed a light kiss on top. Heat rose to her face and her heart picked up pace at the intimate gesture. The clank of forks rhythmically hitting the tin plates halted. Chatter silenced. Every eye in the room looked directly at Hannah and the tall rancher before her.

"Hannah, you look lovely this morning," he said, releasing her hand slowly, but keeping his eyes firmly directed at hers. "I would love some coffee."

As Will and the cowboys took a seat, the hum of conversation buzzed again. Hannah scurried to the kitchen to get breakfast for Will and his men, listening to the barely restrained congratulations offered Will's way. When she glanced over her shoulder, his face reddened.

When she entered the kitchen, Betty grinned foolishly. She patted Hannah on the arm and followed behind her with two plates. Keeping hold of the coffee pot, Hannah took the third plate in hand. As they neared Will, he kept his attention on her. She set the plate in front of him, never looking away from his intent stare. She smiled again as she filled his coffee mug.

Will introduced his two men as Jed and Hawk. Both looked very young, probably a good four years her junior. While they said little, both men were very polite, thanking her as she refilled their mugs.

"Have you eaten?" Will asked.

Hannah shook her head. With the flutter of her stomach and the heat rushing to her face every time he looked at her, she did not think she could eat a bite.

As the diners passed their plates down to the end, Hannah went to retrieve them. Betty quickly shooed her away. "You best be on your way dear. I'll see to the dishes."

Will and his men were finished their meal so Hannah donned her bonnet. Taking a deep breath to calm her nerves, she met Will out front.

"I hope you don't mind riding," Will said. "The trip is much easier on horseback than in the wagon."

Hannah tried to hide her surprise. She had expected he would bring the wagon. She was just a young farm girl the last time she rode astride. Looking from the stirrups back to Will, she forced a smile. Relief flooded her when he cupped his hands together to help her onto the horse. By the time she had her skirts arranged, Will and his men already mounted their horses.

The ride was pleasant as they passed over rolling hills and dipped into shallow valleys. Some of the five mile journey wove through tall pine tree forests, while the latter part gave way to grassy lands.

When they crested the last hill, Hannah soaked up the majestic view. To the west, the bright grayish white granite rock was sparsely dotted with pine trees and shrubbery. These amazing mountains looked as if they had been forced up through the grassy lands by some extreme force. The contrast of the rock was stark against the backdrop of deep blue sky and rolling green grass below. Breaking up the expanse of green, clusters of cattle were overseen by the cowboys.

In the bottom of the valley, there was a flat area, where several buildings stood. One looked to be the barn. Next to it stood the nondescript bunkhouse and a small shack. Then Hannah saw it—the ranch house—nestled near the mountains and buffeted by a small shimmering lake. She thought the whole scene to be the most picturesque place she had ever seen. She was so engrossed in the view she missed seeing Will dismiss Jed and Hawk.

"This," he said stretching his arm across the expanse, "is Colter Ranch."

"It is breathtaking," Hannah said as she unconsciously brought her hand to rest over her heart. "I have never seen anything so glorious."

"Come, let me show you around." The pride in his voice was evident.

Will led them down the rest of the road, before making a large circle around the grounds. Now she understood why he hadn't wanted to use the wagon, for the tour would have been much too long on foot. Circling to the east, they moved past the barn.

"This is where we stable and corral the horses. We also have two milk cows and a few pigs. Over there is the bunkhouse where the cowboys live. There is a large open room where they take their meals and play cards in the evenings. The other room houses all of the bunks, which is very similar to the Mother Load at the boardinghouse. That," Will said, pointing to the small shack, "is Rosa's place. She does all of the cooking, cleaning, and laundry. Then we have the smoke house next to the bunkhouse. Snake manages all the butchering and smoking of the beef we supply to the boardinghouse, fort, and other locals."

They continued on around toward the ranch house. "This is my home. It's not much, but will do nicely for now. Someday, I want to build a much larger house out of wood planks, instead of the log cabin. I dream of having a large porch on the back to sit in a rocking chair while gazing out on the lake."

"It sounds lovely," Hannah whispered, catching his vision.

Stopping in front of the house, Will dismounted. Reaching up, he placed his hands on her waist and easily lowered her to the ground. He allowed his hands to linger a few breaths, his closeness sending all her senses wild. Taking her hand, he led her to the house to give her the grand tour.

"In here, we have a full kitchen, stove and all. That took some doing to get it shipped from Santa Fe, but I know Rosa was happy for it. The table is rather crude. Something I put together for the short term."

He pointed out the fireplace in the sitting room, which was a continuation of the kitchen and dining area. She noticed two doors off the length of the room, most likely bedrooms. While the house had paned windows, the curtains hanging over them were more utilitarian than decorative. Hannah thought the place could use a few homey touches.

Picking up the blanket and basket of food Rosa set out, he held out his arm for Hannah. She placed her hand in the crook of his elbow and they strolled leisurely toward the lake. It was so peaceful and serene. She loved it.

Once they were near the shore of the lake, Will set the basket down and spread out the blanket. He helped her get situated before taking a seat next to her. He propped one arm up on his bent knee. The other leg was stretched out and he leaned back on the other arm, mere inches from her side.

Content to leave the basket untouched for the moment, Will looked off towards the lake. "When I left Texas, I didn't want to go," he confessed. "I thought that would be my home forever. I was born there and I was going to grow old there." He picked at the cloth covering the basket. "But, God had other plans for me. And now here I am.

"When I first saw this patch of land, we were coming from the north—" He pointed to the trail. "—instead of the south like we did today. I knew when I saw it, this was home. Everything about it spoke to me, to the depths of my soul. In a brief moment, I saw it all—the house, the ranch—" He turned and looked at her. "—a wife, and lots of children. In that instant, I knew this was God's gift to me—this magnificent land."

Hannah felt his eyes on her, but kept hers fixed on the lake. She could see the draw of this land. She felt it too. It was that sense of belonging. "Thank you for bringing me here. It is incredible," she said turning to look at him.

Will leaned closer and her pulse raced. Bringing his hand to her neck, he gently pulled her face towards him. Closing the distance, he kissed her. She closed her eyes and leaned into his strength. He responded, trailing his fingers down her neck, sending shivers up her spine. This kiss was different than before. It held such promise and hope and it was utterly delightful.

A soft rustling nearby caught her attention and she hesitated, pulling away. Glancing over Will's shoulder Hannah saw Ben touch the brim of his hat before moving his horse along. She smiled knowing the older man was slyly acting as chaperone.

Will dropped his hand to the blanket, putting some space between them. "What about you, Hannah? What are your dreams?"

Contemplating the question, she reached for the basket and began setting out the meal. Between bites of bread and cheese, she tried to articulate the dream she once had. Drawing her knees to her, she placed her arms around them and propped her chin on top.

Sighing, she answered, "A year ago, my biggest dream was to be a mother and grow old with Drew." A few tears slid down her face as she continued, "Then trouble forced us to move. I didn't want to leave, for I wanted to raise my children there. When we left Ohio, I felt my dreams were dead. Slowly, on the trip here, I began to see Drew's dream and tried to make it my own, starting a new life in a new land."

She paused swiping at the tears. "We left Ohio shortly after our second anniversary and I didn't understand why my dream of being a mother was still unfulfilled." Hannah paused, uncertain if she should have shared such a personal thought. Yet, Will seemed to listen with genuine interest. "Then, when Drew died in the avalanche in the San Francisco Mountains and when I realized I was with child days later, the dream seemed more like a nightmare. The child was my last link to him, yet I didn't want to go on without him."

Her words caught and she was surprised at how raw the emotion still was. Will reached out and took her hand in his, softly running his thumb over her knuckles.

"Then, once I started working at Fort Whipple, just as some of the sadness started to lift, I lost my baby."

"I know."

"How?"

"I was there that day." He took both her hands in his. "I had just moved into the line in front of you for some dinner, when you collapsed into my arms. I had no idea who you were, but I prayed for you because I knew you would need it." He paused, his voice growing quiet. "It wasn't until later—when I met you at the boardinghouse that I realized it was you."

The distant lowing of cattle seemed louder in the lull. Hannah struggled to maintain some composure. How strange that he should have been there that day and turn out to be the man who caught her. How mysteriously God worked—that he would send this man to pray for her in the midst of a crisis. Had she just glimpsed the Almighty's plan for her life?

"I'm sorry that you lost the baby."

She managed a slight smile as she pulled her hands from his, clasping them around her knees again. She was not done answering his question.

"After the baby was gone, I could have died inside. But for the grace of God and the kindness of dear friends speaking truth to me, I would have. Working at the boardinghouse was exactly what I needed—days full of work and under the watchful eye of motherly Betty." She smiled at that.

"It wasn't until very recently that I began to dream again. I still long to be a wife and mother. And, even though some part of Drew will always be with me, I am ready to look forward." *With you.* Her thought startled her. Was she really ready to let go? "Some women long for adventure and excitement. In the last year, I've had more than I thought I would have in all my life. I want to stay here, marry again, and raise a family in this beautiful land. Nothing more."

She glanced over at Will. The expression on his face was one of understanding and longing. She didn't know why, but she felt drawn to this man. He was noble of character and deep of soul. So different from Drew, but so perfect for her.

Nervously, she laughed off the heavy feelings stirred by their conversation. Hoping to lighten the mood, she said, "So, tell me about your cattle."

For the next fifteen minutes or so, Will explained in great detail the size of his herd, his business strategy, and his plans for the future of his ranch. He spoke with such confidence, definitely very experienced in ranching.

As the conversation lagged, Hannah stood. She didn't want this day to end but it must. Will took the cue and stowed the picnic items back in the basket. Throwing the blanket over one shoulder, he carried the basket on one arm, offering the other to Hannah.

"Thank you so much for showing me your wonderful home. It is so peaceful here," she said as they neared the house.

Will left her near the horse and went to deposit the picnic basket and blanket inside the house. When he returned, she thought he was going to help her mount the horse for the ride home, but was caught off guard when he moved closer. His eyes searched hers as if looking for something he lost. She leaned toward him, as he kissed her again. So sweet was the kiss, she lingered in his arms when he pulled away. How could he communicate so much in one action? She wanted to remain here forever.

But reality must prevail. She stepped back and he helped her mount the mare. They rode in silence back to town, both deep in thought.

As they neared the boardinghouse, boarders lined out the door, signaling that supper was in full swing. Will lifted Hannah down from her horse. Pausing he looked as if he was about to say something, then he stopped and kissed her hand instead. Wishing her a farewell, he mounted his horse and took the reins of her horse. Once at the top of the hill, he turned and waved.

Hannah waved back, wondering if she might just be falling in love with the quiet rancher.

Chapter 32

Prescott

August 15, 1864

Today was bittersweet. As much as Hannah tried to forget the date, she could not. Today would have been her third anniversary with Drew and the memories consumed her. A sadness hung around her shoulders and would not lift. Why couldn't she just forget?

After snapping at Betty as they washed the breakfast dishes, Hannah mentioned the significance of the day. Then she picked up a basket and walked out the back door. When Paul followed a few steps, she yelled at him and told him she was going to search for wild cherries along the river. He stopped and let her go, despite the risk. A few times on the walk to the creek, she felt like someone was watching her, but when she glanced over her shoulder, no one was there. She knew it was risky—venturing out alone—there was always the threat of Apache attacks.

Stopping by the creek, she watched as a leaf floated in the gurgling water, carried over rocks and rushed downstream. Was that what life was like? Getting hung up on rocks one moment and then being swept away the next?

Her memories of Drew were starting to fade. It was over seven months since the tragic accident claimed his life. If their baby had survived, he would be a newborn now—and fatherless.

The thought was too much. Hannah fell to her knees and sobbed, grieving again for her losses. *Lord, when will this grieving end?* Months of pain came rushing forth. Minutes rolled by, drowned by her tears. The flood of grief kept swallowing her in its depths, forcing her under. She cried out to God. *Help me! I cannot bear this any longer!*

Just when she thought the grief would not let go, she saw an image in her mind of a gentle father picking her up. Sitting in His lap, she sobbed until there was nothing left. He gently stroked her hair and whispered words of love. Her Heavenly Father cared and held her in His strong embrace—one that could overcome the despair of her heart. She sat there, soaking in His glory, soaking in His healing, until she began to feel whole again.

Standing, Hannah wiped her eyes with her handkerchief. Breathing deeply of the fresh pine, she let the Father's peace settle around her heart.

Not ready to be in the company of others, Hannah moved further upstream until she found the wild cherries. Dropping them slowly into her basket, her mind moved on to other thoughts.

Several weeks passed since she visited Will's ranch. Her face flushed as she thought of the kisses they shared. Strange how one moment she could grieve her dead husband then the next think of the new man in her life. And this new man was affecting her like no other. Something deep inside her longed for his presence. While she loved Drew dearly and shared a good life with him, something about Will made her feel at home. She could never explain it. Somehow, she managed to fall in love with the handsome rancher from Texas. He eased his way into her heart when she was not looking. She missed him and wished she knew when he would be in town again.

Picking up the full basket, she found Paul nearby, keeping watch over her unannounced. When she moved forward, he fell into step beside her silently with rifle at the ready.

They headed back to the boardinghouse where Betty waited in the doorway. Taking the basket of cherries from Hannah, she told her that Lieutenant Harrison was waiting for her out front.

Squaring her shoulders, Hannah walked around front, not really wanting a surprise visit from Joshua today.

"Lieutenant, this is a surprise," she greeted, knowing her smile must have looked forced.

Joshua wasted no time getting to the point. "Would you walk with me for a few minutes?"

She nodded.

They strolled toward the town square, but not before Hannah noted he came to town alone. She hoped everything was fine with her friend.

"I have some news," he said without emotion.

"Yes?"

"I have been promoted to Captain."

"That's wonderful!"

When she turned to look at him, he looked forlorn which caught her off guard. Surely this was good news, right?

He turned toward her and took her hands in his. "I'm leaving. With the promotion, I am being reassigned to the southern end of the territory."

"When do you leave?"

"Tomorrow morning."

"So soon?" She would miss his friendship.

"Yes," he paused. "Hannah, there's something I've been meaning to say to you for some time. I love you. I have loved you since we came to Fort Whipple. Maybe even before then, I don't know."

Hannah's heart lodged in her throat. This could not be happening. Not today. Not with him.

"What I'm trying to say is that I can't see my life without you in it. Hannah—" He stopped short, moving toward her.

He was going to kiss her!

As he closed the distance, she hesitated only a moment before taking a large step backwards. Joshua was obviously not expecting that, for he dropped his hands to his side. His eyes widened and his jaw went slack. She felt terrible for him, but was certain she had done nothing to encourage such thoughts.

Growing nervous, Joshua said, "I was hoping you would agree to become my wife."

His eyes pleaded with her, finally unveiling the depth of love he kept hidden from her before. That made this so much more difficult. "I can't marry you."

"I know you don't love me the way you did Drew, but our friendship could grow into love in time."

Her heart ached for him. "Captain," she said, choosing the formality to help emphasize her point. "While I treasure your friendship and will forever be in your debt for your kindness, I cannot marry you. I'm sorry, but I do not love you, nor do I believe that our friendship would ever be more. You are a good man and you deserve someone that will love you in return. I am not that woman."

He stared into her eyes looking for confirmation that her words were true. His pain was evident. He was dumbfounded and could not speak. After a few moments, his shoulders slumped forward in resignation. Finally, with great sadness he said, "Goodbye, Hannah." Then Captain Harrison walked away.

"Go with God, my friend," she whispered as she watched him ride out of her life, sorry for the pain she inflicted with her refusal, though not regretting her decision.

Gathering her wits, she straightened her back and returned to the boardinghouse. It was time to start the evening meal. Rubbing her fingers on her temples, she walked through the back door. She stopped suddenly when she saw the shelves fully stocked with Colter beef. Her questioning gaze was quickly answered by Betty.

"Will was here. He stopped by with more smoked beef."

Her heart dropped to the floor. "He was here? Did he ask for me?"

Betty looked away, and Hannah knew the answer before she spoke. "I'm sorry dear. He did not."

Hannah wanted to run away and cry. Instead, she picked up pots and pans slamming them about on the stove to soothe her frustration. What was happening? Why did Will leave without speaking with her at least for a minute? She thought they were growing close. She thought he cared for her. Had she completely mistaken the message behind those kisses?

Is this awful feeling the same thing she just caused Joshua to feel?

Will was excited to see Hannah today. He knew she wasn't expecting him, but he wanted to surprise her. He needed to deliver more beef and pick up a few supplies. He also hoped to have some mail from his sister Julia in Texas, now that there was regular mail service to points east. But what he really wanted was to see Hannah. He hadn't stopped thinking of her since she visited the ranch. She obviously admired the magnificent piece of land that was now his home. He thought of those kisses often. She was so sweet to the taste. Her skin was so soft to his touch. He was definitely falling for her. There was a small part of him that felt complete in her presence. Who was he kidding? He was in love with Hannah Anderson!

Since that day at the ranch, Will did everything with a new perspective. He hummed as he worked with the horses. When riding he sat taller in the saddle. He was happy, even joyful. Ben noticed the change and questioned him about it. He told his old friend everything, how he was in love with Hannah, how he wanted to make her his wife.

And he knew the exact moment he was sure he loved her. He asked her the simple question of what her dreams were. He was surprised when it affected her so. When she said she longed to be a wife and mother, that's when he knew. He knew he wanted to be the man of her dreams. He was going to ask Hannah to marry him, but he had to come up with something special.

For days, he thought of how he would propose. Today, he would ask her if she would have dinner with him at the hotel in two days. Then, he would come back to town with flowers on that day. He would take her to dinner, asking for a quiet table where they could talk. Then he would ask her. It was a good plan and he was sure it would work.

Whitten pulled the wagon to a stop in front of the boarding-house. Will grabbed the first crate of meat and carried it into the dining hall. Hannah was not there, but Betty was. No matter, he was not leaving town without asking Hannah to dinner. He chatted with Betty for a minute while she emptied the crates. Hannah still wasn't back from whatever chore she was working on, so he decided he would come back after they loaded supplies from Don Manuel's store.

As he lifted a crate of flour into the wagon, Will saw Hannah walking in the town square. His heart leaped at the sight of her—before he noticed she was not alone. Dropping the crate into the wagon, Will watched the scene unfold. Hannah was walking next to Lieutenant Harrison, the two talking with rather serious expressions. She stopped and turned towards him. Then Harrison paused, turning toward Hannah. Will's heart pounded loudly in his chest as Harrison took Hannah's hands in his. Will's jaw tensed and his eyes narrowed. What exactly was going on? Then, Harrison moved forward to kiss Hannah.

Will could not watch the rest of the act of betrayal. He turned away, his heart shattering. Betty was wrong. Hannah did not love him, she loved Harrison. She made her choice.

Anger boiled to the surface as the truth sank in. Hoisting another crate he shoved it into the wagon. How could he have been so foolish? Was she just toying with him that day at the ranch? How could he have been so wrong?

Lifting another crate from the stack to be loaded, Will shoved it into the wagon bed with such force, the wagon rocked forward. Crate after crate suffered a similar fate, until the wagon was loaded. Task completed, Will mounted his horse and mumbled something to Whitten.

Pointing Jackson toward home, Will resisted the temptation to glance back at Hannah. Strong determination and a severely broken heart forbade it.

Will was in a foul mood all day, well actually for two days, ever since he saw Hannah with that lieutenant. Today was supposed to be the day he would ask her to be his wife. Instead, she had picked the military man. Dropping the saddle onto Jackson's back with thud, he felt a little remorse. It wasn't his horse's fault that Hannah was a shrew. Maybe that was being a bit harsh, but it made him feel a little better.

Jackson wasn't the only one who suffered his wrath. Last night, Jed said something that set Will off. He didn't even remember what it was. All he remembered was that he nearly decked the young man—poor Jed. Ben's warning glare was the only thing stopping him from making a complete fool of himself. Then, this morning, the kitchen filled with tension after Will barked at Rosa for not making his eggs scrambled. In truth, he hadn't asked her to make them that way and he had treated her unfairly. He was acting boorish. And all over a woman.

Growling in frustration at himself, Will mounted Jackson and turned him eastward. Covington reported this morning that he saw some signs of an abandoned camp at the far end of Will's property.

He was going out to see if the camp was from Apaches, Mexican cattle thieves, or someone else.

Dad-blame it. He sighed. There was another thought of Hannah. Why couldn't he just get her out of his mind? How could she have affected him so deeply and so quickly?

Unlike many men he knew, Will had never found love in Texas. He hadn't missed it then either. He loved working with the cattle, rounding up the strays, branding the calves, and driving the herd to market. He never had time for love. He didn't have time to be lonely. But, now he was lonely—lonelier now for having loved Hannah and lost her than he was before he met her. Why did her face haunt his dreams? The laughter, the teasing, the moments of introspection. He wanted it to stop. He wanted to forget her and have the pain go away. But he couldn't.

Getting impatient with his lovesick thoughts, he forced his mind to other things. There were still no letters from his sister Julia. He sent a letter from Santa Fe over nine months ago. He sent letters in the spring through the military post. He was sure she received at least one of them. Why hadn't Julia sent any letters back? Was Reuben being ruthless with her, not letting her send anything out of his hatred for Will? A pang of guilt pierced his already broken heart. He should have brought Julia, even though it was against his father's last wishes.

Maybe his own pain was shading his thoughts. Perhaps Julia found a handsome rancher to court. More realistically, Reuben would be the one to find her a wealthy rancher with no concern for age or looks or character. Still, Julia was strong willed and could stand her own against their brother. He respected her much more than he'd ever respected Will. Will was certain Reuben didn't love Julia, for the only thing he loved was money. But respect for one's sibling would take one far enough. At least he hoped that was true.

Spotting the ashes Covington mentioned, Will focused his attention on his surroundings. Judging from the few remaining ashes, the camp was several days old. Dismounting his horse, he took a closer look. There were signs of boot prints, so it was unlikely the camp was Apache. Looking carefully at the area around the fire remains, he spotted a small piece of bright red fabric. Unless there were settlers in the area with Mexican blankets or throws, he had a gang of Mexican cattle thieves on his hands. They were probably scouting the herd to make plans for when to strike. Will would have to step up the number of men on the outlying areas especially at night.

Mounting Jackson, he turned the horse toward the ranch. He only went a short distance when something spooked the horse. Seeing the rattlesnake after Jackson, he was unprepared. His mount reared up suddenly, frightened by the snake which quickly slithered way. Will lost his balance and tumbled backwards over Jackson's hind quarters. His breath rushed from his lungs as his body hit the ground hard. His head whipped back making contact with something hard. Pain seared through his head. He had to get back on Jackson. As Will tried to stand, his head started spinning and he dropped to the ground, everything going black.

Ben was getting worried as the sun lowered in the sky and no one heard from Will since the morning. He couldn't shake the ominous feeling. Something was definitely wrong. He saddled a mare and went to get Owens to ride along.

Just as he stepped into the yard from the bunkhouse, he saw Jackson loping toward the corral in full gear but missing his rider. Fear gripped Ben as he shouted for all the men to gather. Running from bunkhouse the men saw their boss's mount and knew he was in trouble. The only way a cowboy sent his horse back without him was if he was dead or unconscious or too injured to ride back. Ben hoped it was the latter.

Gathering Owens and Whitten, Ben gave instructions to the rest of the men to watch for Will to return. If either party found him, they were to shoot twice in rapid succession. If three shots, then they should prepare for injuries. Mounting their horses, the men set off at a gallop towards the east. Ben figured the best place to start looking was at the reported site of the abandoned camp.

Light faded quickly. Ben and the other men grew quiet. An air of anxiety hung about them, as they knew they would never find their boss in the dark. As they rode over the last rolling hill on the eastern edge of the property, Whitten spotted Will's lifeless form.

Ben stopped his horse next to this man who was so much more like a son than a boss. He feared the worst, seeing that Will was unresponsive. Ben felt around for signs of life and injury. No broken ribs, but his chest rose and fell with the breath of life. Arms and legs were okay. Lifting Will up, he saw the dried blood on a rock in the fading light of day. Searching for where the blood came from, Ben found the injury. The back of Will's head was coated with dried blood. How long had he been out here?

He instructed the men to fire off three shots to warn the others they were coming in with injuries. The men secured Will's limp body to the extra horse. The return trip would be agonizingly slow, especially in the dark with an unconscious man and when every second counted. Ben hoped Covington heard the three shots and rode out to find the doctor as planned. They would need him there when they got back.

It was the better part of an hour before Ben, Owens, and Whitten carried Will into the ranch house. Rosa already had water boiling and bandages ready.

"Where's the doctor?" he asked.

"Covington rode out for him over an hour ago, but hasn't returned," Snake answered.

This was not good.

Chapter 33

Hannah spent the last two days vacillating between hurt and anger. She still didn't know what caused Will to ignore her. Betty was not able to offer any suggestions either. She said he seemed in a very pleasant mood when he delivered the beef, although somewhat preoccupied. Before he left, Betty said he mentioned he would be returning.

Two days went by with no word. Maybe she was reading into his actions. Perhaps he was on a tight schedule for the day and could not wait for her to return. Or he might have been called away for something important back at the ranch. No matter what explanation Hannah came up with, it did not ring true. Will didn't come to town often. Usually when he did, he planned a full day. This was completely out of character.

After a busy day at the boardinghouse, Betty retired early. Hannah unpinned her hair, letting it fall down her back. As she brushed out her hair, she prayed. *Lord, I don't know what is going on with Will. I love him, Lord. Please calm my fears and help me not to worry.*

As she set her brush aside, she reached for her night dress. A loud banging noise from the front door of the dining hall made her jump. She cautiously walked toward the front door and opened it. Paul stood outside with rifle in hand. A young man was with him.

"Mrs. Anderson?" Covington asked, bursting through the dining hall room.

Hannah blinked as she realized the man was one of the Colter Ranch cowboys. He was breathless and obviously distraught.

"Mrs. Anderson, you have to get your things and hurry!"

Confused, she asked, "Why?"

"It's Boss. He's hurt and I can't find Doc Murphy. You have to come and help."

For moment, Hannah thought she would be sick. Will was hurt?

"What happened?"

"Don't exactly know ma'am. He didn't show up for supper and Shepherd was worried. I was to stay behind and ride for the Doc if I heard three shots, the signal for injuries, cause I'm the fastest rider in the bunch. So, when I heard the shots—that's what I did. Only I couldn't find Doc Murphy. The army at the fort said he was out in Peeples Valley and wouldn't return until tomorrow. Mrs. Anderson, you're the only one that can help. Everyone knows you saved that soldier's life a few months back. You've got to come now."

"Let me get some things." Glad she hadn't yet slipped into her night dress, she gathered her medical supplies. Not knowing the nature of his injuries, she brought the most useful items. Stepping out into the night, Covington helped her up on his horse. He climbed up in front of her, telling her to hold on tight. She guessed that he had expected the doctor to have his own mount. She placed her arms lightly around his waist. When he shot the horse off in a fast gallop, she tightened her grip. This was insane, riding this fast at night in no moonlight. She prayed the young man knew the way well enough to keep them from crashing down a ravine or into a tree.

Before she knew it, Covington brought the horse to a stop in front of the ranch house. Inviting light poured from the windows, unaware of the gloom around them. Covington dismounted quickly. Then taking her by the waist, he set her on the ground. She ran through the front door, headlong into Ben.

"Where's the doctor?" Ben questioned Covington with a frown while he steadied Hannah.

"He's out in Peeples Valley. Too far to ride out and get him tonight, so I brought her," he answered pointing at Hannah.

Taking Hannah's hand Ben dragged her into Will's room.

"What happened?" she asked, fear edging her voice.

"He was thrown from his horse. Hit his head hard on a rock, back here," he said, pointing to the left side of his own head. "Do what you can."

Nothing could have prepared Hannah for the sight before her. Will's motionless pale form lay in the center of the bed. His eyes were closed and sunken into his skull. He seemed eerily still. Her breath caught. Was he dead? She kept her focus on Will, angling her head towards Ben to ask him, but he already left the room.

She didn't think she could do this. Despite how hurt she had been that he didn't ask for her when he was in town, she loved this man. She wasn't sure if she could think clear enough to help. *Help me, Lord. I need your strength and wisdom.*

Hannah made her way to his bedside. She placed her hands on his head trying to focus on what to do. She felt his arms and legs for broken bones or other injuries. She found the cleaned head injury on the back left side of his skull. A knot the size of an apple started to form. They needed to put cool water on it to help bring down the swelling. As her hands continued searching his limbs for broken bones, tears clouded her vision. Feeling nothing broken, she pressed her hands on his abdomen. His body flinched and she grew concerned. She wasn't sure if that meant an internal injury or just bruising. Hoping it was the latter, she continued to examine him.

Finding nothing else, she left his side and returned to the main room holding her shaking hands to her side. "I need some cold water. As cold as you can get it."

"What do you think?" Ben asked after motioning to Snake to go get water.

"The swelling on his head is pretty bad. We need to try to get that down and the only way I know how to do that is with ice or cold cloths. He may have some bruised ribs, too. I couldn't find any broken bones. I would feel better if the doctor were here to take a look."

"You just tell us what you need, Mrs. Anderson, and we'll see to it."

Fear consumed her. The pressure was too much. How could she help him? She was not a doctor. Hannah excused herself from the room, bile creeping up her throat. Running out the front door, she lost her supper on the front lawn near the hitching post. *Oh, God. Please help him.* She prayed sinking to her knees, tears streaming down her face.

Ben lifted her back to her feet, his worry evident. Gripping her shoulders, his gaze pierced through her panic. "You have to stay strong. You are the only one who can help him."

Snake returned with cool water. After taking a sip to calm her stomach, she took the bucket into Will's room. She soaked a cloth in the cool water and placed it over the lump on the back of his head.

When his body started convulsing with a seizure, Hannah screamed for help. Tears streamed down her face as Snake and Ben pinned Will to the bed until the shaking stopped. Hannah continued her ministrations, despite the feeling that nothing she did would save him. She stayed by Will's side throughout the night, continuing to place cool cloths on his head injury. She thought the swelling had lessened some.

Will did not have any more seizures, thankfully, by the time Dr. Murphy arrived the next morning. He must have come straight from the fort upon returning. The doctor examined Will and reported his findings. "He has some bruised ribs on his left side in addition to the bump on his head. There are no signs of internal injuries."

Hannah and Ben both let out a breath at the news.

"Keep doing what you are doing until the swelling is gone."

"How long before he is awake?" Ben asked the question that was on the tip of Hannah's tongue.

"Head injuries can be unpredictable. We just don't know how these things work. He may wake up soon, or he may never waken. When he does come to, he may not remember things or he may have some permanent damage. I just have no way of knowing for certain. Mrs. Anderson, I will leave him in your care. In the meantime, I will stop by every few days to check on him. If you need me before then, send someone to fetch me."

Tears pooled in Hannah's eyes at the news. He may never wake up. Would she lose the second man she gave her heart to? Was she cursed? She dismissed the thought quickly. She knew God had not abandoned her. She prayed he would not abandon Will either.

Hannah woke, stiff and sore. She had fallen asleep kneeling next to Will's bed, his hand in hers. She begged God for Will's life. She pleaded. She sobbed until she had nothing left. It was a week since he was thrown from his horse, left to wander the unconscious realm. She barely left Will's side. She couldn't. She wouldn't.

Last night she got into an argument with Ben over the subject. Ben tried to order her to rest in the other bedroom while he cared for

Will. She refused, screaming hysterically at him. Eventually she got her way.

Hannah was utterly empty, drained of all emotion now. She had nothing left. She hoped that it was true—that the Holy Spirit would really pray when she couldn't—because she couldn't any more.

She checked Will's head injury, relieved that the swelling had not returned.

She was so tired, having barely slept in a week. She would just sit in the chair next to his bed for a moment.

Hours later, she woke to Martha Murphy shaking her. "Hannah, Hannah," Martha repeated. "I've been trying to rouse you for several minutes now. You look terrible. Come with me."

Half dazed, Hannah followed Martha into the adjacent bedroom. Pushing her toward the bed, Martha said, "You lie down now and rest. Dr. Murphy's orders. We're here now and will see to Mr. Colter's care."

Too tired to protest, she complied.

Sometime later, Hannah shot upright in the unfamiliar bed. She heard strange murmurings from the room next door. She eased out of bed and walked towards Will's room. Cracking the door open, she saw Dr. and Mrs. Murphy and Reverend Read surrounding Will's bed. They each had a hand on his arm or head and were praying fervently for healing. Relieved that he was in good hands, she returned to bed.

Again, she woke with a start. As the fog lifted, she saw Martha hovering over her. "Hannah, come eat some supper with us after you freshen up."

Martha had laid out a fresh dress for her. Pouring some water into the wash basin, she cleaned and changed clothes. When she entered the room, Martha, the doctor, and the reverend were already seated around the table. How strange it felt to be dining with a group of people in Will's home without him. At the thought, she looked towards his closed door before sitting in the remaining chair.

"Mrs. Anderson," Dr. Murphy started. "You have done a marvelous job of caring for Mr. Colter, but at your own expense." Martha's glare didn't deter him. "If you don't care for yourself as well and let others help, I will send you back to Lancaster's."

Her head snapped up at the seriousness of his tone. She nodded compliantly.

"He's right. Mr. Colter is in the Lord's hands, not yours," added Reverend Read. "You must let God do the work."

Tears trickled down her cheeks as she turned her head to look away from the group. Martha grasped her hand and tenderly patted it.

"Hannah, I know it's hard, especially when you love someone so deeply and have been hurt before, but trust God. He is working on mending Will. You will not lose him."

She wished she could believe Martha. She ate in silence as the others carried the conversation. She felt great remorse for not having told Will she loved him. She remembered their conversation by the lake. When she told him she dreamed of being a wife and mother, she also dreamed of him by her side. Now he could die without ever knowing.

After the three visitors left, Hannah opened the door to Will's room. Ben was sitting in the chair next to the bed, his head bobbing up and down as he slept. She wasn't the only one worried.

Not wanting to disturb Ben, she knelt next to Will on the other side. She placed her face on his hand, tears falling softly on his skin. She stayed like that for a moment, before standing and leaning close to his ear.

"I love you, Will Colter," she whispered in his ear. "I love you more than anything. Please don't leave me."

She kissed his forehead, before running from the room overcome with despair.

Chapter 34

Will looked around, frightened. He was somewhere in pitch black darkness. Holding up his hand in front of his face, he could see nothing. Where was he? He tried to cry out, but no sound would move past his lips. His limbs felt heavy, weighed down. He could not move. Panic started to rise. Again he tried to call out, but couldn't.

What was that? He thought he heard a sound. A woman's voice. Someone who meant something to him. Who was it? *Who are you?* He wanted to shout. Where was he? What was going on? Why couldn't he see anything, say anything?

A door slowly creaked. Bright white light filled the opening. It hurt his eyes and he squinted. There was a figure standing in the doorway. Who was it? Was that a man? A woman? He couldn't tell. The bright light was making it difficult to distinguish.

He saw a face flash before his eyes. Smiling. Strawberry blonde hair. He knew this woman. Then it was gone. Only the figure in the flood of white light remained.

"Who are you?" Finally he could speak.

No answer.

"What do you want? Where am I?"

Still no answer.

The woman's face flashed before him again. Who was she? She was someone important to him. His mother? Sister? Wife?

It hurt to think. A constant pounding was beating between his ears. Had he fallen? Was he hurt? What was going on?

The ghostly figure just stood in the doorway. Not saying anything. Not moving into the dark room, nor moving away from the room. He noticed that none of the bright light was shining past the doorway into the room. It was as if the light was swallowed by the darkness at the threshold.

Still the pounding. It hurt. He couldn't think.

There, again, he thought he heard a woman's voice. It was dim and in the distance. What was she saying?

"I love you, Will Colter."

There was more, but it was muffled by the drumming beat in his head.

Who was she?

Again, she spoke. "I love you more than anything. Please don't leave me."

She loved him. Who was she? She didn't want him to leave. He wasn't going anywhere. He couldn't go anywhere. He tried, and his limbs were still immovable. Who was she?

He felt a moist drop of water—was it a tear, her tear—on his face.

The drumming beat threatened to extinguish the fleeting recognition. Who was she?

Hannah. It was Hannah. It was his love, Hannah.

What did she mean, don't leave? Where was he going? Why couldn't he see her? Why was that figure standing in the doorway?

The figure started to come into focus. It was a man. Something was very familiar about the man. Where did he know him from? He had always known him—at least that is what Will thought. No. Not always. Since he was a young man.

Who was he? Who introduced him? Was this man his father? No. It was his father that had introduced him to this man. Who was he? The drumming in his head hurt so bad. Make it stop.

Hannah. Why couldn't he talk to her? To tell her he loved her? Would she be able to hear him if he shouted? He opened his mouth desperate to tell her. No sound would come. He kept trying. *Hannah. Hannah. Never will I leave you. I love you.*

The figure moved forward into the room with startling swiftness. Who is he? He was certain he knew this man.

Yes, that's who it was.

"Don't take me with you," Will pleaded. "I can't go with you yet. Hannah needs me."

The figure said nothing, but gently cupped his hand behind Will's head. Instantly the drumming stopped, the figure departed, and he was left in pure darkness again.

He heard the woman again. Hannah. His Hannah. She was crying. She was holding his hand. Why was she crying? What was wrong? Hannah.

"Hannah," Will spoke his voice barely audible but it cut through the silence.

She looked up from her weeping and stared into his eyes. The startled look on her face went to confusion, then to relief.

"I love you," he said. Had she not heard him?

"My love, why are you crying?" he asked his voice hoarse.

"Will? Are you really alive? Are you really okay?"

What did she mean? He wondered. What happened?

He lifted his stiff and heavy arm, relieved that it finally obeyed his command. Cupping her face, he wiped away the tears from her cheek. His heart soared when she turned her lips and placed a kiss in the palm of his hand.

Hannah blinked, shocked at the sound of Will's voice. Had she dreamed it? Did he just speak her name? Could she dare hope?

Looking up, she saw the most beautiful sight. Will's golden brown eyes were open, staring back at her. Tears of joy streamed down her face. He was alive, awake! He moved his hand to cup her face and she turned placing a kiss in the palm of his hand. He came back to her! *Praise God! Thank you, Father.*

Overwhelmed with emotion, she tried to compose herself before speaking. "How are you feeling?"

"Stiff and sore. It hurts some when I breathe deep," he said lightly touching his bruised ribs. "What happened?"

Hannah moved from kneeling next to his bed, to sitting on the edge. Wiping her tears with her handkerchief, she answered, "From what we were able to piece together, about ten days ago you were riding in the far east section. Your horse threw you. You hit your head pretty hard." She choked on the words. Taking a deep breath, she continued, "It was hours later that Ben went looking for you because you didn't show up for supper. They sent Covington out for the doctor but brought me when the doctor couldn't be found."

"Ten days? I don't remember any of it."

"You've been unconscious this whole time. What do you remember last?"

Will thought for several minutes. "I remember being angry about something. I snapped at Rosa in the morning over something stupid." He paused, then whispered, "I was angry with you."

"At me? Whatever for? The last time I saw you was the day we spent here. We had the picnic by the lake. When you came with the delivery for the boardinghouse, Betty said you left abruptly. I was crushed. I had been looking forward to seeing you."

When she mentioned the boardinghouse, she saw a frown pass over his face. He looked like he was either angry still or trying to remember something. Maybe both.

"I saw you with Harrison. I saw you kiss him."

That's what this was all about. He had seen Harrison talking to her that day and must have seen when he tried to kiss her. "That's impossible. I never kissed him. What you saw," she said, her voice taking on a sharpness she hadn't intended, "was Captain Harrison coming to tell me was leaving. When he tried to kiss me I backed away because I don't love him. I love you." No need to mention that Harrison asked to marry her, again.

Will looked down at his hands. Several emotions passed across his face. Anger, regret, pain. Then as if a light dawned, he looked up and asked, "You love me?"

"Yes, Will Colter. I love you! Why else would I sit by your side for ten days begging God to spare you?"

His laughter sounded so good, washing away any irritation she had a moment ago.

"I love you, too, Hannah," he said smiling.

Standing, she returned his smile. "There's a whole ranch full of people that are going to want to know you are okay. Rest now. I will be back to check on you later." She squeezed his hand, then left, closing the door behind her.

Walking outside, she headed toward the bunkhouse. Before she made it there, Ben rode up on horseback. He must have seen her out of the house and been worried.

"He's awake."

Ben let out a *whoop*. "When did he wake up?"

"Just a few minutes ago."

"I'll have Covington ride for the doctor, then I'll be in shortly."

Hannah nodded returning to house. Joy filled her soul. *Thank you Lord for your mercy.*

A few days passed and Will continued to heal from the injuries. Dr. Murphy checked on him several times and was scheduled to return this morning. Hannah fluffed another pillow, placing it behind him as he leaned forward. Then she handed him a plate of bacon and eggs for breakfast. She sat in the chair next to his bed as he ate, studying him. Each day he grew stronger.

A light knock on the door alerted Hannah to the doctor's arrival. "How is our patient doing?" Dr. Murphy asked looking at Hannah.

Before she answered, Will said, "I am just fine Doc. Ready to get back to work."

Dr. Murphy laughed. "That's what all men say. But, let's not rush things. You've suffered a serious injury that will take more time to heal."

Will scowled as he finished his breakfast.

"Let's get you out to the table this morning," Dr. Murphy said. "I would like to run through some tests to check your memory and cognitive abilities."

Hannah stood. Taking Will's plate she left the room.

A few minutes later, Dr. Murphy assisted Will to the kitchen table. The doctor asked for some paper and a pencil as he eased Will into the chair. Hannah retrieved the items and set them on the table. The color drained from Will's face. He braced his palms against the table, straightening his arms. She witnessed his dizzy spells many times over the last few weeks, and each time she worried he might land on the floor. A few seconds passed before Will dropped his hands to his sides, the dizziness gone.

"First, let's test your memory," Dr. Murphy said. He had Will list off his family members names, and Hannah confirm the ones she knew. Then he had him recite Psalm 23, which Will recited to perfection. Dr. Murphy asked him the names of each of his men, each of the horses, all recounted accurately.

"Next, let's try some math," Dr. Murphy said as he jotted several problems onto a sheet of paper. "Can you cipher these?"

Will took the paper and stared at it for a moment. Taking the pencil in hand, he quickly jotted the correct answers to the various problems. When he pushed the paper back across the table to Dr. Murphy, he smiled.

"Very good," Dr. Murphy said. "Next, let's try some reading." He wrote a few sentences on the reverse side of the paper then handed it to Will.

Will lifted the sheet of paper. Staring at it, his expression went from hopeful to confusion to disappointment. Hannah waited silently cheering him on.

Will cleared his throat. "Is it right side up?"

"Yes," she whispered.

Will stared at the paper some more. A few more minutes passed before he tossed the paper aside in frustration.

Dr. Murphy said, "Tell me what you just experienced. Were you able to recognize the letters? The words?"

Will looked down, ashamed. "It's like I know they are words. Even some letters look familiar but it's like the letters danced on the page. I don't know." He looked away, shoulders slumped.

"Let's try this," Dr. Murphy said, writing out the letters of the alphabet in order. "Can you tell me what each of these letters are?"

Again, Will stared at the page. Hannah watched, holding her breath. Perhaps something would be familiar.

Will shoved the paper away again, seemingly distraught. "Why can't I read? Why can't I make sense of the words and letters, but I can solve math problems as quickly as always." He slammed his hand down on the table causing Hannah to jump. "It doesn't make any sense!"

She hurt for him. How awful it must be to have learned a skill, know that you once knew it, only to have it taken away.

Dr. Murphy placed his hand on Will's forearm. "The mind is a complex thing and we know very little of how it works. I've seen patients who were unconscious as long as you with far less cognitive ability than what you are displaying. The reading may come back in time, but you will have to work for it, practicing daily despite the frustration."

Will refused to look up. "I am feeling tired and would like to rest now."

Hannah's heart ached for him as she watched the doctor help him back to his room.

When Dr. Murphy returned to the kitchen, he said, "This is a difficult thing to face. I wish I could tell him he will be able to read again, but I just don't know. However, I think with time, if he starts with the basics, it may come back."

Hannah nodded.

"Has he been able to get around better?"

"Yes. As you saw, he barely needs help getting from place to place—even then it is mostly if he has overexerted himself."

"Well, tell Will I'll come to check on him the day after tomorrow. Keep him off horses until then. I want to see for myself just how mobile he is before we let him try that."

Hannah nodded and walked Dr. Murphy to the door.

Hannah sat next to Will as he worked on writing the alphabet. When a knock sounded at the door, he dropped the pencil a bit too eagerly and rose to answer the door.

"Dr. Murphy," he greeted.

"Will, Mrs. Anderson," Dr. Murphy said, entering the room. Setting his bag on the corner of the rough wooden table, he glanced over at the papers on the table. "Ready to get started?"

Dr. Murphy pulled a chair away from the table and motioned for Will to sit. He instructed Will on raising his legs one at a time, then together.

As they worked on several agility tests, reality set in. Hannah did not need to hear Dr. Murphy's diagnosis to know that Will no longer needed her help. He recovered enough to take care of his basic needs. This past wonderful week was coming to a close, signaling Hannah's departure. She needed to return to the boardinghouse and her job. But, every intricate part of her soul longed to stay here with Will. She never wanted to leave his side again. She wanted to be his wife—though he had yet to ask.

Truthfully, she knew for days the time had come for her to return to her life. She put off the decision for the better part of the week until Ben—not Will—asked her this morning when she would be leaving. Will was there, overhearing the conversation, yet remained silent. When she glanced over at him, he looked away. What did that mean? Did he want her to stay as much as she wanted to stay?

While Will continued the exercises, Hannah stood and walked into the room that had been her home for the last several weeks. She pulled her carpet bag from under the bed, tossing it on top of the bed with a frustrated sigh. She was an unmarried woman in an unmarried man's house—a man now well enough to care for himself. No matter her desires, she must leave.

Folding her other dress neatly, she laid it in the carpet bag. Retrieving her Bible from the night stand, she laid it on top of the dress then clasped the bag shut. She tried not to give in to the loneliness that she knew was coming.

After she and Will declared their love for each other, Hannah thought with much confidence that he would ask her to be his wife. But he hadn't. Hadn't hinted at it. Hadn't mentioned it. Had he even thought of it? Maybe it was too soon. Maybe he need more time. Maybe he thought she needed more time. Sighing, she commanded her thoughts to stop. There was no point in trying to guess his motives. If he wanted to marry her, he would ask in his time. And if not... She didn't want to think on that.

Taking one last glance around the bedroom, she picked up her bag and shut the door on her way out. Dr. Murphy just finished with Will. They both turned to look at her.

"Hannah," Will started.

"Dr. Murphy," she said, cutting him off. "I saw you brought your buggy. Perhaps I could trouble you for a ride back into town."

"Certainly," Dr. Murphy agreed.

Will turned to the doctor. "Can you give us a minute?" The pained look on his face stabbed at Hannah's heart. Perhaps she should have given him more warning.

Dr. Murphy nodded, pulling the door closed behind him as he exited the ranch house.

Will reached out his hand and took the carpet bag from Hannah. Once he set it on the table, he took her hands in his. Looking down into her eyes for several silent seconds, he seemed torn.

"Thank you, Hannah, for everything," he said softly.

She willed the tears not to pool in her eyes but they didn't listen. When she looked away, Will lifted her chin so she would look at him.

"I love you," he said before placing a soft kiss on her lips. Pulling her into an embrace, he rested his chin on the top of her head. She wrapped her arms around his waist holding tightly, desperate to take a sweet memory with her.

His voice was husky, when he said, "I'm going to miss you."

She stepped back wordlessly wiping her eyes with her handkerchief. She started to reach for her bag, but he lifted it from the table then motioned her towards the door. She walked through into the bright sunlight. After helping her into the buggy, he handed her the bag.

"I'll come see you soon, I promise," he said, lifting her hand to his lips. When he stepped back from the buggy, Dr. Murphy *hupped* his horse into motion, leaving a part of Hannah's heart behind. As the wagon climbed to the top of the hill, she turned and waved as the tears rolled down her face. Will waved in return. *Please come soon.* Her heart called out.

Chapter 35

Colter Ranch

August 26, 1864

Will climbed into the saddle firmly strapped to Jackson's back. The stallion snorted, then eagerly moved forward at his command. He breathed deeply of the muggy air. The huge white clouds littering the sky reflected the sun's bright rays, making him squint. Pulling his hat low over his eyes, he savored the feel of riding in the open country again. While he rode for a few hours each day in the week since Hannah returned to town, today marked his longest ride yet.

Hannah. The woman consumed his thoughts and his prayers. Every morning and every evening for the past week, he prayed, seeking God's guidance on how to proceed with her. As his memory returned in the days following his awakening—as he called it—Will remembered the scene he witnessed between Hannah and Harrison. Her explanation made sense and he believed her. Yet, for days he held on to the hurt and anger, not caring that he misunderstood. This morning, he finally let it all go. And, with letting go, came a love so deep for her that he knew she would become his wife.

But, before he could ask her to live life by his side, he needed to ask her forgiveness. He knew he hurt her immeasurably by his silence the day he wrongly assumed she loved Harrison.

As Jackson climbed the hill toward town, Will grew nervous about seeing Hannah. This morning, he took extra care getting ready. He shaved the stubble from his face. He wore his best shirt. He even brushed the dust from his trusty hat and shined his boots. He wanted to look his best for his future wife.

Wife. He grinned at the thought. Who would believe this thirty year old rancher would have found his wife in the middle of the Arizona Territory? He hardly believed it himself.

When he told Ben of his plans, Ben insisted he accompany Will to town, mumbling something about not missing Will's proposal for anything.

As the pair rounded the last hill, they saw a group of roughly twenty wagons pulling into town. Will's heart sank at the sight. Prescott was going to be crazy—it always was when a wagon train arrived. Already a line formed outside the boardinghouses, the restaurant, and the hotel. Apparently none of the new arrivals wanted to cook dinner, Will thought wryly.

Glancing over at Ben, he saw his questioning gaze. Sitting taller in his saddle, Will refused to be deterred from his mission today, although his patience may be challenged. With a slight motion of the reins, he urged Jackson forward down the hill into the fray. Stopping in front of Lancaster's, he dismounted and tied his steed to the hitching post out front. Stepping to the back of the line, he waited his turn, despite his desire to run inside to sweep Hannah away.

The man in front of him turned. It was his friend Mr. Boggs. "Mr. Colter. What brings you to town today?"

"I'm here to visit someone."

Mr. Boggs smiled knowingly before commenting on the growth of the town. "With the train that just got in, we'll probably have to start building a school and church."

"Are there enough children for a school?" Will asked.

"As of today, there are twenty or so school age children."

Will raised his eyebrows, surprised so many children lived in the area. "How is life as a big elected official?"

Mr. Boggs smiled. "Not sure yet. Legislature sessions don't start for two weeks yet. We'll probably be meeting in Don Manuel's store, since he's headed back to Santa Fe."

"Why would he be pulling out when so many people are arriving?"

"Not sure. Don't worry, though. Gray & Company just opened a store on Montezuma Street. They are shipping supplies up from La Paz along the Colorado River. There are rumors that William Hardy is considering opening a store in Prescott as well."

Will was constantly amazed at how much changed in the town in matter of weeks. He and Boggs continued to discuss news of Prescott while slowly moving through the line.

As Will and Ben moved into the dining hall, he caught sight of

Hannah. She pressed the palm of her hand to her forehead with a frazzled expression resting on her face. When she looked his way, he smiled sheepishly and waved. Instantly her face lit up, almost as bright as his heart.

"Will, Mr. Shepherd," she said pouring them both a cup of coffee. "What brings you to town this busy day?"

"You," Will said not missing a beat. Her face flushed before she turned toward the kitchen waving a hand in the air.

Balancing four plates of food at a time, she served the last round of guests. As she set the last plate before him, he commented, "I'm surprised you had enough food to feed this crowd."

Taking a seat across from him, she explained, "When the scouts at the fort saw the wagon train, they sent someone to town to let us know we had new neighbors to welcome. Betty and I doubled everything. We did not want a repeat of last month's chaos—running out of food when a surprise wagon train arrived."

"You look lovely," Will said, swallowing his last bite of food.

She snorted. "I look like I've been mauled by a wagon train." Sighing, she added, "But I am so glad to see you. I thought maybe you'd forgotten about me."

"That is not possible, Hannah." *And if I have my way, you won't have to worry about that again.*

Slowly, the rest of the crowd departed, leaving Ben, Will, and Hannah sitting in an empty dining hall. Betty peeked around the wall separating the room from the kitchen. When she saw he was here, she bounded over, beaming.

"Will, Ben, so good to see you. How are you doing Will? Any more dizziness? What about weakness?" Betty mothered him.

"I am just fine. Still have trouble reading, but I hope with time it will come back."

"Good, good," she said, patting him on the arm before clearing the empty plates from the table.

Ben stood and asked, "Betty, could you use some help with dishes?"

Will and Hannah stared, while Betty's eyes grew wide in surprise. "I'd love some help. Aren't you just the gentleman?" she asked while some added color crept to her face.

Ben, turning to Hannah, said, "You just sit here with Will for a bit, or maybe take a walk with him to keep him out of trouble. I'll see that Betty has all the help she needs."

Hannah shot Will a questioning look and Will just shrugged his shoulders. He was surprised by his old friend's behavior, but thankful that Ben had skillfully orchestrated exactly what Will wanted, time alone with Hannah.

"Would you like some fresh air?" Will asked as he stood.

"Yes, but can we sit on the bench out back? I'm rather worn out from feeding such a large crowd."

Offering his arm, he led her through the kitchen and out the back door, carefully closing it behind him. She took a seat on the bench—the one where he accidently spied on her months ago. The thought brought a smile to his lips as he sat, angling to face her.

"How are you, Will, really?" Worry etched lines in her brow.

"I am doing well. I have been riding most of the day for the past few days. And I'm starting to feel like myself again." *Except that you are not with me.*

"What about the reading? Any progress there?"

"It's frustrating. I know that I know how to read, but I just can't seem to make sense of what is before my eyes. But, considering how bad a head injury can be, I am thankful that is the only thing I'm struggling with."

"I'm glad."

The breeze rustled through the pine trees, blowing the loose tendrils of Hannah's hair. She might think herself disheveled, but he thought her the most beautiful creature alive.

"Hannah," he started, suddenly feeling very nervous. Taking her hands in his, he asked, "Will you forgive me for assuming the worst when I saw you with Harrison? I acted terribly and I am sorry that I hurt you."

"Will, I already forgave you," she said smiling up at him with those beautiful blue eyes.

Relieved and emboldened, he continued, "This last week without you has been twice as much time as what I ever want to be apart from you again. You are part of me and I am empty without you."

Standing, he pulled her to her feet, retaining his hold on her hands. "What I am trying to say, is that I love you." He swallowed, hoping his nerves would calm. "Will you marry me?"

She went quiet and his heart started pounding. *Please, Hannah, say yes.*

Then, she stood on her tiptoes and flung her arms around his neck, lowering his face towards hers. She kissed him, squarely on the lips, her body melting into his. When he recovered from the shock, he returned her kiss. Letting his hands explore her back, her neck, her face. He finally settled them around her waist. Pulling back, he searched her eyes. He saw her answer there, but he still wanted to hear it.

"Is that a yes?"

"Yes," she vehemently replied, her eyes reflecting a deep love. "Yes, I will be your wife."

He pulled her close again, content just to hold her for a moment. Whispering in her ear, he said, "One last request—can we marry soon?"

"Are you free next Saturday?" she replied, before he covered her mouth with another kiss.

"Hurry up, Hannah," Betty said. "You don't want to be late for your own wedding."

As Hannah placed her Bible on top of the contents of her case and snapped it shut, she looked around the private rooms at the boardinghouse—her home for the past four months. As excited as she was to become Will's bride this afternoon, she would miss her dear friend Betty. For almost a year she lived in close quarters with the kindly mother figure, first on the Santa Fe Trail and then at the boardinghouse. Hannah smiled as she remembered how Betty seamlessly taught her how to cook over an open fire along the trail. And buffalo chips! She almost forgot about the only fuel to be found on the open prairie. It was Betty who comforted her when Drew died and helped her look forward as the grief passed. She hoped their friendship would continue, despite the distance to the ranch and the busyness of the boardinghouse. Taking a deep breath to calm her nerves, Hannah picked up her bag and walked out the door.

Will sent the wagon in for her bright and early this morning, so she could bring all of her things with her. There wasn't much, but certainly too much for horseback alone. She suspected he also wanted to make sure she journeyed in comfort. Ben helped Betty up to the wagon, then Hannah. Taking the seat next to Betty, Ben clucked the wagon into motion. Paul rode alongside on a borrowed horse.

As the wagon topped the last hill, Hannah was struck anew at the magnificent scenery. This beautiful valley was going to be her home with Will. They would walk along the lake in the evenings. Perhaps have a lazy Sunday afternoon picnic on its shore. She would start a garden in the spring near the house. This winter would be a perfect time to spruce up the inside, adding curtains and such. She would grow old on this ranch at Will's side.

A brief flicker of a memory of Drew came to the forefront of her mind. What if she lost Will? *Please, Lord, let me grow old with him.*

She closed her eyes, listening to the soft rushing of the breeze. She would not fear. God was with her. He had not abandoned her in the darkest days of grief. Instead, He spread before her a dream unfolding—one where she would have a new name, married to the handsome rancher that captured her heart after so much tragedy— one with her Lord by her side.

She opened her eyes as Betty patted her hand. "All is well, dear."

Hannah smiled as Ben pulled the wagon to a stop. He helped the ladies down, while Jed and Hawk unloaded her things. "We'll see your things inside for you, ma'am," Jed said.

As Ben escorted her and Betty towards the lake, Hannah's pulse quickened. She looked over the crowd gathered. Many of their friends were there. Dr. and Mrs. Murphy, Mr. Boggs, most of the boarders from the boardinghouse, all of Will's men, Rosa, and even the two ladies Hannah had worked with at the fort were there. Captain Harrison, of course was not, having been reassigned the very next day after speaking with Hannah. It was probably for the best.

Will stood, waiting for her near the shore of the crystal blue shimmering lake. He wore a dark brown tailored suit that fit him perfectly. She glanced down at her own dress, the brown calico she wore especially for him on the fourth of July. With less than a week to plan the wedding, she settled on her newest dress, not knowing it would match his suit so perfectly.

Betty unhooked her arm from Ben's and took a place standing next to her son, while Ben led Hannah all the way to Will's side in front of Reverend Read. Looking into Will's eyes, she barely noticed Ben stepping back to stand on Betty's other side. Will smiled at her then nodded to the reverend to begin the ceremony. Hannah recited her vows to Will fully aware of everything about this precious man. She smiled as he recited his vows, tears threatening in the corners of his golden brown eyes.

When the vows ended and the good reverend gave permission for Will to kiss his bride, he gave her the most devilish look. Her heart quickened as he cupped her face with one hand and pressed the other hand against the small of her back. He lowered his lips to hers in a sweet kiss. She felt his careful restraint.

Before moving completely away, Will whispered for her ears only, "There's more where that came from, Mrs. Colter."

Hannah's face flushed at his teasing, while the reverend announced them to their friends as Mr. and Mrs. Colter.

Rosa, Martha, and several other ladies, prepared an enormous buffet of food. While Hannah longed for time alone with Will, she enjoyed the celebration with friends. Throughout the meal, while many well-wishers came and went, Will stood by her side. After he finished eating, he placed his arm around her waist and kept it that way, making her feel secure.

As the sun dropped lower in the sky, their guests departed, leaving the newly wedded couple to their solitude. They sat next to the lake, in the same spot where they had their picnic not so long ago, and watched the sun set over the mountains on their first evening as a couple.

"Hannah, I love you so much," Will said, taking her face in his hands. Then he kissed her with all of the desire that a man has for his wife. She could really get used to this.

When he pulled away, his voice was husky with emotion. "Shall we retire to our home, Mrs. Colter?"

Standing and taking his offered arm, she said, "I would love to, Mr. Colter."

Author's Note

Now for my favorite part of the book – the Author's Note. I love this part because it's where my favorite authors have clued me in to what is historical fact versus imagination. It's that nice little bit of closure.

When I started writing my debut novel, I knew two things: one, that it would have something to do with Prescott, Arizona, and two, that someone would die. In fact, the first scene I wrote was the avalanche scene in the middle of the book, which changed very little through revisions and editing. The raw emotion came from my reaction to my mother's unexpected passing almost ten years ago. There was much healing in the act of writing that scene. I hope if you have lost a loved one that this scene and this book has somehow helped with your healing process.

As a transplant to the great state of Arizona, I learned quickly that I knew very little about the history of the state. Once I discovered the state became a territory in the middle of the Civil War, the ideas for this book began to take shape. I researched the political motivation behind the forming of the territory during such a tumultuous time in our country's history.

Then, in my research, I came across the letters Jonathan Richmond wrote to his family while traveling with the Governor's party from Cincinnati, Ohio. I was hooked. I had to write about all of the amazing things Jonathan and the governor's party experienced on their travels, from the five hundred Indians at Fort Larned, to Gray's Ranch, to finding the Indian woman's severed head, to Devil's Gate, to Sante Fe, to the snowy inauguration. Many of the events of the journey were inspired by his firsthand accounts.

Of course, when writing an epic tale about a wagon train journey, one must understand many things: mode of transportation, what kind of supplies were needed, what was the terrain like, what was a woman's role on the wagon train. These details were important to painting an accurate picture of life on a wagon train. I came across a wonderful book about the history of the Santa Fe Trail which provided a great deal of detail to help make the journey come to life.

While I tried to keep facts and the real historical characters as accurate as possible, this is still a work of fiction. The major area where I took some creative liberty was with the First Cavalry Company of the California Column. I needed a way to include Lieutenant Harrison from very early in the journey and I wanted him to be trained by the real Captain Benjamin Davis. Captain Davis trained the First Cavalry Company before heading east to fight in the war. While the First Cavalry Company traveled all over the western territories, they were not part of the governor's party and there is no record of them traveling to Fort Larned, though other companies of the California Column traveled as far east as Fort Leavenworth.

The details about Prescott are my best representation of events and details of the earliest days of the town. While Lancaster's Boardinghouse is a figment of my imagination, it was inspired by the account of a woman nicknamed the Virgin Mary who ran the first boardinghouse in town. Much of the first Fourth of July celebration came from accounts of later celebrations.

Most of the political characters mentioned in the book were real and I did my best to understand more about who they were, what they looked like, etc. Those characters include: Governor Gurley (who died from appendicitis in Cincinnati, never setting foot in Arizona), Governor John N. Goodwin, Secretary of Territory Richard McCormick, General Carleton, Jonathan Richmond, Bob Groom, Captain Walker, John Boggs, Major Willis (the first commander at Fort Whipple), and King Woolsey. All conversations and interactions with these characters are how I imagined they might act or talk or think and in no way represent any actual documented conversations.

I hope you have enjoyed this journey with Drew, Hannah, and Will as much as I have. No journey would be complete without thanking a number of people who helped make this book possible.

My parents – thank you for teaching me about Jesus early in life. I have been blessed to call him savior because of your influence. You have always encouraged me to grow and stretch beyond myself. Thanks, Dad, for the support as I struggled to figure out what this whole writing thing is all about.

My husband – Wow! It's finally done—my first novel. Thanks for listening to the hours and hours I talked about the history and research and my characters. And thanks for always asking how my writing was coming, even when you'd rather talk about football. I love that we share a love of history and writing, even if it works itself out differently.

My critique group: De, Aunt Tami, Kristen, Sherri, Kris, and Kurt. Thank you for taking the time to read this book and providing such wonderful feedback. Thanks for being honest, even when I didn't want to hear it. This final version is reflective of your great ideas and suggestions.

My editor, Fae – Thank you for your help and your enthusiasm.

My in-laws – Thank you for encouraging me in this new venture and for your prayers. I love being a part of your family.

The Women's Ministry at Mission Community Church – Thank you all for helping me grow in my journey and for the constant support by prayer, email, and Facebook. Knowing that you believed in me has pushed me to make this book the best that I could.

My Lord, Jesus Christ – Thank you for inspiring me when I was discouraged. Thank you for showing me where to take the story when I was lost. Thank you for helping me write a story to point others back to you and your character. Take this book and make it what you will. As one changed forever by your love, I know you can do anything!

Book Club Questions

1. Why do you think Hannah had a hard time trusting Drew when he decided they would move to the Arizona Territory?

2. Jed's first impression of Hawk was very negative. Yet, as the story unfolds we learn that they both have much in common. Has there been a time in your life where you've misjudged someone? How did you feel? What did you do differently when you realized you misjudged that person?

3. Both Hannah and Will experienced tremendous hardships in this book. Can you relate to one of them more than the other? Do you find it difficult to keep your faith in the midst of many trials?

4. Grief is tough. Some days are good. Some are bad. Sometimes things hit you when you least expect it. For me, Mother's Day is always a tough day—even a decade after losing my mom. Has this book changed your view about grief (whether your own or someone close to you)?

5. Has this book changed your view about the struggles pioneers faced in order to settle the West? How has your view of your life changed as a result?

KAREN BANEY, in addition to writing Christian historical and contemporary fiction novels, works as a Software Engineer. Spending over twenty years as an avid fan of the genre, Karen loves writing about territorial Arizona.

Her faith plays an important role both in her life and in her writing. She is active in various Bible studies throughout the year. Karen and her husband make their home in Gilbert, Arizona, with their two dogs. She also holds a Masters of Business Administration from Arizona State University.

To find out what happens to Julia Colter, Will's sister, pick up Prescott Pioneers 2: *A Heart Renewed.*

Headstrong. Unconventional. Until life turns upside down…

Julia Colter struggles to accept life under her controlling brother's greed. The suitors he selects would benefit him, but are far from the ideal husband for her. When her rebellion against her brother puts her life at risk, she turns to her friend for help.

Adam Larson longs to train horses and plans to head west to the Arizona Territory to see his dreams fulfilled. When his sister's best friend shows up in the middle of the night, he agrees to help her flee. The decision changes his life, in more ways than he expected.

Can Julia forget the pain from her past and open her heart to love?

Prescott Pioneers 2:
A Heart Renewed

Chapter 1
Star C Ranch, Texas
July 4, 1864

"You cannot be serious, Reuben!" Julia Colter shouted, not caring that she might wake her niece and nephew from their afternoon nap. Pacing back and forth across the length of the kitchen, she stopped in front of her older brother, her temper flaring almost as hot as the stove. "He is balding and fat and twice my age!"

"You will marry who I say!" Reuben thundered. "I expect you to treat Mr. Hiram Norton with the upmost respect this evening. He has shown great interest in you and the least you can do is be civil with the man."

"But, I could never love him!"

As Reuben shoved her violently up against the wall, Julia's breath left her lungs in a rush. Digging his fingers into her arms, she could feel the bruises starting to form. His brown eyes darkened with unrestrained anger as he glared down at her. She swallowed in fear, stunned by his abrupt action.

"Stop, you're hurting me," she said, trying to break free from his vice like grip.

He raised his hand as if he meant to strike her—something he had never done before. The action startled her to silence. Instead of hitting her across the face, as she thought he might, Reuben returned his hands to her upper arms squeezing even harder.

Leaning so close the heat of his breath warmed her cheeks, he said, "You have no idea what hurt is, Julia. You are an insolent little whelp. You will paste a smile on that tart little face of yours. And you will do your best to win his affections or," his voice menacing, "you will suffer my wrath, the likes of which you have yet to see."

Releasing his hold, he pushed her so hard that she tumbled to the floor in a heap. As he turned to walk away, he added in a sinister tone, "It would be best if you get used to the idea of Hiram Norton and give up fanciful notions of love, dear sister. You will not have that luxury. The sooner you come to accept that, the better it will go for you."

She sat in stunned silence as Reuben stalked to his office down the hall. Tears streaming down her face, Julia bolted to her feet, running out the front door of the ranch house to the nearby stables, still frightened by her brother's brutal behavior.

The smell of hay and horse assaulted her delicate senses as she selected a gentle mare. Throwing her saddle on the horse's back, she led her from the barn. Once under the open blue skies, she shoved one foot into the stirrup, swinging her other leg over the mare, riding astride. Nudging the mare into a full gallop, Julia fled to the one place she would always feel free—the back of a horse in the wide open pastures.

Reuben may be her guardian now, but she had only to endure a few more years of this before she would be of age and in control of her life. If only she could stop him from marrying her off before then.

At seventeen, she considered herself too young to get married, though many women her age and younger married. She wasn't ready. She didn't pine for the responsibilities marriage entailed. She liked her freedom. But, when she was ready to marry, she would marry for love and not because Reuben wished it.

Certainly, she would never marry Hiram Norton. The thirty-seven year old rancher was the exact opposite of what Julia wanted for a husband. His short stature and fading hairline made him look even older. He had a reputation for loving excess. When it came to food, his waistline showed the results of that love. There were other unsavory aspects to his reputation as well—including rumors that he frequented the saloon and brothel.

No, the man for Julia would be young and handsome. His

character would be impeccable, his honor undeniable. Land, money, and wealth held no importance to her. She only cared that her dream man would be able to provide for her and their family.

As the wind tangled her long, sandy brown curls, she continued to press the horse for more speed—needing it to soothe her fear and anger. In the distance the herd of longhorns kicked up dust. The sight sparked a memory of Will, the kinder, more honorable of the Colter brothers, sending her mind racing in another direction. So many times he'd taken Julia out to the pasture, teaching her how to rope, ride, and work with the cattle. Some thought such behavior unacceptable for a lady. She was glad to learn these skills. Should her handsome young dream man end up being a rancher, he might appreciate her ability to work the ranch by his side.

Why hasn't Will written? The thought of him brought fresh tears as memories of his hasty departure flooded her mind. Not only had she buried her father, but she also lost the brother she was close to—all within a few short weeks. Almost a year ago, following her father's death, Reuben forced Will to leave the ranch when he had been deeded the house and ranch. While Will and Reuben both received half of the herd and the financial holdings, Will was left with no home or land. Unable to find anything close, he moved to the Arizona Territory, leaving Julia behind. Alone.

The only time she heard from him was in November 1863. Will wrote that he, his men, and his cattle arrived safely and set up their new home near the Granite Creek settlement in the Arizona Territory—wherever that was. No other letters came.

Despite the thirteen year age difference between Will and Julia, they adored each other. She followed him everywhere, never far from his side even when he worked with the herd. When she needed protecting, it was Will who came to her defense.

Oh, how she could use his protection now. If he were here, he would stop Reuben from forcing her to marry that awful Hiram Norton.

But, he wasn't here. He was in a distant territory, far from Texas, far from her aid. Her father left her in Reuben's care—not Will's—even though Will would have been the better choice as far as Julia was concerned.

Their father never saw the evil that clouded Reuben's heart and he knew nothing of his manipulative ways. In her father's eyes, Reuben was as good of a son as Will. If her father knew of Reuben's late nights in town or of his forceful tactics for bankrupting other ranchers and taking over their lands, he turned a blind eye. She found it hard to fathom that father could have missed such thinly concealed behavior.

As the mare started to struggle for breath, sides heaving with great effort, Julia eased up the pace. She was so torn. She had thought more than once to runaway to Arizona, but was afraid Reuben would find her and drag her back. Now he wanted her to flirt with Hiram Norton and get him to marry her. She had no desire to do what Reuben was asking. Mr. Norton may be wealthy, but he was twenty years older than her. There was something indecent in that alone. Nothing about him or his character appealed to her.

Realizing she was nearing the outer pasture, Julia turned the mare around to head back to the ranch house. She did not want to risk angering Reuben further by being unprepared for their dinner guests. *Lord, please don't make me have to marry that repulsive man. Will always said you could work things together for good. I am not seeing much good right now. Please give me the strength to make it through this evening meal.*

As she pulled the mare to a stop in front of the stables, she slid off the horse. One of the young cowboys, Bates, took the reins from her hand.

"Miss Colter, you best hurry," he said, nodding toward the lane leading to the ranch house.

A cloud of dust at the far end of the lane indicated their guests were already arriving. Julia shot a quick word of thanks to the friendly cowboy before picking up her skirts and running to the house. Reuben stood waiting with fury written on his face.

Rushing down the hall she slammed her bedroom door shut. She splashed some water on her face, wiping away the dust from her ride.

"Where have you been?" Mary's panicked voice preceded her entrance into Julia's room. Reuben's normally calm, quiet wife seemed rather anxious as she picked up the corset she laid out.

"Riding."

"Whatever for?" came the squeaky, agitated response.

Julia tore off her day dress, tossing it over a chair. As Mary came to assist her with the corset, she took her last deep breath of the evening. She hated the confining contraption. Once the stays were tightened, she lifted her arms as Mary helped settle the lovely yellow silk down over her shoulders.

"You should have been in here an hour ago," Mary lamented. "Now there is no possible way we can fashion your hair into ringlets. The other women will think you don't care about your appearance."

They would be correct, Julia thought. "You fret, too much," she replied, brushing out her tangled curls. She would be content with twisting her unruly hair into a chignon, despite how much it fought against the pins.

"Go on. I'll finish," she instructed Mary, hoping to have a quiet moment to compose herself before entering the fray.

Mary hesitated for a brief moment before softly exiting the room. Taking as deep a breath as she could, Julia let it out in a heavy sigh. Undoubtedly, Hiram Norton was already here, waiting for her in the other room. Pasting a smile on her face, she squared her shoulders and left the solitude of her room.

"Hiram," Reuben said as Julia approached, "I do not believe you have met my sister, Julia."

It took every ounce of courage to hold her smile steady and extend her hand towards Mr. Norton's rotund frame. Taking her hand, he placed a sloppy kiss on top. "Reuben, where have you been hiding this lovely filly?"

Filly? The distasteful comment sickened her.

"Mr. Norton, a pleasure to meet you," Julia said with more decorum than she thought she possessed. As soon as his hold lifted, she discretely wiped the back of her hand on her dress.

"Miss Colter, you are absolutely stunning," he replied, allowing his lustful gaze to rove over her neckline, down her curvy figure, making overtly inappropriate stops along the way.

She fought to tamp down her mounting abhorrence. As the guests were seated around the table, she eagerly helped Mary set out the food.

Still irritated by Mr. Norton's uncouth comment, she decided to fight back as she took her seat. "Mr. Norton, my brother tells me you have been very successful with your ranch, despite the Union's blockade. Tell me, how do you do it?"

Reuben's eyes narrowed slightly, letting her know he caught her barely hidden sarcasm.

"My lovely Miss Colter, such matters are too complicated for your simple mind to understand."

Another mark against Mr. Norton—condescension towards women, she thought, keeping the sweet smile firmly in place. Lobbing a spoonful of potatoes on her plate she waited for him to continue.

"However, I shall endeavor to enlighten you," he said with an air of superiority, snatching the potatoes from her hand. "While the Union may have blockaded our route to drive cattle to the New Orleans market, they have made no such effort to stop us from driving to points north or west. It seems that as long as we aren't supplying the Confederate Army, they care little where we sell our cattle. We have simply changed our route north to the railways in Missouri. While I don't care for the Union and their imposing ways, a profit is a profit. And I have made significant gains by being one of the first Texans to sell to eastern markets by way of Missouri."

"If a large profit is to your liking, why not drive the cattle west towards the California market where prices are more than triple that of the eastern markets?"

Reuben shifted in his chair uncomfortably. His darkening eyes warned her to hold her tongue. She knew she should have heeded the warning, but she preferred being forthright. Let Mr. Norton find that out now.

Mr. Norton laughed off her question, causing her to dislike him even more. "You are a spirited little woman, I will give you that. But your comment shows your youth and your naivety."

Taking not one, but two large pork chops from the platter she handed him, he said, "While the prices west are much higher, so is the cost to drive the cattle such a great distance. The length of time it takes to drive the cattle to California is almost three times as long as the northern route. It is also much more dangerous. There are many more Indians and cattle thieves westward. It would simply not be profitable to drive the herd west."

His snooty tone grated on her nerves. When she opened her mouth to speak, Reuben interrupted. "Perhaps, dear sister, you should leave the business matters to men. I'm sure you would be much more interested in knowing how Mrs. Withers' new baby is faring."

Mrs. Withers quickly picked up the conversation, monopolizing both Julia and Mary's time. While Julia was surprised Reuben even knew the woman had a child, she was thankful for the opportunity to ignore Mr. Norton.

As the conversation continued, she felt something brush against her knee then move away. She kept her focus on Mrs. Withers' overlong description of her young son and on eating the meal, until she felt the unmistakable presence of a man's hand move above her knee. She stole a glance and confirmed Mr. Norton's hand rested most inappropriately on her thigh. Angling her legs further away from him as discreetly as possible, her stomach churned. When Mr. Norton pressed closer, she thought she might lose her dinner. The man appeared to have no limits.

Standing abruptly, she said, "If you'll excuse me. I'm not feeling quite myself." Without waiting for a reply she hurried to her room.

Reuben scowled after his sister. Her behavior had been completely unacceptable, despite his attempt earlier in the day to reason with her. This silly idea of marrying for love must have worked its way into her thinking from the stories their father told of their mother. No one married for love.

He certainly hadn't. While Mary was pleasant looking enough and easy to control, he did not love his wife. He had married her to increase his social standing among the area ranchers—something his father never seemed to care about. Her father had been one of the wealthier men in the area and he was easy to win over. In fact, Reuben thought, most everyone he met was easy to manipulate— except Will and Julia.

It didn't matter. Will was gone and out of the picture. He was no longer a nuisance, even though it was Will's fault that he was in such a financial mess. When he left with half the herd and half the financial holdings, Reuben was unable to pay debts to some very powerful men—a situation he was desperately trying to resolve.

The last bite of his pork chop churned in his stomach as fear gained a foothold. He needed Hiram's money from the marriage arrangement to Julia. It was his only hope of turning things around.

As his guests finished the meal, Reuben stood. "Gentlemen, shall we retire to the front porch for some refreshments and cigars?"

The men eagerly nodded, obviously wanting to be away from the women as quickly as he did. As Hiram stood, Reuben pulled him aside. Speaking loud enough for the others to hear, he said, "We'll join you in a moment. Hiram and I have a few business matters to discuss."

Leading Hiram back towards his office, Reuben hoped Hiram would still be amiable to the agreement they discussed several days ago at the saloon, despite Julia's less than enthusiastic attitude this evening.

Before he offered a seat, Hiram took one, starting the conversation on his terms. "Julia is quite lovely. You've been holding out on me. When you asked for such a large sum, I assumed she must be dreadful to look at."

"So you are pleased?"

"To a point. While she'll keep me entertained, she needs to learn to control her tongue, especially in front of guests. I'm surprised you haven't dealt with this already."

Reuben frowned. If only Hiram knew what he was up against. With any luck, he wouldn't find out until after his wedding day. "Well, Father has only been gone a short time. He doted on her, so it will take some time to teach her to properly respect a man."

"Ah, there's the catch. I'll have to train her myself then." Hiram laughed. "It will be a fun challenge—breaking her. Too bad you didn't have more time to do the job yourself. You could get a much higher price for her, as beautiful as she is."

The price he was asking was enough. Normally prone to greediness, when it came to selling his sister's hand in marriage, he felt it prudent not to get too greedy. He was running out of time and needed to pay his debts soon. Once that pressure slackened, he could focus his energy on rebuilding his wealth.

A brief hint of remorse came over Reuben. Had he stooped so

low that he was selling his sister for money? But, it was not as if he were selling her to a brothel. No, he was just selling her to a wealthy rancher. She would live in luxury. What could be bad about that?

He knew living with Hiram Norton would not be pleasant. The man had a reputation for being ruthless to his business associates, to his women, and even to his mother. He had no limits. He made Reuben look like a saint. Julia would undoubtedly be miserable married to him until she learned her place.

Chiding himself, he refocused his attention back to what Hiram was saying. He needed this man's money, not a sudden case of conscience.

"After we have our cigars," Hiram was saying, "then, I will take Julia for a walk. See if I still fancy her. When I return, we will announce our engagement. It will be short. No longer than a month."

Reuben held back a gasp. He hadn't expected Norton to want a short engagement. "You know what the townsfolk will say with such a hurried wedding. They will think my sister has been compromised."

Pulling a large stack of bills from his coat pocket, Hiram slammed it down on the desk. "I don't think you will care too much what is said about your sister's reputation. Who knows, what they say may end up being true anyway."

The dark look on Hiram's face sent shivers down Reuben's spine. Ruthless seemed a rather inadequate word to describe the man before him. He had to make sure Julia did not ruin this deal, for he did not want the added pressure of Norton's anger.

Mary knocked on Julia's door not more than ten minutes after she left the meal. Her voice was timid when she spoke. "The men have retired to the front porch for cigars. Reuben requested that you return to the parlor with the women."

Sighing, Julia did as instructed. She listened to the gossip of the rancher's wives and wished her friend Caroline Larson was in attendance, so she might actually be able to enjoy the evening. The

Larsons owned a ranch to the east of the Star C and they had been longtime family friends. Before father passed away last year, the Larsons were always invited for every social gathering—sometimes they were the only guests. Since then, Reuben saw little use for Mr. Larson's moral ways and only included them on rare occasions to pacify her or his wife.

Not paying attention to the boring conversation, Julia missed seeing the men return from the outdoors. Mr. Norton's hand on her forearm jolted her from her thoughts. "Miss Colter, I was hoping you might take a walk with me."

"And who will be acting as chaperone?" she replied coyly, not wanting to be alone in his presence.

Mr. Norton laughed, a sound she was beginning to detest. "Silly girl, I am much too old for a chaperone. I assure you, your reputation will be safe with me. I simply want to stroll for a few moments with a beautiful woman on my arm."

She thought a stroll might be too much for the man. He was sweating profusely and seemed to have difficulty walking the distance to the door, as his breath came in short, heavy bursts. She looked to Mary for support. She smiled and nodded her approval, oblivious to Mr. Norton's reprehensible behavior. As Reuben stood next to Mary, his eyes narrowed with a silent warning. Heeding the unspoken message, she stood and accepted Mr. Norton's arm.

Outside, the air barely cooled in the waning sunlight. Julia grew warm in a matter of seconds. She wished she thought to grab her fan when a sour odor wafted from the man at her side. Averting her face, she tried to catch an untainted breath of air. Unsuccessful, she decided parting her lips to breathe through her mouth might be preferable.

Nearing the stables, Mr. Norton stopped abruptly, turning towards her. The quick motion—seemingly impossible coming from the man who seemed to struggle walking much of a distance— frightened her. Sucking in air quickly through her mouth, a slight tickle lingered in the back of her throat, almost bringing on a cough.

When he spoke, his voice took on a sinister edge. Even in the dimming light she could see the contempt in his eyes. "Miss Colter, while I admire your feisty spirit," he said as he grabbed her wrists. "It would serve you not to embarrass me again, especially by questioning my business practices in a room full of my peers. I can make your life most unbearable if you cross me." Without warning he pulled her close and crushed his mouth down on hers as his hands took great liberty in exploring her body.

The shock of his action took a moment to register. Once it did, Julia brought her booted heel down hard on the top center of his foot, just as Will showed her. He dropped his hold instantly, crying out in pain. As he limped toward her, she ran for the front of the house to put some distance between them. She stumbled on a rock, giving Mr. Norton time to catch up. He grabbed her bruised upper arms with surprising strength.

"Do not ever do that again," he said in a hostile tone. "Do you not know that Reuben has promised you to me? Make no mistake, *Miss* Colter, I am a powerful man. If you want to live a decent, peaceful life under my roof, you best lose some of your haughtiness. Or, I will take whatever measures necessary to force it out of you."

She blinked, trying to absorb all that he said. Was he saying that Reuben already agreed to her marrying this loathsome man? An ominous chill swept over her as he continued his intense stare. Her heart beat rapidly within her chest as her panic rose. She could not—would not—marry this dreadful man!

Dropping his hold on her, Mr. Norton extended his arm and placed her hand in the crook. "Smile," he commanded as he limped to open the front door.

Though her smile came insincerely, his seemed quite pleased. He crossed the room slowly, still favoring his injured foot, before stopping in front of Reuben and Mary. "Reuben, it gives me great pleasure to announce that Julia has eagerly agreed to accept my offer of marriage. She was so delighted that she agreed to a short engagement. We will be married in a month." His fingernails dug into her arm daring her to speak otherwise.

The smirk on Reuben's face told her this had been their plan all along. Such a public announcement, even though it was completely false, would be difficult to break. *Lord, help me. I cannot marry that man.*

Books by Karen Baney

For more information about Karen Baney, the history behind the books, or other books written by her, please visit www.karenbaney.com.

Prescott Pioneers Series
A Dream Unfolding
A Heart Renewed
A Life Restored
A Hope Revealed

Contemporary Novels
Nickels